With Catlike Tread

Connor checked the street. I turned my head to do the same. No movement, no lights, no curious neighbors with sawed-off shotguns. Nothing. I turned back to him. He was fluid, graceful. Review the scene. Move with purpose. Repeat. Building to abandoned car. Car to light post. Light post to doorway. Doorway to body.

Oh, my God. Body. I hadn't seen him before. A T-shirt, baggy blue jeans, and battered tennis shoes. Untied laces. Pool of red seeping along the concrete. Connor knelt and reached for the man's wrist. He didn't react.

"Connor?" I called to him.

He stepped into the street, staying low as he returned. When he was within reach, I lunged, wrapping my arms around him and holding on as tightly as I could.

"Are we waiting for the police?" I asked. He pushed his sunglasses to the top of his head and I could see his eyes. Grass green. No sign of stress. Or fear, or panic. His calm slid into me like honey. . . .

Also by Gabriella Herkert

Catnapped

DOGGONE

An Animal Instinct Mystery

Gabriella Herkert

AN OBSIDIAN MYSTERY

OBSIDIAN
Published by New American Library, a division of
Penguin Group (USA) Inc., 375 Hudson Street,
New York, New York 10014, USA
Penguin Group (Canada), 90 Eglinton Avenue East, Suite 700, Toronto,
Ontario M4P 2Y3, Canada (a division of Pearson Penguin Canada Inc.)
Penguin Books Ltd., 80 Strand, London WC2R 0RL, England
Penguin Ireland, 25 St. Stephen's Green, Dublin 2,
Ireland (a division of Penguin Books Ltd.)
Penguin Group (Australia), 250 Camberwell Road, Camberwell, Victoria 3124,
Australia (a division of Pearson Australia Group Pty. Ltd.)
Penguin Books India Pvt. Ltd., 11 Community Centre, Panchsheel Park,
New Delhi - 110 017, India
Penguin Group (NZ), 67 Apollo Drive, Rosedale, North Shore 0632,
New Zealand (a division of Pearson New Zealand Ltd.)
Penguin Books (South Africa) (Pty.) Ltd., 24 Sturdee Avenue,
Rosebank, Johannesburg 2196, South Africa

Penguin Books Ltd., Registered Offices:
80 Strand, London WC2R 0RL, England

First published by Obsidian, an imprint of New American Library,
a division of Penguin Group (USA) Inc.

First Printing, August 2008
10 9 8 7 6 5 4 3 2 1

For Great-grandma with the mashed-potato hair, who dreamed big and told great stories;

For Grandpa Baumann with his Pillsbury Doughboy laugh;

For Ed, Joe, Sherry, Florine, Marschel, Greg, Debra, John, Teresa, and Spurr—artists all;

And for Ker and Koko—it's okay you're remedial;

With special thanks to Kristen and her team—you make me better than I am.

Chapter One

FORTY-SEVEN MINUTES TO NAKED.

I looked at the text message again. I'd never been the sort to turn my cell phone on the second an airplane landed, but then again, my messages were getting better. At least my propositions weren't coming from strangers anymore. I caught my seatmate glancing at my screen. She was a grandmother in a housedress who'd spent the journey from Seattle showing me pictures of gap-toothed adolescents and waxing rhapsodic over their amazing achievements.

"Porn," said Grandma, sighing. "I miss it."

I tried to cover my choke with a cough and reached for my carry-on.

WHERE? I typed, lining up in the airplane aisle behind the harried parents of screaming twin toddlers.

ANYWHERE.

I shook my head and tapped, WHERE R U?

SECURITY.

SAFE SEX?

FLIRT!

U STARTED.

I shuffled off the airplane and into the terminal. The airport was bright, the tinted windows blocking the brutal glare of the San Diego sun. I walked beside the moving sidewalk, too impatient to stand and wait to be transported. I saw Connor through the Plexiglas at security, the sun streaming behind him, giving him a sort of halo effect. I might not know him well, quickie wedding and all, but I suspected my husband's angelic glow was a lie. As if to prove me right, he looked up from his cell phone to watch a twentysomething hottie in a tight, short dress walk by him. I snapped my phone closed and moved past the checkpoint.

"I can come back if you're having a guy moment," I drawled.

Man, he looked good. Really good. Michelangelo's David with clothes and a navy haircut. I tried to smooth my hair. No man should look that good when static electricity was turning me into a jeans-wearing Medusa. He grinned. Amused. Fine. I'd just be cool. Oh, what the heck. Amused could be done naked.

Connor pushed a loose curl behind my ear, then kissed the skin beneath my lobe and whispered, "Forty-three." He grabbed my hand and steamrolled toward baggage claim.

"I'm sorry, Commander, but this trip is official business, and the law firm of Abercroft, Hamilton, and Sterns does not finance booty calls. It's against our expense policy."

He leaned closer. "Forty-two."

"That's it?" I asked, half running to keep up. "I don't see you for three weeks, fly for hours behind hyperactive five-year-olds, and all I get is a peck? I must look really bad."

He stopped. Turned. Let his eyes wander from the top of my head to my toes, then back up, stopping at his favorite parts.

"Or not," I said weakly, covering my cheek with my hand.

"Not." He started pulling me again, but I balked under the baggage claim sign.

"Um, Connor?"

"Yeah?"

"I didn't actually check any luggage." I half turned, showing the carry-on bag I had draped over one shoulder.

"That's it?"

"Yep."

"One overnight bag for a week?"

"Well, um, yeah." I shrugged.

"You are the weirdest woman. But I like that. One

suitcase. Forty." He took my bag and herded me out the door into the bright sunshine.

"Because I can fit my jammies in one suitcase?"

"You're not going to need pajamas."

An older woman in a gray suit looked over her shoulder at us, silver eyebrows raised. What was this, Shock a Senior Day?

He stopped next to a convertible. Black. I couldn't help smiling. Honestly, sometimes the guy thought he was James Bond. The convertible was at short-term parking, which was half the distance and twice the price. Money well spent. He tossed my case into the car before backing me up against the hot metal and really kissing me hello. I wrapped my arms around his neck and kissed him back. Connor could kiss.

"Get a room," an old guy muttered as he climbed into a Buick in the next slot.

"Great idea," Connor whispered, reaching behind me to open the door.

"You are a bad influence." I slid into the passenger seat, fanning my face with one hand. "But we have a great car."

"We?" he asked, getting behind the wheel and reaching across me. I felt the tingle slide all the way down my spine. I swatted at his hand, but he just opened the glove compartment and took out the parking ticket, holding it up for me to see with his most innocent expression. An angel he was not.

"We. California is a community-property state. I never thought I'd own even half a BMW." I looked over at him. "Impressive as it is, if you stole this car I never saw you before."

The engine roared to life and Connor drove toward the exit. He moved his hand to my thigh, and I could feel his heat through the denim. I gave him my best what-are-you-up-to look, like I didn't know, but he didn't move his hand. This flirting thing was fun.

"What's the new case about?" he yelled over the rush of sound. Once the car was in fifth gear on the freeway, he returned his hand to my thigh, migrating just a little north.

"Fraud. One of those identity-theft things," I yelled, stroking the back of his hand. "Except that my thief is bolder than most."

"Bolder?" He slid his fingers up two inches of denim.

I pushed him to the relative sanity of my knee. Crashing wouldn't be good here. "Yeah, bolder. My guy isn't just in it for the money. He wants the fame, the attention, the invites to the swankiest parties in town."

"I'd pretend to be somebody else to get out of one of those things."

"I bet you look great in a tux. Very man-about-town."

"I'd look like a waiter."

"Well, a waiter in a nice restaurant, anyway." I laughed.

Weren't we the normal married couple? Recently married, with the flirting and sexual tension, but normal. From the outside, anyway. So what that we got married after knowing each other less than a week? So what that "knowing each other" was mostly biblical even then? Or that the same could be said of the fifteen or so days we'd spent together in the six months since we'd been married? We didn't fight about money or sex, but that was probably a good deviation from the norm. We did fight about my job as an investigator for a law firm, but mostly because I'd nearly gotten myself killed on a missing-pet case. What were the chances that would happen again? I rubbed my wedding ring with my thumb. I even had the outward trappings of a run-of-the-mill wife. Normal.

Except that half the time it felt like I was pretending to be married and Connor was just a figment of my imagination. A very good, very vibrant imagination, but make-believe nevertheless. If this were my version of normal, there would be a lot more panic: hyperventilation and hand-wringing followed by drunken excuses and annulment. What the heck? If I was going to hallucinate a hot husband, a hot car, and the promise of hot sex, I might as well enjoy it.

"Or you could wear your uniform," I suggested. "Sort of a blond Tom Cruise. Now, he's cute."

He squeezed my leg and I squirmed with a laugh. Now he knew I was ticklish. Another late-to-the-party discovery.

"He's short. Besides, you wouldn't throw me over for a midget actor in an ice-cream suit, would you?"

"I would if he'd give me a deal on chocolate–chocolate chip. Men are great, but they're not dessert."

He lifted my hand and kissed my fingers, then my palm. "Depends."

I curled my fingers over the spot. "Watch the road."

"Yes, ma'am."

"So, anyway . . . my identity thief gave this interview to some right-wing radio guy all about how he had amnesia for years and wandered around homeless. Then, one day, he just woke up and remembered who he was."

"Rich and famous. That's handy," he said, pulling onto the San Diego Coronado Bridge. I grabbed at his arm, craning for a better look at the view.

"Amazing." I leaned back in my seat. "What? Oh, yeah. He remembered he was rich. Not so famous, though. My guy, the real guy, he's practically a hermit. Makes Howard Hughes look like a party animal, which is why John Doe—that's what I call my mystery man—why John needed to do interviews. He wanted to raise his profile. Become *Time*'s Man of the Year." Since profile raising does not come free, a line of credit was established.

"Gutsy," he said.

"Maybe, but definitely not genius material. Still, he did me a solid. The bank that let John withdraw upon demand hired us. A potential fraud with an important customer's money freaked them out enough to send me down here on their dime. They preapproved a week, although that might have more to do with me not having to stay in a hotel. I have to work, of course, but I figure with you working during the day it'll be fine. I might not be able to keep it to the nine-to-five, but we'll have some time together."

"We could afford you coming down from Seattle whenever you want, Sara."

"This is better. Besides, I don't have much vacation time saved up. Prestigious law firms do not allow their serfs out of work often. It gives them ideas."

Connor touched my cheek. "I've got some ideas myself about that."

We were pulling onto Orange Drive, heading toward the Hotel Del Coronado. I wanted to go see the old hotel, maybe check out the ghost stories. I looked at Connor. Maybe we'd do that later. It was weird. I never thought of myself as half of a couple before. Planning little adventures for the two of us. It was amazing how quickly I was adjusting to this new two-person configuration. Connor pulled in front of a high-rise, parking in a red zone. Apparently he was also seeing some advantages in the relationship. I smirked.

"Welcome home, Mrs. McNamara," he said.

I giggled. He yanked my suitcase off the backseat and sprinted around the car. We laughed and chased into the building, stopping for a mind-blowing kiss just inside the door. Seven floors in the sluggish elevator and he had my shirt mostly unbuttoned, sending tingles down my back. Ten floors and we could have been arrested.

His condo was at the end of the hall. We kissed and touched, and he fumbled with his keys. I leaned back against the door, pulling him closer into me as the door opened behind me. I grabbed for him to keep from falling backward.

"You must be Sara."

Connor pushed me behind him with enough force to have me stumbling, grabbing for my open shirt. I struggled with the buttons, peering around his shoulder to gape at the intruder.

"Either that or you got some 'splainin' to do, Lucy," the man—boy, really—in front of Connor drawled.

A younger, darker version of Connor waggled his eyebrows at me. I stood horrified as the Norman Rockwell portrait of mother, father, brother, and sister stood framed in the open doorway, all assessing me and my state of undress. Oh, my God. Their resemblance was unmistakable. They had to be his family.

"You ever think of calling first?" Connor asked harshly, sexual frustration evident in his voice.

Great. Terrific. Now, not only was I seducing their firstborn in a public hallway, he was openly resenting his own family. Family. As in stuck-for-life relationships. I'd barely considered meeting his family. If I had, I wouldn't in my wildest, darkest dreams have imagined this nightmare.

"I couldn't stop her," Connor's father offered. "You know how your mother is when she gets an idea in her head." He shrugged, turning up his hands and not seeming even a little embarrassed. "Ryan, Siobhan, come into the living room. You, too, Liss. Let's let them have a minute."

His mother looked like a Madonna, all serene and unnerving. His sister seemed to share my mortification. Ryan gave me a leering wink before he turned away.

Grimacing, Connor looked at me. I kept one hand over my mouth to keep from retching. The other hand clutched my blouse closed. In the hallway.

"God, Sara, I'm really sorry. I didn't know they would be here. They don't usually drop in unannounced. They were probably just anxious to finally meet you." He reached for me but I jumped away. His family. Naked. Hallway. God.

"It's okay," I choked. *They don't* usually *drop in?* It was so not okay.

"I'm sorry."

"No big deal. I just met my in-laws while stripping their eldest in a public area. At least, I assume that's who those people were. I mean, maybe they're just voyeuristic burglars, or we interrupted the plumber fixing the sink." I concentrated on buttoning my blouse. Maybe he'd confirm one of my wild suggestions. Even a lie would be good here.

He shook his head.

"I'm sure I'll be able to look them in the face again. In about a hundred years." I put more room between us, rubbing my arms. When did it get so cold in this hallway? "Could you fix yourself?"

He looked down. His T-shirt was half-untucked, and the top button of his jeans was undone. He looked . . . mauled.

"They know we're married, Sara." He straightened his clothes.

"There's knowing and then there's knowing, Connor. This would be an overshare." With a groan, I covered my face with my hands. A phone rang behind me as he tried to pull me into his arms, but no way was I going for that.

"They're grown-ups, babe. I don't think we've shocked them."

"Oh, God," I moaned.

"Uh, Sara?" The younger brother was back. "The phone's for you."

Not exactly saved by the bell since it was five minutes too late for premortification intervention. Timing was never my strong suit.

"Thank you."

"I'm Ryan, the younger, smarter, better-looking brother." Ryan flashed dimples at me.

"Hi."

"Hi. You're nothing like I was expecting."

"Ryan, shut up," Connor snapped. He moved to crowd his younger brother back toward the interior of the apartment, but Ryan didn't budge.

"I'm not sure I want to know," I said.

"No, it's good."

"Why don't you take it in the bedroom, Sara?" Connor suggested as Ryan reached for my hand.

"Particularly since the hall has gotten so crowded," Ryan choked.

"The phone. I meant the phone." Connor pushed Ryan back.

Ryan grinned and shifted his weight to avoid being moved. With his green eyes, he could pass for the Cheshire Cat before his disappearance. Well, if the cat had been a surfer dude. Connor was flushed, finally sharing my embarrassment. Served him right.

"I could try to distract the 'rents for you, but short of setting fire to the place you won't have time to get that shirt off a second time. She's very focused, our mother. Which is too bad, because that's a sexy bra," Ryan assured me.

"Uh, thanks."

"Anytime."

"Ryan, get the hell out," Connor snapped, closing the front door in his brother's face. "Sara, this isn't as bad as it seems."

"Oh, I'm pretty sure it's every bit as bad as it seems."

"I'll get rid of them."

"Permanently?"

Connor looked shocked. "They live about ten minutes from here. Siobhan, maybe a half hour. I could probably buy until tomorrow."

At any time in the future, in a mere thirty minutes his entire family could descend. Very convenient. "I was kidding."

"I'll send them home. Then, when they come back, you can meet them normally."

I stared at him. *Yes, please, new in-laws, if you could just leave me with your sex-starved son and his misbuttoned jeans, I'll be ready to exchange personal chitchat over dominoes some evening very soon.* Honestly, for a smart guy . . . I took a deep breath.

"I'm going to answer the phone. If I'm lucky, it's an emergency that requires my immediate attention. If I'm really lucky, I'll fall and smack my head on a table lamp and wake up having lost my own identity."

"Honey—"

"Don't 'honey' me. Just"—I pointed toward the apartment—"deal. I'll be right back."

Connor opened the door and held it. I walked past him and toward the bedroom I could see at the end of the hall. I saw his family milling about in the living room. I closed the bedroom door behind me and picked up the phone.

"Hello?"

"Hey, Sara."

"Joe." I sank down on the bed. At this moment I wished I were in the office, having this conversation with Joe over the wall of our shared cube. Even Abercroft,

Hamilton, and Sterns looked good compared to the family homestead, complete with appalled in-laws. I wanted to blurt it all out, but Joe and I didn't have that kind of relationship. Neurotic blathering I saved for my best friend, Russ.

"You okay?" he asked.

"Fine."

"You don't sound that good."

"It's nothing."

"O-kay. If you're sure." That was the closest Joe had ever come to asking a personal question. I was touched.

"Really. It's fine. What's up?"

"You got a call. The receptionist misdialed and transferred it to me. It took a couple of minutes for me to figure out he really wanted you, and by then I thought I should just try to get the information before his medication wore completely off."

"What?"

"Think weird with a capital weird. Acted like Deep Throat."

I was intrigued. Given the scut work that a new associate like Joe got to do for the firm, he was experienced with weird. If this guy was tripping Joe's meter, he must have been odd indeed.

"His name is DeVries. I guess you called him. He wants to meet you tonight. Nine p.m. He actually said, 'Come alone.' "

Joe recited an address. I opened the bedside table for a pen. It was neat. Four paperbacks, all thrillers, a su-doku·book, a bag of candy, and a technical manual of some sort. I took out a pen and checked the bottom drawer. More manuals. No porn. No little black book. Interesting. Did he clean them out before I came?

"I checked him out. I didn't have much time, but I did do a background on this guy. He's nuts. Extreme right-wing, conspiracy theories, and a criminal record."

Oh, brother. I should have done that before I'd left. Instead, my first call had been to Connor. It was a work trip and I had husband on the brain. Henry DeVries was just the guy who talked to the guy I was looking for, but if I'd been doing my job thoroughly, I would have done exactly what Joe did. And I would have had plenty of time to do more than scratch the surface.

"What kind of criminal record?" I asked.

"A lot of arrests. The most recent was inciting to riot. If you go back far enough, you get assaults and even a couple of domestic-abuse arrests."

"Convictions?" I asked. Not that it really mattered. Anybody who'd been arrested enough probably wasn't someone you should plan assignations with. I stroked the comforter. It felt like silk. Brown and blue stripes, masculine, but still silk. My brain flashed on Connor in this bed. His parents were probably thinking the same thing I was: *Sara Townley is a sex fiend.*

"Sara, listen, this guy was off the chart on the phone. A colorful past or even a public persona is one thing; crazy so you can't hide it is something else. I also checked the place. It's not the same address as the radio station. You should make sure this meeting is in public. Or better yet, take him with you."

"Him?"

"The guy. The husband."

"How do you know—"

"Russ has a big mouth. Take him with you."

"I am perfectly capable of doing my job without him."

Chapter Two

I left a voice mail for Tom Senthe, the bank middle manager who was handling the fraud investigation from their side, then braced myself and went back into the living room to face Connor's family. I explained that I had to meet someone with regard to my case. Everyone smiled politely—until Connor insisted on knowing the address.

"Absolutely not," he yelled. Actually yelled. At me. After the surprise family reunion and the sexual frustration. He had nerve.

"This is my job, and I'll do whatever I want to."

"You will—" he started, before his mother smacked him in the back of the head.

He turned, his green eyes wide.

"Mother—" he began.

"Don't 'Mother' me, young man."

Everyone got to their feet and started moving toward the front door.

"Nice to meet you. I'm Siobhan," his sister whispered as she walked past.

His father patted my shoulder. "I'm Dougal. We'll wait for you in the hall, Liss."

"Don't worry. She can take him," Ryan whispered in my ear, kissing my cheek.

"Do you have any idea where—" Connor began, his voice once again even.

"Of course I do. I've lived here longer than you've been alive, Connor. But we do not yell like we are four years old," his mother said.

"No yelling, but hitting is okay," he muttered.

I bit my lip. He sounded like a kid. My Navy SEAL–trained, tough-as-nails husband being scolded by his five-foot-nothing, one-hundred-pound mother. Fascinating.

"Sara has a job to do. You"—she poked his chest with one well-manicured finger—"will respect that. I'm Alyssa, dear. Welcome to the family."

Connor stiffened.

"Connor will go with you."

I froze. My mother-in-law scared the hell out of me.

"Agreed?" she asked.

Connor and I exchanged a look.

"Yeah," Connor said.

"What?" Alyssa asked sharply.

"Yes, ma'am."

"Yes, ma'am," I repeated.

She smiled. "Good. I'll call you tomorrow, darling." Connor leaned down and accepted her kiss.

"We'll arrange a proper introduction, then." Alyssa said, kissing my cheek and breezing out the door.

Connor drove in silence. As the sleek condos and manicured lawns became small shops and then depressed high-rises and boarded-up warehouses, I reflected on how my day had gone to hell. One minute Connor had his hands inside my blouse, the next I was hanging out in Beirut, trying not to show fear. It was hard to imagine that things could actually deteriorate from flashing his parents and yet . . . here we were. Note to self—the next time some source insisted on a gang-zone rendezvous, I was going to decline the invitation. Awkward social situations, even those that included my new in-laws, weren't a legitimate reason to say "please can I" when offered an escape that led directly to hell. If I hadn't taken the call from the office . . . Oh, who was I kidding? I would have volunteered for death row rather than make small talk with his family. They'd been very nice. Extremely polite. It creeped me out.

Ryan seemed okay. Smart. Funny. Flirtatious. Connor without the grown-up gene. A little shorter, a little darker, the same green eyes. His father had barely spoken. Strong and silent, or calculating the slut factor? Hard to tell. He had silver hair and crisp golf clothes. His eyes were blue, his tan deep.

His sister, Siobhan, was like the negative Polaroid of all of them. Her mother's frame with a brittleness that screamed discomfort. Her father's eyes in a watered hue, more pastel than sapphire. Ryan's pleasantness without his confidence. Connor's . . . what? She'd barely spoken since the hallway striptease. Okay, then. Connor's ability to keep his mouth shut.

Alyssa McNamara was gorgeous. Mahogony hair and chocolate brown eyes. All dancer's grace and fashion sense. I felt like a polyester giant next to her. "Call me Liss," she'd said. "We'll have to plan an outing. Get to know each other. Maybe go shopping." Shopping and family obligation? Root canal. Cosmetic brain surgery. Voluntary commitment for psychiatric evaluation. All higher on my list of must-dos. And that was before she'd done the scary-matriarch thing with the head slap.

I glanced at him. They definitely had that in common. What did he expect? I didn't do family.

"That's it. You wait here," I said, reaching for the door handle.

His arm flashed, locking me into my seat. He was scanning the street, barely turning his head. His body language radiated alert status.

He might have a point. I looked at the steel-gated windows with the gang tags. A charred Honda was the only vehicle on the street. It had a certain get-the-hell-out air to it.

"I'll come with you," he offered.

"Absolutely not. We talked about this. My case. My problem. You are here strictly as a chauffeur, Connor, and even that's against my better judgment. Besides, DeVries is squirrelly. He's not expecting two people."

I sounded confident. Yeah, the neighborhood was a little, um, lived-in, but I'd been in bad places before, and the informant was legit. This meeting wasn't exactly my dream scenario, either, but no way was I acting the delicate flower in front of Connor. He was too alpha not to put his oar in.

"He'll cope." Connor got out of the car. "Slide across."

I reached for the door handle.

"No, Sara."

I got out and came around the car. I gave him my look, the one that said, *Don't mess with me.* He stared back. Short of manhandling me, which he'd never do, he'd have to respect my autonomy. Patience. What I needed was patience. I waited him out.

"Fine." He tried to sound reasonable. "We'll go together."

I wasn't so stupid that his suggestion didn't sound good. Smart, even. Then again, if I gave him an inch I'd never get the edge back.

"No means no. I've got it covered." I frosted my look a little more.

"Humor me," he said.

"There you are with that Tarzan-and-Jane thing again. Knock it off, Connor. It's getting on my last nerve." I glared. "Besides, he'd make you as GI Joe in ten seconds, max. I don't think that will encourage him to open up, do you?"

"You don't know that."

"You've got the army crew cut. Believe me, it's obvious you're military."

"It's not a crew cut." He reached up and smoothed down his hair. I had to fight against softening. He looked like a little kid pushing down cowlicks.

"I could be a skinhead," he continued. "I bet this guy loves skinheads. Probably hangs out with them."

"Then it will be quite a cultural experience for me. I'll tell you all about it when I get back." I turned away.

He caught my arm. "I'm not letting you go alone."

I stared at my hand, then skewered him with a look. "You don't *let* me do things. I decide and then I do them."

He let go. "You're mad about the parents, I know. I'll admit I was out of line when I told you not to meet this guy by yourself. And Ryan doesn't know when to quit, but—"

"I like your brother. This isn't about him. Or your parents, or even you, Connor. It's about me doing my

job, for which I neither need nor want your assistance."
What was with him withstanding my most withering
look. I'd frozen muggers dead with it. I lifted my chin
another inch. I was still looking up at him. The height
mismatch was not helping. Next time I'd stay on the curb
when trying to back him off. Christ, he was stubborn.
Pigheaded. Damn alpha males everywhere.

"Okay. Go ahead. I'll wait here."

I stared with narrowed eyes. He couldn't possibly
think that reverse-psychology thing was going to work.
I waited. He thought that if he said left, I'd go right.
Please.

"Fine." I turned and marched across the street.

"Terrific," he mumbled.

"I heard that," I called over my shoulder.

I kept my back straight. He was infuriating: pushy and
arrogant and without the least little bit of faith in my
abilities. Well, I'd show him. A voice inside my head
whispered that this might not be the best time to insist
on independence. I squashed it. I'd been in worse spots.
Heck, I'd been in more uncomfortable spots today. I
could handle this. Keeping my spine straight, I headed
toward the radio studio.

The building looked like the others. It had heavy
metal gates in front of the window and a rainbow of
graffiti across its face. Hard to imagine that it housed
state-of-the-art equipment that allowed DeVries to
broadcast remotely. It looked more like a down-on-its-
luck warehouse. I moved from the door to the window
and cupped my hands, trying to peer through the fencing
to the window beyond. Maybe he'd stood me up.
Thank God.

I didn't mean that. I wanted this informant to show.
I wanted to make progress on this case. I wanted Connor
to see what I could do and that I didn't need his help
to do it. I just would rather do it at the beach, with
sunshine and smiling faces.

An engine sputtered, and a rusty Nova crept out of
an alley fifty yards away.

"He's not there," Connor called, sounding entirely too
happy about it.

"I'm going to see if there's a side door."

Of course I was. I wasn't giving up just because I could feel a hundred eyes peering at me from behind barred windows and the hair on the back of my neck was standing up. I was a professional. I rounded the building and Connor moved parallel to me, staying in my peripheral vision. I should tell him to stop. A dog started vocalizing. I looked up. He was sitting at the edge of the building, a black Lab mix of some sort, looking pretty good for being homeless. She stared at me with dark eyes, her song hitting a high note. It was like she was talking to me. Not barking, not growling. More of a Scooby Doo sort of thing.

"It's okay, girl." She sang another couple of chords. Stopped. Stared. Barked. Maybe she thought she was a whale. It was more like that than a dog. She growled. Usually dogs liked me. Two homeless guys abandoned a doorway, moving fast. The dog started vocalizing frantically, running up and down the scales.

"Gun," Connor yelled.

I turned and stared. Sun glinted off metal in the open car window. The shots were loud. No one ever tells you that. Really loud and distant at the same time. Glass shattered behind the building's metal grate. I couldn't move. Connor hit me with a flying tackle. We hit the ground rolling. My breath came out in a whoosh. He log-rolled us into the alley and behind the garbage bin. My ears were ringing and the world had gotten very fuzzy. Air. I needed air. Breathe. In. Out. Breathe. Shots pinged off the metal. An engine revved and tires squealed. Then silence.

I remained still. Frozen. Waiting. A minute passed, then another. I started to feel Connor's weight on me, squeezing my lungs. He was sweating, his body damp— or maybe that was me. I couldn't tell where he stopped and I started. His heart beat so hard, so loud I could feel it in my body. He rose on hands and feet, lifting his weight off me. I clung to him, then let go. I could feel the ground now. Hard. There was a rock digging into my back. My cheek stung. I checked my arms and legs. Moved my fingers and toes. There wasn't any pain. No blood that I could see. I was alive. He was alive. Amazing.

Connor ran his hands over me. For the first time since I'd known him, his touch wasn't sexual. I winced when he reached the lump on the back of my head, but otherwise his check hadn't elicited any additional pain. Alive. We were alive. Fine. Cold. I was cold. He rubbed my hands but I could barely feel it. It was like I was watching us from a distance. He swam in and out of my vision.

"It's okay, babe. It's over." He glanced over his shoulder, shifting his weight and peering around the garbage bin. "They're gone."

"People were shooting at us, Connor." Was that my voice? I sounded calm. Really calm. As if getting shot at were normal. Was it normal? It was starting to seem normal. That couldn't be good.

"Yeah, but they're not anymore." He brushed my hair away from my face. "You hurt anywhere? Your neck? Your back?"

My head pounded. I started to sit up. He pulled me into his arms, wrapping himself around me. He was so warm. I squeezed closer. I was cold. He was warm. I wanted to crawl inside him and stay there.

"It's okay. It's okay," he soothed. His voice was so gentle even while his heart pounded. That was strange. My heart rate had slowed and his still pounded. He shuddered against me, then pulled away.

"Do you think somebody called the police?" I asked. "Oh, my God. The dog. Do you see the dog? Is she hurt?"

"She's fine. Got away clean." He kissed my hair. "I'm going to check the street. Stay here." He turned and crouched next to the garbage can.

I panicked.

"Connor." I grabbed at his arm.

"It's okay, babe."

It wasn't okay. It wasn't nearly okay.

"No."

He brushed my hair, stroking my arm.

"My job now," he said.

His face showed nothing. He was calm. He was back

in control. This was his realm. His zone. It might be my case, and there might be bad guys with guns, but he had me covered. I knew he could get hurt. I knew he could. But it didn't feel real. At that moment he was a superhero. My superhero. Invincible.

"Be careful," I whispered before kissing his cheek.

"I'll be right back." He kissed me hard and moved from the bin to the building, flattening himself against the brick. I got onto my knees and crawled to the edge of the garbage can. I didn't have a good view of him, so I moved around the can to keep him in sight.

He checked the street first. I turned my head to do the same. No movement, no lights, no curious neighbors with sawed-off shotguns. Nothing. I turned back to him. He moved. He was fluid, graceful. Review the scene. Move with purpose. Regroup. Repeat. Building to abandoned car. Car to light post. Light post to doorway. Doorway to body.

Oh, my God. Body. I hadn't seen him before. A T-shirt, baggy blue jeans, and battered tennis shoes. Untied laces. Pool of red seeping along the concrete. Connor knelt and reached for the man's wrist. He didn't react.

"Connor?" I called to him.

He stepped into the street, staying low as he moved toward me. Gripping the edge of the garbage can, I put all my energy into wishing him back to me. When he was within reach I lunged, wrapping my arms around him and holding on as tightly as I could. I needed to touch him. He was back. We were together. A man was dead but we were okay. He rubbed my arms.

"Are we waiting for the police?" I asked, staring into his eyes. Grass green. No sign of stress. Or fear or panic. His calm slid into me like honey.

"I doubt anybody called them."

"You're kidding. No, of course you're not. You already told me no one would call the cops, didn't you? Sorry. What are we going to do? We could call them from the car."

"Honey, we're going to call the cops. But not from here. From someplace safer."

"Yeah, okay."

"I want you to stay behind me. Behind but close. Really close."

I nodded, chewing my lower lip. I was going to be so close we could pass for Siamese twins.

"He's dead, isn't he?"

Connor nodded.

"We're going to the car. When we get there, you're going in first on the driver's side. Get across and down as fast as you can. Got it?" I nodded.

I wondered if he felt it. The man. Did he know he was dying? Was it quick? Of course it was. How long had we been in the alley, a minute? Five minutes? The man hadn't been on the street when I'd walked by the first time. He'd been alive. Now he was dead. I clung to Connor.

"We're going to move fast, stay low. Ready?"

I clutched at his waist. "Ready," I whispered.

We ran.

Connor made a deal with the dispatcher to send a detective to us instead of making us go back to the scene or to the police station. Being charming paid dividends. The cop who met us at the coffee shop an hour later was in his early thirties, Hispanic, with broad features and the paunch of an ex–high school football player gone to seed. He slid into the booth across from us. After meeting Connor's eyes for a brief moment, he turned all his attention to me. Connor bristled beside me. I almost laughed. It wasn't really funny. The cop wasn't really flirting, but Connor was jealous. It was just so normal. So everyday.

Connor slid an arm along the back of the booth, playing with my hair. The cop seemed amused when Connor introduced me as his wife. The cop shook my hand, lingering over the gesture. I let him.

"Why were you in that neighborhood, Mrs. McNamara?" Officer Hector Montoya asked.

"I use my own name, Officer. It's Townley, but you can call me Sara."

He preened under my smile. Maybe it was relief, but I felt a little light-headed with the emotional swings of the day. Montoya was attractive. He was flirting, and I flirted back as if I hadn't just seen a guy gunned down in the street. I sipped at the lemonade. Tart and sweet. Adrenaline and relief. Flip sides of the same coin. Second wind, maybe, but I was feeling better. More in control.

"Sara." He smiled back.

Connor stiffened fractionally. I slid closer to him. He wrapped one of my curls around his finger and tugged. I glanced at him and rolled my eyes before turning back to the cop.

"I was meeting Henry DeVries. The radio guy?" I made it a question.

"Ah." The cop wrote in the notebook he'd laid on the table.

"You ever listen to him?" I asked.

"Can't say I do."

"But you do know who he is?"

"Yes, ma'am. I mean Sara." He sent another grin my way. He was laid-back, not pressing. Probably updated at the scene first. He wasn't rushing.

Connor tightened his grip on my hair just enough for me to feel it. Without looking, I reached up and unwrapped his fingers, taking his arm from around me and placing his hand next to his orange juice. A mouse swatting at a lion's paw.

"I was supposed to meet him at nine," I continued.

"He set the time?"

"Yes."

"He set the place?"

"Yes."

"Not exactly Beverly Hills," Montoya remarked. "Why would he want to meet you there?"

"I got the message secondhand. It came through my office. Apparently Henry DeVries was insistent. He didn't say why."

"You knew how dangerous the street was before you went?"

I glanced at Connor. If I hadn't, Connor had filled me in pretty thoroughly before we'd headed out. "I needed to talk to him."

The cop looked at Connor. "You have anything to say about that?"

"It's her show."

That was a new one. What was he up to? Montoya looked at him with something like pity. Violation of the guy guide: Never let the little woman run the show. If only Montoya knew . . .

"Why were you meeting him?" The cop directed the question to me.

"He interviewed someone I wanted to get in touch with."

"Who?"

"Charles Smiths."

Montoya looked surprised. He sipped his coffee. "The philanthropist?"

"Yes," I confirmed. I looked directly at Montoya. Smiled. Still. I wasn't lying but I wasn't sharing either. I knew I wasn't much of a poker player. Connor could always read whatever I was thinking on my face, even if he ignored it on occasion. I didn't look away. Maintaining eye contact was the key to not looking shifty. The cop didn't even blink. If he was reading me, I couldn't tell. He could draw to an inside straight.

"There must be easier ways," Montoya suggested. "Smiths is famous. San Diego's mental health facility was built by him. Or by his money, anyway. Not just that, either. There are scholarships. Even one for the kids of local cops. If you wanted to meet him, why go through DeVries?"

"I was looking for Charles Smiths, and he'd recently done a radio interview here in San Diego. I contacted the station to see if they had a phone number for him, and Henry DeVries called back."

"And DeVries set the time and place?"

"Yes."

"If Sara never talked to DeVries directly, I guess he wouldn't have been expecting you, Mr. McNamara?" Montoya asked without even glancing Connor's way.

"It's Commander." Connor shrugged.

I could see where Montoya was going. If that was DeVries in the doorway, maybe whoever had set him up planned a two-for-one. Me and him. DeVries claimed to have important information about Charles Smiths and my mysterious identity thief. Mind-blowing, Pulitzer Prize–winning information. When Joe had relayed the message, I'd thought it was hype. Why would anyone give such vital insight to a credibility-testing, right-wing blowhard? What information could it be, anyway? Smiths was practically a recluse whose only mention in the press or anywhere included reference to the many people helped by his generous financial contributions. He would have been socially bulletproof from everything but the most heinous of accusations. I winced. Well, if Henry DeVries was the guy in the street, he'd never had a chance to share anything with me. Nor would he. Meaning there was no reason to want me dead. It might explain the timing, but surely there were easier ways to get to him. Less public ways.

"So take me through it, Sara," Montoya went on. "You arrived when?"

"Ten minutes to nine, maybe. I got out and went over to knock."

"Where were you, Commander?" His emphasis mocked Connor's rank. My husband really did have remarkable self-control. He didn't react at all to the snideness of the comment.

"At the car."

Montoya raised his eyebrows.

"Like I said, her show."

"What happened after you knocked?" Montoya turned back to me.

"Nothing, so I knocked again. When there was still no answer, I went around the side to try to look in the window."

"Did you see the man in the doorway at any time?"

"No. I think I heard the door open. Or maybe it was the lock. I'm not sure."

"Did you see the car?"

"Sort of."

"It was coming toward you?"

"It's all kind of a blur. Yeah, it was coming toward me, I guess, but all I really remember was Connor yelling and then I hit the ground."

"Good move. Might have saved your life."

"I didn't mean I hit the ground. Not like that. Connor knocked me to the ground, actually. He saved my life. I just stood there with brain cramps." I smiled at Connor. Had I said thank-you?

"You saved me," I said. "Well, you and the early-warning canine alarm, anyway."

The cop cleared his throat. I leaned back, taking Connor's hand under the table. Considering we'd been within range of automatic gunfire less than an hour ago, I was feeling pretty good. We were okay. I was back on the case. A real case. Real enough to warrant machine-gun fire. Okay, that maybe wasn't the best sign, but it did mean that this wasn't just some paper-pushing case. I wasn't half-naked in front of Connor's parents anymore, and if the case was important, I wasn't going to have much time to do the family-bonding thing. Everyone would understand. Yeah, things could be worse.

"What did the guy who got shot see? Have you had a chance to talk to him yet?" I asked.

Montoya and Connor exchanged a look.

"Oh," I said. He was dead. I didn't know him. Never actually met him. But he'd been standing twenty feet away from me less than an hour ago, and now he was dead. "Poor Henry."

"I thought you'd never met him."

"I didn't."

"But you got a good enough look to identify him? How? Have you seen a picture of him?" Montoya probed.

I shook my head. "I guess . . . I mean, I assumed . . ." I looked at Connor. He was watching the cop. "It wasn't Henry DeVries?"

"You don't seem surprised he's dead, Commander."

Connor shrugged.

"Would you be surprised if the ID turns out to be someone other than Henry DeVries?"

"I'm not prone to surprise, Detective."

If it wasn't Henry DeVries, who was it? Okay, the neighborhood was terrible. People probably died there all the time. Not when I was standing near them, thank goodness, but a coincidence? They couldn't honestly believe . . . No way. Wait a minute. I looked from Connor to Montoya and back again. Was there a book they gave the XYs when they were born? A gift basket that included blue booties and the guy guide to keeping the little woman on the sidelines? Fine. They were so not getting away with it.

"Why'd you leave the scene?" Montoya asked. Damn. He used the same smile when he was asking dangerous questions as he did when he was making idle chitchat.

"It seemed prudent," Connor offered.

"People were shooting, Detective. We thought to get out of range, but we did call nine-one-one and tell them where we'd be."

"Which must explain how you found us, Detective," Connor added.

The two men had an eye-to-eye standoff. Montoya looked away first.

I needed to get rid of the cop. No problem. He'd handed me the spin. In that neighborhood a body wouldn't be news. He could chalk it up to gangs or drugs or bad timing. I'd play along. He was giving up more than he was getting. If he wanted me out of the way, he'd have to accept that I wouldn't return his call the next time he tried to pump me for information. And there would be a next time. This body, DeVries or not, was connected to my case. My case. Montoya was coming late to the party. I had the upper hand.

I glanced at Connor. He was staring at me, one eyebrow slightly raised. Connor was another story. There was no chance he'd check out, given today's dramatics. I'd get more space from my shadow. No, avoidance wouldn't work with Connor. But I didn't know him well enough to know what would work. It was a drawback to the wake-up-married approach we'd taken. Maybe not a drawback, exactly. I smiled. Figuring out how his head worked might be as much fun as figuring out his . . . well, the rest.

"What about you, Commander?"

"Sorry. I drifted off for a minute there. What did you ask?"

"When did you see the victim?" Montoya asked.

"Peripherally, after I'd seen the car."

"Can you describe it?"

"Nova. Not in great shape."

"Did you get a license number?"

"It happened pretty fast," he said.

He was hedging. Maybe it was a hesitation in his voice, or the almost imperceptible slowing in the thumb stroking my hand, but I knew Connor had something.

Montoya stayed for another ten minutes, asking routine questions while flirting with me. If he got anything important out of the Q & A, I didn't hear it.

"What didn't you tell him?" Connor asked as soon as Montoya was out of earshot.

I shifted in the narrow booth, looking at him with my most innocent expression. "How do you know I held something back?"

"Educated guess."

"Well, stop it. You're creeping me out." I gave an exaggerated shudder.

He shook his head. He could read me the riot act, but it would come back to bite him. He knew that. Particularly since I'd bet my last dollar that he hadn't exactly owned up to everything he knew or suspected either. He had to know that sooner or later I'd figure out he hadn't exactly been forthcoming either. No sense setting himself up to crash and burn. He wouldn't make an obvious mistake like that.

"What didn't you tell the police?" I stared. It wasn't a question.

"It is creepy." He stared back.

I laughed.

"I'll show you mine if you show me yours," he offered.

"You're terrible." My cheeks warmed. I shouldn't feel embarrassed. Well, it wasn't embarrassment so much as sexual energy, but we were in a public place. "It's a deal."

He kissed me to seal the bargain before throwing a five-dollar bill on the table and getting up. In the parking lot he put the top of the convertible up.

"Hey, Connor. That's her." There she was again. Smooth black hair. Big brown eyes. No blinking.

"Who?"

"The dog."

Connor looked up. "Must be a thousand Labs in the city."

"It's definitely her. Do you think she's following us?"

Connor moved beside me, opening the door and pushing me into the front seat.

"Let's go."

"Maybe we should see if she's okay. She might have gotten hit with glass or something. Or she could be hungry. We ought to get her something to eat. To thank her for trying to warn me."

Connor pulled out of the lot, checking the rearview mirror. "She's fine."

"You don't know that."

"I know we're getting out of here."

"If she wanted to attack us, she could have done it already."

We merged onto the freeway. I guessed he wasn't an animal person. Maybe he was just a cat guy. Flash, the cat who reigned supreme at my apartment building, was slavishly devoted to him.

"What didn't you tell the cop?" he asked.

"I didn't tell him that Charles Smiths is missing more than two hundred thousand dollars, and the bank who hired my firm is convinced that the thief is the same guy Henry DeVries interviewed," I shared as we pulled out of the lot.

A corner of his mouth quirked up.

"How did he manage that?"

"Charles Smiths opened a personal line of credit on-line a few months ago. No problem; he's worth millions. Then there was a lot of activity on the line, and an automatic fraud alert kicked in, shutting off the account. The bank's policy is to try to notify the holder of the account. They left messages, but due to privacy rules all they did was say it was the bank and that they had an important business matter to discuss, with an eight-hundred number to call. No one ever called back, which isn't that surprising, since lots of people delete calls like that from their answering machines. But the strange thing is, Charles Smiths never called to complain that his account was shut off. He didn't call to complain about the activity either. On the other hand, he didn't pay. Then some clerk noticed an irregularity. The new account opening-document signature didn't match the original. The bank figured Smiths didn't know about the account."

"So?" Connor changed lanes, going around a slow-moving Mustang with a granny at the wheel. "Why didn't they just ask the guy if the account was his?"

"Politics. When the average guy gets his identity swiped, the banks figure it's the cost of doing business. They file an insurance claim, then pretty much turn all the cleanup over to the poor slob on the wrong end of things."

"Okay."

"When a major customer is involved, the banks simply refund the amount wrongfully withdrawn without the customer having to do a thing or, if the bank's really lucky, knowing a thing. It's like getting hacked. If everyone knows your most valued customers are at risk, sooner or later you don't have any valued customers. You have to eat the loss anyway, since they're big enough to scare you with pulling their accounts, and the loss in customers just isn't worth the insurance check. It's kind of backward, really. For nickels and dimes, the banks report and the insurance companies pay. For big dollars, or important clients, the bank bites the bullet and plays see-no-evil and especially tell-no-evil."

When my boss had briefed me on the case and told me that, I'd groaned. The reaction had earned me a ten-minute diatribe on understanding that our clients weren't like other people. Morris Allensworth Hamilton IV, pin-striped and constipated senior partner in a major Seattle law firm, included himself in the elite class of bank patrons whose world would not be cluttered by such mundane considerations as identity theft. That he clearly

thought peons like me deserved whatever happened to
them would have been funny if it hadn't included his
complete inability to perceive any reason any person
on earth would choose to pretend to be one of us.

"How do they know the real Smiths didn't make the
withdrawals? Christ, the guy could just deny it and end
up with a quarter-of-a-million-dollar lotto win."

"They don't. They hire an investigator. In this case,
me. Which I was carefully doing at my desk until Charles
Smiths gave an interview on the radio. Because Charles
Smiths's accounts were under a fraud watch from the
bank, they were notified when it happened. They do a
whole Big Brother thing to anyone on their radar. Newspaper alerts, new credit application check, a daily Google.
The bank told me. I confirmed that the real Smiths
signed a charge for the Geek Squad to set up a new TV
in Seattle an hour before the interview in San Diego.
The radio station confirmed the Smiths interview was
done in person. Voila. Smiths didn't do the interview.
Two different guys impersonating Smiths simultaneously
struck the bank as an unlikely coincidence, so here I
am."

"What's the point?" Connor asked.

"If the interviewee and the thief are the same guy, I
need to confirm it without letting Smiths know that the
bank has given hundreds of thousands of Smiths's dollars
to a thief. If this guy is just a nut giving interviews, I
need to find that out, too."

"What will the bank do?"

"If the thief has the money, the bank will quietly write
it off. I'll probably have a word with the guy and try to
convince him that next time he'll go to jail, but the bank
won't really go there. Too much bad publicity, and it
would get back to Smiths. On the other hand, if Smiths
set up the account and made the withdrawals, the bank
will send a gentle reminder that obscene wealth can lead
to forgetting little things like owing a quarter of a million
dollars, and to please pay."

"Nice clients you have."

He had a point. It didn't seem right somehow to help
out the bank when they were willing to let real people

suffer the pain of identity theft at the same time they protected those actually in a position to defend themselves. On the other hand, the bank was getting screwed, too, so technically it is a victim and I wasn't actually employed by the forces of evil. It was just hard to tell them apart. In my heart of hearts, I'd be happier if I were sticking up for the *little* guy. With banks and millionaires, little became relative pretty fast.

I was getting so paranoid. Too much *Sopranos*. From now on I was sticking to PBS. Now I was wondering what other motivations the bank might have. If this were really on the up-and-up, wouldn't they go to the cops, ask for discretion? The logic made a sort of stupid sense, but maybe there was more going on. Something I didn't know about. Like what would the bank really do with this guy if I found him? Talk to him? Why? What would be the point? If they weren't willing to go public, they couldn't have him arrested. They'd already cut off access to the accounts. It had to be the interview. Maybe DeVries did know something. What?

Connor exited the freeway and we were once again in civilization. "Your turn," I prompted.

"My turn?"

"C'mon, Con, give. I told you. You left those cops thinking this was some sort of random violence. You don't believe that."

"They haven't tagged the DB yet."

"English, please."

"We don't know who the victim is yet."

"It's DeVries," I insisted. "Oh, I get it. We weren't formally introduced, and just because he was the man standing near me at the exact time and place where I was supposed to meet Henry DeVries doesn't mean the dead guy has anything to do with me. Convenient." There I was, thinking again.

As much as I was enjoying playing cat and mouse with Connor, it would be kind of a relief if this was just bad timing. Who was I kidding? That brainless I could never be. Of course, if the body in the street turned out to be someone other than DeVries, like a drug dealer or a known terrorist or something, maybe. But even that didn't play. Why pick that moment? It had to mean something.

"He was just a guy walking out of a building," Connor said as casually as he could. He should work on that delivery.

"What do you mean?" I played along.

"I mean that if I'm some radio shock jock with an agenda that makes Rush Limbaugh look like Jesse Jackson, I wouldn't agree to meet anyone at my place of business. I wouldn't even concede that I had a place of business. I'd sure as hell be watching my six."

"Your six?"

"My back."

"Right. But I called him."

"You called a number a voice on the phone gave Joe. It's not validation. We don't know that this thing has anything to do with him or you or your case."

"You're saying that I just happened along a neighborhood difference of opinion?" We were back to the really-big-coincidence theory.

"Jesus, Sara, you saw the place. That neighborhood probably has blood on the sidewalk twice a week."

"Lucky it wasn't my blood," I said.

"Yeah, lucky," he muttered.

Chapter Three

I watched them from the deck. He was bigger and broader than Connor. Mahogany-skinned and bald-headed, both of them glistening with sweat in the early-morning sunshine. I couldn't see Connor's expression, but their body language told me this wasn't a casual chat. I drank a little more juice. Connor had been gone more than an hour. At his running pace, that probably meant ten hard miles. While I'd bet they worked out every day—their respective zero-body-fat bare chests clear evidence—I doubted most days required that kind of stress relief. Face-to-face, still talking after the run was over. A colleague. Since the mystery man was also Connor's first call after yesterday, Mr. Bald Is Beautiful was probably a friend as well. They were definitely up to something.

A dark shape emerged from the foliage next to the walkway. Looked up at me. Damn. There she was again. That was definitely the same dog. How the heck could she have followed us home?

I went back into the apartment and had a quick glance around. Connor would suspect, of course. He wasn't stupid. And he knew me better than I knew him. It was all I could do not to pull the fire alarm to get a couple of alone minutes in his place to have my first good snoop. He worked out. I snooped. Everyone had their own stress remedies.

He rolled his socks into balls, all facing the same way. He had exactly eight each of his foundation garments—T-shirts, socks, boxer briefs, and one pair of silks that seemed startlingly out of place and worthy of further investigation. I bet he'd never bought socks because he ran out of clean laundry. That alone was pretty disturbing, but it didn't tell me anything other than that opposites attracted.

His closet was the same: several uniforms ranging from desert fatigues (who ironed stuff like that?) to the blinding white formal wear I'd teased him about. Shoes and boots, all highly polished. Then there was a tuxedo, two business suits, and four pairs of chinos. Jeans, button-downs and polo shirts, and sneakers rounded out the closet. And all of it organized by type of clothing. Really disturbing.

It was a little endearing, too. There were two empty drawers and ten extra hangers. Mine, I'd guess. It was sweet and thoughtful, and he'd never admit he'd done it to make me feel more at home. Too squishy for a SEAL.

The rest of the condo was more of the same. His reading tastes were eclectic, spanning from *Architectural Digest* to Harlan Coben thrillers. He used a bookmark instead of turning the corner of the page. We probably shouldn't share. The furniture was nice but unmemorable. The television was huge and plasma-screen. Fruits and vegetables lined the shelves in his refrigerator, and there wasn't any spinach liquefying in the crisper drawer. His cupboards held no snacks, sweet or salty. He ate Kashi cereal. No Lucky Charms. We were going to have to agree to disagree there. The second bedroom seemed unused and the guest bathroom was so pristine I wondered if anyone ever came to stay.

When Connor came in, I was sitting on the floor in my bra and panties, rummaging through my carry-on suitcase. He might not notice, but I was wearing a matching set.

"This outfit works for me," he told me, leaning against the doorjamb, enjoying the view.

I turned my head to look at him, haughty and half-naked.

"Gee, thanks."

I went back to digging through my clothes. I was shooting for nonchalance.

"I'm looking for"—I pulled up a pair of jeans—"these. Why is it that if I need something, it's always on the bottom?" I shook the denim, sat down, and pulled them up my legs.

"Murphy's Law. You could have waited for me to shower."

"Somehow I thought that might take a while, and I want to get started checking out what happened last night."

"Why do you want to do that?"

"A man is dead. If it turns out to be Henry DeVries, it could be related to my impostor."

He didn't say anything.

"What?" I couldn't take it.

"Is it too much to ask that you let the police handle it?"

I looked up at him. Like he was going to? I couldn't tell if he thought I'd buy it or if he was just making general conversation. I wouldn't take it personally if he was trying to trick me into signing up for the snake-oil-of-the-month program—not that I'd tell him that. He'd never scam me about something important. Well, nothing like other women or impending financial disaster or anything, but he'd definitely tell the protect-the-little-woman whopper if he thought he could get away with it. That was fine. It was his responsibility to try, and mine to catch him at it. No problem. I was up to the challenge.

"Is that what you're planning to do?" I asked, wide-eyed and innocent—except for the mostly-undressed part.

Ah, a gentleman. He was struggling with it. I saw it in the tightness of his jaw. Dishonesty didn't sit well. I shouldn't play with him. He was out of his league, poor lamb.

"Don't you think that's the right answer?" he asked, dodging.

"Answering a question with a question won't do it, Connor. You have no intention of letting these sleeping dogs lie. I saw your face last night. You're mad. You're not just going to wait around to see what the police find out."

"Adrenaline, that's all. This morning it makes more sense to leave it to them."

"You mean it makes more sense for me to leave it to them."

"Well, yeah."

I laughed. Hard to get mad at a guy this terrible at bullshit. I pulled a T-shirt over my head. He straightened, then sagged back against the doorjamb. He'd had a tough couple of minutes. First I refused to let the shooting go, and then I put on clothes.

"Are you going to tell me what you're going to do?" I stood up and put my hands on my hips, throwing in a little stink-eye for good measure. What would he do? Try another lie? Distraction?

Stall. "I never said I was doing anything."

"Who's the Adonis?" I asked.

"Who?"

"Tall, black, beautiful." I rolled my eyes. "Better runner than you."

He sighed. "Blue. His name is Blue."

"He's black and he's Blue?" I laughed at him. Sometimes he didn't realize when he was being funny.

"Yeah."

"And you met at some unholy hour to go for a casual jog the first morning I was here?"

"I run with him a lot."

"Instead of staying with me? I don't think so. If there's one thing I'm pretty sure about, Connor, this early in our marriage, it's that racing out of our bed isn't something you'll do often."

Point for me. I didn't think I'd be doing it much either, but now wasn't the time to say so.

He reached out and put his hands on my hips, reeling me closer. "You didn't try to talk me out of going."

"God was still sleeping when you left. Stop changing the subject."

He pulled me close enough to kiss beneath my ear. I felt the current travel down my spine.

"What was the subject?"

I took his wrists and pulled them away from my body. "I rest my case."

I reached up and patted his cheek like a kid. His body didn't get the "kid" message.

"You make me sound like a sex fiend," he said.

"You are a sex fiend."

He laughed. There was no real way to argue with that in his present condition. "That's why you married me."

I went to the dresser and picked up a brush, pulling it through my curls. No sense giving him a second look at the Medusa curls. This was more for effect and because I was enjoying playing with him.

"True. Actually, not true. I'm not sure why I married you. Or, to be more precise, I'm not that clear on how it actually happened. The sex-fiend thing was a pleasant postnuptial surprise." I shook my head, very model-like and dramatic. The crazy curls marred the moment, but he sucked in his breath anyway.

I could have told him why I'd married him. I'd thought about it endlessly. Obsessed over it. How does a thirty-five-year-old woman wake up next to a one-night stand and agree to a quickie Vegas wedding? I could pretty it up with knowing my own heart and waiting for Mr. Right, but that was all crap. I did it because he dared me. He'd asked and I'd laughed. Tsk, tsk. Afraid of marriage? Of men? Hell, no, I wasn't afraid. I was married.

"Postnuptial surprise?" he asked. "You've got to stop hanging out with all those lawyers."

"What did you ask him to do?"

"Who?"

"Don't play blond, Connor. It's not convincing. Blue. What did you ask him to do?"

I pulled him back on track. I wasn't ready to share that he'd outmaneuvered me with the whole wedding thing. Or to find out whether he thought he'd outmaneuvered himself at the same time.

"You have a one-track mind."

"What did you ask him to do?" I repeated.

"I asked him to check out the car. I also asked him to do a background on DeVries."

"See how easy that was? It didn't hurt a bit, did it?

If your friend is going to do the paper-trail stuff, I should try to talk to some of the people in that neighborhood. Maybe I can pick up some good gossip." I knelt and took a hair toy from the suitcase, turning to look in the mirror as I tried to wrangle my curls into a bun.

"You don't have to go back. Blue's going to check it out. Believe me when I tell you that if there's anything to know, he'll find it."

"Maybe. There could still be something worth finding at the crime scene itself."

"I don't want you going back there."

I met his eyes in the mirror. "It's broad daylight. The place is undoubtedly still overrun by the boys in blue. Besides, I'll have company."

"Who?"

"Pavarotti."

"Who?"

"Pavarotti. Our four-footed friend from last night. I figured she's a tenor. I know there are a couple of other famous ones but I couldn't remember their names, so she became Pavarotti. She must have followed us home."

"You named her." He shook his head.

"Of course." The bun wasn't working. I took it out and watched my hair go back to wild curls. I was never going to look put together. Maybe I should just face facts?

"It can't be the same dog. She couldn't have followed us. It's got to be twenty miles."

"I'm telling you."

"I'm telling you not to go back to talk to the neighbors until I can go with you."

Oh, he didn't just say that. I stared at him. Put the brush down on the dresser top. "I don't take orders, Connor. I thought we'd established that last night."

"That came out wrong."

"Gee, you think?"

"I've got to go into the office. It can't be helped. Wait for me to go with you." He held up his hands. "Please."

I slapped a hand to my forehead. "I almost forgot. Some captain called. He said that your morning meeting was pushed to two o'clock, but he wanted you to meet with, um, somebody at nine. I wrote it down." I pointed to the night table.

He picked up the sheet of paper and read. He crumpled the paper.

"Trouble?"

"Tomás Gutierrez. SecNav."

"That clears it right up."

"Secretary of the Navy."

"Ah, the big cheese. Got it."

"Okay. I'll work it out. I can be out of there by four thirty. Five at the latest. We'll go back then. Together."

"I'm going to need a car."

"I'll drive us later."

I stood up and went over to stand in front of him. Hands on hips. Not smiling. Not cooperating. Basically being me.

"I want to get there while the police are still discombobulating the neighbors."

"People don't discombobulate." He shook his head.

It was a good word.

"In that neighborhood, they don't," he said. "Not for the cops. They've seen too much. Wait for me."

"I'll be fine. I'm wearing my most do-not-be-alarmed-by-me-I'm-harmless clothes. I'll rent a nondescript car. I'll hang out. I'll make unsuspicious small talk. I'll blend so well you'd think I was a smoothie. I'm going. Stop worrying."

He groaned. "Call me the second you're out of there. Take the cell phone. I want it with you at all times. One hour. That's it. If you're a minute late . . ." he threatened.

"I know." I smiled. "You'll send in the marines."

"Better. I'll send in the SEALs."

Accord. Great. I released my hair, pulled my T-shirt off, and unsnapped my jeans.

"Do I have to wait?"

"You're dangerous," he said.

I slid my hands across his chest. Hard muscle encased in silk. "Pots and kettles, buddy."

Chapter Four

The phone rang.

"McNamara," he barked.

"Townley." I used my stern voice. I could barely hear him over the cough of the engine.

"Hi." His voice slid toward honey. I could feel it in the pit of my stomach.

"Hi, yourself. Is this a bad time?"

"No. Where are you?"

"Headed back toward the water, I think. Damn," I yelped. "Sorry." The gears ground noisily. I'd worry if ruining the transmission of this behemoth didn't seem like an act of mercy.

"No problem."

"I wasn't apologizing to you. I was talking to the guy I just cut off."

The engine grind rose an octave. It went from car failure to cat crisis. I closed my eyes in protest. Not a good idea. When I opened them again I had to jump on the brakes to avoid the back end of a fancy-schmancy car whose bumper was worth more than this entire car on its first day.

"Sara, what the hell is all the noise?"

"I rented a car. Shit. Sorry."

I waited while he cursed. I empathized. "Sara?"

"That wasn't my fault. He was tailgating," I yelled over the rumbling engine.

"Maybe you shouldn't talk and drive."

Everyone was a critic. He hadn't tried to steer this bus.

"I'd be fine if— Hang on a second."

The tires squealed, followed by a *chump-chump-bang*. That was new. Not good, but new. I took a deep breath and held it, waiting for the crash.

"Sorry," I yelled. "Jeez, some people don't know how to share the road. Anyway, I'm back."

"Pull over."

"I can't do that. Grenville might not start again."

"Who? No, never mind. Just get off the road."

Middle lane. Uncooperative, life-threatening heap of a car or, in the event of a collision, missile. The traffic on both sides was going what felt like a hundred miles an hour with two-inch clearances. Changing lanes wasn't in the cards.

The coffee I'd been drinking roiled in my stomach. I reached across to open the glove compartment. Surely the last renter had stocked up on the antacids. The compartment wouldn't open. I banged on it and banged again. It popped open and launched the contents onto the passenger seat. Maps, air-pressure gauge, condoms, and duct tape. Hey, I was a believer in safety first, but I wasn't sure if that meant the condoms, the duct tape, or both.

"Sara?"

"I think I know where I am now."

"Just pull off and I'll come get you."

"I've got the hang of it now. Idiot," I yelled. "That was totally his fault."

"Get off the road."

The phone went ominously silent. I wiped the sweat from my forehead.

"Sara?"

I dropped the phone and grabbed for the steering wheel with both hands. I eased into the sudden break in traffic and took the exit, made a quick left, and pulled into a parking lot. I leaned back against the headrest. Who needed cardio?

"Sara!"

"You don't have to yell."

"What happened?"

"I parked."

He blew out a breath. I could picture him in some bland government office, pacing, eyes closed. He did not like being out of control. It could have been worse. He could have been in the car with me.

"Okay. Parked is good."

"Two slots together. I didn't even have to parallel park, which is good, since Grenville is a bit on the recalcitrant side."

"Who is Grenville?"

"The car."

"This thing has a name?"

"I named him."

"Of course you did."

"I thought it would help us bond. Improve our relationship, which frankly hasn't been that great so far, what with the stalling and backfiring and teeth rattling. My head hurts worse than it did after the Aerosmith concert."

"What the hell kind of car did you rent, anyway?"

"I tried to go to Rent-A-Wreck, but their cars there were all too nice. Totally false advertising. So Ryan arranged one of lesser appeal."

"You called Ryan?"

"More like I conjured him."

"And he let you go into that crummy neighborhood in a beater?"

He sounded mad. It wasn't Ryan's fault. He'd only been trying to help, which was more than Connor'd done by ducking out of the condo while I blew my hair dry. As if a little thing like no transport to the rental car place would dissuade me. It was so ungallant, I knew he'd done it to discourage me. Ryan's turning up on the doorstep had saved me from figuring out the whole taxi-or-bus thing to get a car.

"Ryan doesn't *let* me do things, Connor." I permafrosted my voice. It might be enough to cool his tongue, if not his temper. I didn't want Connor taking a bite out of Ryan for being a good guy and doing me a favor. Besides, I wasn't stupid. It was daylight, for Pete's sake. And no one, *no one,* would try to steal this thing, bright light of day or no.

"Right." It came out cranky, but he clearly didn't want to start World War III over something that had already happened. Either that or he thought he was more lethal in person.

"Absolutely right. And I don't want you blaming Ryan for this. I know how to take care of myself."

Ten seconds. Twenty. A minute. Maybe he counted to cool down. Maybe he was quietly breaking office furniture. Hard to tell. I could hear him breathing, so I was pretty sure he hadn't had a heart attack from the strain. I'd give him a couple of minutes to get the temperature gauge back down to nonexplosive. I stretched, moving my head from side to side. I reached my arms over my head and twisted at the spine. The lack of shock absorbers had compressed my spine in ways that told me I wasn't as young as I used to be.

"Connor?"

"Yeah."

"I don't want you taking it out on Ryan. He was only trying to help."

Silence. How did he do that? The emotional control was remarkable.

"I mean it," I told him.

He sighed. A heavy, meaningful, against-my-better-judgment-and-only-because-right-now-my-little-brother-is-not-close-enough-to-maim kind of sigh.

"I hear you. Was it worth it?"

"Not so far. I left a lot of cards on doors but no one's really talking. It's early days. This part of the job is all shoe leather and patience." I looked down at my sneakers. "Oh-for-two. "Do you still want to meet for lunch?"

"Yeah. I'll pick you up."

"No need. I'm already downtown. Can we eat down here? I can see the marina. I'm not sure which street exactly, but it looks pretty close. There's got to be some good places down here."

"Um."

"What does 'um' mean? Don't worry if you can't do lunch, Con. You're working. I understand. It's not a problem."

I wanted to see him, but I also wanted to appear rea-

sonable about his work. Something told me I'd need to
be able to say 'I support your job' later. Probably when
I wanted to do something he didn't like. He'd only have
an hour for lunch anyway, best case. If I focused afterward, and he worked a regular day, we could meet at
his place by five, five thirty at the latest. We'd have
fourteen hours without interruption. I had plans for
those fourteen hours.

"It'll need to be someplace casual, though," I mused.
"I'm still dressed in jeans. Otherwise, I'll have to go
back to your place first to change."

He hesitated.

"The club is casual. Are you near the Marriott? It's
probably easier now that you're parked to just walk
over."

The Marriott sounded high-end. Oh, well, if he didn't
mind I didn't.

"I can see it from here. You're probably right. I
wouldn't want to give up a primo parking space. When?"

"The Yacht Club is on the boardwalk between the
convention center and Seaport Village. It's right near
the hotel. Anybody can tell you where."

"Yacht Club? It sounds swanky."

"It's not. Everything on the water is called a yacht
club."

"Okay. Meet you there in a half hour."

"Sara?"

"Yeah?"

"I'm sorry I yelled at you."

He led a very sheltered life.

"You don't know what yelling is." I laughed. "You've
got to ask Russ to show you sometime. He screams in
three languages, and includes hand gestures and, when
he's really in the zone, projectiles. It's a force of nature.
Frankly, you're an amateur. If you want, I can score you
some lessons."

Just the thought of my over-the-top best friend and
neighbor Russ standing in my living room gesticulating
wildly while Connor sat on the couch with a bemused
expression had me laughing out loud. We'd probably
have to do the coursework in small doses. Ten minutes

at a time so Connor didn't accidentally drop Russ out a window to get it to stop. I loved them both, but they were night and day. Connor, unflappable and patient. A deep thinker and, sometimes, a nontalker. Russ, hilarious and flamboyant. An emoter and, always, an oversharer. My men.

"I'm sorry anyway."

"You're forgiven."

"Seen any more of your friend the explorer today?"

I sighed. I'd been looking for her. "No. I'm kind of bummed about it."

"Well, I'm glad you haven't run off with another suitor."

I laughed. "That's nice, honey. Hang up, now, Connor."

Chapter Five

"**Y**ou said casual," I hissed in his ear, balking just inside the foyer at the Yacht Club. "And you never mentioned your family. Again."

"It is casual, and I thought you might not show after last night."

He had a point about the no-show. "In what universe? If lunch costs more than I make in a year, it is not, by definition, casual."

I squeezed his hand hard enough to stop blood flow. Men. Two days in a row making the less-than-stellar family impression. I might not be the most sensitive of women when it came to dress code, but I didn't want to go to the ball as the Little Match Girl either. They'd think I was a complete idiot. I looked around. The men wore creased golf slacks and crisp shirts, while the women were in silky dresses and heels. I saw pearls. There were at least three trophy wives, and enough plastic body parts to run a Barbie chop shop.

Connor leaned down and whispered in my ear: "I think you look great."

"That'll help, Connor. You get to be the navy recruiting poster boy while I'm shilling for Save the Children."

He choked. I glared. It wasn't a cough. It was laughter, and he was about to get himself hurt. Blood would show on that uniform.

"It is not funny."

A solemn face and dancing eyes did not solace bring. "It's just family, honey. No one will notice."

I wasn't going. It was as simple as that. He couldn't

make me, and he'd never cause a scene in the middle
of the Yacht Club. Then again, he'd tricked me into
showing up in blue jeans for a family get-together at the
Marriott, so he really must not have cared what people
thought and was stupid enough to try to convince me to
go in since I was already there. He'd already risked a
scene. I could be screaming right now. I could have my
hands around his throat and there wasn't a woman in
the place who'd interfere if the facts were known.

"You don't actually think a public place is going to
protect you, right?"

He stopped. Turned. Sighed. "I don't suppose you'll
think I have a good reason."

"I think reason has left the building."

"My mother said she expected you, and she did mention it last night, but mostly I thought you'd suddenly
have something you had to do on the case if I told you
my parents would be here."

"Gee, you think?"

"They won't care what you're wearing."

"Honest to God, Connor, are you trying to be dense?
Your family already thinks I'm some sort of sex fiend.
Now they'll add garage-sale fashion sense and total social embarrassment to my list of nonqualities." I dropped
his hand and stepped away, pushing my hands through
my hair.

"Sara, it's no big—"

"Sara, Connor, have you been waiting long?" His father walked up and clapped a hand on Connor's shoulder, smiling down at me. I tried to smile back. He'd be
okay. He'd still have one son who could father children.

"Admiral McNamara." I held out my hand, wondering
if "psychotic break" showed in my expression. The older
man took my hand and pulled me in for a quick hug,
kissing my cheek.

"Dougal, remember? Or 'hey, you' if it's easier. Have
you seen Alyssa? She should already be here." Leaving
an arm around my shoulders, he steered me toward the
dining room. I caught the look he exchanged with Connor. Obviously a man who'd seen plenty of combat in
his time. As we walked through the dining room, I was

uncomfortably aware that I wore the only pair of jeans in the room.

Connor's mother and his sister, Siobhan, sat at a table on the deck, their eyes shielded by sunglasses. If either thought anything about the way I was dressed, they didn't show it. Whoever said ignorance was bliss had never been clueless about the dress code in front of their in-laws and their friends.

"Sara, we're so glad you could make it." His mother smiled easily.

Connor held out a chair and I sat down, keeping my back to him. I didn't think I was going to be able to keep my mood out of my expression if I looked at him. Dougal took a chair next to Alyssa, and Connor sat next to me, leaving Ryan's chair the only empty one at the table.

"Thank you for inviting me—I mean us." I could feel myself redden. *And next time would it be too much to get that invitation in writing, with a suggested form of dress? A little insight to keep me from looking like a total idiot in front of my scary mother-in-law?* I took a deep breath. It wasn't their fault. No, it was Connor's.

"You were right the first time," Ryan said as he arrived at the table, going around to kiss his mother and tug on Siobhan's ponytail. She swatted at him, a half smile touching her pale face. He knelt next to me, pinning me to the chair with an exuberant hug and kiss. He was like a big friendly puppy. I felt my anger cool.

"You're much better-looking," Ryan said. "We had to invite him to get you to come, but now that you know us, feel free to leave him home." He threw a punch toward Connor's arm. "Hey, didn't he warn you about the dress code? They're used to button-down anal-retentive types here. A sexy pair of jeans like those are likely to cause a riot. That's why I never wear them." He grinned at me.

Bless him. No guile, straight to the obvious. He really was charming.

I smiled back. "A public service."

His grin broadened. "Exactly. You're smart and beautiful. Hard to imagine there are two of us in the same family. What are the odds?" Ryan straightened and brushed at the crease in his trousers. He pulled his chair around Connor's, wedging himself between us. Connor glared at him, but I moved over, giving him room. He'd come to my rescue. If it were up to me, he could sit anywhere he wanted.

Connor heaved a sigh and moved his chair.

"There. That's better. Where's the food? Have you ordered yet? I'm starving."

We took a couple of minutes to place our orders. When the drinks came, the interrogation began.

"So tell us everything, and don't leave out the good parts," Ryan said.

"What do you want to know?"

"Well . . ." Ryan leaned close and waggled his eyebrows at me. His teasing relaxed me, and I almost, but not quite, forgot that I was underdressed at this little soiree. Whatever grudge Connor might harbor about the car, he owed Ryan big-time for saving his butt at lunch.

"How did you and Connor meet?" Alyssa jumped in, smiling an apology at me. Maybe she thought her youngest was being pushy, but I welcomed his directness. I tried not to flinch as her under-the-table kick to one of her offspring went wide. I assumed she hadn't deliberately targeted me.

"I already told you that," Connor protested.

" 'Las Vegas' is hardly a complete answer, dear."

Everyone looked at me.

"We met in Las Vegas."

"See?" Connor asked. No one so much as looked toward him. This hot seat was apparently a one-seater.

"At the half marathon. Actually, I'm pretty sure Connor was there to run the full marathon, even though he denies it."

"So he waited until you were exhausted and couldn't get away to ask you out." Ryan blew out a heavy sigh. "Typical."

Ryan's unrelenting teasing of his older brother was starting to make me feel a little sorry for Connor.

"Pretty much, yeah," I said.

Everyone laughed. The waiter came with our lunch.

"How did he ask you to marry him?" Siobhan asked. "Was it romantic?"

"Very."

"It was?" Connor seemed incredulous. It wasn't traditional, sure, but it had been romantic. Sneaky and underhanded and totally sweet.

"I thought so."

"Let me guess. He used the champagne-and-flowers approach? Probably some schmaltzy music. Some guys have no imagination." Ryan shook his head, biting the head off of a piece of broccoli.

"No champagne, no flowers. No music, either, unless you want to count the sound of the slot machines."

"He proposed in a casino?" Alyssa sounded appalled.

"He didn't propose, exactly."

"What did he do?" Siobhan asked, leaning forward.

"He offered me half his nickels."

Ryan choked on his beer. Connor pounded him on the back a little harder than he probably needed to.

"I always knew we'd have to pay somebody to take him off our hands," Ryan mocked.

His parents laughed. Even Siobhan smiled a little. This family thing wasn't so bad. They were nice.

"I thought it was sweet," I said, deliberately fluttering my eyelashes at him. Connor's cheeks pinked.

"Sweet," Ryan said, rolling his eyes at me. Connor put his hand on the back of Ryan's neck. To an undiscerning eye it might look like brotherly affection, but I had a sneaking suspicion that Connor was squeezing. Ryan's eyes widened and he yelped.

"Hey, sweet is good. I like sweet. I'm always saying there just aren't enough sweet guys out there. I mean sweet he-men types. Don't you think so?" Ryan squeaked, pulling away from Connor's hand.

"Mmmm," Dougal said.

"Sweet is fine, Connor," Alyssa agreed, ganging up on him.

"I didn't have any left." I tried to rescue him. "Nickels, I mean. I didn't have any left. They give you these buckets to hold them in. You probably know that. Anyway, I'd been playing the slot machines and I'd run through my ten dollars. Connor was playing the machine next to me and he'd hit a jackpot. He had, like, fifty dollars' worth. Anyway, he said he knew a way I could have half his nickels. I asked him how, and he said I could marry him."

"Aw, that is sweet, you old softie." Ryan punched Connor on the arm. Connor punched him back half-heartedly.

All Ryan's clowning had made it impossible for me to stay mad. Connor owed him big-time.

"What did you say?" Siobhan asked.

"I laughed." They did, too. "And said no."

"No, thank you," Connor corrected. "Her rejection was very polite."

"Then he said he'd bet me all the nickels that I wouldn't have the nerve to say yes. I said he'd run screaming in the other direction if I said yes, which he denied."

"He's more a crier than a screamer," Ryan suggested.

"Sshh." Siobhan waved him off. "So you said yes."

"Not right away."

"Tease." Ryan threw an arm around me.

"He started shaking the bucket. Taunting me. Fifty dollars in nickels makes a lot of noise. He just kept shaking the bucket, pushing it toward me, then pulling it away. I realized the people around us were listening. When they knew that I knew they were there, they started yelling. 'Do it.' 'Get it in writing.' 'Take the money.' 'Marry him.' 'Run.' It was crazy."

"Somebody told you to run?" Alyssa asked, laughing hard, leaning into the story.

"Cynics," Connor said.

"People started tossing nickels into Connor's bucket. Just a couple at first. Then more. A little old woman, she must have been eighty, dumped her whole bucket into Connor's and said her contribution entitled her to Connor's 'service.'" I made air quotes. "Every other Tuesday."

"Hey, I'm a catch."

"Pretty soon he had a whole bucket of nickels. I didn't have any. What's a girl to do?"

"So you got married." Siobhan sighed.

"Less than a half hour later. I still don't know how he arranged that." I sipped at my water.

"I had nine hundred and eighty-seven dollars and a willing woman. I was unstoppable."

"Con-nor," a female voice purred.

Arms wrapped around him from behind. Ryan froze beside me.

Siobhan went pale. Dougal stood up, glancing at Alyssa. Ryan leaned back, sliding an arm around the back of my chair. His body language screamed *intrusion*.

"Lily." Connor pulled her arms from around his chest, but she slid around to the front and sat on his lap, kissing him on the lips. Definitely an ex. Still possessive, too. Ryan's arm came off the back of the chair and pulled me a little closer protectively. I didn't move.

Connor pulled his head back, standing up and forcing her to stand, too. He held her away from him and looked at me.

"I didn't know you were in town. You should have called."

The invader pouted. She was dressed in a short green dress, showing long legs in high heels. Her blond hair was down and straight. She had that hot-date look that some women seemed to pull off effortlessly. So Connor's past would never wear jeans to the club. Bully for her.

"I'd like to call you something," Ryan muttered.

"Sara, I'd like you to meet Lily Dawson." Alyssa smoothed over the moment with a page from Miss Manners. "She's an old friend of the family. Her mother and I were at Vassar together. Lily, this is—" Alyssa began.

"My wife," Connor broke in.

He said it with pride. I began to breathe again.

"Excuse me?" The color drained from Lily's face.

"My wife."

"Sara Townley," Alyssa began again. "Our daughter-in-law."

"I hadn't heard. Congratulations." Lily smiled at me, her eyes glittering. "You'll have to excuse me, Stella. I've been living in New York for the last couple of years and haven't had a chance to catch up with Connor yet."

The family was silent, the moment dragging awkwardly. Siobhan kept her head down, while Ryan looked resentful. Connor's parents exchanged a long look. Everyone was waiting for me. Connor looked more resigned than fearful. I could explode or just laugh the whole thing off. I was jealous. I'd never been jealous before. About anyone. I wasn't sure what to do. Connor's green eyes bore into me. She was standing next to him, all polished and perfect, and he was staring at me, oblivious. He might just be putting a good face on it, but if so, it was convincing. A ghost of a smile touched his lips. Waiting for me. Either way.

"My name is Sara." I stood up and moved around Ryan's chair, holding out my hand. "I'm happy to meet any friend of Connor's."

Lily let my hand hover while she stared at me. She used a toothpaste smile and finally offered just her fingertips. I hated people who did that. What did she think? I was going to kiss her hand?

"How do you do?" Lily asked me, staring at Connor.

"I'm very well, thank you." I dropped Lily's dead fish. Ryan stood up and moved to the back of my chair, holding it for me. Well, I knew whose side he was on. I smiled at him and he winked back.

"Sara was just telling us about how she and Connor got married. One look and he was a goner." Ryan sat down and casually draped his napkin across his knee. "Couldn't wait to get married. Rushed right off then and there. I guess when you find the right one, nothing gets in the way."

"How is your mother, Lily?" Alyssa asked. "I haven't seen her since the silent auction."

Dougal stepped toward the empty table to his right and took one of the chairs. He brought it over next to his and held it while Lily sat down. Connor gave him a slight shake of his head, but he just shrugged. I guessed this was going to play out. There was something off about Lily. Whatever it was, I'd rather know what was coming. Connor and his father sat down.

"Can I see your ring?" Lily asked sweetly.

I held out my hand with its plain band. Lily reached

across to take my fingers, the square-cut diamond on her own left hand catching the light. For an engaged woman, she was pretty quick to fondle somebody else's husband.

Siobhan took an audible breath and the whole table went still. Ryan's hand gripped my shoulder.

"We haven't exactly had time to go shopping yet," Connor mumbled.

What was he talking about? I loved my ring.

"Connor hasn't seen anything good enough for Sara," Ryan offered. Siobhan reached out a hand and touched my arm. Alarm bells clanged in my head.

"It's very"—Lily rolled wide gray eyes to me—"sweet."

The energy at the table was toxic. What was going . . . the lightbulb went off. Ex with a capital E.

"You'll have to excuse us, Lily. We haven't had a chance to get to know Sara yet, so we planned this family lunch to get better acquainted. I'm sure you understand." His mother tried to save him, her face grim as she looked from Lily to me.

"You should make him buy you an engagement ring," Lily said. "He's very good at engagement rings. This one belonged to his grandmother. He insisted I keep it." Lily held her hand up, admiring the ring on her own hand before batting her eyes at Connor. His face was completely blank. Yep. Dead man walking.

There was no way I was letting this bitch have the upper hand. Even if it was wearing a diamond big enough to play baseball on.

"No point, really," I said, smiling at her. "We're not engaged."

"Of course. But you should get him to buy you one anyway. You never know."

"She knows." Connor tried to catch my eye, but I didn't acknowledge it. I breathed calmly. In and out. Air was a really good tool for dealing with malevolent forces. She was deliberately provoking me. That was a mistake she'd live to regret.

"I know the ring he bought me was a wedding ring." I folded my hands on the table, the platinum band visible. "Actually, he bought me two. One when we actually got married and this one. Platinum. Sort of a this-is-really-working-out-upgrade. Guess he really meant the whole forever-and-ever thing."

Connor's shoulders relaxed a fraction. Lily's smile never faded, but her eyes went hard. Nasty and cold. What had Connor been thinking?

"Funny he doesn't wear one, then."

"I don't need a ring to remind me," Connor said. "I know I'm married."

"I'm sure he does, Susie. Connor was always very reliable that way. Unlike some people." Lily turned toward Siobhan. "I ran into Jack the other day. You should have called me, Siobhan. At the Sheraton, although I heard he put a deposit down on a new place. One of the penthouse suites near the marina. That's terrible for you."

Siobhan went deadly white. Her mouth opened, but she didn't say anything.

"No one wants you here," Ryan threw in, his face red, his napkin jumping as his hand clenched around it.

"I'd like you to stay," I said, smiling.

"Of course. Didn't Connor tell you? I'm practically family, Sandra."

"It's Sara. Which I'm sure you know."

My voice sounded good. Calm but not cold. Nothing to hint that she was in dangerous territory. Hopefully my expression matched. It wouldn't make a difference if she did suspect. I was about to toss away the Miss Manners trophy forever. It was too late for Lily to save herself.

"I'm surprised you want to stay, since it seems like you've already managed to do everything you wanted to do today. You've made the innuendos. I get that you and Connor were an item and that he gave you the ring. I know you still wear it. You managed to hurt a very nice person for no other reason than that you could. Is there anything else on your agenda, Lily? Any other big, crawly secrets you want to fling my way just to amuse yourself?"

That was exactly what it had been, too: an ambush. My second in two days. Never let it be said that I didn't

learn from my experiences. I was firing back with both
barrels.

"I-I don't know what . . ." Lily stammered, taken
aback.

"You know. I know. Everyone knows." I leaned forward and held my left hand out for Lily. My wedding
band glittered in the sun. "This one is a wedding ring.
Believe me when I say no one is ever going to confuse
the two."

"Game, set, and match," Ryan said, clapping softly.

I touched his shoulder and shook my head. "Is there
anything else you'd like to know?"

Lily seemed dumbstruck. Dougal kept his coffee cup
near his lips to hide a smile. Alyssa looked from me to
Lily and back. Siobhan stared at the table, while Ryan
practically pulsed with energy. I met Connor's gaze. He
mouthed, *I love you.* I rolled my eyes. He was sweet.

"Wait," Connor said. "There's one more thing."

He just couldn't resist coming in like a knight on a
white charger. I knew he knew I didn't need a rescue.
That was enough. I'd let him wear the superhero suit.
He didn't owe me a fix, but I knew he'd feel better if
he tried.

"I want to apologize to my family. Especially Sara and
Siobhan." Connor turned to Lily. "I inflicted you on
them. I won't do it again."

"Connor, I know you're upset, but we've been important to each other too long—"

"You're not important, Lily. Sara's important. Siobhan's important. Next to them, you're so unimportant
you're invisible."

Lily swung hard, the slap cracking against his cheek.
He didn't even clench his fists. If he'd ever had any
emotional investment in her, it was long gone. Even so,
she'd taken a full swing. Maybe I should rescue him?

The room went silent.

"You can go now," I told her.

Lily turned on her heel and left.

Chapter Six

The rest of lunch was an anticlimax. Siobhan was subdued. Connor's parents stuck to impersonal topics, and Ryan steamed. Weirdly, it seemed like only Connor and I were unaffected. I made deliberate attempts to include Siobhan in conversation, but she was woolgathering somewhere distant. Ryan acted like he owed someone a black eye and was worried he'd deliver late. I might not understand the nuances of the family, but things seemed really off to me. After paying the check, Connor pulled me toward the parking lot.

"I'll get it back," he promised, walking too fast for me to comfortably keep up. Grenville stuck out like a sore thumb in the parking lot. I was feeling far more kindred with it than I had before lunch.

"Get what back?" I asked.

"The ring."

"What?" He didn't really think I cared about that, did he? That already seemed like a lifetime ago.

"Yes?" He made it a question.

"Don't be ridiculous, Connor."

I stopped short. We needed a translator. I wasn't mad. I was busy. He looked bemused—eyes cloudy, lips parted, genuinely confused.

"I didn't protect you. I should have."

"From what?"

"Lily."

"Why? I thought I handled her pretty well." Now I was a little puzzled. Actually, I'd thought I was in the zone. Rude, no doubt, but highly efficient and downright righteous about the whole thing.

"You were great." He grinned.

"Thanks."

"You're welcome. And you're not mad?"

"No."

"Why not?"

"I could maybe explain why I was mad if I were, but clarifying the negative seems tricky. I don't know why I'm not mad. She's a bitch. I'm chalking up your relationship with her to ignorance and hormones."

Connor shook his head. "Thanks, I think."

"You're older. You're wiser. And since I intend to keep your hormones all to myself, Lily doesn't seem relevant."

He stared. "So we're not fighting?"

"I'm not fighting. I've got to go." I crossed the last few yards of the parking lot to Grenville and pulled on the door. It opened, hanging lopsidedly. I got in and banged the door shut.

"And I'm not in the doghouse?"

There was nothing I could do if his conscience bothered him. Except take advantage of it—and him—when the opportunity presented itself.

"Sara."

"I've got to get back to work. We can talk later." He reached in and took the keys out of the ignition.

"Give me my keys."

"Calm down." Bad move. His face told me he knew it the second the words were out.

"I'm perfectly calm. I'm also in a hurry." I held out my hand imperiously. "Now give me my damn keys."

"You shouldn't drive when you're upset."

"I am not upset." I said it through clenched teeth. Maybe the idiot needed me to yell to feel better. "I am perfectly fine to drive. And I really need to go."

He crouched next to the door. "Just tell me what to do."

I shook my head. Now he was driving me crazy. "Nothing. I'm not mad. Really. Now can I have the keys? Please?"

He reached through the open window and tucked my

hair behind my ear. He always tried to distract me with touch. The irritating thing was that it worked so well I couldn't even blame him for sticking with it.

"Sara?"

I held out my hand silently.

"We need to talk."

"Sure. We'll talk later. All you want. I promise."

In ten seconds I was going to fake a major meltdown so I could forgive him and move on.

"You shouldn't drive like this," he tried again.

I glanced through the windshield. "Hmm. You're right."

"I am?" Now he was suspicious of too easy. I had him off balance, that was for sure.

I pushed open the door. He stepped back out of the way.

"We need to talk about this," he insisted.

"What is it with you and talking?" I marched toward the Yacht Club. "There's nothing to talk about. I'm not mad. I'm not upset. I'm not plotting your imminent demise. Lily's useless and vindictive, but your taste in women is improving. Problem resolved. I've got things to do."

"Where are you going?"

"I'm going to call a cab."

"I'll take you."

"No. Go back to work."

"I'd rather—"

"Sara, Connor. Did you forget something?" Siobhan was wrapping a scarf around her head, her keys in one hand.

"No." Connor cut her off. Jeez, what was he thinking? Siobhan didn't need the short tone from him, not after putting up with the lunchtime festivities. I wanted to reach over and smack him in the head.

Siobhan stopped, biting her lower lip. "Is anything wrong?"

"Yes," Connor said.

"No," I said. I stepped on his foot. Hard. "Your brother is an emoter. I don't get it myself."

Siobhan smiled. It looked forced. "I never thought of him that way."

"You should."

"Sib, Sara and I need to—"

"Actually, Siobhan, could you do me a huge favor?" I asked.

"Anything."

"I rented a car this morning. It's a little on the unreliable side, and Mother Hen Connor is turning gray just thinking about it. Do you have plans this afternoon?"

"No, I'm free."

"I would understand if you're busy."

Siobhan stood a little straighter. I suddenly wondered what she did during the day. She didn't seem to have a job, or at least, no one had mentioned one. If she'd been a stay-at-home wife, with the recently removed husband her house must seem like anything but a haven. I could see her cleaning, cooking, entertaining the pig's associates. If Jack was really gone, Siobhan would probably welcome the distraction.

"I didn't have anything planned, really," Siobhan insisted.

"If you don't think you'd be too bored, maybe we could see some of the sights. I've never been to San Diego before, and Connor has to work."

"I would like that." Siobhan smiled. It wavered a bit, but she hung on.

I glanced at Connor. He was staring at me. I gave him my most innocent expression. He wouldn't welcome having his sister weaned from his protective cocoon. His eyes narrowed. He thought I was up to something. Who, me? I glanced at Siobhan. I'd look out for her, but a little mischief making might be just what the doctor ordered. Siobhan could do worse than catch a little revenge fever. Maybe she'd give me some pointers about fitting in while I was corrupting her. Quid pro quo, as they said at my law firm. Connor did not seem convinced.

"You're going to do the tourist thing?" Deeply suspicious, but what could he do?

"Sure." My smile was at maximum wattage. That alone should have him on pins and needles all afternoon. So what if he knew I was up to no good?

"Don't let her talk you into anything, Sib."

Chapter Seven

"There's a great maritime museum, if you'd like to try that," Siobhan asked.

"Not really. I was lying."

She flinched. "Lying." Her eyes were glassy.

"Not to you. To him. Your brother. He hovers."

"He does."

"Let's put it this way: Girdles give you more breathing room."

She rested her hands on the steering wheel and stared straight ahead. She hadn't started the Mercedes, and the summer heat was turning it into an oven. She didn't seem to notice.

"Does it bother you?"

"What?"

"Me talking about him like a husband?"

She shook her head. "I'll take you home now."

"Oh."

She turned the key. The car rumbled to life and the air poured out cold. My car took ages to cool off. This one had an instant-Arctic feature.

"Siobhan, it's okay if you haven't got time today. I understand."

"You want to go out with me?"

"Just not a museum."

She turned and smiled at me. A genuine smile. A McNamara smile. "No. That's fine. We could go shopping."

"I'm not a big shopper."

"Okay, uh, how about—"

"I need to do a couple of work things. How'd you like to tag along?" I asked.

"Really?"

"Yeah." I pulled Detective Hector Montoya's card from my wallet. "I want to go talk to the cop from last night. See if they identified the body."

"Body?" Siobhan turned. Her eyes were as big as saucers.

"Didn't Connor tell you?"

She turned and started the car. "Connor doesn't tell me things he thinks would upset me. No one in my family does."

Uh-oh. Danger, Will Robinson. "Maybe we shouldn't—"

"I'm sick of museums, too." Siobhan said. She pulled the car out of its slot. "What's the address?"

"Skyline Drive."

"Oh."

"Really, if you don't want to go, I understand."

"No. I want to go. I'm tired of being the fragile daughter."

I had no idea what to say to that. Frankly, she seemed fragile to me. Protected by her family. I envied her a little. Not that I was a delicate flower. I wasn't. But it would be nice if someone thought that way about me once in a while.

"You know what? Let me call first. See if he's there. No sense making a wasted trip."

I dialed. "Detective Montoya, please."

He wasn't at his desk, so I left my number. Taking Siobhan to a bad neighborhood was one thing. Doing it as a fool's errand was another.

"He wasn't there?" she asked.

"No, but maybe he'll call back this afternoon. We can meet him then. Let's try the radio station. The real one, not just the warehouse where we were last night. We'll save the war zone for when the cops are available."

"What radio station?"

I scrolled on my phone. "Towne Center Drive?"

Siobhan's shoulders relaxed. Must be a better part of town. I gave her the address and she punched it into her GPS unit.

On the drive, I told Siobhan the story from the night before. She didn't ask questions, just absorbed the details. There was no lecture on the dangers of not staying at my desk or rants about crazy women. She barely spoke. If Siobhan shared Connor's views on my job or my most recent escapade, she kept it to herself. She pulled into a parking lot.

"Ready, Watson?" I asked.

She smiled. "After you."

We walked into the station and over to a receptionist.

"Hello." The receptionist smiled. She was well coiffed and manicured, wearing a stylish suit. She would need the jacket in these arctic indoor temperatures. She made a better match to Siobhan than I did.

I slid my card across to her. "I'd like to talk with Henry DeVries's boss, please. I don't have an appointment, but it is important."

"I'm sorry, but our management team doesn't see anyone without an appointment." She slid the card back.

"I have vital information about Henry. It's a police matter." I tried again, pushing the card back.

"Then the police will contact us." She boomeranged my card, her smile never fading.

"The detective assigned to this case is Hector Montoya. I think your boss would like to talk to me before he gets here."

"I don't think so."

"Listen, Miss, er, Philmar." I read the name off the rack of business cards on her desk. They'd actually printed cards for her with the title of "receptionist." "I think—"

"I am Siobhan Reed." Siobhan pulled a gold-filigreed card from her purse. "I would like to see the owner immediately, please."

The receptionist's eyes widened. She took the card, looked down, and swallowed visibly. "Of course, Mrs. Reed. Right away. Would you like to wait in our conference room?"

"That would be fine."

I followed, dumbstruck, behind the two elegant women. We were offered deep leather chairs in a teak-lined room. Iced cappuccino quickly followed. I waited until the receptionist scurried away.

"How did you do that?"

"Family connections." She smiled wanly. She didn't seem that thrilled by them.

The door opened and a man burst in.

"Mrs. Reed?" He held out a hand. "Pike Overthal. I'm the manager here. Mr. Rooten isn't in the office just now. If he knew you were coming . . . well, he told me to take care of you. 'Anything she needs,' Mr. Rooten said."

Siobhan shook hands without standing.

"Can I get you anything else? Something to eat. One of the girls brought some cookies in this morning. Homemade. Real tasty."

Siobhan smiled. "No, thank you, Mr. Overthal. I'd like to introduce you to Sara Townley."

I stood to shake his hand.

"Nice meeting you, ma'am."

Ma'am. He had two decades on me. Those family connections must be pretty strong indeed.

"Sara has a few questions to ask you."

We sat down. Overthal turned his attention to me like an eager-to-please puppy. He leaned forward onto the table.

"Anything."

"Has Henry DeVries come into the office today?"

Overthal blinked. "Henry DeVries doesn't come into the office, ma'am."

"Never?" That surprised me. How could he do a radio show without the studio?

"No. Runs his show on remote. Tapes most of them in advance from his own place."

"Is that the warehouse in Bay Terrace?"

Overthal looked from me to Siobhan. "What's this about?"

"Last night there was a shooting in Bay Terrace. A man was killed."

He leaned back and steepled his fingers. "You think it was Henry?"

"I don't know. I'm asking you."

If Pike Overthal was upset at the thought of losing a valued employee, it didn't show. I expect Morris, my boss, the anal-retentive senior partner, would be even colder if I went to the ever-after.

Pike reached forward and punched a button on the speakerphone in the middle of the table.

"Agnes?"

"Yes, sir."

"See if you can get DeVries on the phone."

"It's only two o'clock, sir."

"I don't care. Wake him if you have to."

"Yes, sir."

"What's your connection, Ms. Townley?" Gone was the enthusiastic sycophant. Maybe he wasn't just a pencil pusher. This Overthal sounded like a real journalist.

"I was supposed to be meeting him."

Overthal shook his head, his eyes cagey. "Now, I know that's not true. Henry didn't meet people."

"He did interviews." I sipped coffee. I could feel the buzz surge in my bloodstream. Apparently the good stuff came with more caffeine.

"Not the way you mean. He sometimes had conversations with the fringe, if you see my point. Guys who had the same conditions of anonymity and need for security. He didn't meet with society types or their friends."

"He agreed to meet with me to discuss an interview he did with Charles Smiths."

Overthal's face closed up. Recognition for sure. But what else? Was it just a reporter trying to get beneath a story, protect a source? Or did he know something he wasn't going to tell me?

"What about Smiths?" Overthal said.

"It was his information, not mine." I could lie, too. "He wanted me to look at a copy of the transcript of the interview to see if I could come up with some answers for him. Maybe som explanation for why Smiths would do an interview now, when he's been deliberately avoiding the spotlight for so long."

"Why would he think you knew?"

I reached into my pocket to make sure I'd picked up my card from the receptionist. She'd never even glanced at it. The hard cardboard reassured me that she couldn't tell him anything.

"Because I called him to ask about the interview. I work in Seattle. Smiths is a major donor there, and he doesn't give interviews. I thought that if I could figure out why Smiths chose to speak with DeVries, I could use it to get close to him. Maybe open him up for some of our local causes. He's a big giver in San Diego, and Seattle could use some of that generosity."

"Okay." He sounded doubtful.

"He's never participated in any of our annual fund-raisers for the mental health facility or the arts. We have the annual charity ball in a few days," Siobhan offered. "We help a lot of important causes, from cancer research to prison reform."

Less than an hour in my company and I'd turned Connor's little sister into a liar. I was nothing if not efficient.

"When I called, I left a message for DeVries." I said. "When he called back he said he'd talk to me if I went through the interview with him and answered some questions he had."

"What questions?"

"We never got to that. We played phone tag and set up the meeting for last night. It was interrupted by the shooting. DeVries hasn't called back. Naturally, I wondered—"

Overthal clicked the phone on. "Agnes, bring a copy of the Charles Smiths interview transcript into the conference room right now." He hung up before she could answer. "Tell you what, how about we go through it together while we're trying to find Henry?"

It was a trap. He was curious. Maybe even a little paranoid, although we were up to something, so maybe a little paranoia was warranted. No wonder DeVries had worked for Overthal. The had a lot in common. It didn't matter. I wanted to see the transcript enough to risk his suspicions. "That would be fine."

The phone rang. "Yeah," Overthal snapped, leaving the phone on speaker.

"Sir, I haven't been able to reach Henry DeVries. I've left messages. Mr. Rooten is on the phone for you."

"I'll take it in my office." Overthal stood. "If you'll excuse me for a minute . . ."

"Certainly," Siobhan said.

Overthal left the room.

"Nice fib," I complimented her.

"It just takes over, doesn't it?"

"That's always been my excuse."

"Let's not tell Connor," Siobhan suggested, pink in her cheeks.

Oh, yeah, let's not. "Agreed. But listen, Siobhan, they know you. Sooner or later this guy is going to want to ask more questions and they know how to find you."

"He won't call."

I thought about the bulldog look on the manager's face. "He will."

"Lower-level executives don't call Reeds asking for information. Jack and I are the golden couple of San Diego society." She sounded better. "We attend ten-thousand-dollar fund-raisers for the homeless in designer clothes. We have absolutely no contact with anyone who has anything to say other than 'Thank you' and 'You amaze me, Dr. Reed.' And even that is only whispered by 'our equals.' " Siobhan used air quotes. "Jack makes sure of that."

"Well, then the owner will call."

"He won't call me."

I felt bad about Siobhan being the only point of contact for these guys. Maybe I should just leave my card.

"He'll call my grandma Gertie."

Oh, no. More family drawn into my web of lies.

"Grandma, being a left leaner, will tell him to get lost."

"If that's the case, why did they play leapfrog when you dropped your name?"

"Because his second call will be to my conservative husband."

"This is the one with the new marina condo?"

"Right."

So maybe it wouldn't go anywhere. I hadn't even met Siobhan's husband and given the circumstances, she'd have no reason to tell him anything. I couldn't see a

guy newly released from the constraints of matrimony
following around the wife he left to find out how she
spent her day. I was a little surprised a news guy
wouldn't know the ins and outs of the local high-
powered marriages, but maybe that was a good thing.
Lily knew, because she knew the family, but maybe
Siobhan's significant other was keeping his mouth shut
outside the close personal relationships. For her sake, I
hoped so. Siobhan didn't need the gossip mill churning
over her marriage. She didn't seem like the sort to tell
the girls at lunch to mind their own business.

The door opened and Agnes stepped in. "Mr.
Overthal said he wanted this. His office door is still
closed." She placed a bound transcript on the table. "Do
you need anything else, Mrs. Reed?"

"Nothing, thank you."

The girl left.

I picked up the transcript and pushed back my chair.
"I don't think we need anything else, do you, Siobhan?"

The corners of her lips twitched up. "We'll get
caught."

I opened the door a crack and looked out. The hall
was empty. We had a straight shot past the awed receptionist to the front door. "The trick is to act like you're
not up to anything. You're the great and powerful Siobhan Reed, remember? Clerks do not ask questions."

Siobhan stood, tugged her jacket down, and put her
scarf around her hair. She slid her sunglasses on. "Right
behind you, Holmes."

Chapter Eight

Trying to read in the car as Siobhan rocketed away from the radio station was making me carsick. Opera blasting from the speakers as getaway music wasn't helping.

"That was so much fun," Siobhan enthused. "Is your job always that much fun?"

"Sometimes people shoot at me."

"Yes. I suppose that's not fun. But exciting. Nothing exciting ever happens to me. Do you know I didn't think about him the entire time we were in that place?"

I didn't need to ask who "him" was. My cell phone rang, and I closed the transcript.

"Sara Townley," I yelled. I reached forward and turned down the CD. The relief to my brain was instantaneous, but my ears still rang.

"I'm sorry. Who?"

"It's Detective Montoya."

"Hi."

"Hi. Listen, I got your message and I'd like to talk with you. Can we meet?"

I glanced at Siobhan. She was conducting the opera with one hand, driving like a banshee. Adrenaline poisoning.

"I'm not alone."

"The commander struck me as a stick-like-glue kind of guy."

I grinned. He would if he could. "It's not him. I'm actually with my sister-in-law." I had in-laws. How weird was that idea?

"I could meet you later," Montoya offered.

Later meant Connor and the glue thing. I held the phone to my chest. "Are you over it for today or could I talk you into another meeting?"

Siobhan beamed. "Another? Really?"

"With the police?"

"I'd love to do the police."

I shook my head. We had lying, stealing, and doing the police. Connor was going to kill me when he found out. What the heck? She wasn't thinking about "him" anymore.

"Do you mind if I bring her?" I asked Montoya.

"Not at all." I could hear a smile in his voice. "Where do you want to meet?"

I held the phone against my chest. "Where should we meet him?"

"How about Café Lulu? It's in the Gaslamp Quarter. F Street."

"Café Lulu?" I asked into the phone.

"It'll take me a while to get there. How about an hour?"

"See you then." I hung up.

"Café Lulu it is. One hour."

"We're close," Siobhan said. "We've got time to run into Artesia and get our nails done."

I looked down. Then I looked over. Siobhan's nails were perfectly painted, her hands soft-looking and delicate on the steering wheel. In contrast, it looked like I used mine as shovels. No chance I was putting them in front of a stranger.

"That's okay. If you want to go, I'll just hang out and read through the transcript. Try to see if there's anything useful in it."

"I don't mind waiting with you. It'll be fun."

I could see that the adrenaline was wearing off. Siobhan had stopped tapping her hands. The color in her cheeks was fading, and she sagged a little in her seat. Well, sagged as much as a could-be charm school instructor with perfect posture could ever sag.

"It doesn't take two to read a boring transcript, Siobhan. I appreciate the offer but if I want to get this thing into my hard head, it's probably better if I try to find a quiet place and concentrate."

"If you're sure, maybe I'll just go ahead and get a little reflexology and an aromatherapy treatment."

I hoped neither of those things would leave a mark.

"Sounds perfect. Take your time and I'll meet you at Lulu's afterward."

"I'll drop you off."

"Thanks."

I ordered a latte and found a table near the back. Three pages into the transcript, I wished I'd ordered espresso. I was running into a little postshooting, post-sex, post-ex-fiancée lull myself. Or maybe Henry De-Vries was the most boring interviewer on the planet.

"Hi, Sara."

I looked up. "Detective Montoya." I closed the transcript and flipped it, facedown, onto the chair next to me. Good thing he wasn't gunning for me. He could have shot me from less than a foot without me ever knowing he was there.

"Can I get you a coffee?" he asked, a bright smile lighting his features.

"My hair already hurts, thanks, but you go ahead."

He laughed. "That's a lot of caffeine. I'll be right back."

My phone rang. "Sara Townley."

"I thought you were sightseeing."

"Connor? How did you know . . ." That wasn't good. How much did she tell him? Everything? "What makes you think I'm not?"

"You're not."

"You're right. I'm not sightseeing. Unless you consider good looking Latin men landmarks."

"What?"

"Gotta go. Hot date with a hot guy. Hate to make him wait." I hung up and turned the phone off. It didn't compare to a virulent vixen over veal chops, but it did perk me up a bit.

"Is he the jealous type?" Montoya asked as he took the seat opposite me.

"Who?"

"Your husband. I didn't exactly bond with him last night, but today I feel sorry for the guy."

"Why?"

"Men married to women who wear the expression you were wearing when you were on the phone deserve pity."

I laughed. "He's tough."

"He's overmatched."

"Are you always such a sweet talker, Detective Montoya?"

"As long as he's not here, call me Hector."

"So, Hector, did you identify the guy in the street yet?"

"Not yet."

"Henry DeVries had a criminal record. His fingerprints were on file. Identifying him should have been a snap, pardon the pun."

Montoya sipped his frozen drink. His brown eyes were steady. He was flirting but his heart wasn't in it. He was here to work.

"Pending notification of next of kin, we haven't officially identified the body yet. My turn. What would a thousand-dollar-an-hour Seattle law firm want with a right-wing talk-show guy one step up from public access?"

"And here I was thinking you hadn't been busy, Hector. No comment."

He smiled. "It's going to be hard to take our relationship to the next step like that, Sara."

"This from a man who won't confirm what we both already know. You're right, Hector. Our future doesn't look bright. But I'm going to give you another chance. Any witnesses?"

"Other than you and your lesser half?"

"Yes."

"No."

I leaned closer and looked straight into his eyes. "Are you lying or just not sharing?"

He leaned in. "Maybe I'm telling the truth."

"That would be a disappointment."

He leaned back and laughed. A couple of women at a table behind him did double takes and started a whispered conversation. Probably checking his ring hand.

"I am truly sorry for my shortcomings." Hector put a hand over his heart.

The woman behind him gave me a thumbs-up sign and fanned herself. I nodded my agreement.

"What?" He looked over his shoulder.

"I was just agreeing with the women behind you, who think your shortcomings aren't readily apparent."

He blushed. "Thanks." He looked down, sipping his drink.

"So, no witnesses, huh?" I asked again, trying to take advantage of his discomfort. "None of the neighbors saw anything? What about the two homeless guys?"

"In the wind. Funny you didn't ask about the other radio station employees. I mean, DeVries ran his show out of that location. Twenty-four-seven station, there would be sound engineers, whatever, pretty much all night."

No way was I falling for that. Montoya had to know as well as I did that DeVries's location was a remote. "Exactly. Have you had a chance to talk to all of them yet?"

"No point. DeVries worked alone. His show was remote. His feed went back to the main station on Towne Center Drive and was sent out from there. But you already know that."

I was busted. I knew it. He knew it. Then again, if I didn't object to a blatant liar why would he?

"I do?" I went with Marilyn breathiness and sandstorm eyelash twitching.

This time his smile started slow and stayed lazy. And lethal. Guess it wasn't all work with him after all.

"Is that why you wanted to see me?" I asked.

"Well, one reason, anyway. I could have read you the riot act over the phone but it wouldn't have been as much fun. For the record, Sara, you are not to interfere with an ongoing police investigation. You are not to contact the principles in this investigation, nor are you to leave anyone with the misapprehension that you are in the employ of the San Diego police, or any other police, for that matter."

"I never said I was a cop, and I'm surprised they remembered my name."

"I went with the description."

The station had Siobhan's name but he was going off my description. They might not have even mentioned Siobhan. A stranger asking questions could be sacrificed to the cops. A society doyenne who knows your boss and your boss's boss, not so much. Interesting. "Oh. Do I want to know?"

"It was flattering. Well, half-flattering."

"I'm guessing the receptionist was the unimpressed one."

"Could have been worse; she could have called security and had you thrown out. That station has more than its share of questionable visitors. They've got full-time security."

Siobhan was right: The old guard hung together. I wanted to know if they called Montoya or if I came up when he went to them, but I couldn't figure out how to ask.

"Sara, I need to ask you some other questions."

"Okay, but I don't promise to answer."

"Of course you don't. Is there any chance that you were the target?"

"Think I'm that much of a pain?"

He shrugged. "Do you have any connection to San Diego other than your husband?"

If the radio station employees hadn't seen fit to share my connection to Connor's family, I wasn't going to. "I met Shamu once as a kid."

"How long have you been in town?"

"A day."

"Ever been here before?"

"Nope."

"Who knew you were going to be in that neighborhood? Anyone from your work?"

Joe. That was a dead end. "No one."

"Your family? Friends?"

"No one," I repeated.

"Except your husband."

"He saved me."

Montoya leaned forward and rested his arms on the table. "Any rough spots in your marriage, Sara?"

I shook my head.

"None? No fighting? No money trouble? No misunderstandings of any sort?"

"He hates my job."

"Would a near miss help him convince you to leave it? While he gets to play hero?"

"Nobody kills a perfect stranger to make a point." Montoya jumped the curb with that one. "Connor's not like that, and if he were, he wouldn't miss his primary target."

"He's a SEAL, Sara. They're wired differently."

"I doubt the navy keeps psychotics in their ranks. He's been in the service his entire adult life. They would have noticed."

"Meaning you wouldn't? I didn't get the impression you'd known him long."

I squirmed in my chair. Hadn't I just calculated it yesterday? Sixteen days together. Six months total. "I know him. Look, Detective—"

"Hector, remember?"

"Detective. I don't know if you're trying to scare me or unnerve me or what, but I am not the target. Connor is not some puppetmaster. Stop wasting your time chasing us and find the guy who killed the as-yet-unidentified body in the street. Your street, by the way."

Montoya grabbed my hands and held them tight. "On my street, a political figure was gunned down with a military weapon. He was shot from a fast-moving vehicle. He was struck once, in the aorta. What the armed services refer to as center mass. With a navy wife standing next to him."

"Sara?" Siobhan stood just outside my peripheral vision. Her voice quavered. "Am I interrupting?"

"No. He's leaving."

"Sara—" Montoya began.

"It's Ms. Townley." I pulled my hands free. "And we're through."

Montoya stood. He held the chair for Siobhan and she

slid into it, perching on the edge. "Take care of yourself, Sara. Ma'am."

"Is everything okay, Sara?"

"Yeah."

"Want me to get some coffee? Or we could eat."

"I was thinking a drink."

Siobhan stood. "What would you like?"

"I'm thinking a grown-up drink."

Her eyes went wide. "Are you sure everything's okay? Who was that guy?"

"He's the end of a perfect day. Actually a perfect afternoon that started with lunch with my husband's ring-wearing evil bitch of an ex while inappropriately dressed in front of my new in-laws, and ended with veiled threats from the police. Of course, it's better than yesterday, when I was naked before nearly being shot. Yeah. I was thinking a just-the-girls, never-repeat-a-thing-you-hear, drink-as-big-as-a-bathtub sort of outing."

She giggled. "I thought you were great at lunch. And the radio station. And probably with the threatening policeman. I mean, he didn't look at all scary to me, but that was probably because you took care of him, too. Really, you've been amazing all day."

"I'll think so, too, in about two hours," I agreed.

"We should go to my house. Then we won't have to drive."

"Connor's house. No ghosts there."

Her smile faded.

"Hey, I'm not prying."

"He's a good man. He is." She pulled the keys from her purse as we walked to the car. "We need to go to the store."

"He doesn't keep alcohol at his house?" I thought about it. "He definitely has beer."

"I need rum."

She made mojitos, which didn't taste like alcohol. By the third glass we sipped while sitting on the deck overlooking the water, I was thinking of Montoya as a bug on my shoe. Lily was somewhere beneath him. Connor was doing okay despite the haze, but Siobhan's husband was a bastard even through the anesthesia. She cried a lot. Except it wasn't like she was crying. I lifted my sunglasses onto my head and peered closer. It was more like she was watering. She talked. She joked. She clinked glasses. And she watered.

"Are you okay?" I asked.

"Lily is a"—hiccup—"not-nice person."

"If I were that much of blight on the face of humanity, I would understand if someone tried to drown me in the soup of the day," I offered.

A cough.

"I mean, you couldn't blame someone for performing a public service like that, could you? Then again, any woman who doesn't take an engagement ring off after the guy marries someone else is so pathetic we should probably sympathize." I swirled and drank.

Hiccups.

"Until you realize that she has to be pretty damn stupid to take shots at a woman wearing the wrong clothes in front of her new in-laws. I mean, after that, laying her out in the entryway just seems like such a minor transgression, what would stop me?"

"I'd like to see that," Siobhan whispered.

"I'll get you a ringside seat."

"I'm a mess," Siobhan said miserably.

"Allow me to refer you to the aforementioned dress-code violation."

A feeble chuckle. She picked up the pitcher and topped off her glass.

"Whatever you're paying for your mascara, it's totally worth it," I said.

"Thanks."

I handed her a paper towel. We'd had a sloshing situation earlier.

"Really, if I were crying that hard I'd look like a raccoon in a clown's nose."

Her chuckle had more body. She patted her face with the towel.

"I also honk like a goose. It's loud and very not-pretty."

"I bet you never cry."

She had me there. Or if I did cry, I did it in the shower where no one could see. I'd also deny it to my last breath.

"Want me to ask Connor to beat him up? He owes me for his misspent youth."

"No. That's okay."

"The offer's open."

She dabbed some more. "I'll have to see her again. We're on the same committees. We go to the same places." Siobhan's lips trembled. She seemed so fragile, so unsure of herself. Not at all like Connor or Ryan. Or the parents, for that matter. I'd bet Jack was a real piece of work.

"I could invite her the next time somebody shoots at me. It would look like an accident." I toasted her with my glass.

"This morning I think Connor confided in a friend of his, the two of them plotting like I wasn't there when the shooting started." I leaned back and closed my eyes.

"Blue," she said.

"You know him?"

"They're thick as thieves."

"Don't suppose you could get him to tell you what's going on?" I turned my head to look at her.

"Blue or Connor?"

"Either."

She shook her head.

"Which is another reason I've got to do it," I told her.

"Do what?"

"Surprise him. Take care of my own troubles." I raised my glass. "Unfortunately for Lily, she's the obvious choice."

"For what?"

"To make a statement. To show Connor and this guy Blue and my idiot boss, Morris— Have I told you about him? He's an idiot in a pinstripe suit. Anyway, to show all of them that I'm tough and smart and take no prisoners."

Siobhan giggled. "Bummer for Lily."

"You know it." I slouched deeper into my deck chair.

"Jack will be mad, too."

"What's he got to be mad about?" My voice echoed in my head. Siobhan stiffened. "Sorry. It's your business."

"Jack's a good man. He's having a hard time right now, that's all. I mean, I don't always understand the pressure he's under with the practice. He's a doctor, you know. It can't be easy for him, working with her."

"Who? Lily?"

"Her aunt Gretchen. She's generous. I know she supports Lily financially and gave Jackson his start in his practice, but, well, she's a difficult person."

"I've met her niece. I'm guessing *bitch* is the word you're looking for." I sipped. It was hot in the sun and I was thirsty.

"It's hard work. Jack's told me. Dealing with everyone else's issues and problems. There's never room for your own. If he's said it once, he's said it a thousand times— no one thinks of the therapist."

"He's a shrink?"

"A psychiatrist. Yes. Didn't I tell you?"

"No. You said doctor."

"It's a high-profile practice. That adds to the pressure. I mean, Gretchen Dreznik is huge. She wrote the book."

I set my glass down and sat up. I swayed a little. I couldn't have heard that right. Jack. Gretchen Dreznik. Psychiatrists.

"What's your husband's name?"

"Jack." She drained her glass, sighing.

"Jack what?"

"Jackson Reed. Psychiatrist to the stars." She let her hand hang next to her chair.

Uh-oh. Dreznik and Reed. Psychiatrists. I was drunk, but not so far gone I failed to recognize that having my new brother-in-law's name turn up in one of my cases was bad news. Jackson Reed. Psychiatrist to the stars. The biggest constellation being a millionaire named Charles Smiths.

"I should do that," Siobhan said.

"Do what?"

"Make a statement."

"Good idea." I doubted Connor would appreciate that advice either.

"How?"

"How what?"

"Do you make a statement?"

"Well, rum helps." I leaned forward and refilled my glass. I had no idea what I was going to do about Jack. All I knew was that today, I deserved another glass.

"We've got rum. What else?"

I stared at her. "Are we talking statement with a small s or a capital one?"

"Capital. Definitely capital."

"Then there's only one thing a girl can do to go into the world ready for battle."

Siobhan leaned close. "What?"

"Have you ever heard of going commando?"

Chapter Nine

"**H**ow's the hangover?"

"If you don't want your shoes to find out, you'll give me that coffee." I kept the cover over my head to shield me from the sun. Siobhan had taken a cab home around dinner time. I had lain down for a second.

"What time is it?"

"Eight a.m."

"In the morning?"

He lifted a corner of the sheet and held the cup while I sipped. My mouth tasted like the inside of a cave. "I will never drink again."

He crouched next to the bed. "I thought you weren't that upset yesterday."

"I wasn't."

"So what was with the hot-date hang-up and the drunken journey to Jamaica?"

"Forget the other man. He was blind-date hideous. As for the foreign adventure, Siobhan makes good mojitos. Or at least they seemed good yesterday."

"Siobhan was with you?"

"Ugh."

"Siobhan doesn't drink."

"Ugh."

"Is she okay? Did she say anything?"

Probably. I just couldn't remember what. "Girl pact."

"What does that mean?"

I pulled the sheet back over my head.

"It's that son of a bitch she's married to."

Jack. Shit. I'd forgotten.

"Go back to sleep," Connor soothed. "I've got to go to the office. I'll be back for dinner."

"Um." Should I tell him about Jack? Montoya? Siobhan's card at the radio station? Not yet. I didn't know anything yet. One thing at a time. Number one with a bullet, ha, Jackson Reed and his connection to Charles Smiths. So Jack's name was in a file. Big deal. He'd probably treated hundreds of people. I pushed the sheet back. Connor was gone.

I showered for a long time. I drank two pots of coffee. I took more than the daily allowed dose of aspirin. It took a couple of hours, but I stopped wanting to die.

I called Joe at the office.

"You do not sound good," Joe said, sounding like he hadn't slept for a week.

"Hangover."

"Of course."

"Has anybody called there looking for me?"

"Like who?"

The police, maybe. "Anyone?"

"Not that I know of."

"Could you keep your ears open? Maybe cozy up to Elizabeth the Evil and see if anyone has called our esteemed senior partner wanting to know about the case I'm working on?"

"Cozy up to Liz? I'd rather eat dirt."

"Fine. Then search her desk when she's not looking."

"What am I looking for?"

"A cop named Montoya."

"Morris hates cops. Even if he didn't, there's that pesky old attorney–client privilege thing. You're home and dry."

"Smiths isn't the client."

"Then you're on a street corner soaking wet. I can come up with about fifty bucks for bail."

"Which I won't need if Montoya's not getting anywhere. Listen, I need something else, too."

"More than risking my job and the wrath of the world's scariest woman? Did you give me a kidney I don't know about?"

"I'll cover your Snickers bill for a month."

"Six weeks."

"Five, and you're risking diabetes. I'm thinking about your health here."

"Agreed. What?"

"I need everything you can get on the doctor who treated Charles Smiths."

"Isn't that your identity-theft victim?"

"Yeah."

"Why?"

"He's my brother-in-law."

"The victim?"

"The doctor."

"So?"

"You're right. It's probably nothing. But—"

"He's family. Got it. How deep do you want me to go?"

Information was power, and I needed some of that. "Center of the earth."

"I'll e-mail you."

"Thanks."

An Internet search didn't yield much. Jack was mentioned in newspaper accounts and journal articles, but always as a second banana. Lily's aunt got all the real ink. She was some sort of über-expert big on the talking-head tour. I couldn't resist checking out Charles Smiths, too. I'd gotten the file initially, but the thief had been my target then. Now I couldn't help but be curious. Smiths brought up hundreds of hits. There were a couple of stories about large donations (he must donate anonymously most of the time) and a couple mentioning the interview. The rest seemed like other guys with the same name. I had more Google hits than the real Smiths did.

When in doubt, knock on doors. When you have a hangover, take a cab. I went back to the neighborhood where I'd gone to meet Henry DeVries. It hadn't improved. The business owners didn't know anything new, and if they'd heard rumors since my earlier visit, my persistence wasn't impressing them enough to share. I couldn't even tell if they were stonewalling or really didn't know anything. It was pretty tough going in my condition. I gave it two hours and headed back for a nap.

* * *

"I thought we ought to get acquainted," Lily said, looking beautiful and polished and perfect sitting on Connor's couch in his condo. She'd helped herself to a glass of something. I sighed and came the rest of the way into the apartment.

"Funny, I don't remember inviting you."

"Oh, I've never needed an invitation. I'm family."

"Guess he never took back the keys." I sat down on the couch opposite her. Calling the cops would be an overreaction. Of course, it wouldn't be as obvious a ballistic moment as throwing her off the balcony. "That was trusting of him."

"Connor and I have always been each other's best friend."

"Up until the moment you cheated on him, you mean."

"Let me guess: Little brother has been telling stories. Ryan has never been my biggest fan. A little sibling rivalry. You shouldn't take everything he says as gospel."

"Rivalry? Looked more like gastric distress to me. And I'd chisel his words into stone tablets before I believed a word coming out of your mouth."

A whisper of a smile touched her crimson lips. Not enough to require Botox. Very forward-thinking of her.

"I believe in being honest with people," Lily said, holding up her hand to admire the ring on her third finger.

"Me, too. You're honestly a bitch."

"Leaving Connor was a mistake. One I intend to rectify." She adjusted the band so the diamond caught the light.

"Bummer for you. I don't share." I sat back, fighting the urge to cross my arms. I wanted to exude calm certainty. Best not to dwell on the smooth coiffure, tailored dress, or perfect features of this woman who'd shared Connor's bed.

"You should go, Sara. You're not our people. But then, you know that, don't you? It's impossible to miss."

"Your"—air quotes—"'people' being nonhumans? Toxic blowup dolls? Vicious former friends?" I tried her hint of a smile.

"My aunt is always trying to get me involved in her causes. She's very big on the dregs of society. Out of respect for her, I've spent hours reaching out to the lowest classes, sharing meals and conversation with prostitutes, thieves, and criminals. No matter how much time I spend with them, they will never be my people."

"Antisocial birds of a feather."

She leaned forward, resting her elbows on her knees. Her smile was ice-cold. Not unlike her heart, I suspected.

"Between you and me," she began, "it doesn't suit. I'm happier without those unfortunate influences. Which is why I've decided to take Connor back. He's on my level. But having said that, I know how to make myself understood by the"—she looked me over, from wild curls to unlaced sneakers—"inferior."

"Go ahead. Grunt. I'll try to keep up."

"You can't compete with me. We both know that. Connor's mine. He always has been; he always will be."

"Thanks for loaning him to me last night. That was sporting of you." I stood up. What was I doing sharing veiled sexual references to Connor with this woman? "I don't believe in owning people, Lily. Connor's hands aren't tied. He can make any choice he wants. He made it clear he's already done so."

"Only because he didn't realize I was available."

"Telling you to get lost definitely happened after you hung out the welcome mat. Speaking of welcome, you've outstayed yours. Get out."

Lily stood, brushing manicured hands over hips to smooth her skirt.

I called a locksmith the second she was gone. I didn't want Lily sneaking up on me while I slept. She definitely had an air of Lizzie Borden about her. Ryan turned up as the locksmith was leaving, his keys in hand. Did everyone in the free world have a set to this condo?

"I hate to break the news to you, Sara, but my brother doesn't know anything about women." Ryan held the sliding door open and we dropped onto deck chairs with cold bottles of beer in hand.

"Truer words were never spoken." I took a swig from my beer, watching a tourist boat chug toward the marina.

"It's not just you, either. His name is pretty much mud all over town. Mom told me she was going to talk to Connor. She was not happy that you were forced to endure a scene on your first official outing."

"I thought he was pretty good at the end."

"I would have hit her back," Ryan said with relish.

"No, you wouldn't."

"Oh, yeah, I would."

"I just can't see a McNamara man hitting a woman, Ryan."

"There's an exception to every rule." Ryan looked over his shoulder into the shadowed apartment. "Where is he, anyway?"

I sighed. "Still at the office. He had some important meeting with his boss. I'm starting to feel neglected. I tried calling but he didn't pick up the phone. I was going to ask him what he wanted for dinner, like a good wife, then see if he'd pick it up on his way home."

He laughed. "Good one . . . Did you really take Siobhan with you yesterday afternoon?"

"Word travels."

"She called me. Then she wouldn't tell me anything." I grinned. "Maybe you've got loose lips."

"If you hadn't met my brother first, I'd show you."

"Behave, little boy."

"Yes, ma'am." Ryan propped his feet up on the table, leaning back into his chair. "So are you going to tell me what you girls did yesterday?"

"We're not girls," I scolded, mirroring his posture.

"You're not. Siobhan is."

"Your sister is a grown-up."

"Well, in some ways maybe." He frowned. "Whatever you were doing, it's the most alive I've heard her in a long time. Thank you."

"Connor might not be so thrilled."

"If he doesn't have a sense of humor, to hell with him."

We clinked bottles.

"I think the womenfolk were chasing bad guys while Connor typed reports. Am I close?"

"No comment." I didn't need Ryan putting it like that to Connor. After my run-in with the cat-sitting murderer earlier in the summer, I'd promised no more personal confrontations without backup. I had a feeling Connor's idea of backup wouldn't stretch to include inviting his sister to witness the fireworks.

Ryan cleared his throat to cover a laugh. "I'll bet. Is he still waiting for the other shoe to drop?"

"He thinks I'm mad."

"Mad as in angry or mad as in hatter?" Ryan asked.

"I doubt he distinguishes the two."

"At least you're not a shrieker." Ryan chuckled softly. "Or a hitter. He's lucky. If your felon-chasing, badass self had been on the other end of that slap he took, we'd still be picking him up off the floor."

"You've got that right. What do you think set Lily off, anyway? Siobhan said that Lily is famous for her control. I've got to tell you, she didn't strike me that way at the club."

"Gee, I don't know. Giving Connor a lap dance before he introduced you as the missus seemed calculating to me. Maximum damage, minimal personal risk. There's no way she could know you'd clean her clock. Maybe she didn't take her medication. Or maybe it was her time of month."

I looked over at him. "And you think Connor's stupid about women? If you ever repeat that in my hearing, I'll beat you up every day for a solid month so you understand that there is no safe day for the likes of you."

Ryan grinned. "I will heed the warning. That's why I'm the 'lucky with women' brother. I know my audience. Of course, unlucky Connor managed to end up with a fox like you." He leaned his head back against the cushion of the chair, a slight smile still evident.

"Yeah." My chair scraped against the redwood as I moved a couple of inches away. I closed my eyes and relaxed against the canvas. "You think I'm a fox?"

"I wouldn't push you out of bed."

I turned my head and glared at him through my sunglasses. "That's on the wrong side of the little-brother line, but thanks."

"My pleasure." He pulled his sunglasses to the end of his nose before doing a Groucho Marx eyebrow impersonation. "And I mean my pleasure."

"Just knock it off."

He sighed. "I'll try but I can't make any promises. I'm a male in my prime. Besides, since Connor was stupid enough to get involved with someone like Lily, sooner or later you're going to realize I'm the smarter brother. A far better catch. And did I mention I'm in my prime?"

"You did."

"It bears repeating."

"Shut up," I told him. Ryan was fun. I'd never had a brother or even wanted one. Suddenly I was seeing how much I'd missed. I picked up my cell phone and dialed Connor's number. Still no answer.

"Ryan?"

"Yes, O hot one?" he asked, his eyes closed.

"Can I ask you a personal question?"

"Prime. One hundred percent."

I shook my head. "Seriously."

He opened his eyes and looked at me. "Seriously prime."

"You seemed angrier about Lily than Connor. He was mad for us, Siobhan and me. You seemed mad for yourself."

"It's no big thing."

"I think it is."

He looked away, staring out at the water. I waited.

"It's okay if you don't want to tell me. I mean, we only met a couple of days ago, even though it feels like I've known you a lot longer."

"You're tough. You'll hang in. You're not like . . ." His voice trailed off.

"She left him?" No way. If that were true, what was the big production about at lunch? I thought her spin earlier was a lie, but if she had left him, maybe she did think all she had to do was crook her little finger and he'd come back.

"When? Why?"

"Doesn't matter now. He's with you. You're sticking." He hadn't moved, and yet all his easy slouch was gone.

"I am." I raised my bottle to my lips before realizing I'd drained the last of my beer. We watched the boats in silence for a couple of minutes.

Ryan cleared his throat. "Why do you think he never told you about Lily and everything?"

"It's the past."

"Hmm. It's not like they were ever actually married or anything." Ryan leaned toward me. "You're not like other women. You're not obsessed with shit that doesn't have anything to do with you."

"Technically, I think lunching with my husband's ex-fiancée who's still wearing his grandmother's ring has something to do with me."

He laughed, relaxing back into his chair. "A mere technicality. You've got a great story for the grandkids, though. Beauty and the Bitch." He laughed again.

I joined him. It seemed funnier now than it had at the time. I wondered about running into Lily. Whatever her history with Connor, that meeting was no coincidence. She'd been loaded for bear. Ready to make a scene, whether at Connor's expense or Siobhan's, I couldn't be sure. Either way, she'd been okay with burning her bridge. I hadn't thought so at the time. I'd been smug in my handling of her, but now I wondered. Whatever Ryan's issue with Lily, something big and ugly was still lurking. Something told me Lily wasn't done yet.

"Did you know she does some charity thing with Siobhan? Your sister told me, like they were friends, maybe. Even now. All that at lunch and Siobhan never said a bad word aginst Lily. Jack either."

Ryan's body tensed. He put his bottle on the table with a dull thud. "Of course not. Siobhan never has a bad thing to say about anyone. People who know that, well, they take advantage. You should try to get Siobhan to go out to dinner with you and Connor."

"What about you? Do you want to join us?"

"I'm not good with crying. You don't need me there. You and Sib can do that woman-bonding thing that makes no sense to us alpha males."

"Which makes Connor . . ."

"A hostage," Ryan supplied.

"Well, I can tie you to a chair if that makes you feel more manly."

He got out of the chair and strode to the railing. He held his shoulders stiffly, his entire posture screaming anger. Then his shoulders slumped. He turned to face me, leaning back against the railing.

"I can't be around her. She's my sister and I love her, but I just want to shake her. She caught him doing his secretary and stayed with the asshole. Now he's buying some penthouse screw pad with her money, and she spends all her time crying or moping. She probably wants him back. How stupid is that?" His hands were gripping the railing behind him so tightly that his fingers showed white.

"Even so."

"Even so what? I think I ought to kick the crap out of that dirtbag." He pounded the railing.

"That's not a good idea, Ryan."

"Why not? You think he's going to whine to Siobhan about it?"

"I think he'd have you arrested."

"Not if he knew I'd be back." Ryan's voice was low and mean.

"Use your head, Ry."

"I'd rather use my fists."

"But then Siobhan would pay."

"And he just gets away with it?" He looked over at me, his voice rising.

"I never said that." I smiled.

Ryan stood straighter and stared. "You never did, did you?"

"Nope."

"Did I ever mention how much I liked your style at lunch?"

"You did."

"Lily's warped but not stupid. She understood you were taking her down. Jack's not like that."

"Too subtle for him, am I?"

He stared. "I've got a feeling you've got range."

"You know, I really do. Bummer for him."

"So, what's the plan?"

Two birds with one stone. Work my case and help Siobhan take out the trash. "First, we have to see if Connor is in the mood for an adventure."

Chapter Ten

"**I** love this breaking-and-entering stuff," I whispered in Connor's ear.

"Shh." He dropped to his knees in front of Jack's office door, reaching into his pocket for the small leather case.

"I want lock picks for our first anniversary."

"Quiet."

I listened while the tumblers clicked. "And maybe some sort of alarm detection thing."

"I've created a monster." He stood, opening the office door and ushering me inside. He closed the door and locked it. We bypassed the reception area and headed straight to a door marked with a gold-plated JACKSON REED, PSYCHIATRIST.

Fifteen years of treatment with the good doctor and Charles Smiths was still hiding in his house. In Seattle, where he wasn't doing interviews with Henry DeVries. I couldn't deny it: Dr. Jack Reed had gotten him away from the place of his childhood trauma—only to have an identity thief set up shop a few miles from the house where the real Charles Smiths's parents had been murdered? Across town from the crime scene where the only man who spoke to the thief was also murdered in cold blood? A small world was one thing. This was something else.

No wonder the head games Jack was playing with Siobhan were making her nuts. He was in the industry. He had to know he was pushing her buttons, undermining her confidence. I didn't even know him and he was making me crazy.

Jack's door was unlocked. We went in and Connor shut the door, moving to the windows and closing the curtains before pulling a penlight from the backpack. He pointed the beam at me. I blinked.

"What is the first rule?" Connor asked.

"Never wear white after Labor Day?" I shielded my face with an arm.

"Never get caught. Which is what happens when you talk too much before you've secured the premises."

"Enough with the spotlight already. What's next, rubber hoses? Don't worry so much. Ryan's watching. He'll call if the big bad wolf comes creeping down the lane. C'mon. We've got serious snooping to do."

He shook his head, his lips twitching.

Okay, so it wasn't the traditional dinner-and-a-movie date night with the husband. Sneaking around. Unlawful entry. Plotting against Jack the Bastard. I loved this stuff. Maybe I could talk Connor into taking me to the base. I bet they had some cool toys over there that would seriously expand the scope of my imagination. I glanced at him. He'd say no. He already thought I was nuts. In a good way. Probably.

I used my flashlight to assess the room, taking in filing cabinets, expensive furniture, and original art. Psychiatry must pay pretty well. Jack was definitely living the good life. I made a mental note of the layout. Connor moved toward the computer. I took the file cabinets.

"What do you think we're going to find?" I asked while flipping through files, using my flashlight to read. "This is mostly billing stuff." Which included first-class tickets to Seattle billed to Smiths, C., every other week. Nice work if you could get it.

"Check the other cabinet. Look for any files marked 'personal' or 'miscellaneous.' They might be under his name or the practice's name." Connor pushed a PalmPilot into the port.

"Hey, can you just do that?"

"Do what?"

"Put a different Palm into his dock and get it to download?"

"It has to be the same type of device. And you need the pass code."

He never looked sexier to me.

"That's cool."

He looked up. Smiled wickedly.

"Having fun?"

"Oh, yeah." I turned back to the files. "Okay. Here's one. 'Dreznik Reed, professional services corporation. Partners, Gretchen Dreznik and Jackson Reed.' Nothing." I looked over my shoulder. His attention was elsewhere. I pulled the file marked "Smiths, C." and slid it into my backpack. "Psychiatric services, blah, blah, blah. You want any of this?"

"Grab anything you think might give us an edge and we'll copy it before we go. Just make sure you know where it came from so we can put everything back in the same place."

I hesitated. Maybe I didn't want Jack to know I'd been looking for Charles Smiths either. On the other hand, I definitely didn't want Connor to know I was working on my case, and it was going to take Jack longer to realize I'd stolen a file than it would for Connor to realize I was copying one with my identity victim's name on the label. Theft it was.

"Okay, but wouldn't it be considerably creepier if he knew someone had broken in?" I suggested. "I mean, the whole point of this is to get under his skin, right? To play with his head? To make him straighten up because he's sure he's being watched. Having somebody break into my place would do that to me."

"You doing something I should know about?"

"I haven't been conserving water." I looked over my shoulder and frowned. "Just today, for example, I showered twice. Once by myself and once . . . well, let's just say that shower lasted a little longer."

"Stop showering by yourself."

I giggled. "There's an idea."

I moved to the cabinets behind the door. "They're locked."

It took Connor less than a minute to find the key in the pencil cup. He held it up.

"Nice," I complimented, taking the key from him. I started with the S drawer.

"We only need the financial stuff, Sara."

"Just making sure this is all patient files." Smith, Smith, Spurr. No Smiths. I flipped through a dozen files in each direction. No "Smiths, C" in the patient records. Billing but not patient.

"Anything?" he asked.

"No. Just the medical mumbo jumbo."

Connor was busy jotting into a notebook. Charles Smiths could be misfiled. Then it could be anywhere. Damn. I thought I was onto something.

"Okay. Potential dynamite at the ready." I picked up the folders I'd pulled from the billing cabinet. "I'm ready to copy. You know what we need?"

"What?"

"One of those little cameras. We could take pictures of every page. Very Maxwell Smart."

"He wasn't that good at his job."

"Maybe not, but he had fun stuff."

"You want a shoe phone?"

I laughed. "My birthday is coming up."

"I'll keep it in mind."

He walked me over to the door, cracked it, and peered out. The outer office was empty. He shepherded me, keeping near the walls and away from the front window. Stealthy. Very professional. I didn't see any lights or hear any cars. The outside light was enough to work by. We went to the copy machine tucked away behind a cubicle wall.

"Be sure to copy with the lid down. We don't want a green glow through the window."

"Could be aliens." I dumped my stack next to the machine.

"Well, neighbors have a tendency to call the cops to report little green men."

"Maybe they'll send the *X-Files* guys to investigate. That'd be great. That guy is really cute."

He put his hands on his hips and shook his head. "You're married, remember?"

I winked at him. "Married doesn't mean dead. Go sleuth some more while I finish this up."

I clicked off my flashlight and copied pages, using the light from the machine to read. I should tell Connor about Jackson. Or at least mention that his name had come up as part of my investigation. Except Connor had been quick to agree to this felony when he thought it was just to help Siobhan. I doubted he'd be as thrilled if he knew I was once again working a case that led to grounds for my arrest. Of course, we were together during this B and E, so it would leave him with a do-as-I-say-and-not-as-I-do problem.

What were the odds? Just because Connor's brother-in-law treated Charles Smiths, it didn't mean Jack was involved in DeVries's death. Philandering jerk was one thing, deep conspiracy killer another. So my thief chose a San Diego radio guy to tell his life story to. Smiths had lived in San Diego for years before moving to Seattle. It made a twisted sort of sense that his ties to Jack's hometown left enough of a trail to make it the likely location of an identity theft. Still, most of these cases were hackers with no connection whatsoever to the actual victim. It felt . . . off.

I finished copying and went back to Jackson's office. I stood in the doorway and watched Connor work. Efficient. Catlike. Soundless. Every move deliberate. It was like watching a dancer. He was good.

Walking to the windows, he pushed the drapes to one side. With the moonlight streaming through the window, I saw him jam a wadded-up piece of paper into the lock.

"We're coming back?" I asked.

He looked over his shoulder and smiled.

"Maybe."

"You take me to all the best places."

He rolled his eyes, closing the drapes. I blinked, trying to adjust to the darkened room. I clicked my flashlight on and went back to the file cabinet, returning folders to the drawers. Finished with my task, I turned back to Connor, spotlighting him with my flashlight. I watched as he turned the desk phone over and used a screwdriver to open the casing.

"What are you doing?"

"Nothing." He didn't look up.

"Oh, my God, you're bugging his phone."

"Look for a safe."

"Where'd you get it?"

"We need to move, Sara."

I walked around the room, peeking behind paintings. If I were Jackson, where would I hide my safe? Well, there was no plastic dog poop. From Siobhan's description, he seemed like a plastic-crap kind of guy. Okay, so if I had an office with a safe, where would I put it? I went back to the bookshelves. Fake book, maybe.

Connor finished at the desk. He found the safe in less than a minute, in a pot holding a ficus. He pulled the tree out easily and set it on the floor. I went over to him and flashed my light into the hole. There it was. I was impressed.

"How did you know?" I asked.

"It's fake."

I reached out and touched a leaf. Glossy silk. "So?"

"There are plants in the outer office. They're real."

"So?"

"In this place they probably have a service that comes in and takes care of them. Waters them, feeds them, whatever."

Light dawned. "If you already had someone on the payroll to take care of the plants, why would you choose fake? Got it. You're smart. I like that in a guy."

He reached out and touched my cheek, then crouched down to examine the safe.

"I'm guessing it's his birth date," I offered.

"Because . . . ?"

"From what Ryan told me, Jack is the center of his own universe."

Connor glanced down at his notebook and punched keys.

"Where'd you get the date?" I asked.

"It's on his calendar."

"I rest my case."

The safe opened on the first try. "You're smart. I like that in a woman."

I knelt next to him and leaned in. "That's good to know," I whispered in his ear.

Connor pulled three envelopes and a ring of keys out of the safe.

"Get the pack," he said.

I got up and took the backpack we'd brought from the desktop. I unzipped it and peered inside.

"What do you want?"

"Passport."

Searching the contents, I came up with the blue-covered book. I held the backpack with my chin so I could flash light on the inside. A nice-looking guy. The name Jackson Reed. Date of birth.

"We could have gotten the code from here," I said.

Connor reached out a hand. I watched as he swapped our passport for one he'd taken from the safe.

"What are you doing? And where did you get a fake passport so fast?"

"Not fake—expired. I got it from their house. I'm making sure he can't wander out of the country anytime he chooses."

"You think he's going to leave?"

"I don't know. Better to be sure."

"Wouldn't it be a good thing? For Siobhan, I mean. If he went away?"

"Eventually."

"But not until she's taken back her life?" I guessed.

He nodded. I knelt down and wrapped my arms around him from behind. "You're a good guy."

He reached back and wrapped an arm around me. "Thanks."

"A good guy with an expired passport. An irresistible combination." I kissed the back of his neck.

"Remember that for later."

The second envelope yielded two electronic passkeys.

"Black bag," Connor said.

I let go and searched the backpack, handing him the nylon bag. I watched as he used a black box to clone the electronic card keys. Then, he made impressions of the safe keys using a ball of plastic putty.

"Where did you get all this stuff?"

"As I said, I got the passport from Siobhan's

house. The reader and key-impression material I borrowed."

"I'm guessing you can't just go to the library and check that stuff out."

"Depends on the library."

"How do I get a card?"

He shook his head. Opening the last envelope, he exposed stacks of hundred-dollar bills, maybe fifty thousand bucks' worth.

"Wow," I said. I'd never seen that much money before. "Where do you think he got it?"

Connor hesitated, then put the envelope back in the safe with the rest of the items and replaced the plant.

"We're going to leave it?"

"Yes."

"Why? Wouldn't it make it harder for him if it went missing? Especially if he's planning to run?"

"I don't want him knowing we were here. He might check the money."

"And we don't have stacks of Monopoly cash to swap it with? Bummer."

"Roger that."

I glanced at my watch. "We're at nineteen minutes."

He glanced at his watch. "Confirm nineteen."

"I love it when you talk spy."

"Feel free to repeat that after we're out of here."

"Aye-aye, Cap'n."

I went over to the file cabinets where I had set my copies. I stuffed them into the backpack as Connor resettled the ficus. He reached out his hand and I took it. We were moving to the door when the phone rang. I froze. It rang again. Connor went back to the desk and turned up the volume on the answering machine.

"This is Security One Services. If either Dr. Dreznik or Dr. Reed is available, please call immediately."

"Oh, my God. We must have tripped security," I said, starting to sweat. Probably not *we*. It must have been me. When? They were just calling now. Maybe a neighbor walking his dog or something had seen the light? Whatever. We had to get out of here.

Connor turned the computer back on.

"What are you doing? What about the first rule?"

"Breathe, Sara."

I raced over to him and grabbed his arm, my eyes moving back to the door. "We've gotta go. We're caught."

Connor tapped a few keys. He picked up the phone and dialed.

"This is Dr. Reed, Jackson Reed," he said calmly. How could he do that? Stay so cool. I was on the verge of panic.

"Zero-zero-seven-H-I-P."

He had the code. He must have. He was just going to play through. Act like nothing was wrong.

"Zero-zero-seven-H-I-P. It was a false alarm."

It was going to work. Jesus.

"You, too." He put the phone down.

I stared, putting a hand on my chest to try to keep my pounding heart from jumping out.

"Way to stay calm there, Twitchy."

"I don't have as much felony experience as you, sailor." I fanned my face. "I nearly wet my pants. You were great, though."

"Thanks."

"I mean amazing." I was definitely jumping his bones at the first available moment. There was nothing he couldn't do.

"I'll be more amazing later," he said, practically reading my mind. So maybe I was drooling a little bit. Who could blame me? The guy was talented. And gorgeous. And felonious. What was a girl to do?

"Promises, promises." I laughed and leaned over to kiss him hard. God bless adrenaline. "Mmm," I said, moving closer.

Connor pulled away. "Right," I said. "Business first. I admire your professionalism."

"Thanks."

I looked at my watch. "Tsk, tsk. Late again. Will you never learn?" I grinned.

I smiled back.

Five minutes later Connor was driving us away. Ryan was in the back, all nervous energy.

"What'd you get?" Ryan asked as we drove through the neighborhood.

"Nothing earth-shattering," Connor said.

"I bet you got something good." Ryan said, leering at me in the passenger seat.

I checked my outside mirror. No one behind us. We were clear.

"Not much, really. It wasn't as interesting as my boss's desk."

"You've broken into your boss's office?" Ryan sounded impressed.

"Once. Well, actually Connor broke in twice, but that was before I got really good at it. Now I could break in all by myself."

"Which you are absolutely not going to do," Connor said.

"Absolutely not," I assured him with my fingers crossed.

It was his fault. He taught me how. I couldn't be expected not to use what I knew. That would just be wasteful. Besides, it wasn't like I would do it to hurt someone. Well, other than Jack, of course. My intentions were pure, my aims just.

"I mean it."

"Yes, dear. Whatever you say, dear." I leaned toward Ryan. "He thinks everything's about him. I only married him to pick up some marketable skills. As soon as I figure out how to swipe the Hope Diamond, I'm outta here."

"I'll run away with you," Ryan offered.

"That's generous of you, but I'm pretty sure you're too young for me."

"Get 'em young. Train 'em right. You could be my teacher."

I looked at him. He reminded me of my best friend, Russ. Well, not the flirting part. Russ was gay. But other than that, they could be twins. Funny. Sweet. Up to no good ninety percent of the time. People I wouldn't mind needing bail with.

"Maybe you're too old for me," Ryan came back. "How old are you, anyway?"

Okay, maybe not.

"Thirty-five, and I am aging like fine wine, little brother-in-law, while you are still toddling." I channeled Catherine the Great.

"Toddling." He laughed, leaning between the front seats to look into my eyes. "Great word. Maybe we should reconsider the age gap, though. Men are sexually mature earlier than women, you know. We could, if you'll excuse the expression, reach our peaks together."

"That's a sweet offer, Romeo," I said. "But it turns out I'm already involved with someone. He may not be younger than me, but he does fine."

"Actually, he is," Ryan said.

"Shut up, Ryan," Connor said.

"You see, Sara? He may be younger than you, but he's already reached the old-geezer years with that attitude."

"What do you mean?"

"Listen to him. A little innocent flirting and he gets all aggressive."

"Not that. What do you mean, he's younger than me?"

"It's not enough to do you any good. You really have to go with the much younger man to get the most bang for, and from, your buck."

I groaned. I pushed Ryan back and looked at Connor. "How old are you?"

He glanced at me, then carefully returned his gaze to the road in front of us. Oh, my God. He was younger than me.

Connor sighed. "Thirty-two."

"What?"

"Does it matter?"

"Yes, it matters."

Of course it mattered. He was younger than me. I was a cradle robber. Well, maybe not Charlie Chaplin cradle robbing, but still.

"Why?" Connor asked.

"What do you mean, why?"

"Why does it matter?"

"Because it does. I never dated anyone younger than me before."

"We're not exactly dating, Sara."

"You know what I mean."

"He withheld material information from you," Ryan goaded. "You can probably get an annulment on those grounds." Ryan reached over and grabbed my hand. "This is your chance, darling. Throw him over and run away with me."

He grinned at me. I looked at Connor. He was ignoring Ryan and concentrating on the road. Okay, so maybe it wasn't a huge deal. It was only three years. It just felt weird. Our little escapade had completely eliminated my bad mood after the disaster at lunch and now, over something totally unimportant, I felt my hackles rising. Maybe I was premenstrual.

"I'm talking to your brother," I said to Ryan, freeing my hand.

"Butt out," Connor told him.

"Hey, bro. No problemo." Ryan leaned back, raising his hands in surrender.

"Are you mad about this?" Connor asked.

"Why didn't you tell me?"

"Why would I? It doesn't matter to me. Are you saying it matters to you?"

Maybe. No. Of course it didn't matter. Heck, if I wasn't going to throw a tantrum because another woman was wearing his ring, the relative number of candles on our birthday cakes shouldn't throw me.

"What else haven't you told me?" That came out a little harsh. Apparently I *was* going to let this get under my skin.

"Nothing important, Sara."

"I'm not sure you understand what's important, Connor."

"You're probably right there."

"He's always been a little slow," Ryan offered.

"Hush," I said.

"Mind your own business," Connor said.

"Jeez. Some people are in a bad mood."

"What else?" I repeated.

"Nothing. I swear."

"I've never liked surprises, Connor. Maybe you should know that."

"Okay. No surprises." He checked the rearview mirror. "Well, maybe one."

"What?" I couldn't guess. Tattoos? No, I would have seen them. Prison record? The navy would have thrown him out. Love child? God, I hoped not.

"Damn," he said.

"What?" Ryan asked.

Connor pulled the car over onto the shoulder and killed the engine. The interior of the car was strobed by light.

"I think the police want to talk to us."

Chapter Eleven

"**Y**ou know, your little brother takes after you," I said when we got home.

"What do you mean?"

"He was Mr. Cucumber when that cop pulled us over." We went into the kitchen and I poured a couple of glasses of juice like I'd lived there all my life.

"It was just a broken taillight."

I handed him a glass.

"But he couldn't have known that. It had to cross his mind that we were about to go to jail for B and E on a family member. I mean, being arrested probably wouldn't kill me, especially since you'd be in the next cell, but I can't see your parents, or his college, or his future employers being that excited about a criminal record. For that matter, I doubt it would do your career any good, either."

He drank. "An arrest does not a criminal record make."

I straightened and looked at him, excited despite myself. Maybe a prison record wasn't a reach. "You've been arrested?"

"I didn't say that."

"For what?"

"I didn't say that I've been arrested."

"You didn't deny it, either. C'mon, Connor. Tell me." I pulled at his shirt, working on being my most beguiling. "Tell me."

I was nuts. A checkered past would be a pretty interesting new fact about my husband.

"There's nothing to tell."

Yes, there was. I could feel it. Or maybe he was just going to make something up. There was something predatory in his green eyes. Lust. He might be considering fabrication in exchange for clothing. Well, I supposed that if he was going to go to that much effort, the least I could do was play along.

I peered at him with half-closed eyes. "Tell me."

"It won't be that easy."

"I'll get it out of you."

"Promises, promises," he repeated my earlier taunt.

I'd make him wait. Not long. Just long enough to play with him a little. I'd show him he wasn't the only one with a little self-discipline. I stepped back. "Business first. What do you hope to get from that?" I asked, pointing to the open backpack I'd put on the kitchen table.

"A clue. More than one."

"Ah." I licked my lips. "Clues." His hands came down as he stared at my mouth. There was no aphrodisiac as strong as Connor wanting me and making no secret about it. I had to take a couple of deep breaths to keep from reaching across the table and ending the game. I cleared my throat.

"Gambits cleverly disguised as a PDA," I said. "Very tricky. And what do we hope to learn from these breaking and entering toys, Dr. Watson?"

He moved closer, reaching out for me. I shook my head and sat down at the table. He gave a heavy sigh and sat across from me. Yes, playing with him was definitely the right answer.

"I'm Sherlock. You're Watson. And they're tools, not toys," he told me. He leaned back in his chair, putting his hands behind his head. It screamed, *If you can wait, so can I.* A challenge.

"I get it. I do. I even put a little kit of my own together after we broke into that impound yard, complete with sleeping aids and dog chews for antisocial rottweilers. Even if it didn't yield nuggets of information, I suppose you could always make the stylus into a weapon." I pulled the tiny pointer from the outside of the case, pointing it at him.

"I'm a SEAL, not MacGyver."

"I loved that show."

"Figures."

"So?"

"I used it to download Jack's information off his computer."

"Obviously. Slick, but don't you already know your parents' phone number?"

"Bigger picture, hon."

I scrunched my nose, tugging at the collar of my T-shirt. I could talk business while ratcheting up the sexual tension if he could. Connor started to rise.

"I still don't get it," I said.

He sat back down, his eyes glowing. Plotting as foreplay. Yes, he was definitely going to accept that challenge.

"Jack's a geek. He loves all the whizbang stuff."

"I'm still going to need a bigger hint."

"Most people use their PDAs for phone numbers, maybe their schedule. Jack uses his for everything. Expenditures. E-mail access. Surfing. His broker." He tapped the PDA against his palm. "Anything and everything anyone might want to know about Dr. Jackson Reed in a handy five-by-five container."

"That is so *1984*," I said. "If he used it like that, it's kind of surprising he left it in his office."

"This one isn't his; it's mine. I downloaded his information."

"Of course you did." I was still impressed he knew how to do that. He was a continual surprise, this husband of mine.

I reached over and picked up the PDA, doing my best to give Connor a view down my shirt. He took in an audible breath. Good.

I smiled at him and hit the power button on the PDA. I tapped the icon for his address book, scanning the names.

"Now that we have all this vital information, shouldn't it be useful or something? I mean, it's only a clue if you can do something with it." Maybe I was missing the forest for the trees, but darned if I could see any way to get Jack by knowing when his next dental cleaning was.

I opened his scheduler and started flipping through Jack's most recent appointments.

"Patience," Connor advised.

"Is that like telling me to keep my shirt on?" I looked up at him through my lashes.

"I would never say that."

"To anyone?"

"To you."

I fought the grin. "Glad to hear it. I'd hate to think the honeymoon was over."

He leered. "It's not."

An entry in his datebook jumped out at me: *L.D., Hippo.* I flipped pages. Weekly. Going back months. "Oh."

"What?"

"Nothing." Jack couldn't be that stupid. Not without multiple blows to the head. Ryan would kill him. Connor would drop his dead body off the pier. Both would be mercies compared to his mother-in-law's wrath.

"That wasn't a nothing 'oh.' That was a something 'oh.'"

"Jack had what looks like a standing date, er, appointment. Tuesday afternoons at noon."

"He was cheating on Siobhan?" Connor asked, his voice tight.

So Siobhan never told him. I bit my lip. Thank God I hadn't let that cat out of the bag. If Connor were my brother and my husband were a lying, cheating son of a bitch, I wouldn't tell him either unless I wanted to be a widow. Which I would, except I'd prefer the self-help route. Ready or not, Siobhan was going to have to get ready for this hitting the fan.

"Probably. Don't take this the wrong way, Connor, but are you surprised? I mean, they are separated. A girlfriend isn't that far a leap. It might also mean there's no chance they'll reconcile. Your sister is pretty fragile. She might go back if that were an option. Forget everything. Or pretend to. If he's involved with someone else that might close a door she needs to stay shut."

I set the PDA down. Connor paced. This was going to be bad. I could feel it.

" 'L.D., Hippo, 555-8412.' " I recited.

"What?"

"The Tuesday appointment. 'L.D., Hippo, 555-8412.' "

He stared.

"It's in his address book, too."

"Lily," he said, so softly I almost didn't hear. L.D. Lily Dawson. Jack was a colossal ass and Lily was an evil bitch. Connor's ex evil bitch.

He did seem upset. His face was flushed, and his hands were clenching and unclenching. He did still care about her. Watching him hurt my heart.

"They're friends," Connor whispered.

"I think they're more than friends now, Connor."

"Not Jack and Lily. Siobhan and Lily. They're friends. Even after we broke up Sib kept in touch. Cared about her. This is going to kill her."

He was upset for Siobhan. Not for himself. The tightness in my chest eased a little. "It won't be good."

"They deserve each other."

"Truer words," I conceded. "Since he's not going to refer to his lover as some sort of humongous mammal, I assume that must refer to a place."

"His boat, the *Hippocratic Oath*."

"Clever," I mocked.

"That's Jack."

"And stupid. I haven't met the guy, but why would he choose your ex? Maybe he wants to get caught."

"Or he's rubbing Siobhan's nose in it."

I thought back to my afternoon with his sister. She'd talked about Jack without judgment. I remembered thinking she didn't realize he was going out of his way to be a bastard to her. Denial. Self-protection. Both. But a lie like this . . . it was inevitable it was going to come out. This wasn't selfishness on Jack's part. It was deliberate violence.

"He needs to be stopped," I said. I no longer felt any guilt for what I'd done.

Connor stopped pacing. Stared at me. I could practically hear his gears grinding.

"What did you do?" he asked.

"I sort of borrowed something," I confessed, not feeling at all repentant.

"Honey, you're welcome to anything I've got. It is a community-property state," he stated solemnly. He sat back down at the table. "Well, everything but my 'Beat Army' sweatshirt, anyway. I'm sentimental about that."

"It wasn't that sort of something."

"Let me guess, you hot-wired that rattletrap you've been traipsing around in all day."

"I don't know how to do that." Another interesting sideline. The man was multidimensional. "Do you?"

"I plead the Fifth."

"Is that what you got arrested for? Would you show me? Every girl can use a few mechanical skills."

He laughed. "No comment on the first, but as for the second, sure. We'll make it the advanced course in Sneak One-oh-one." He drained his juice. "So if you haven't graduated to grand theft auto yet, what did you take?"

"Some papers from Jack's office."

"That's why we were there, Sara. Our motives weren't pure."

"Actually, I took some other papers from his office."

"Why?"

"That would be part two of my confession."

"How many parts are there?"

"Two. Well, three, maybe, but no more."

"Okay."

I fidgeted, folding my legs under me and playing with my hair. I wasn't worried that my behavior would shock him. He hadn't seemed the least bit disturbed by the scene I'd made at lunch. He owed me a couple of minor transgressions. No, it wasn't what I'd done that was the problem. It was Jack's connection to my case. Connor wasn't going to take it well.

"I took a billing file."

He seemed surprised. "Fraud."

"What?"

"You think he's stealing from his patients. Lord knows he's taken enough of Siobhan's money. Or the insurance companies. He's overbilling."

Connor wanted Jack to be guilty of something. Something more than cheating on his wife. Something that would give Connor the leverage to get Jack out of Siobhan's life. Given Jack's choice of adulteresses, I didn't blame him.

"The forgive-no-one, coldhearted, I-will-definitely-send-you-to-prison insurance companies?" I guessed.

"Stands to reason."

"And it plays into your hands."

"Maybe." He reached for the backpack.

I pulled the pages from the backpack, handing the crumpled folder to him. He raised one eyebrow and took it.

"Whoever this guy was, he was paying a pretty penny to get his head shrunk. The invoices were paid." He flipped pages. "By check. Damn. No insurance."

"It could explain the cash in his office."

Connor leaned back and stared at the ceiling. "It's possible." He pinned me with his eyes. "Why did you take it?"

"Curiosity killed the cat."

"So tell me, kitten, what was so interesting about this one?"

"Charles Smiths is the name of the guy my identity thief has been impersonating."

His eyes widened. He picked up the folder and opened it, his finger running down each page.

"You do have a way with dropping bombs into conversation."

"At least I'm not boring."

He looked up. "Not boring, no."

"Could be a typo on the file folder." He played devil's advocate. "Everywhere else they use this guy's Social Security number. 'Smith' is not exactly uncommon."

"You could be right," I agreed. "And even if it is Smiths, there're probably lots of them, too."

"But you don't believe it?" he guessed.

Coincidence never sat well with me, either. "No."

"You have a reason to doubt it?"

"That would maybe be that part two I was talking about," I confessed.

"Not boring." He grinned. "Tell me."

"Don't get mad."

"That's not a promising start."

"My Charles Smiths is under a psychiatrist's care. Has been since his parents were killed."

"How do you know?"

"It was in the brief from the bank. They told me to justify their demand that I not speak to Smiths in person. He was in a delicate emotional state. Shouldn't upset him. Any bad news, blah, blah. I thought it was a euphemism for rehab. I also thought it pretty convenient for the bank, who didn't want to tell him, anyway." Stealing documents from the office could clue Jack in to our evening adventure. Pick 'em.

"What was Smiths being treated for?" Connor asked, still in the casual conversation mode.

"Initially, some sort of adolescent something or other. No one seemed to know. But later he was treated for post-traumatic stress."

He was processing. It didn't show on his face, but I could swear I heard his wheels turning.

"He's starting to look like a suspect, Connor."

"A suspect in what?"

"Whatever's going on with Charles Smiths. Whatever got that radio guy killed, assuming it *was* the radio guy in front of the warehouse." I pulled my legs out from under me and shifted in my chair. "You're the one who doesn't believe in coincidence, Connor. Whatever he's been up to, it could come out. It could blow up. In Siobhan's face, maybe. Suddenly this thing is about your family."

"He's no family of mine. I tolerate him because Siobhan wants him. I'll keep my mouth shut if she decides to take him back, but he is *not* my family."

I thought about that, chewing on my thumbnail. "You don't feel like you have to be loyal to him for Siobhan's sake? I mean, as satisfying as it might be to get some real dirt on Jack, Siobhan might be the one to pay."

"I think it would be in Siobhan's best interest—in everyone's best interest, really—if Jack were helped out the door."

Tough love. Families appeared pretty complicated from the outside. If I were his sister—thank God I wasn't—I'm not sure I'd appreciate his commitment to expediting my husband's exit. And I was a lot tougher than Siobhan. She might never recover. Then again, Siobhan's fragility might be all about the treatment she was getting from her I'll-screw-you-and-your-friend husband.

"I think that would be the best thing, too," I agreed.

"You're smart. You haven't even met him yet and you know he's no good. I wish Siobhan could see it."

"Maybe you should help her see it. You could tell her what we already know. About Lily, I mean."

Would I want to know if it were me? Probably. Would I want my brother to be the one to tell me? Couldn't see myself enjoying that.

Connor sighed and rubbed his hands over his face. "I can't tell her. Not yet. They're already separated. It would be like rubbing her face in it. I'm not going to do that to her unless I can't see any other way. I wouldn't want her to do it to me."

"Maybe knowing he'd do that to her, to you, to your whole family . . . well, maybe she'd see him a little clearer, be a little surer. Or she might be so outraged that Jack did that to you, she'd choose."

"He didn't do anything to me."

"He picked your ex."

Connor leaned forward and reached for my hands. "Lily is past. I'm only upset for Siobhan's sake."

"I know."

"If you know, then why—"

"He might not know you're past her. He didn't pick Lily out of a phone book. Jackson deliberately chose her. Someone who still has a connection to your family. He made sure that if Siobhan found out, she wouldn't have anywhere to go."

I lifted his hand and kissed his wrist. "You don't want to tell Siobhan about Lily because it would hurt her more. Do you think her decision would be different just because the roles are reversed? She wouldn't tell you, either, even if she knew. She wouldn't go to your parents or your brother because it might get back to you and you might get hurt. He isolated her. He also made sure he could screw you while he was banging your exgirlfriend. He's evil."

He cupped my face with his hand. "I can't tell her."

"All I'm saying is, Siobhan isn't the only McNamara Jack seems to have a problem with. He must really hate you, too, Connor. You should watch your back."

"This is about Siobhan, not me."

"He's bad news for your family. It's a pity you don't own a house," I said.

"Why?"

"We could bury him in the backyard. I bet that guy Blue would help us."

"I bet he would."

"We need to handle this so Siobhan thinks it was all her idea," I stated. "Then she can take pride in taking control of her own life. If you're not going to tell her now, and it ever comes out about Jack and Lily, you should act shocked. Siobhan wouldn't want to think you knew and didn't tell her, even if your intentions were good."

"You're a constant surprise. For someone with no family, you're pretty good with the dynamics."

"I have Russ."

"Coconspirators aren't family."

"So says a guy who was a willing accomplice less than two hours ago. Along with his brother, I might add."

"So how do we convince my sister that eliminating Jack was her plan?"

"We act casual. Mind our own business, which, in this case, is our investigation into Jack."

"Good thing it's an act, because I'm not sure you've got the mind-your-own-business gene."

"Accomplice, remember?"

He smiled at me. "I'll keep you anyway."

"Thanks." I yawned.

"You ready for bed?" he asked.

We had a plan we couldn't implement until morning. Which just left the night to get through. Suddenly I had a second wind. This newlywed stuff was great. "What are you suggesting?" I asked.

"Why, nothing, ma'am." He stood and came around the table to help me out of my chair.

Good manners or sexual impatience? I really hoped he wasn't a Miss Manners devotee. I tipped my head back and looked him in the eye. "You sure?"

"Absolutely." He crossed his heart and held up a hand in the Boy Scout salute.

I tried not to laugh. I put my hands on his chest and eyed him with mock suspicion. Without warning I stepped closer and pushed hard, forcing him to stumble back.

"Race you," I yelled, already whirling and running from the room.

He chased.

Rounding the corner, I launched myself onto the bed. I turned over and sat Indian style, raising my arms over my head in triumph. "I win."

He shook his head. "What did you win?"

I beckoned with one finger. He knelt on the bed in front of me and I rose to my knees, stripping off my shirt and flinging it toward the door. I took the hem of his shirt and he raised his arms to help. His shirt landed on top of mine.

"How does this differ from me winning?" he asked.

"I get to be on top."

"Sounds good to me."

Chapter Twelve

"**H**ow was the run?" I asked as Connor walked into the kitchen. I'd made coffee, and Connor helped himself to a mug. He was shirtless. Glistening with sweat. His running shorts clinging to one of his better assets. I enjoyed the view.

"Good. You should have come."

"Only nut jobs run at five a.m., Connor. Everybody knows that." I shuddered and burrowed deeper into my cup.

He laughed.

"Not only that, but this happy-morning-person thing has to stop before somebody gets hurt. And by somebody I mean you." Of course, I hadn't complained when he'd spent a half hour nudging me from sleep before the run.

"Sorry, ma'am. It won't happen again." He sat down at the table across from me and glanced at the files I'd spread across the tablecloth. "What's this?"

"Background. Now that we know Jack is connected to Charles Smiths directly, and to John Doe by one degree of separation, I thought I should go back through everything in case something new jumped out."

He glanced at his watch. "Jumping before seven. You are on the hunt."

"There's a lot to get through. First, the cops formally identified Henry DeVries."

"How'd you get that?"

"Joe, the associate attorney who sits in the cube next to mine. He got it from the police report."

"Why would they give him that?"

"Phone calls from scary law firms tend to yield results. He used his senior-partner baritone. He's been practicing in case the real senior partner ever falls down an open elevator shaft."

"Any chance of that?"

I held up my hands. "I'm hoping you'll alibi me."

"No problem."

"I'm still looking for John Doe."

"Find anything?" He helped himself to a piece of toast from my plate.

"First, there's this." I handed him a file. "It's the transcript from DeVries's interview with John. I stole it when we went to the station."

"We?"

Uh-oh. "Me. I meant me."

He let it go. "What's your idea?" He sipped. Grimaced. Got up and dumped his coffee before pouring a glass of juice.

"Bad?"

"Don't worry about it. You're smart and sexy and fearless. With those other talents, capable of making drinkable coffee would be too much to ask."

"Smart aleck."

He winked, resuming his seat at the table.

"DeVries was a conspiracy theorist, right?" I began. "The Oliver Stone of radio. But look at this." I pointed. "Question: 'When did the government take over your life?' Answer: 'When my parents were murdered.' Okay, that makes sense. His parents were a big deal and their murder was all over the papers. Lots of ways John knows about it. But then DeVries asks, 'Do you think the government had your parents killed?' Answer: 'Yes.' DeVries says, 'Of course,' and moves on to the next question, but John keeps talking. He says, 'Yes. They had the red-eye.' "

"So. He's unbalanced. He probably sees the government as some sort of monster."

"That's probably what DeVries thought. He blew by it because he knew the guy was crazy but didn't want to confuse his listeners with logic."

"I'm not following."

"How come impostor John's description matches that of the only other eyewitness to the murder of the real parents?"

He sat up a little straighter. I handed him a piece of paper and watched him read. It was a statement taken from Maria Gonzales on June 12, 1981. Her occupation was listed as maid. The report was taken after La Jolla police had responded to an anonymous 911 call in which the caller claimed to have heard shots. At the scene, the dead bodies of Martin and Andrea Smiths were found in their home. The only official witness described a strange red glow just prior to seeing Mrs. Smiths fall to the floor. Maria claimed to have heard no shots.

"Where'd you get this?"

"Seattle PD's own Sergeant Wesley."

"You're kidding."

"No. Apparently he's forgiven me for my"—I made air quotes—" 'exuberance' during my missing-cat case last June. He was friendly in a snarly sort of way. He called in a favor and somebody in La Jolla faxed it over. They wouldn't send it to Joe. I guess fear of litigation doesn't last longer than the statute of limitations. They wouldn't send him anything from archives."

"As usual, you're two steps ahead of safe. Wesley and at least one person at the La Jolla Police Department know you're asking questions."

"I played desk jockey. How is that unsafe?"

"What's the case status?"

"Still unsolved. The cop who took the report, Officer Esteban, is retired. I'm going to wait until a reasonable hour, then call him and see if he'll talk to me."

"Us," he said.

"What?"

"Talk to us."

"Don't you have to work?"

"Try to make it afternoon. I'll work it out."

"Okay," I said. "You're looking kind of grim, Con. What's the deal?"

He looked at me. "You're starting to read me pretty well."

"Thanks, although you don't seem that happy about it."

He hesitated. Preparing to tell a protect-the-little-woman lie, no doubt.

"I don't like your job."

"I do."

We exchanged Mexican-standoff stares. He sighed. "I know."

I sat down and shuffled papers. I pulled the interview transcript with Henry DeVries from the middle of the stack and placed it on top. "DeVries asked about the murder of his parents when John Doe did the interview. Now that we know Charles Smiths really was a little out there psychologically, it also supports why my boss was so adamant about my not going to talk to Smiths. Nothing loses clients faster then bringing up bad memories. Some random guy talking about the murder of his parents would qualify. When DeVries asked, John said, 'They brought the flag.' "

I picked up another folder. Dug through the pages until I got to the autopsy report. Attached to it was a color photo of the crime scene. Smiths senior was wearing a navy blue suit. His wife's dress was nearly a match. Both bodies were splayed against a white tile floor, with crimson pools near their heads.

"It's a couple of dead people," Connor said.

"It's red, white, and blue. Maybe he did add the red light after the fact, but if he did, how do you explain the flag?"

"It's still a stretch." He downplayed the connection.

"So, it's a stretch. The question is, how did John know about both the glow and the colors in the hall?"

"He doesn't, and he guessed. He didn't mean anything by the flag thing. Maybe there was a leak and John did his homework."

"Why?"

"Why what?"

"Why go to all that trouble? Come on, Connor. You're going to rip off somebody's identiy. You track down their Social Security number and start applying for credit cards, car loans, whatever. You get as much as you can as fast as you can. Why would anyone take the time to learn every little detail about their victim?"

He leaned back in his chair. I let him think while I refilled my coffee. There wasn't an explanation.

"It could be just what you said the first day, Sara. John Doe wanted to steal more than money. He wanted the whole life. So he found out every detail."

"Or . . ." I prompted, returning to my chair.

"Or he already knew the details. Maybe he knows one of the witnesses."

"Or maybe John Doe knows Charles Smiths. He's the one who'd know all the details, not just the murders. If we can find Smiths, I think we can find John Doe."

Connor leaned back and steepled his fingers. "Did you meet Smiths?"

"Blackout, remember? I never saw him, but I know from talking to neighbors that Charles Smiths is living in a house outside Seattle. He gets grocery deliveries and the cable guy installed a new TV two weeks ago. The same day as the interview. That and ke keeps a really low profile."

"Roger that."

My brain was running overtime. I shouldn't. Only a manipulative, evil bitch would even consider it. Although in my own defense, my motives were pure. Okay, not Ivory soap, but not cheap jewelry either. Maybe I wouldn't go to hell. Well, straight there, anyway.

"What?" Connor asked.

He'd know I was the source of all evil. He'd never agree. He was Mr. Direct. No shading, no creative interpretation of facts and events. His approach didn't play to my strengths.

"What?" he repeated.

"Do you believe the ends justify the means?"

"No."

"Didn't think you did." I sighed.

A corner of his mouth turned up. "Tell me."

I hesitated. "What if . . . for the sake of argument . . . I'm just sort of brainstorming here. . . ."

"Sara."

"If I were going to review the facts of this case, I'd

say that John Doe knows Charles Smiths, and Jack knows Smiths, and Jack is defrauding Smiths. John Doe is talking to Henry DeVries, who is now dead."

Connor coughed back a laugh. "You think Jack killed Henry DeVries?"

" 'Think' "—I twirled my hair—"is a little strong. I'm really looking for something closer to 'sell.' As in sell the idea of Jack maybe, possibly, perhaps being involved in the shooting."

"Sell? To who?"

"I don't know. Maybe Detective Montoya would be interested."

"He won't."

"But he'd sort of have to ask some questions to eliminate the possibility, don't you think? The kind of questions you'd ask a suspect's wife." I sipped cold coffee. It was bitter on my tongue.

"You want the police talking to Siobhan?"

"She's not stupid."

"Except when it comes to men."

I couldn't argue with that. "If your sister thought her husband was doing anything she thought would damage your family, she'd change the locks."

"Damage us how?"

"You said it, Connor. Intestinal fortitude, not Jack's forte. If he were going to kill someone he'd have to hire the gun. Where would an upper-crust shrink find a professional killer?"

Connor's cup hit the table hard.

"In the military. Or ex-military. But since Jack never served a day, he'd go to someone who had. Like someone in his own family. My family."

"Take a breath, Connor. We're making it up, remember. Anyway, Montoya isn't the only stop on this bus."

"Who?"

"Charles Smiths. It's three degrees of Kevin Bacon, but Jack, our would-be assassin, is connected to him, too. If Smiths were in danger, he'd want to know. Even my boss would want me to say something. Dead clients, particularly millionaires, are bad for the firm's bottom line."

"O-kay."

"Since I'd be talking to Charles Smiths anyway, it would be foolish to miss the opportunity to see if I could find out a little more about the billing problem. And by a little more, I mean the kind of thing that holds up in a court of law. Since I'll already be there."

"Efficient."

"And with any luck, productive. By the time Siobhan has a chance for second thoughts, perception would be reality and Jack would be bye-bye."

As plans went, this one was good. Machiavellian, with a touch of Mother Teresa. Montoya would get to spend a few days chasing his tail. Connor would get to play protective big brother. Siobhan would be rid of Jack, and I would be running my case without interference.

Connor was watching me. More like trying to drill into my brain.

"Do you do this often?"

"Plot the overthrow of the world?" I guessed.

"Yeah."

"Well, I'm not a virgin." I stared at him. He could make a fortune as a poker player. "We don't have to, if it's freaking you out. I know it's not your style."

"Don't sweat it."

"You're not repulsed by how bent I am?"

"I'm stuck on you not being a virgin."

Chapter Thirteen

"**H**arrison Nilford Jr., aka Henry DeVries," a disembodied baritone said. The beautiful running partner Blue. Connor and Blue were at the office. Connor assured me that I was getting the information at the same time he was. I wasn't sure I believed it.

"Bio?" I asked.

"Think Limbaugh, then turn right. Lots of stories about the establishment. Likes to blow hard about society types not living average. Comes from money. Figures. Harvard dropout. Premed. A couple years under the radar, then a bunch of arrests for hard living and bad judgment. No convictions."

"You get anything on the license plate?" Connor asked.

"Hoping for stupid criminal tricks, Rock? No such luck. The plate was a fake."

"Rock?" I asked.

"It was too much to hope for, I guess," Connor said. "What else did you get?"

"Radio shock jock for the last eighteen months or so. Lots of conspiracy theories and antigovernment crap. Publicly, he was tight with a militia group based out of some farm near Chiapas, Mexico. Ethnic cleansing of indigenous people. You know the drill."

"And privately?"

"It's just gut, but I wondered if maybe he was on the feebs payroll and tired of slumming. My contact went tango quincy as soon as I dropped his name."

"Tango quincy?" I asked.

"Too quiet," Blue said.

"That's something. It might even lead away from Jack. An informant for the government would have plenty of enemies of his own," I said, leaning on the porch railing and gazing at the bay. The view was so perfect.

"Could," Blue conceded. "Not just the feds, either. DeVries was pitching a book. I couldn't get details. DeVries was paranoid, but he'd sold it as an exposé of the political secrets of San Diego society. Deep, dark local history. Maybe one of the Junior League's gone red."

"Doubt it." Connor threw cold water on the theory.

"Why not?" I asked. "It's motive."

"Where would one of them get the gun?"

"They ain't that hard to acquire, man."

"True. But an M-sixty is a sloppy weapon. Where would the crew team learn to put two in center mass?"

"That's hard?"

"It's not something anyone could do," Connor said. "Anything else?"

"The cop, Montoya, he'll be looking to talk with your lady."

Dread slid into my stomach. "Why?"

"DeVries's quarters were tossed, and the satellite station where the meet was supposed to happen . . . well, last night somebody decided to redecorate with a Molotov. It went up like the Fourth of July."

"Shit," Connor muttered.

"Roger that. Now that they've confirmed DeVries, they'll want to talk to his last appointment again."

"That woman can find trouble without half trying."

Blue laughed. "Can't they all?"

"You know I'm still on the phone, right?"

"Who's cover?" Blue asked.

"What's cover?" I asked.

"Okay, Sara, now, don't blow a gasket—" Connor began.

"Cover is something that will make me blow a gasket?"

"Oops. My bad. Looking forward to meeting you in person, Sara."

"I owe you, buddy," Connor muttered.

I heard a door close. I waited a moment, but when it seemed clear that Connor wasn't going to elaborate, I prompted him. "What are you up to?"

"Nothing."

"Liar. Cover? Explosive potential. You might as well tell me. I'm going to figure it out anyway, and then I'll definitely go ballistic on you."

"Ballistic. Nice word."

"Good vocabulary. Bad end result," I assured him. "Just because I can't reach you right this moment doesn't mean you won't pay when you get home."

"I only did it because I'm concerned about you."

"Building a rationalization before you even confess? That's a bad sign."

He sighed. "Cover means coverage."

"You're having me watched?" The nerve. I leaned over the railing, scanning the street. It could be anyone. No. He'd pick a man. Another military type. Maybe someone from his squad. From this height, I couldn't guess. "What does he look like?"

"Look like?"

"I want to see if I can spot him."

"No."

"You're mad? You're kidding me. You invade my privacy and you're mad?" He was nervy.

"Sara, get in the damn house."

"No."

"Yes. Now."

"Look, Connor—"

"You look, Sara. Didn't you hear anything I said this morning? This isn't some civilian. Whoever took out DeVries was a pro. If he thinks you know something, he could be targeting you right now. This whole thing is getting dangerous. Get in the house. Away from the windows."

Despite my best intentions, he was making his point. I went back inside and closed the sliding glass door.

"At least tell me his name."

"Whose name?"

"Your cover guy."

"You're inside?"

I let the silence hang. If he was going to freak me out, he shouldn't have it easy.

"Sara?"

I sighed. "Yes, Mother, I am safely tucked in."

"Thank you."

"You owe me."

"Noted."

"So tell me about him. It is a him, I presume. You'd never assign a woman to be 'cover.'" My air quotes were lost on him. "Women can't be trusted to take care of themselves, after all."

"Let me out of the doghouse, will you? His name is Troj. He's on my team."

"Troj?"

"Trojan."

"His parents named him after a condom? You sent a guy named for a prophylactic to 'cover' me?" More quotes. "That is very, um, open-minded of you."

He chuckled. "I can be open-minded. It's not his name. It's his call sign. Sort of a team nickname. He got it because he went to USC. The Trojans."

"An entire school committed to safe sex. That's nice. When are you coming home?"

"Depends."

"On what?"

"On whether you're going to be lying in wait with a frying pan."

"I don't cook."

"I didn't say you did."

"Assume for a second that I'm not planning widow-hood. Imminently, anyway."

"I'll be out by sixteen hundred."

I calculated. Four o'clock. Too long. I debated telling him I didn't plan to stay his prisoner and lose a whole day. No point. He'd say no and I'd do it anyway. I sat down on the couch and propped my feet up.

"Why did Blue out you?" I asked. "Tell me you were having me followed?"

"Entertaining himself."

"And why do these other guys agree to follow me around all day? They must have better things to do."

"Same reason."

"I hope I don't disappoint."

Chapter Fourteen

Changing the guard was a mistake. I spotted him immediately. The elusive Trojan might have been mist. The infamous Blue, not so much. Even in this mostly minority neighborhood, there just weren't a lot of hard-bodied black men in that size. I'd gone back to reinterview two neighbors who'd left me messages after finding my card on their doors. It was always the same. Had they seen anything? Had they ever seen DeVries with another man? Could anyone describe any Caucasian, male stranger, thirty to fifty years old, whom they'd seen in the area in the last two weeks? Two hours and I had nothing. Not a description, not a friend of DeVries, not a lead. I was hot and cranky, and seeing Connor's best friend trying to blend into a building was the first interesting thing that had happened to me all day.

I crossed the street and walked over to him. He stayed very still. "Hello, Blue."

"Hello, Sara. You shouldn't be in the open."

"He'll be mad."

"Roger."

"Probably told you to hog-tie me if you had to."

"Roger."

"That's not going to work out."

He smiled. "That's confirm."

I smiled back. Reasonable and pretty to look at. If I had to have a shadow, I could do worse. "What happened to the condom guy?"

His smile widened. He offered me an elbow and escorted me to a shiny new SUV. I let him help me into the passenger seat and bathed in the air-conditioning when he turned the car on.

"The condom guy had to report for duty. You're stuck with me."

"That is a burden." I lifted my sunglasses to bat my eyelashes at him.

"My ex-wives thought so."

"Wives as in plural?"

"Three and counting."

"You're kidding."

"No, ma'am."

"Fools."

"You flirtin' with me, Sara?"

"You mind?"

"Not even a little. Maybe we shouldn't tell Con, though. He seemed a little agitated this morning."

"I think he should cut back on the caffeine. Where are we going?"

"Condo. He mentioned he was going to give coffee a wide berth going forward."

I clicked the seat belt closed. "He told you I make lousy coffee, didn't he?"

"Robert Michael Todd. Serial number 686-41-0804."

I shook my head. "Name, rank, and serial number? I thought we were bonding here."

"Robert Michael Todd. Serial number 686-41-0804."

"Does he tell you everything?"

"You planning on making him pay?"

I leaned back in my seat. "He's a SEAL. He can take care of himself."

"I've got five bucks on you."

I peppered him with questions on the way back to Coronado. He answered none of them. He was so good at the dodge, I barely noticed he kept changing the subject. I didn't learn anything about Connor or his family. The team was not described. The job not mentioned. If I had to be that circumspect all the time, my head would explode.

We pulled to the curb in front of an ice-cream cart and got out. The line was long. Tourists and locals trying to get a little relief from the heat. For me, it was bliss. The air-conditioning had chilled me effectively, and my thin Seattle blood was once again craving deep warmth. I ordered an ice cream sandwich. Blue shook his head and ordered an old-school Popsicle. I reached into my pocket for money but he waved me away.

"Afraid I'll compromise you?"

"Afraid I'll let you." He smiled

"Sweet talker."

We unwrapped our treats and took a seat on a bench to eat them.

"What has he told you?" I asked.

"What I needed to know about your case to be cover."

"He must have told you more than that. You did all that legwork. Besides, I saw the two of you together the first morning I was here. That was before things came off the rails yesterday." My ice cream was melting and I had to lick fast.

"But after your meet with DeVries."

I nodded. "He was already worried. So he called on his best friend."

"He's covered my six a time or two."

"Six means ass?"

He smiled around his Popsicle. "Pretty much." His phone beeped. He flipped his wrist to open it.

"Todd . . . You want me to take her? . . . Anything else? . . . Over." He snapped the phone closed.

"Connor?" I guessed.

He looked at me for a long moment. With his sunglasses in place, I didn't have any idea what he might be thinking. Did having Connor's six include lying to his wife? Finally, he nodded.

"Did he try to call me?"

"No."

"Because if he had, he would have been yelling loud enough for me to hear, right?"

Blue shrugged.

"So he's updating you but keeping me out of the loop. Did he tell you to lock me in the dungeon?"

Blue fought a grin. "You can see the light of day as long as you don't drift from the team. Especially if you don't tell him."

I nodded, locking my lips and throwing away the key. "Where did he want you to take me?"

"Nowhere."

"Where did you think he wanted you to take me?"

"A face-to-face with a cop named Montoya."

"He's jealous."

Blue shook his head, reaching over to put his Popsicle stick in the trash. I handed him my wrapper and napkins. He threw them out.

"Connor said Montoya left a message but you haven't called him back."

Uh-oh. "We didn't exactly leave our last meeting on a positive note. I'm giving Montoya a little time to pull his head out of his behind. I'm surprised he called Connor, since Montoya thinks Connor might have killed Henry DeVries to teach me the perils of modern marriage."

"What?"

"As much as said Connor might have had someone shoot at me so I'd go home to barefoot and pregnant."

Blue crossed his arms. "This was after the meeting with the three of you?"

Damn. Busted. "Sara Townley. Rank: she who must be obeyed. Serial number: none of your darn business, since it seems like an easy way for you to steal my identity." I crossed my arms, trying to channel haughty.

Blue smiled. "Name, rank, and serial number has a lot of words with you. The cop was an overreaction?"

"And then some."

"Hmmm."

"Hmmm what?"

Blue leaned back. What was it with these navy guys? Didn't anyone ever teach them to think out loud?

"Going to tell me what you're thinking?" I asked.

"Montoya says Con is a person of interest. He tells Connor you're a person of interest."

"What does that mean?"

"Divide and conquer, maybe. New relationship under

pressure. Doesn't matter. Connor's not going to let you in a room with Montoya until you've got a lawyer."

"I didn't do anything."

"Not the point."

"He knows I didn't do anything."

"Still not the point."

I had to move. I got up and strode down the block. "Will Connor take a meeting with the cops?"

"We in a hurry?"

"What?" I was three feet ahead of him. "Oh. No. Sorry."

"No problem."

"You didn't answer my question."

Blue didn't bother with the personal statistics.

"Are we suspects?"

"Connor's take, for what it's worth, is that Montoya wanted to get you alone. Guess he doesn't know Montoya wants to get you alone again."

"Connor believes Montoya sees me as the weak link or a hustle?"

"Montoya's familiarity was mentioned."

Connor was sweet in a Mayberry sort of way. For a guy trained to kill people. "Does he think I'm going to run off with the police?"

"He's not taking chances. He invoked."

"What does that mean?"

"Connor told the cop not to talk to you without the lawyer."

"Did he tell you I work for a bunch of lawyers?"

"He mentioned it."

"What else did he mention? Other than my case and my coffee making."

"Not much."

"Would you tell me?"

"Not likely."

"Well, did you respond when he told you this 'not much'?"

"Nothing to say but the obvious."

"What's that?"

"Don't fuck it up."

"That's sweet."

"We're being followed," I said, glancing over my shoulder.

"Since we hit the neighborhood," Blue confirmed. He was on the street side of me. When tourists passed too close on the sidewalk, his hand on my back shifted me away from them. Yet he seemed totally unconcerned about our stalker.

"This is going to seem totally weird to you, but . . ."

"You've seen him before."

"Everywhere. I swear, I'm starting to dream about that dog."

"Just enamored. Seems harmless. Keeping his distance."

I stopped, turned. The dog stopped but didn't run away. I crouched. Held out my hand. The dog sat down and licked her lips. Blue shielded me from the ambling people and their stares.

"Come here, Pavarotti," I cajoled.

"Pavarotti?"

"She sings."

"You named the dog."

"Of course. Does she look homeless to you?"

"Cujo is probably male. Even the homeless care about their pets. Maybe more than they do about themselves."

I looked up at him. "Sounds like you know."

No shrug. No confirmation. Still, a glimmer of something real. I turned back to the dog. I'd spent all morning looking for a witness. Someone who'd been there the night Henry DeVries was killed. Someone who might have seen the elusive John Doe. And here she was. She'd been everywhere I'd been. Seen every person I'd seen.

"Ever had a dog, Blue?"

"Probably has rabies."

I grinned at him. "So much for harmless. I have a cat. Flash. Did Connor tell you? She saved my life once."

"Okay."

"No, really. She did." I squinted through my sunglasses. The collar was nearly invisible in the black coat of the Labrador, but it was there. "The thing is that cats aren't dogs. I want to have an up-close-and-personal conversation with that dog. If Pavarotti were a cat, I'd have to wait her out. But I'm thinking a dog might be more easily persuaded to work on my time schedule. She doesn't seem afraid. Just cautious."

"Hot dog," Blue suggested.

I pulled out a crumpled five-dollar bill and handed it up to Blue.

"On me," he said. "Stay here and stay down."

I took a business card out of my pants pocket. My last one. I pulled out the pen I'd used earlier and jotted a note on the back of the card. *If you knew Henry De-Vries, I need to talk to you. I have important information. Please call or e-mail. Sara Townley. P.S. I like your dog.*

Blue came back and handed me the hot dog, nicely grilled.

"I'll need something to tie my card to her collar."

"She has a collar?"

"Not homeless after all."

Blue went back to the hot-dog vendor. He came back with a twist tie. I handed him the card and he used a pocketknife to drill a hole in the corner, attaching the plastic tie and twisting it shut, leaving enough extra to do the same to the dog's collar. He closed the knife and returned it to his pocket. He held out his hand.

"I'll do it," I told him.

"I'll take care of it."

"She has rabies, remember?"

"Which Connor will not appreciate me exposing you to."

I stood and the blood rushed to my feet. I reached out a hand and held on to Blue while my equilibrium came back. I stumbled backward, and he placed a hand on my arm to steady me. The dog took two paces forward and cried deep in her throat. Blue moved me onto the grass and I sat down. Pavarotti belly-crawled a couple of feet closer, whining.

"It's okay, puppy. I'm all right."

She tipped her head to one side, ears pricking.

"You need this more than the dog." Blue handed me the hot dog. "Eat."

I shook my head. "I need to talk to the dog."

Blue sighed. "She needs to talk to the dog. Eat. I'll get the dog."

"Don't scare her."

"I'm not going to scare her."

Blue took a step toward Pavarotti and she popped up, prancing back. He took a step forward. She took one back and one to the side. Another dosi-do and sideways move and the dog and Blue were equidistant from me. Pavarotti looked from him to me and back like she was at a tennis match.

"Back away, Blue."

"I will get the dog." He moved forward and the retriever moved away.

"Sit, Blue."

He lifted his head. The dog did, too, ears high. Blue moved back and sat on a bench. She sat on the grass. I leaned forward and set the hot dog on the lawn between her and me. Her nose twitched. I patted the grass. She lay down.

"It's okay, Pav. The hot dog is for you." The dog stayed, staring at me.

"She's not going for it," Blue called from the bench.

Pavarotti's head turned toward him; then she slithered closer to the treat as if to call him a liar.

"That dog does not want food," Blue said.

Without taking her eyes off him, she leaned over and snagged the meat from the bun, chomping down.

I chuckled. "You have a way with women."

"Contrary females."

The dog finished the bun and licked her lips. I patted the grass beside me and she crawled closer. When she was within reaching distance, I held out my hand to be sniffed. Her nose twitched, and I leaned forward enough to lightly touch her fur. I stroked her. She moved closer, rolling onto her back and exposing her belly.

"Definitely a girl," I told Blue.

"I could have told you that just by the way she listened to me."

"She's sweet." I rubbed her chin and she vocalized, a deep vibration in her throat. I tied the card to her collar. She sprawled, stretching long. "Maybe I should take her home. I mean, it's clear to me she has a family. She's not afraid or anything. I wouldn't want her just roaming around. She might get hurt."

"I thought you wanted the dog to take a message to the enemy."

"Well, I do, but not enough to leave her on the streets. No, she should . . ." I stood. Pavarotti jumped up and raced past me down the street. She stopped on the sidewalk and turned, barked once, and was gone.

Chapter Fifteen

"**D**on't you have class?"

"More than you know," Ryan said soberly. "Or I'll ever be able to show you, more's the pity."

Blue had handed me off to Ryan midafternoon. He hadn't said it, of course. That would have risked life and liberty, not to mention bodily injury. On the other hand, Blue had stuck to me like gum on my shoe all day until the second Ryan had turned up.

"You're a bunch of male chauvinist pigs."

"But I've got a nice ass."

I rolled my eyes. "I meant"—exaggerated sigh—"don't you have to go to college once in a while?"

"It's summer vacation."

"It is?"

"Yeah. August. Hot as hell. No school."

"Then don't you have a job?"

"From what I hear, keeping an eye on you is forty-plus hours a week." He raised his bottle and saluted me from the chaise next to mine. "I'm applying."

"You're annoying," I told him, clinking bottles.

"Didn't take you long to figure him out," Connor said, coming onto the deck still dressed in uniform.

"Hi, honey, how was your day?" Ryan asked.

Connor reached over and took the beer from his hand, draining it and handing the bottle back. Ryan took it reflexively. He shook his head and got up to disappear into the apartment. Connor kissed me once, twice, three—

"Get a room," Ryan said, handing Connor a beer. "So we've been recapping the visit so far. We've got the dead guy, Grandma's ring, Siobhan's breakdown, and the SEAL team assignments. And then there was nearly getting caught having sex in the hallway."

I slapped a hand against my forehead. "Brain cramp. What was I thinking?" I drank deeply. "It hasn't been our best week."

Connor smiled. "It had its moments."

I tried to do stern. "Do you ever stop thinking about sex?" I turned to Ryan. "Does he ever stop thinking about sex?"

"No," they said in stereo.

"Family trait." Connor shrugged.

"High sperm count," Ryan agreed.

I laughed. "Honesty. I admire that in people."

Connor leaned close enough so only I could hear. "I have plans for you."

His breath tickled my cheek. I could feel the warmth of his lips near my ear. So his one-track mind wasn't such a bad thing.

"What do you have in mind?" I whispered.

He leaned closer. "I want to see Shamu."

"What?"

"That's what I want to do this afternoon. Pretend you don't have a job I hate and play tourist." He kissed my neck. "Play with you."

It was . . . I don't know . . . normal. No chase scenes, no family angst, just Connor, Ryan, and me playing tourists. Eating too much. Getting sunburned. Pretending. I offered him my hand.

"Sea World it is," I agreed.

"Not me. I don't do that kiddie stuff."

"C'mon, Ryan. It'll be fun."

"It'll be an afternoon spent watching you covered in whale spit and fraternal drool. Pass."

We parked in Balboa and walked. It was at least ninety degrees, and my curls clung to my temples. Connor put sunblock on my nose. He held my hand and pulled me around like a schoolkid on a field trip.

"So what are we going to do about Jack? How deep do you think he's involved?" I asked.

He shrugged.

"You're right. Let's talk about something else."

"Okay," he said.

"Go ahead," I said.

"What do you want to talk about?"

"I don't know. Pick a subject."

This ought to be good. On the one hand, we had the manipulative, ring-wearing former fiancée. On the other, we had the secret job. Then there was always his bank balance.

"I'm better responding."

"Tell me something I don't know. Tell me about your parents. How did they meet?"

We moved over to the edge of a pool where sea lions were swimming and sunning. A redheaded girl about five years old smiled at Connor through a chocolate mustache. He flirted back. The girl lit up, laughing, before clinging to her mother's leg and hiding her face.

"She dumped a blind date for him."

"For who?"

"My father."

"You're kidding?" That didn't sound like his elegant maternal unit.

"No. Her godmother set it up. Grandma Gertie."

I closed my eyes for a minute and tried to remember. "The left leaner." We walked toward the otters.

"What?"

"Siobhan mentioned her. I think she meant liberal."

"That's Grandma Gertie. She set Mom up on a double date with a guy who went on to draft the subpoena for Jerry Rubin for the House Un-American Activities Committee."

"Left-leaning Gertie?"

"The shock was supposed to make liberal lovers more appealing to my mother. Gertie's, well, one of a kind."

I laughed. "What happened?"

"My dear mother set fire to the table."

I sucked in a breath, covering my mouth with a hand. "Oh, my God. Deliberately?"

"She denies that. According to her, her date was an octopus. When she jumped to her feet in protest, she tipped the table in this Italian restaurant in Georgetown. The tablecloth caught fire. My dad played the hero with a pitcher of water. Two weeks later they got married."

"Impulse runs in your family."

He shook his head. The otters splashed him. I laughed. He wiped the spray away.

"How many times do I have to tell you?" he asked. "It's instinct. It's certitude."

"Nice one, double word score."

We moved on, drifting with the crowd. "Impulse or instinct, we get it right. My parents have been married forty-four years next month. They spent a decade getting to know each other, then had kids. They're happy. They still like each other. Not many people get that."

"You're right. They do seem"—I searched for the word—"symbiotic."

"Very nice." He complimented my vocab choice.

I tipped my head and brought my shoulders up in an aw-shucks way, batting my lashes. His hand found the small of my back, then underneath my shirt. Just fingertips. Public place. It was sweet and sexy. In this mood he was irresistible. He kissed my nose. I Eskimo-kissed him back.

"That's a happy story."

"Yeah. I guess. I never really thought about it."

"Tell me about Ryan."

"What about him? He's great. I like him. He's also a pain in the butt, but then, what little brother isn't?"

"Pretend I don't know anything about little brothers."

We entered the stadium and picked our way to a bleacher seat near the top.

"He's a lot younger than me, so we didn't hang out much growing up."

"What's the deal between Ryan and Lily?"

"Loyalty. Ryan thinks I got shafted and isn't shy about saying so."

"You don't think it's more than that? Don't you think he's a little over-the-top when it comes to her?"

"For him, it was all her fault. He picked a side. But I know I wasn't a great boyfriend."

"Universal truth number four hundred and ten, Connor: Cheating isn't about the person you're with. It's about the person you are."

He smiled, still facing forward. "That's good."

"True, too, but I stole it. You remember my next-door neighbor Russ?"

"Hard to forget Russ."

"Well, he said it first. Actually, he said it, and then we painted it on the wall of the apartment he shared with a wandering boyfriend right before Russ moved out."

"That sounds like him."

I nudged him, lowering my voice. "We used jack-o'-lantern orange. The no-good creep is probably still trying to cover it."

He laughed, putting an arm around me. "Revenge is sweet."

We watched Shamu jump through a hoop, then take a fish from the mouth of his trainer. A wave washed over the edge of the pool, and a group of kids screamed and backed away, wiping at wet faces.

"Ryan seems more than loyal," I observed. "It's more like rabid."

His body tightened. "He's a good guy."

"He's a great guy. An amazing flirt. Very funny. If I were into younger men . . ." I sat up straight and turned to face him. "Wait a minute. Your parents got married after two weeks and they're about to celebrate their forty-fourth anniversary." I glared.

"Yeah."

"Crap."

"What?"

"Nothing."

"What?"

"He wasn't lying. The rat. Ryan was telling the truth. You're younger than I am."

"Don't sweat it. I like older women."

Brat.

Chapter Sixteen

"*Hello, John Doe.*"

I stared at the screen. The cursor blinked rhythmically. I was drinking my morning coffee. Connor had made a pot before he left. Very domestic.

Balboa Park. Two p.m. Five-five. One twenty. Curly dark hair and blue eyes. I looked down. *Blue T-shirt. Jeans.* I hit send.

He'd offered the meeting and asked for a description by e-mail, calling himself lostboy81. Lost boy. Maybe *con man* would have been more accurate.

I dialed the phone. "Bank of Puget Sound, Ted Singh speaking."

"Mr. Singh, this is Sara Townley of Abercroft, Hamilton, and Sterns."

"Ms. Townley, how good to hear from you. Do you have an update for me?"

"Yes, sir. I have a lead on the man I believe gave the interview with Henry DeVries. I hope to meet him today. Have you changed your mind about having the police question him?" I sipped coffee. I felt a little sick thinking about turning over a dog lover to the cops, but he was a probable felon.

"There has been a development, Ms. Townley. The account has been resolved."

"Resolved, sir?"

"The line of credit has been repaid in full."

Oh. "Then the case is over?" Fine. I could stop feeling like scum for parting a nice dog from her master, and move on to learning the McNamara family handshake.

"No. We would still like you to meet with this man."

I leaned back in my chair. That didn't seem right. Why would the bank want me to continue? They got their money back. "To what end, Mr. Singh?"

"We would like you to question him on how he managed to access our client's personal information."

"I'm sorry, Mr. Singh, but I don't understand. I assumed you confirmed that all remaining accounts were legitimate. Has there been another attempt to access customer accounts from this direction?"

"No, no, nothing like that. It's routine."

I waited. He didn't expound. Not that clients were required to share their internal thought processes with me—they weren't—but this wasn't tracking.

"Routine, sir?"

"For our internal review. We would like to test our procedure. Determine if this could have been avoided."

"Avoid what? The client paid the money, right?"

"I have already given my new direction to your firm, Ms. Townley. I would appreciate your updating my colleagues in the La Jolla branch two days from now. You will be dealing with Mr. Philip Carson."

"Certainly, sir."

He hung up without saying good-bye. I checked my e-mail. There it was: new instructions from the senior associate assigned to the bank's account. *Continue to pursue all leads to make personal contact with the individual who claimed to be Charles Smiths during an interview with Henry DeVries. Fully debrief said individual to determine access to personal information and/or banking procedures to determine if process improvement is recommended. Expenses preapproved through end of week.* A client who wanted to leave their lawyers on the clock. Curiouser and curiouser.

I got up and took my coffee and the DeVries transcript to the patio. It was a spectacular day. Cobalt blue sky, warm breeze off the water, perfect. Unless you were Henry DeVries.

I leaned on the railing. I leaned farther. They were standing less than twenty feet apart. The man and the dog. I couldn't really tell from this distance, but I'd bet five bucks their brown eyes held the same intensity. I lifted my cup in salute. Blue, from his position lounging against a building, lifted a paper cup in return. I wondered why he was watching me from across the street. They were busted. He could annoy me from inside the condo.

Pavarotti turned her head toward Blue. Then she looked back at me and was gone. I guess she thought I only needed one babysitter at a time. Well, if the man was going to waste his time loitering outside Connor's condo, I should find a use for him. The rental car was giving me black lung, and I wanted to try to find Charles Smiths today. I'd researched the property records online—San Diego county was very progressive—and found a house in the name of a holding company owned by a limited liability company owned by a trust whose beneficiary was none other than Charles Smiths.

I grabbed the paperwork off the printer in Connor's office and headed out.

"Mornin'," Blue said as I approached.

"Why didn't you come in?"

He shrugged.

"You know we've met, right? That I can pick you out of a lineup? That you're a huge guy hanging out in one hundred and ten degrees?"

"You suggestin' I'm not invisible?"

"No. I'd never do that."

He sipped his coffee. Iced. His only concession to the heat. Personally, I felt like my scalp was on fire. "You busy?"

"Remote surveil."

"Right. Well, how remote is remote?"

He smiled. Wicked grins must be navy-issue. "What have you got in mind?"

"A road trip. I've got an address I want to check out."

"And you're signing up to have me bird-dog you?" He shook his head. "What're you up to?"

"Connor talks too much."

"We gettin' arrested?"

"No."

"Too bad." He took keys out of his pocket and pointed toward his shiny SUV. The car beeped.

I gave him directions. He didn't chat. He didn't play the radio. The truck silenced all the sounds outside the vehicle. I couldn't hear him breathe. I might have gone deaf. I was going to wait him out. People always filled silence with chatter. It was a great interrogation technique. I would stay completely quiet and he wouldn't be able to take it and he'd tell me things. About Connor. Things I didn't know. Real insights. The kind of things only a best friend would know. The sort of stuff that would take me years to find out for myself. He'd tell me. He wouldn't be able to take it. The void of sound would crack him.

"So, how long have you known Connor?" I asked.

No reply.

"It's just that you guys seem like best friends or something. You probably know him pretty well."

Silence.

"He tell you anything about me? Other than that I needed a keeper?"

Nothing.

"Do you suffer from transient muteness?"

"No."

He pulled next to a curb and turned the truck off. He removed a black nylon case from the glove compartment and put it in his pocket. "Ready?"

"Sure. I've got nothing else to do. I'm just sitting here talking to myself." I got out of the truck and stood on the curb, waiting for Blue to join me.

"House is a block down on the right," he said. "I'm point, which means you stay behind me. You end up in front of me, I pick you up and carry you out."

"Like I'd let you."

He stepped closer, blocking out the sun. He was bigger up close.

"You're point," I conceded.

There was a privacy fence and the front gate was locked. There was a bell. We rang. Once, twice, three times. No sign of movement. Nothing.

"This is probably the wrong time, but I should mention that I can't get caught. My boss doesn't want me actually approaching Charles Smiths. He made kind of a point of it."

Blue looked at me. "Don't worry about it. If we get caught, Con will kill both of us before you get fired."

"Comforting," I told him.

The neighbors had a hedge that proved prickly but not obstructive. We circled to the back, and Blue took two steps and was on top of the fence. He reached down and pulled me up like a doll. We hit the far side together. His shirt rode up and I saw the gun.

"We don't need a gun."

He put a finger to his lips.

"We would have knocked on the front door if the gate hadn't been locked."

He tapped my lips.

"Fine," I whispered.

He rolled his eyes.

The house was nice but not spectacular. The windows on the ground floor were shaded. The doors were locked. The grass was mowed but dry.

"Doesn't look like a millionaire bachelor pad, does it?" I asked.

No reply. Shocker.

Blue climbed on top of the fence at the side of the house where the wood ran close to the eaves. He stayed low on the roof and moved toward the back of the house, peering into windows. He dropped from the roof and landed on the grass next to me, rolling and getting to his feet in the same motion. A giant Nureyev.

"Anything?" I asked.

"Nothing. Time to go."

"We haven't learned anything yet."

He repeated the over-the-fence maneuver and we were once again whacking our way through the hedge.

"I would enjoy partnering on these little adventures more if you didn't think you were the Sphinx."

He walked fast. Maybe not fast, but his legs were long and it seemed like racing to me. When we were back in the SUV, he pulled away from the curb and headed out of the neighborhood.

"You didn't learn anything?" he asked.

"Well, he lives within his means."

"That all?"

"Pretty much. Did you see anything different in the upper windows?"

"Nothing."

"It was a wasted trip then."

"I mean nothing. Absolutely nothing. No furniture, no rugs, no pictures on the walls. Nothing."

I thought about that. "Maybe he just lives on the ground floor. Some people do that."

"No light fixtures."

"No one lives there."

"Roger that."

"Damn. I thought I was onto something. It took me two hours this morning to wade through all the layers to find any real estate holdings at all."

"What do you mean?"

"It's layered. Held by a bunch of intermediaries."

"An investment."

"Maybe. But if Smiths were in the investment business I would have found more than one. And if that were the case, they wouldn't bury them layers deep. The attorney in the cube next to me, Joe, does a lot of real estate work. He puts each new property into an entity to shield it from liability. You know, in case some neighbor falls and sues."

"Okay."

"This was in a trust. In a something else held by something else. And it was in the big one. The one that controls all the others."

Blue turned toward the water and pulled into a parking lot.

"Where are we going?"

"Lunch. We need to refuel and reassess."

My stomach rumbled on cue. "Lunch," I agreed.

Chapter Seventeen

"**S**he's smart. Sneaky, too." Blue winked. He held the phone away from his ear so I could share Connor's total lack of enthusiasm.

I could picture him at his desk. Cursing wives and friends. Rubbing at his temples to relieve the pressure. I was a little surprised he was buying it. Blue was a highly trained operative with sniper experience. He could probably track a target through dense jungle without so much as a ripple in the vegetation. Then again, Connor had sent someone I'd seen before with orders to lock me in the condo. I wasn't blind, and Connor should know better than to try to control me like that.

"I would have, but she told me she'd make a scene on the street. You already have cop trouble. I didn't think you'd want me to add to it. It was a field decision."

A field decision. Made me sound like an enemy of the state.

"You want me to follow her into the women's fitting room?" Blue sipped his beer. I toasted him with my lemonade. "She's trying on dresses. I didn't think you'd want me to maintain line-of-sight under the circumstances."

I covered my mouth to muffle a laugh. Dresses. Except for the wedding dress he'd bought me and a stop-traffic mini he'd asked about when he came to visit, I didn't own any. Connor would assume I was up to something.

"Not your fault," Blue assured him. "No. I didn't lose her." Blue sounded a little put out. "No. She's washing her hands. Yeah. We ought to recruit her. The team could use somebody with her skills. Okay. Fine. Got it. Out.

"He wants to talk to you." Blue handed me his phone.

"You're still a dead man." No sense letting him off the hook just yet. Blue might have been good company, but he was still the keeper Connor had assigned.

"Where are you?"

"I'm drinking with a gorgeous single man who doesn't think I'm stupid."

"I don't think you're stupid."

"Or helpless."

"I don't think you're helpless, either. I think you're beautiful."

I softened a little. He had good intentions; I knew that. He was overprotective and a complete Neanderthal but he meant well. "That is totally not going to work." The edge to my voice had dulled.

"And sexy."

"You are evil and should be destroyed." I said it without heat.

"If you tell me where you are, I could come grovel in person."

"Groveling is good."

"So tell me where you are."

I heard road noise in the background. He'd probably run to his car the second he heard I was out in public. Even with Blue here.

"If I tell you where I am, you'll come and take your clothes off and I'll forget I'm mad."

"Works for me."

It would work for me, too. I groaned. "Hyatt on the water. Patio bar."

"On my way. Let me talk to Blue."

"Do not conspire against me. You've used your one free pass, Connor. I mean it." I was mad. Hurt, too, although I'd deny it to my last breath. I was trying to let it go, play it off, but it was there. He was an ass. Plotting against me. Making my choices. Damn it, he should have told me like we were equal partners instead of keeping it a secret like I was, well, the wife.

"I hear you, Sara."

"Connor?"

"Yeah, hon?"

"Don't do it again."

Blue took the phone. "Roger. Out."

"Bless you," I said.

"I don't know how you talked me into that."

"I appealed to your sense of justice."

"He did say you were a force of nature."

"How does he feel about your recruitment efforts?"

"Not impressed. Specifically, 'Thank God the SEALs don't take women.' "

"That's chauvinistic." Connor would be Connor.

Blue shrugged.

"He say anything else?"

"Montoya is still looking for you."

"Can I ask you something?"

"Can I stop you?"

"Probably not. Why did you tell me all this stuff? What Connor said to you and everything. You've known him for years. You just met me today."

"And that bothers you?"

I stared at him. In for a penny. "Yes. You're his best friend. You're the one who's watching his back. As much as I appreciate your help in giving him a hard time— deservedly so—I can't help thinking . . ."

"He shouldn't trust me?"

"Frankly, yes."

"I've got his back."

I picked at the label on my beer bottle.

"Sara?"

"You shouldn't side with me against him."

"I didn't."

"C'mon, Blue. Everything we did today . . . You chose me over him."

"No, I didn't."

"How can you say that?"

"You can't be controlled. Even he knows that. Trying to dictate is only going to threaten the one thing he wants the most. You. I've known him a long time. He's not sane when it comes to you. He sure as hell isn't the rational guy I've bled with. I didn't choose you. I won't. Ever."

"So why did you help me?"

"I helped him. You were going to do it anyway. I covered you. Which is what he asked me to do. I also softened the ground so you won't resent him. Believe me, Sara, when I tell you I've got his back."

Okay. That was what I wanted. I wanted my own way, too, of course, but even more than that I wanted to know Connor's best friend wouldn't divide his loyalty. I needed to know his teammate would do whatever it took to protect him. Maybe I was controlling, too.

"Fair enough."

Chapter Eighteen

Ten minutes later, Connor kissed the back of my neck. I felt electricity spark along my spine. Okay, so I had already forgiven him. Until the next time, anyway.

"Am I out of the doghouse yet?"

"You should thank Blue, Connor. He did an admirable job of pleading your case, relying mostly on what is apparently a long history of testosterone poisoning."

"Yeah." Connor slumped into the chair next to me. He shook hands with Blue. "Thanks."

"Did you really steal your commanding officer's boat?" I grinned at him, letting him know I wasn't holding a grudge.

"It's not stealing," Blue denied. "Rock referred to it as a reallocation of resources."

"An excellent euphemism for grand theft pontoon." I laughed. "Why Rock?" I asked, directing my question to Blue. "Rock 'n' roll? No, his CDs are mostly jazz, which I personally do not understand, but there you go. Rock-hard?" I slid my sunglasses down far enough to assess him over the top of the lenses. "No, I guess his guys probably wouldn't name him that."

"No," Connor said.

Blue laughed. "Definitely not."

"Dumb as a . . . ?" I guessed.

"Hey," Connor protested.

"That, too," Blue said.

"Okay, I give up. Why Rock?"

"Rockefeller," Blue supplied the answer, even if it didn't make sense to me.

"You want to be appointed vice president?"

The waitress came over and Connor ordered an orange juice, not even acknowledging the blonde's cleavage. Enough stress for one day, I'd guess. "I know. You have a Nixon fetish."

Blue laughed.

"Okay, no Nixon. It has something to do with the arrest? That's it, isn't it? Tax evasion? Criminal ambition? First-degree megalomania?"

"A scandalous past?" Blue suggested.

"Don't help her."

"I know there's something there, but he won't tell me what it is." I leaned forward and stared intently behind my shades. Blue leaned closer and stared back.

"You know, don't you?" I whispered.

"I know everything."

"And you're going to tell me, right?"

"Absolutely." Blue sighed, propping his head on his hand.

"You're my best friend. You're a SEAL. You don't tell," Connor protested.

Blue never looked his way.

"They're smarter, they're stronger, and they don't fight fair. Sorry, man."

"You're dangerous, and I'm breaking this up right now." Connor signaled to the waitress. "I want a beer."

"He wants a lemonade," I corrected.

"Am I on the wagon?"

"I just thought you should have your wits about you when we meet John Doe."

"Who?"

"John Doe, our erstwhile radio celebrity."

He was very still. "When and where?"

"Balboa Park in"—I consulted Winnie the Pooh—"forty minutes."

"How did you find him?"

"He found me. Personally I think it was the dog-o-gram, but he could have gotten my card from anyone

within a five-block radius of Henry DeVries's station
warehouse place."

I watched Connor read. When he was finished, he
leaned back in his chair. He sipped lemonade. He waited
me out. Hell, I didn't know what it meant either. E-
mail from a user calling himself lostboy81. "They"—no
explanation for that—had betrayed him. They had lied
and now everyone would know. Everyone would know
about the red eyes. The red eyes again. Then it gave the
time and place for meeting.

"It's a prank," he said, watching my face.

"Or a setup," Blue suggested.

I shook my head. "I don't think so. Not with the red
eyes. C'mon, Connor. It's exactly what he said in the
police report. The same thing he said during the interview. Whatever the deal is with the red eyes, this guy
can't let it go. They're in everything. The way things that
haunt you get into everything. Except for maybe the
maid, I can think of only one person who could possibly
be that scarred by what happened the night the Smithses
were murdered. That person is the real Charles Smiths.
I think John Doe may actually be Charles Smiths."

"We know about the police report, honey. So do the
cops, the lab, reporters, maybe."

"And everyone they told." Blue put his two cents in.

"Besides, how do you explain the other guy? The one
actually living on the family estate, getting served by the
loyal retainers? They would know if he was the fake."

I held my hair off the back of my neck. Damn, it was
hot. "I can't explain it. Maybe all the servants are new.
Maybe they've been paid off. Maybe he doesn't have
servants. I don't know, Connor. All I know is that nobody cared that this guy swindled two hundred thou
until he went public. Now the person he talked to is
dead and his place looks abandoned."

"What do you mean, abandoned?"

"Did a little recon," Blue said.

Connor sighed. "She loves B and E."

Blue smiled. "Never got that far. Twenty and out. Too
proper a 'hood for the likes of me."

"I thought you were blending very nicely." I patted Blue's hand.

"What about this meet? Can we track the e-mail?" Connor asked.

Blue held up his BlackBerry. "Killed a little time waiting for you. ISP traces to the Santee branch of the San Diego County library. No cameras. No computer sign-in. Only one librarian on duty and she doesn't remember him, at least, not to a voice on the phone."

"He's really good with the whizbang stuff," I said, smiling appreciatively at Blue. He did have a way with women.

"You might try the personal approach."

Blue drained his glass and rose. "Check."

"We also need whatever intel is out there on Charles Smiths and his parents. Pictures," Connor told him.

"Roger that."

"Rendez at the condo at nine thirty?" Connor said.

"I'm gone," Blue said, leaving the restaurant.

"I like him," I said.

"Me, too."

"He told me not to divorce you because of this morning."

"I just wanted to be sure you were safe."

"You just wanted to control my every move." *Control* seemed a little harsh, but there was no upside to arguing fact. Safe, controlled, whatever.

"I love you."

I shook my head, then leaned over and kissed his cheek. "I know."

"Well, I'm glad to know you're not thinking divorce." We stood up, and Connor threw a twenty on the table.

"Me, a divorcée? I don't think so." I laughed and took his hand, looking straight up into his face. "A widow, maybe." I smiled, and Connor followed me out of the restaurant.

Chapter Nineteen

"**Y**ou'll spook him," I said, thrusting my hands into the pockets of my shorts to keep from strangling Connor. "He's already squirrelly."

"It's the squirrelly part I'm not comfortable with, hon. He lies. He steals. For all we know, he had that deejay killed. Maybe even did it himself."

Oh, please. He didn't believe that any more than I did. He was just laying it on thick in the vain hope, that I'd step aside and let him play knight on a white charger.

"Whatever he is, he's unpredictable. A wild card. We need to plan for that."

"We have planned for it. You'll be able to hear everything over the cell phone. If he starts to go off, I give you my permission to ride in like John Wayne. Heck, I'll even do my best damsel in distress for the occasion. But I want to talk to this guy, Connor. He's not going to talk if you're there glaring down at him."

"I'm not glaring."

"You are."

"I'm not."

"Are too."

He shook his head. He should get over it. I wasn't giving in on this one. So far, John Doe was strictly a white-collar criminal. This was my case. He was backing me up. It was broad daylight, for Pete's sake.

"There's no reason to think he's violent, Connor."

"One dead body not enough for you?"

"You heard what I heard. DeVries had multiple volumes of the better-not-run-into-you-in-a-dark-alley crowd.

He had a criminal record as long as your arm. He had a demented fan base. There's absolutely nothing tying John Doe to that shooting."

"I don't need proof. I'm not the cops. Or a judge. I was there when they were shooting at you."

"In my direction. Not at me."

"A distinction you didn't draw at the time."

I scowled, then shrugged. "Point for you."

He put an arm around me. "I'm not trying to score points. I'm trying to keep you safe."

"You can't wrap me in cotton wool, Con. There's something really off about this whole case. I'm going to find out what. With or without you." I looked straight at him to deliver the blow. I didn't want him to think I was mad. I wasn't. I wasn't even challenging him. It was for informational purposes only. He had two choices: back my play or not. Like Connor McNamara would ever pick the latter.

"You'll stay out of reach?"

"Connor?"

"Promise me you'll—"

I pointed. "She look familiar to you?"

Connor turned. Stared. "Well, I'll be damned."

The dog was wearing a red bandanna with a yellow collar. Very colorful. "I'm starting to sense a theme here."

Connor shook his head. His hands tightened on my shoulders.

"Stay away from both of them."

"Don't talk bad about Pavarotti. She saved my life."

"Fine. Stay away from Doe."

I held up the Girl Scout salute. "I'll keep three feet between us at all times."

"Watch his hands. If you see his hands twitch toward his pockets—"

"Drop and roll." I kissed him on the cheek.

He kissed me on the lips. "Be careful."

"I'm always careful."

"Oh, brother."

He gave me a hard squeeze and let go. Connor moved away and walked the perimeter, past the Automotive

Museum to the Air & Space Museum, finally choosing a vantage point on the north side of the Hall of Champions. Then he blended. I could barely tell he was there, and I knew where to look. My cell phone rang.

"Ready?" Connor asked.

"I'm good." I placed the earpiece in and threaded the cord down the front of my shirt, sliding the phone into my pocket. I was nervous. I hoped he couldn't tell.

"We can still call this off. Let the cops do their thing."

"I can't. Connor, I've got to go. If he sees me talking on the phone, he'll blow me off."

"I couldn't get that lucky." He sighed. "Sorry. Okay, here we go."

"Yes, Captain."

"Smart-ass."

"I love you, too." Snarky. That's what I was. Nerves. I had to work on my cucumber.

"I know."

I laughed. "Well, you're not short on ego. Be talking to you."

"Definitely."

I could feel him watching me. It wasn't unpleasant. He was a good person. Overprotective, maybe. Pushy, definitely. But for a guy I'd married after less than a week, I'd done pretty well. I could have ended up with a psycho. Or worse, a mama's boy. I jumped. She was licking my hand.

"Hey, Pav." I held my fingers out to her. "How're you doing?"

She sniffed, then licked again. Not at all skittish. That had to be a good sign.

"You okay after the other night? All that noise? All that glass?" I scratched behind her ears. She closed her eyes and leaned into the caress.

"So, how are you involved in this whole thing? I know you're connected somehow. You've been showing up in lots of suspicious locations. Can't be a coincidence. You a PI? A canine journalist? Pavarotti the Paparazzi?" She sat on her haunches and put both paws on my leg. "Not talking, huh? Don't blame you. Never talk without your lawyer present."

"Move around. Don't make yourself a target," Connor said into my ear.

"I've got to wander." I patted her. "Want to come? My husband is the jealous type, but how could anyone not love you?" I walked back and forth, making little circuits of the plaza. Pavarotti followed at my heels, reaching out occasionally to lick my hand. Tourists came and went, their cameras swinging from neck straps. An older man began to sweep the bricks in front of the Air & Space Museum, removing the debris of the day.

I glanced at my watch: nine fourteen. Our man was late. I stroked the dog's head.

A man came down the walk from my right, past the Starlight Bowl and straight at me, dressed like the homeless: dirty jeans, blackened sneakers, ripped T-shirt. Jacket even in the heat. His hair might be blond when clean, and he sported a couple of days' worth of facial hair. The dog left my side and jogged over to him. They met midway and Pavarotti turned. They came back toward me together. The man's head swept from right to left. The dog looked straight ahead.

"Why are you doing this?" he shouted a good twenty feet away from me. His high-pitched voice screeched. He was hanging on by a thread.

"Charles Smiths?"

Doe took two steps closer. I tried not to look afraid. Not to react. Not to do anything that might set him off. The dog nuzzled his leg and John Doe relaxed.

"Why are you stealing me?" He was plaintive.

"Stealing you? I don't understand."

"You're trying to replace me. To make me crazy. Why?" He lurched toward me and I backed up. Pavarotti barked. Doe hesitated, looking down at the dog for a second. I used the opportunity to slide a little farther away.

I smiled, holding my hands up.

"She's a nice dog. Gentle. Is she yours?"

"Why are you stealing me?"

"I'm not. I swear."

"You're trying to make me crazy. I'm not crazy." He

screamed it in his paranoid nuthouse voice. Nothing was more dangerous than a lunatic.

"I don't think you're crazy. Pavarotti doesn't think you're crazy, either."

"Who?"

"The dog. I named her Pavarotti."

"You want my dog." He reached down and gripped the dog's ruff.

"No. No. I promise you I'm not trying to take your dog. I just kept seeing her. I didn't know her name. I gave her one, just temporarily, until I found out what her real name was. She needed a name. I couldn't just call her 'dog.' That wouldn't be right."

He stared.

"Please. I'm not trying to make you crazy. I just want to talk."

"Liar. It's you. You're the one." He pointed at me, his free arm waving.

"Charles."

"You know me." His voice quieted, his arm sagging to his side. He patted the dog's head. "You know her."

"Um, yes."

"Why won't you tell them?" A tear rolled down his cheek.

"Tell who?"

"Them." His voice rose an octave.

"I'll tell them." I had no idea what he was talking about. He seemed confused. Scared. Okay, crazy. But not dangerous. He hadn't moved any closer. He made no attempt to touch me. And the dog. The dog told her own tale. She wasn't scared. She wasn't trying to get away.

"You will?" he asked.

"Yes. I will."

"My name is Charles."

I nodded. "Your name is Charles."

"And you'll tell them?"

"I'll tell them."

"Promise?"

"I promise."

He reached out, but I didn't get out of the way in time. He touched my hair, petting me with one hand and the dog with the other.

"Pavarotti," he said.

I nodded, holding my breath.

"Thank you," he whispered.

"You're welcome."

He took one step to the left and bolted away, the dog on his heels.

Watching him go, I tried to get my breathing under control. I didn't think my heart could take too many close calls like that. Someone touched my arm and I jumped, swallowing a scream.

"Please don't do that."

"Sorry."

"God, Connor, did you hear him?"

"He's off beam, Sara."

"He's scared. Did you see his face?" I was shaking and sweating.

"Hey, it's okay." He put his arms around me just as his pager vibrated.

Pulling back far enough to look at him, I grinned. "Is that a pager in your pocket or are you happy to see me?"

"A bit of both."

Chapter Twenty

Pablo Esteban lived with his daughter and grandson in a small house north of San Diego. When we arrived, his daughter showed us to a tiny kitchen and went to get her father. Esteban shuffled in a few minutes later and waited while his daughter fixed iced tea for us. She chattered on but he never said a word, the brown eyes sharp in his wrinkled face. I knew men with that look. Connor was a man with that look. Blue, too. Probably a company man, and plenty careful to boot. I wondered why he had agreed to talk to us.

"We were hoping you could tell us something about the Smiths murders. You said on the phone that you worked the case," I began.

"Yes, missus, I did. Long time ago, that." Esteban rubbed his mustache. "Why you want to know 'bout that one? What's so important that brings a little thing like you to my house all these years later?"

"I'm an investigator. I'm looking for a man calling himself Charles Smiths."

The old man nodded. "The boy."

"Not a boy anymore. He's over forty now," I said.

"Suppose he would be. Why are you looking for him?" Esteban sipped at his iced tea, but his eyes never left my face.

"It's sort of a long story. Do you ever listen to KPXY? It's a local radio station."

He shook his head. "With my grandson in the house, there's not much quiet time for listening to the radio.

He's a handful." The man smiled, shaking his head without any sign of regret. "You got kids?"

"No." I shifted a little. Kids. I wondered if Connor wanted them. Did he think about taking our daughter to dance class, or cheering our son at a baseball game? Too fast. We were barely married.

"Plenty of time for that. Wife and me, we didn't have Mercedes until we'd been married more'n ten years. Got to know each other pretty good in them years, too. Knew enough to know we'd make it through the rocky patches."

His rough spots probably hadn't included gunfire and bitchy ex-girlfriends. At the rate Connor and I were testing our relationship, I doubted we'd have to wait ten years before knowing if we'd make it. I was already convinced.

"So tell me about this radio program," Esteban prompted.

"It was hosted by a man named DeVries. He did an interview with someone calling himself Charles Smiths two weeks ago."

"Calling himself? What does that mean?"

"He's an impostor. The real Charles Smiths is in Seattle." At least, that was the story we were telling for now. "That's why I'm here. I'm trying to find the man passing himself off as Charles Smiths."

"Man can call himself anything he wants, I suppose. Who's he hurting?"

"There's money involved," Connor offered.

The old man turned to him and nodded. "They had plenty, even before. I was starting to think maybe she doesn't let you get a word in. My wife was the same." He smiled at me. "Not that that was a bad thing. She was smart. Like this one."

"Thank you."

"Been a long time since a woman wanted to hear this old man ramble. But you're not here to listen to me go on and on. You're here on business."

I smiled at him. "I am, but—"

"No buts about it. A woman with a mission. Now, where was I? Right. Charles Smiths. Parents' names were Martin and Angela . . . Amelia . . . no, Andrea. That's it. Martin and Andrea. Let's see. Call came in about nine at night, I guess." He rubbed at his mustache. "Used to work the night shift in those days. Paid a little better."

"We've seen the police report," I broke in. "We're interested in the witness."

The old man looked toward the ceiling. "A maid. Marta? Maria. Maria Gonzales. Strange girl. Upset but not . . . you know . . . not crying, not screaming. Wasn't like you'd hear about a murder every day, not like now. Composed, I guess I'd call her."

He had an amazing memory. "She gave a statement?"

"To my partner, Jesse Fontura. Good man, good partner. Got cancer bad a couple a' years ago and died last winter."

I pulled the copy of the report out of my pocket and handed it to the old man. He smoothed it across his knee and looked down at it without a trace of a squint.

"I'm interested in anything you might know about this." I reached over and pointed to the maid's reference to a red dot on Mrs. Smiths's white shirt. I glanced at Connor.

Slow, he mouthed.

"Jess, he wrote everything down. Always did. Said he couldn't know what was important and what wasn't till he had some time to think about things."

"Did you follow up on it?" I pressed.

The old man blinked. *Slow, Sara. Don't do anything to put this guy off.*

"Nothing really to follow up on," Esteban said. "There was blood all over that room. Figured some got on her blouse."

"There's nothing that put the kills in sequence," Connor jumped in.

Esteban shrugged. "Forensics wasn't the big deal then that it is now. I watch all them programs. Amazing what you can find out just from a hair or a little skin cell. Things were different then. It didn't seem particularly important, and then, of course, Jess and me was pulled, so we didn't go no further with it."

"Pulled? You mean someone else worked the case?" I got back in the driver's seat. I was perched on the edge of my chair, playing with my empty glass. Connor was definitely up to something, except I couldn't see it. Sequence? What sequence? And why would it matter? I hated being the last one to a party.

"Suits took over. Like your man was saying, money. Talked then and it talks now."

"The only police report we've seen is yours," I told him.

"Wrote it that night. Talked to the maid, waited for the coroner, wrote the report. Next night we go in and there's a note from my lieutenant. We're off the case."

"Who took it over?"

Esteban shrugged. "Wasn't exactly taken over."

"What do you mean?"

"He means the case wasn't meant to go anywhere," Connor offered. "Not every mission is meant to succeed. It might make sense. Someone higher up could have information that changes the parameters. Intel that they can't or won't share."

"Office politics." The old man nodded. "Happens."

"Do you know where we can find the maid?" I asked.

"No. Figure she was an illegal. She was probably gone the next day, back to Mexico. Illegals don't like police."

"Why did she stay until you got there?" That didn't really make any sense to me. If she was an illegal, I just couldn't see her hanging around waiting for the police.

Esteban nodded his approval. A question he would ask. His face creased in a smile. "Always wondered that myself. Most wets, something goes wrong they're already making tracks for the border."

"Any guesses?"

"I guess somebody made it worth her while to stay. Like I said, money talks."

"Was Maria the only witness?" Casually, not making any eye contact, I tried to probe for information about John Doe or Charles Smiths or whoever was really there that night. I glanced sideways at Connor. His face showed nothing. I should not play poker with him.

"What do you mean?"

"There's only one witness statement, Detective," I began.

"I was just a uniform, Mrs. McNamara."

"Sara, please."

"Sara." The old man smiled at me. He was enjoying this. Maybe his life had slowed down, but he had stories to tell. Good old days to recall. No wonder he'd invited us over.

"Is it possible someone else was at the scene that night?" Connor asked.

Esteban sat back in his chair and looked up at the ceiling. He knew something. I could feel it. He was just deciding whether or not he'd share.

"It wasn't about what happened after," Esteban said.

"I'm sorry," I said. "I don't follow."

"Pullin' us off the case, that was higher up. Connections." Esteban nodded at Connor. "You know what I'm talking about."

"Yes, I do."

"Jess and me, we didn't do what we did 'cause we was worried about any of that. It weren't 'bout that. I just want you to understand."

"We do," I assured him. "You did what you did because you thought it was the right thing."

I leaned forward, resting my arms on the table. *Tell me. Trust me.* "What did you do?"

"We kept the boy out of it."

I nodded. No cop would do it now. The risks were too great. The press could find out. The victim's family could sue. The kid could have been the killer. Any one of a million professional, personal, and financial depth charges that would keep even the most moral man away from putting himself at risk for a stranger. In those days, a traumatized teenager still merited kid gloves and paternal protection.

"Charles Smiths?" I guessed.

"Yeah," Esteban conceded.

"He saw his parents murdered," I answered my own question.

"Yes, ma'am, he did."

I looked at Connor. I was trying not to jump to conclusions. John Doe's interview had matched the maid's statement. The details, the description of the murders were too similar. It might still be that Charles Smiths told John. It would explain why Doe would choose Smiths, and how he knew enough about him to steal his identity. Doe could have gotten the information from the missing Maria. He might have had access to the police report and memorized it. Or some third party confidant of either Smiths or Maria could have been the leak. Or it could still be coincidence. Man, it didn't feel like a coincidence.

"Did you take a statement?" I asked.

"We talked to him. Didn't write nothing down."

"Not even your partner?"

Esteban thought about that one. His brown eyes went hazy as he scrolled back.

"Maybe."

"If he did write something down, where would it be? In the file?"

The old man shook his head. "They pulled the case too quick for that. Jess never put his notes in until the end."

I clasped my hands together to keep them from shaking. *Please, let the mysterious Jess be a pack rat.* "Did he throw his notes away afterward?" There was no way Fontura had done that. A compulsive record keeper kept notes. Always.

"Don't think so."

"Where would they be now?" My adrenaline was in high gear. "Did he have a wife? Children? Someone who would have gotten his personal papers when he died?"

"Wife died years ago. 'Bout when my Mercedes was born. Didn't never remarry. Had a son. Miguel. When Jesse died, he brung me a couple of boxes of keepsakes. Never did go through 'em."

"Could we see them?" I asked.

"Ain't here. Not much room, what with my daughter and grandson and all. Didn't want to get rid of 'em, though. Lot of history there. Didn't seem right to just throw 'em away."

"Where are they now?" I persisted.

"Friend of mine lets me keep some stuff in his attic. They'd be there."

"We'd like to see them, if you don't mind, Officer."

The old man sat up straighter, looking me in the eyes without blinking. "You looking to make trouble for that boy?"

"No, sir."

Esteban took a long time measuring me. Weighing my worth, my integrity. Then he treated Connor to more of the same. In the end, I think it was Connor's aura of respectability and the bonds of brothers in arms that swayed him.

"I'll get them for you. Can you come back tomorrow?"

"We'll be here," I assured him.

He ushered us to the door. "I think about him sometimes. The boy."

"You did right by him," Connor said.

The old man smiled a little. "Appreciate you sayin' so. We tried. Skinny little kid. Not tough, not like teens is nowadays. Parents dead. In the big house by himself. Every day the same. Lots of money and nothing else. Just a big empty house and a raggedy old dog."

I stiffened. "A dog?"

"Yeah. Didn't look like no purebred, neither, but that boy, he just kept hanging on to it for dear life. Reckon I don't blame him. Not with the rest and all. I mean, he wasn't never gonna have nothing again. Not really. Course, nobody loves a boy like his dog."

Chapter Twenty-one

"**A** boy and his dog."

"Lots of people have dogs, Sara." We were driving back to the base.

"I know. It's just, well, that's how I think of John. He's obviously older, and Pavarotti isn't the same dog, but isn't he just an emotional kid still clinging to his best friend? Then there's how much John Doe knew about Charles Smiths. What did you think?" I asked.

"I think there are a lot of explanations for how John Doe ended up with the details of that murder scene."

"I'm not saying you're wrong. But don't you think it's at least possible that John Doe is Charles Smiths?"

He checked the rearview mirror and passed a smoke-belching Chevy four-by-four.

"Anything is possible."

"The thing is," I mused, "I'm not sure where that leaves us. We know that Henry DeVries was gunned down. We know that John Doe talked to him and knew things only someone very familiar with the murder of the Smithses could possibly know. We know that Charles Smiths witnessed the murder of his parents. We know Jack is Charles's doctor. Maybe it's time to talk to Jack."

"He's not going to tell us anything about a patient, even if he isn't neck-deep up to no good."

"He's not going to tell you, maybe. I might have better luck."

"No."

Touchy. Not that I blamed him. Jack was not to be trusted. Then again, keeping this enemy close might be worth the price of admission. "I'm not suggesting a solo. Would-be killers definitely require backup."

"I control the sit," he said flatly.

"The what?"

"Situation."

"You ought to come with cue cards."

He took the off-ramp. "I'll work on that. It'll have to wait until this afternoon. I've got another meeting I can't get out of." He glared at me. He did stern very well. "You are not doing this without me."

"I am not doing this without you," I dutifully repeated, putting my hand on my heart.

"I mean it."

"I don't know why you're so suspicious all the time. I said I wouldn't go without you."

"You have credibility issues."

"Hey."

"You know what I mean, Sara."

"I can't believe you're still holding the psycho-killing pet sitter against me. One gun-toting lunatic in six months of marriage is a pretty good track record."

"Three lunatics. The business partner and the secretary. Plus the shooter from the other night. Four."

"That's still not that many."

He groaned. Glancing in the rearview mirror, he frowned, then suddenly changed lanes. I turned around to see. A black Lexus sedan like a hundred others we'd seen.

"What are you going to do while I'm working?"

"You mean whoever you assign to cover me won't keep you informed? Report my every movement? Don't bother to lie, Connor. You're going to. I know you're going to, and you know I know you're going to."

"I wasn't going to lie."

That was probably true. There was no point. He was caught. Besides, I couldn't see him as a casual liar. It would rub his moral streak the wrong way. I'd have to teach him, if he was ever going to be any good at it.

"I'm going to rerun the background check on Charles Smiths. I think I'm going to spend some time checking out Jack, too, if that's okay with you."

"Paper chase only," he said, adjusting the side mirror.

I glanced in my own. The Lexus was still in sight. Still three cars back. Or maybe it was another Lexus. I looked at Connor. His hands were loose on the wheel. He might appear casual, but he was radiating intensity. "Fine."

"I mean it."

"I said 'fine.' "

"You fib."

"You wound me, sir."

He shook his head, his eyes restlessly checking rear and side mirrors. "Somehow, I doubt it."

I ignored that. I might occasionally bend the facts a little. Maybe, once in a while, I embellished. Made a better story. And by *better* I meant less likely to make me look like an idiot, an incompetent, or a nut job. It wasn't an easy road for me. Sometimes I felt like Lucy in the candy shop.

He reached over and pushed a curl behind my ear. He grinned at me. Not mad. Not mad was good. I glanced at the clock on the dashboard.

"When do you have to be at this meeting?"

"Eighteen minutes."

"And it's important."

"Unavoidable."

I leaned forward as far as the seat belt would allow. "Too bad."

"Roger that," Connor agreed with fervor.

He pulled in front of the office and parked. I looked for Blue or one of the other merry men. Today they were invisible. I'd have to try harder. Connor got out of the car and I slid behind the wheel. He leaned into the window.

"Have I said I'm sorry about Lily?"

"Try it without your clothes."

"Roger that."

Chapter Twenty-two

I was pulling out of the gates when my phone rang.
   "Hello?"
   "You never call, you never write. Sniff, sniff."
   "Russ. Hey, honey, how are things in Seattle?"
   "Sad and overcast without my bestest friend. Who never calls, et cetera, et cetera."
   "How's Tony?"
   "Celebrating his taste in men."
   I laughed. I missed Russ. "As well he should."
   "How is Connor? Mourning my absence?"
   "He's hiding it well." I moved into the right lane so I wouldn't have to keep up on the speedway while talking on the phone.
   "What else has been going on?"
   "I've met the family."
   "Dish, girl."
   "Well, the father seems nice. The mother scares me. The little brother is adorable, and the sister is married to a bastard I'm thinking about framing for murder."
   "Ooh, a group project. I'm in."
   "Then there's the ex-fiancée who is still wearing a McNamara family heirloom on the third finger of her left hand. She's drop-dead gorgeous, of course."
   "They all are. Is this the murder we're using to frame the asshole brother-in-law?"
   "I've already got a dead body."
   "Throw one in for luck."
   I laughed so hard I nearly sideswiped a soccer mom in an SUV. She spoke fluid hand gesture.

"I wish you were here." My heart ached a little. Connor might have the Norman Rockwell family portrait, but I had Russ. We were our own kind of family.

"One word and I'm down there removing Barbie's digits, baubles and all."

"You're the best."

"Tell me something I don't know. Listen, sweetie, I have to run, but I wanted to check something with you. The news desk called to tell me someone checked on Alex French's credentials. That wouldn't be you, would it?"

"I should have called. I need to use your alter ego."

"Is it in a good cause?"

"Not at all."

"That's my girl. No worries. The department has strict orders to play along anytime anyone calls to check out Alex. What is she working on today?"

"She's a romance writer working on an article that will serve as psychiatric background for her next book."

"That woman gets around. Tomorrow he's doing a lifestyle piece on up-and-coming male models."

"After the sex change?"

"It'll be a busy day."

"Thanks for letting me borrow your get-invited-anywhere imaginary friend."

"*Mi amiga es su amiga.* Love you, babe. Bye."

I went back to the condo and spent several hours playing desk jockey, chasing background details for our players. It was tedious but necessary. I checked the street every hour or so, trying to spot my shadow. No luck. No dog, either. It was downright lonely. I was debating leaving the condo for the sole purpose of amusing myself by flushing out my protector when Connor strolled in.

" 'Bout time."

He stopped with his lips halfway to my cheek. "For what?"

"I've got a plan."

"Oh, brother."

"It's a good plan."

He rolled his eyes. Ignoring me, he went to the kitchen and came back with an iced glass of something. Not beer. Good. That meant he thought I was going to talk him into something that would require he keep his wits about him. I waited. He drank and paced and finally settled in the recliner opposite me.

"Let's hear it, then," Connor said.

"Jack's got a wandering eye."

"So?" The glass was set down hard. "No. Absolutely not."

"I'm not going to sleep with him."

"You're sure as hell are not." He was yelling.

"I'm merely suggesting that a man thinking with his other brain might be more amenable to sharing what he knows," I said matter-of-factly, as if I'd played Mata Hari before and it was no big deal. Except it was.

"I don't want him near you."

"I don't either, sweetheart." I patted his leg. "I just want to know what he knows about Charles Smiths."

He sighed. He might not have been the one to tell his team I was hot, but I'd lay odds *crazy* came from him. I'd been good all afternoon. I'd done what I was told in the comfort and relative safety of his kitchen. Unfortunately, my good-girl streak didn't run very deep. I was ready for some action.

"So what's the plan?" Connor asked.

"I don't know. Short skirt. Plausible story. I called and made an appointment. I'm a writer. I used Russ as a reference."

"When?"

I needed to learn not to share details. He was too quick on the pickup, and I could do without a brouhaha because I'd started this ball rolling without him.

"From everything I've heard"—I continued on my own agenda—"Jack's got an ego the size of the Space Needle. With the parents' murders, Charles Smiths must be one of the war stories he tells at parties. Names removed for confidentiality, naturally."

"He's a psychiatrist. You're not an actress. He'll see you coming a mile away."

I shook my head. "He doesn't know me. He has no reason to be suspicious. Besides, in my experience, egomaniacs are always sure they're the smartest person in the room. They get blindsided because it doesn't occur to them that they can be had."

I'd done it before. Sometimes Russ and I made a game of it. Usually the more outrageous the story, the more likely we were to be believed. Egomaniacs never called you a liar to your face. They looked down on you with smug expressions and unwarranted complacency that they could not be made a fool of.

"I want this in a public place," Connor said, resignation in his voice.

"I was thinking more along the lines of his office."

"No way."

He'd try to tie me to a chair pretty soon. And he thought I was in danger. Sweet, but foolish. "We can set up backup. I'll be completely safe. You'll be watching out for me."

"Do you have any idea how much he could hurt you in the time it takes me to get into the building? I won't be able to be inside."

"I can take care of myself. He won't be the first octopus I've handled, Connor." I rolled my eyes. "There are a lot of them out there, and I was single a long time."

Just the thought of Jack's hands on me was enough to make the bile rise. If he tried anything, I'd castrate him.

"This is nuts," Connor said for the tenth time.

We were sitting in his car two blocks from the little house that Jack used as an office. We'd stopped at the mall for supplies. When I'd come out of the dressing room, Connor gulped audibly. Yep. There were a few universal truths about straight men. That they were visual was pretty near the top of the list.

"It's a great plan." I tugged at the short leather skirt. Connor watched my every move. It was turning me on. I was definitely going to wear this later. Under different circumstances. He reached out and I slapped his hand away. It was either that or jump him in the front seat of the car in the middle of broad daylight. The sacrifices I made for my job.

"It's not my fault that skirt is giving me ideas."

"Lint gives you ideas. Focus, please." I leaned forward in the seat to check the mute button on my phone. My blue silk blouse gaped open. Connor sucked in a breath.

"Need help?" he offered.

I looked at him, shaking my head, tugging the short red wig over my curls. "We don't have time for your kind of help." I squirmed in the passenger seat. "Or room, frankly."

"I'll buy an SUV tomorrow."

Connor the problem solver. I shook a finger at him. "First rule of spies, remember: Don't get caught. Being in flagrante in the middle of the afternoon in this nice neighborhood in a convertible practically guarantees we'd . . . what was it you called it? . . . botto, something, anyway, flunk the first rule."

"Bolo. We call it bolo."

"Okay, bolo, then. Besides, I thought you were all hot to get the goods on your soon-to-be ex-brother-in-law. What about Siobhan?"

"I'm hot, all right, but it doesn't have anything to do with my sister. You're right. Business first. You good on the plan?"

"It's not that complicated, Connor. I'm a writer looking for background. I get him to talk about himself. That's cake. He's a guy and, from everything everyone says about him, a pompous ass to boot. I try to find out about Charles Smiths in hypothetical terms. I try to get him to describe the real one. Then I seduce him on the desk so you can dissect him with a clear conscience."

"That's not funny. Although it has a certain appeal."

"Relax, Connor. He called to check on my background. He won't ask again."

"He's not stupid."

"Neither are you, but your brain isn't exactly operating at peak proficiency at the moment, is it? What is it with men and the happy-hooker look?" I pulled at the hem. "Even the best of you turns drooly at the first sign of thigh."

"Yeah, well, I'm allowed. I'm not thrilled you're using it on him. We know he doesn't respect women."

"Which is why you'll be listening to every slobbering word. Really, Connor, what's the big deal?"

"The big deal is he's married to my sister and he shouldn't be putting the moves on other women."

"We don't know he'll put the moves on me. Maybe he's strictly into blondes. Does this look okay?" I tugged at the wig. "Am I an ironed Little Orphan Annie?"

"He'll put the moves on you. He's a philandering bastard. Besides, in that outfit, you'd have monks walking into walls. You're fine."

"Fine as in fiiiine, or fine as in Bozo the Clown with breasts?"

He tucked the red hair behind my ears. "Fine as in if he touches you he's going to bleed. Get in. Get what you need. Get out."

I saluted. "Aye-aye, Cap'n." I kissed him. I meant it to be a soothing kiss, but Connor didn't believe in kissing for comfort. I was breathing hard when it ended. I fanned my face. Shook my head to clear it. "Well, okay, then. Relax. This is easy-schmeezy."

"You're probably right. I'm a macho jerk. I hate thinking of you sashaying into his office in that getup."

"I do not sashay."

"You won't have to in that skirt."

"I can handle this."

"I know you can, babe. Jack's dead meat with you on the case. Shit. Let's just do it then. If he lays a finger on you . . ."

"I scream. You rush in and clobber him."

"I like that plan better," Connor told me.

"I know you do, honey. But knocking him senseless doesn't help Siobhan or me. It also doesn't get us any closer to figuring this out. You ready?"

"Yeah," he grumbled.

"Well, here goes nothing." I got out of the car.

I could feel him watching me as I walked to the corner. I put a little more swagger in my step. More hips, more ass. In the little leather mini I felt dangerous. Jack ought to look out. I was coming for him. My high heels clicked against the pavement, the shoes slowing me down. It didn't matter; I knew Connor would be in position before I got to the door. I pulled it open and stepped into the foyer.

"Hello." I adopted a Southern drawl for the mission,

all honey and molasses. "My name is Alex French. I believe Dr. Reed is expecting me."

"Have a seat." The secretary's tone was sergeant gruff. Either she wasn't the warm fuzzy type or my outfit had set her off.

"Thank you. That's real kind of you."

I laid it on thick, a walking, talking Stuckey's pecan roll. I'd bet Connor was smiling. Under all that macho stuff, he really was a softy.

"Ms. French?" Jack's voice was surfer casual.

It matched his look. Sort of. Blond hair, carefully styled with too-perfect-to-be-natural highlights, evenly bronzed skin I'd bet was sprayed on, and casual sailing clothes with a knife-edge crease in the leg. Acting California cool.

"Dr. Reed? I am so happy to make your acquaintance. I can't tell you how grateful I am to you for sharing some of your precious time with me."

His smile widened. Caps.

"It's absolutely my pleasure."

So much for the good doctor's powers of observation. Professionalism didn't seem to be his shtick either. He all but leered at the length of leg I showed in the leather skirt.

"Why don't we go into my office?"

I followed him back and pretended to take it all in with interest. I listened carefully to make sure he wasn't locking us in. Just in case.

"Can I get you anything? Coffee? Iced tea? Something stronger?"

He was pouring doubles at the office? Loosen them up a little, maybe. Probably just the women. "No, thanks. Do you mind if I take a few notes while we talk?"

"No. Go ahead."

Sitting down on the couch, I reached into my handbag and took out a notebook and pen. Flipping open the cover, I checked my notes. They were background, enough to fool Jack in case he glanced at the page while trying to look down my shirt. Overkill, but Connor was committed to the details.

"I'm afraid I'm not familiar with your work, Alex." Jack sat next to me on the couch, too close, and I regretted not taking the armchair.

"That's okay. I write romances." I faked a giggle. "Most of my readers are women, although I can't for the life of me figure out why more men don't read romances. Everything they want to know about women can be found on those pages. Men would find meaningful relationships with women a lot easier if they just did their background work. That's why I'm here. You see, I decided to put some real psychological elements in my next book. Broaden my readership. It's sort of like a thriller but still romantic, you know? I just can't stay away from romance."

"Your husband must appreciate that. I couldn't help but notice the ring."

So he checked for a ring. Interesting. Especially since his marriage was more theory than application. How open-minded of him.

"That." I let an edge creep into my voice. "Well, actually we're separated." Connor wasn't going to take that well, and I knew his hackles were rising on the other end of the cell phone. *Don't worry, baby. There's no chance I'm throwing away a Connor for a Jack.*

"He never trusted me. He was always following me around. Acting like I couldn't take care of myself. A real Neanderthal. I'm sure you've heard it all before." Might as well weave a story Jack would relate to. I was making it up on the fly, but Jack's eyes lit up. Green. Connor's were emerald. Jack's were reptilian. "A divorced romance writer doesn't sell many books. It'll have to be our secret."

Jack leaned in. "I'll never tell," he whispered.

I shifted just slightly. I wanted him interested, but letting him gape at my breasts was making my skin crawl. There was only so much I was willing to do in the line of duty. "I knew as soon as I saw you that we were going to be confidantes." I used a breathiness so campy a reasonable person would have heard it as a cross between Betty Boop and Darth Vader. Not a turn-on. Jack the Letch moved closer. What the heck had Siobhan seen in this sleazeball?

"How can I help?" Jack asked.

"Well, I've been wondering about amnesia. Lots of romances use amnesia, you understand. The hero has forgotten everything but his love for the heroine. Anyway, I'm wondering how something like that could happen. Do you just get hit on the head and forget everything?"

"Sometimes, although that's rare. Usually amnesia affects only portions of the memory. It's often the result of a trauma, either physical or psychological."

"That is so fascinating."

"The human mind, Ms. French, is an endlessly complex and enthralling subject."

"Call me Alex, please, Doctor."

"Only if you promise to call me Jack."

I wanted to gag. "What happens to the blank spot, Doctor? I mean Jack. Say, just for an example, I can't remember who my parents are. Do I know I don't know or do I make something up? Some sort of explanation for how I came to be?" I fluttered my eyelashes. The old tricks were the most reliable. "Always figurin' I wasn't just dropped on the planet fully grown."

Jack slid an arm along the back of the sofa. I wanted that hand someplace I could see it. Then again, it probably didn't matter. If he touched me Connor would find out, and then Jack's limbs would no longer be a problem. Nor would they match.

"Now you've crossed the line to delusional disorders."

"Goodness, I hope I never do that," I said.

"I'm sure you're in perfect mental health," Jack replied.

Clearly you don't know me, buddy. Then again, compared to you, I'm sure I seem in touch with reality. I'm not Narcissus. If anything, Siobhan had understated his ego problem. Connor's sister definitely deserved better. "For the sake of argument, then, delusional disorders?" I asked.

"They take many forms. Some variations are well-known even among laypeople, thanks mostly to television. Paranoia, for example, includes delusions of both persecution and grandeur."

"That is so interesting."

"Then there's Capgras syndrome."

"I never heard of that."

"It's rare. In fact, I'm considered something of the quintessential expert on the topic."

Jack turned away. I glanced out the window and froze. Oh, shit. Connor. Over Jack's shoulder on the other side of the glass. Not ten feet away. He did a brush-off gesture, then pointed at Jack's arm along the couch. I fought a smile.

"Really?" I gushed. "Tell me more."

"When suffering from Capgras a person might believe that someone close to them has been replaced by a double. The double would be identical in looks and manner to the original, but different in a way that only the delusional person could recognize."

"Body snatchers?"

"In a manner of speaking, yes."

That wasn't exactly John Doe. He thought he'd been the one replaced.

"Or, in isolated cases, the delusional individual might think he—or more likely she—was himself replaced."

Direct hit. "I would love to put a dramatic twist like that in my story. I don't suppose you've got a case study you could share with me? For authenticity?"

"Patient matters are confidential, Alex."

"Of course. I wouldn't ask you to do anything unethical, Jack." Like I'd have to ask. "I just thought you could tell me what *could* happen. Hypothetically. To anyone. We could call him, our mythical patient, John Doe."

"Well, I don't suppose I would be speaking out of school if I shared a hypothetical case with you."

So much for ethics.

"Our John," Jack began in a condescending tone that put my teeth on edge, "could be a young man with a metabolic disorder, like diabetes."

"Wait." I held a hand up. "What does John look like?" A guy that busy dreaming about himself wouldn't have enough room in his brain to make it up. He'd probably just describe the real deal.

"It doesn't matter," Jack put me off.

"Sure it does. I'm visual. If I can't see my characters,

they aren't real to me. C'mon, Jack. I'm sure you can paint a picture for me."

"You're the writer."

"And you're the expert," I cooed. I tugged a little on the collar of my shirt. I could see Connor point at me in my peripheral vision. Jack was too busy staring to notice.

"He's young. Mid to late teens. Five-foot-eight or -nine, maybe one hundred and sixty pounds."

"Hair color? Eye color?"

Jack never hesitated. "Blond hair and green eyes."

"Perfect. Identifying marks?"

"You really want detail, don't you?"

"I've got to make him come alive, Jack."

"He has a scar on his chin from a childhood fall."

I touched my chin, marking the spot. "Wonderful. Now I can really see him. So, go on with the medical stuff."

"John Doe's diabetic chemical imbalance results in dementia, which manifests itself in the irrational belief that those closest to him—his parents, for example—have been replaced by their physical and behavioral identical doubles. He could believe that aliens or the government is behind the switch. After a period of time, the gap between reality and delusion widens, and John begins to believe that he himself has been switched as part of the conspiracy."

"How would you treat John if he were your patient?"

"Well, if it were me, I would look for underlying physical or organic indicia."

"Such as?"

My accent was slipping a little, and I kept losing touch with my romance-writer character. Jack didn't seem to notice. While I'd guess he could accurately give my bra size, now that we were talking about his favorite subject, him, all other detail was flying straight past. Connor stepped closer to the glass and I caught my breath. It was so hard not to glance his way. I lost track of what Jack was saying.

"I would look for cerebral lesions and electric disorders," Jack blathered on. "I'd run a CAT scan and electroencephalography. I'd also run a glucose tolerance test and a toxicology report."

"That's a plumb lotta tests."

"It's a serious disorder." Jack leaned closer.

He was looking straight down my shirt. Connor's silhouette loomed closer and I propped my elbow on the back of the sofa, forcing Jack's arm away. I played with my ring, turning it with my thumb, then leaned my head against my hand. The room brightened as Connor moved back away from the glass.

"Perhaps we ought to have dinner tonight?" Jack suggested, touching my leg. "We could get to know each other better. Talk about the work."

"Couldn't it really happen, though?" I asked, moving my leg away.

"What?" Jack sounded distracted.

All that blood flow away from his brain. This is your brain. This is your brain on lust.

"The body snatch. I mean, not technically, of course, but for my book. A little literary license."

"Sure."

"But I'd bet it would be pretty hard to diagnose. It might even get missed."

"Well"—he stroked a lock of my hair, and I tried not to flinch—"it might. It is a highly sophisticated disease, and most psychiatrists—all the medical doctors, certainly— wouldn't have the skills to recognize it."

"The patient, John Doe, well, he'd seem crazy to just about everyone, wouldn't he? He'd say he was being replaced. That people were doubling him. That it was all a big conspiracy."

Jack twisted my hair around his finger. "I suppose."

I reached out and grabbed his wrist. I carefully unwound my hair. "And it would be, wouldn't it?"

"Would be what?"

"A conspiracy."

"Excuse me?"

"No one hears crazy."

Chapter Twenty-three

"That man and his ego in a confined space . . . well, frankly, it defies the laws of physics," I said, sliding into the passenger seat.

Connor did a U-turn without looking away from my legs. It was just a look. Like Jack had looked. And yet one guy made me want to shower—with him—and the other made me need a shower.

"Nice work, Watson. With the description, I mean."

"Why am I Watson?" I asked, reaching for a duffel bag in the backseat.

"Because Sherlock could never get away with that skirt."

"Funny man." I undid my seat belt, yanked my shirt over my head, and replaced it with a T-shirt. The car swerved.

"Christ, Sara. It's a convertible, you know."

"No one saw anything."

Two teenagers in a truck pulled beside us, honked their horn, and gave a thumbs-up out the passenger window.

I waved.

"Jesus."

I kicked off the high heels and skimmed out of the skirt, pulling running shorts up in their place. The tires clicked against the highway reflectors.

"Uh, road," I said.

We moved back into the lane.

"Do you do that a lot?" he asked.

"What?"

"Take your clothes off in public."

"You haven't struck me as a prude up to now, Con."
I jammed the discarded clothes and shoes in the duffel
bag and tossed it into the backseat. I had plans for that
skirt later.

"I'm not objecting. I just wish you wouldn't do it while
I'm driving."

"I'll let you in on a little secret, Connor."

"What?"

"Every woman—well, every woman who plays any
kind of sport, anyway—has changed her clothes in public
without anyone being the wiser."

"Believe me, you strip, I notice."

I patted his arm. "That's sweet, honey."

"Nothing sweet about it."

"Okay, that's horny, honey."

He laughed. "Roger that. What did you think of Jack?
Other than the monster ego."

"Amoral. Immoral. Little dick, but that's mostly just
a guess."

"That had better be all guess."

"Did you catch his description of John Doe?"

"Yeah. Could be hypothetical," Connor mused.

"It's not. That man has no imagination. Sounds a lot
like John Doe, doesn't it? What are the chances the real
Charles Smiths suffers from exactly the same symptoms
we've seen in John Doe? Did you do the math?"

"Yeah. The time frame matches Charles Smiths and
the symptoms match John Doe. Doe and Smiths are
about the same age."

"And physical description," I added.

"Which wouldn't be necessary to steal an identity, Sara."

"Unless you were planning on stealing the whole life.
You said that, Connor. This guy, whoever he is, isn't
just some identity thief. He knows the details of
Charles's life. He wouldn't blow off matching the physical descriptions."

"That's harder to do."

"Unless you're really the guy," I said. "We need to
find someone who goes far enough back with Charles
Smiths to know if John Doe is really him."

Connor started the car. "Want to go to a party?"

Chapter Twenty-four

"It's red." Fire-engine, pay-by-the-hour red, to be precise.

"No flies on you." He grinned.

"I don't do red."

"Your, er, friend"—the saleswoman in the Coronado boutique looked directly at Connor's left hand—"has excellent taste."

"My, er, friend"—my tone got the woman's attention—"doesn't have to wear it. I thought we were going for inconspicuous."

"It's social camo."

"What does that mean?"

"You'll blend with the rubber-chicken crowd. You're the one who wanted to meet someone who knew Charles Smiths back in the day. He's been treated by Dreznik Reed for more than a decade. If John Doe is the real Charles Smiths, Gretchen Dreznik can identify him."

"How do you know she ever met him? Smiths is Jack's patient."

"Gretchen is the commanding officer in that practice. Smiths is rich. Believe me, if he was treated by either of them for a day, Gretchen's met him."

"And you're sure she'll be at this thing?"

"My mom and sister have been working on it for a year. It's the big group fund-raiser. A lot of the local charities participate. Gretchen's woman of the year. She'll be there."

"I can start a fitting room for you," the saleswoman offered.

I'd bet five bucks she'd make a move on Connor the second that door closed. I couldn't fault her taste in men, anyway. "Whatever. I'll need some shoes, too. Size eight."

There was a knock a few minutes later and an arm reached in offering lacy undergarments, silk stockings, and a pair of hooker stilettos. I peeked around the door. Connor grinned wickedly.

"We do have others more suited to a . . . ." the saleswoman said, trailing off while she openly stared at Connor's backside from her position directly behind him. Bitch.

"These are fine." I snapped the door closed. Social camouflage came in layers. Who knew? I struggled into the lingerie. Something told me getting out was going to be a lot easier. I caught myself in the mirror. Hello, Moulin Rouge. The dress went on easier. The neck was low-cut, and the back showed a lot of bare skin dipping to the edge of the silk underwear. The shoes needed an instruction manual—and maybe a helmet—but the overall effect was pretty good. I might even blend in with the club set.

There was a knock. "You about ready, Sara?"

I opened the door for Connor.

"God."

"Thank you."

"You can thank me better than that." Not a don't-worry-about-it peck. This was hot and wet and endless. His hands moved to my shoulders, down my back, and to my hips. Everywhere he touched, I sizzled. I wrapped my arms around him and he lifted me off my feet. I hung from his neck, eyes closed, savoring. Connor's heart beat so loudly I could hear it knocking against his ribs.

"You two okay in there?"

Connor pulled back, breathing hard. He squeezed me harder.

"We're fine," I called back.

"You, maybe," Connor whispered.

"Take my word for it. You're fine, too."

He leaned down.

"We'll be late," I protested.

"That would be a tragedy. Do we have to go?" he asked.

"We're working, remember?"

"No."

Connor wandered away and I went to the register. I turned so the saleswoman could snip the tags from the back of the dress and the top of the merry widow. She scanned them into the register.

"Three thousand, nine hundred and forty-one dollars and eleven cents."

"I beg your pardon?"

"What's going on?" Connor asked, coming up and setting a pile of silk on the counter.

"Oh, my God. You've got to be kidding." I reached over and grabbed the dress's tag.

Connor reached into his wallet and pulled out a platinum card. He handed it over with the frilly stuff. "And these."

I grabbed his wrist. "What are you doing?"

"Paying."

"Three thousand dollars, Connor. For a damn dress. Four thousand with the shoes. Probably five with whatever you just gave her. Five thousand dollars. That's a car."

"Okay."

"Five thousand dollars," I repeated, speaking slowly.

The saleswoman slid his card into the machine. I grabbed him by the front of his uniform and pulled him away from her hearing.

"Don't be crazy, Connor. There's gotta be someplace around here where I can get a dress."

"You're the one who keeps saying we're running late. Besides, you look great."

"Are you insane?"

The saleswoman put the slip on the counter and he stepped forward to sign it. The clerk handed him the bag. He took it and offered me his arm. I ignored him and left the store.

I strode to his BMW, reaching out once to steady myself on a Mercedes. He clicked the locks as I got close and I opened the driver's door, climbing inside. Connor got into the passenger seat. I took shallow breaths, trying to keep from screaming. The ring. The club. The car. The condo. All of it. We were never going to fit. I'd been kidding myself. I held out my hand.

"Keys," I said.

"I can drive."

Breathing hurt. I couldn't let him go and I couldn't keep him. I was ordinary and he wasn't. Everything else and he was rich, too. A real prince. I'd been fooling myself. Seeing practical obstacles like long distance and a quickie wedding. Our differences ran so much deeper. I worked with the rich—the lawyers in my firm, the clients. I wasn't even a person to them. He needed a Lily, not a Sara. Not the cheating part. I didn't wish that on him. But someone beautiful. Accomplished. Rich and talented and amazing. Someone I wasn't and could never be.

I drove like Mario Andretti on caffeine.

He reached over and ran a finger up my stocking to the point where the slit in the dress was. "It is a nice dress."

He either played the stock market, like Warren Buffett, or it was family money. It explained lunch at a place where salad cost thirty bucks. Ryan and Siobhan both seemed okay. Normal. Or maybe they were just polite. Backing his decision to marry beneath him. Beneath him. I sounded like Masterpiece Theatre.

"It should be, for what you paid for it."

"Worth every penny."

"No dress is worth three thousand dollars, Connor."

"When a dress is that right, babe, you've gotta go with it."

"And I object to girl shoes on principle."

"I like them, too."

"I know you do. You're really kind of a prince in that way."

"I'm a prince in every way."

"I know," I muttered. "I think I figured something out."

"Hm?" He pushed a couple of curls out of the way and slid a finger along the clasp at the nape of my neck.

"The car, the apartment, the country club membership. At first I just thought it was a single guy with no student loans and a regular job. I haven't known that many." I shifted gears.

"Single guys?" he asked.

"The gainfully employed. Then I thought, Maybe it's all for show. Not that you bragged about it or anything; maybe you were just one of those people who preferred living well to retirement planning."

"The navy's got a good retirement plan."

"The car could be leased. The apartment sublet from a navy bigwig happy to have his plants watered. And maybe the country club isn't that exclusive."

Who got married without so much as casually discussing money? Wasn't it the biggest cause for arguments in marriages? Hadn't I read that somewhere?

"Where is this going?" Connor asked.

"I'm making a point."

"Okay." He sounded confused.

He probably was. Even I couldn't explain it, really. *It's just money, Sara. Green paper. Meaningless in and of itself.* Except . . . it was the straw. The embodiment of everything Lily had said to me. All the ways they were alike. The last piece of evidence I needed to confirm that Connor and I didn't know each other. We didn't come from the same place or speak the same language. When we stopped being surprised, we'd have nothing in common. No way forward.

"The lease, the workingman's club, the passbook savings. You're not any of those things, are you?"

"No."

"Yeah. That's what I thought."

"You don't sound too happy about it. We don't have money problems. Less to fight about."

Oh, I don't know. I'd bet I was about to pick a pretty good one on just that basis. "I don't know about that."

"We're going to fight about having money?"

"We don't have money, Connor. You do. Your family does. I do not."

"There is no 'mine' anymore, Sara. What I have, we have. You can afford a sexy dress when you want one," he said. "That's good, right?"

"I guess."

I pulled into the parking lot of the Yacht Club and the zoomed past the valet. Pressed and coiffed potential donors chatted under the awning. I pulled into a slot and turned the car off, handing him the key.

"What's the problem here?"

I didn't look at him, keeping my eyes fixed on the hedge in front of me. "You don't tell me things. I don't know which fork to use. These shoes hurt my feet. Take your pick."

"You never asked. Use whatever fork you want. Take them off."

I looked at him then, just for a second, before looking away, blinking fast. Major mistake. I wanted. I needed. I didn't fit. She did. I took a deep breath.

"My family didn't come over on the *Mayflower*, okay?" I said. "I don't get invited to thousand-dollar-a-plate fund-raisers, and I don't have flashy jewelry to wear with dresses that cost more than my car so that I can blend with your ex-girlfriends. Excuse me, I mean ex-fiancées."

"You want jewelry?" He took my hands. I tried to pull away but he held on. I knew he could feel the tremors in them. "What? Just tell me and I'll give it to you."

"You totally missed the point," I said, looking away.

"That much I know."

I gulped. I couldn't tell if it was a laugh or a sob.

"That's progress, I guess." I sighed. "I'm being a bitch. Chalk it up to bullets and adrenaline and forget it."

"And have this come back to bite me? No way. Something's wrong. I'd love to ignore it. Long-term, that's a no-win. I'd rather tackle it than wait. Talk to me."

I shook my head.

"C'mon. Tell me. If you don't, I'm just going to screw it up again."

"You're going to screw it up again regardless."

"Not if you tell me."

"You're a doer. And you have the resources to back it up. Not just money. Will. Nerve. Smarts. It was like when the gun went off. I just stood there. You saved me."

"I love you."

"You're the male version of the fairy godmother."

"Never saw myself that way before." His thumb stroked the back of my hand.

I wanted to believe. "It's true," I said. "She never thought she had to explain herself, either. She didn't ask Cinderella if she wanted to go the ball. Of course she must want to go to the ball. The godmother couldn't imagine anyone who wouldn't. The thing is, Connor, maybe Cinders had big plans with a video and a pint of Häagen-Dazs. Maybe she didn't think the tiara would fit. Maybe that was okay with her."

I looked out the window and watched as an older couple got out of a brand-new Lexus in the parking space next to ours. The man, dressed in a tuxedo, made a production of using his remote to set the alarm. The woman, wrapped in some sort of multicolored shawl with fringe, took his arm and never once looked our way.

Connor reached over and took my hand, interlacing our fingers. He nuzzled my hair. "It fits. We fit."

The was a loud bang against the rear window and I jumped. I saw Ryan, dressed in a tuxedo, move around to the driver's side and open the door. He offered a hand with a bow.

"M'lady."

"Hello, Ryan." I took his hand and let him pull me from the car. Connor unfolded himself and got out.

I took Ryan's arm and let him lead me toward the entryway.

"That is a great dress."

"Thanks."

"Wait." Connor put his hand on my arm. I stopped walking but didn't look at him.

"Give us a minute, Ry," Connor said.

He looked from Connor to me and his smile faded. "Everything okay?"

"It's fine. We just need a minute."

"Sure. I'll be right over there." He nodded toward the doorman. "The devastatingly handsome one." He smiled at me and drifted away, pretending not to watch us.

I turned to face Connor. People walked past, their expressions curious, but no one spoke to us.

"Forget I said anything, Connor. I don't know what's wrong with me. I'm not usually so nuts. Really. Let's just go in and do this. I can be professional if I really put my mind to it. I'll just concentrate on that and try to act normal."

"There's nothing wrong with you. It's been a crazy couple of days, that's all. In-laws and machine guns could make anyone a little nuts."

"You're not."

"I'm a raving lunatic. Trust me on this."

He wasn't. He was perfect. I was a mess.

He lifted my chin. "We're fine. The rest is just details."

"Okay."

"Good." He kissed me lightly.

I gave him a wobbly smile. He offered me his arm but I took his hand instead. We walked toward Ryan.

"A rubber-chicken dinner will fix you right up."

Chapter Twenty-five

The entryway of the club was packed with people, all in their Sunday best. If they prayed, it was at the church of Rodeo Drive. Connor greeted several other officers.

"I'll bet he sets off the detector at the airport," I said. "Friend of yours?"

"The Secretary of the Navy."

"How many words a minute do you think he can type?"

"Funny."

It wasn't. Maybe I ought to get a billboard painted: I DON'T KNOW WHY HE PICKED ME EITHER. All caps. Big font.

"And her? Trophy wife?"

"Soprano at the Met."

"Very cultured of you to know that," I said. To my right we had important politicos. On my left, mink-clad—in August in San Diego, no less—operatic superstars. Elegant naval officers and, drumroll, me. *Work. Concentrate on the job. Gretchen Dreznik. Famous psychiatrist and potential lead to the elusive Charles Smiths.*

"Where are the parents?" Connor asked Ryan.

"They're here somewhere. They bought a table."

"What about Siobhan? Is she coming?"

"Doubt it." Ryan sounded annoyed.

"What's the problem?" Con asked.

"The worthless bastard she's married to made the guest list."

"You're kidding," I said. *Ooh, the gang's all here. Ter-*

rif-ic. Apparently Jack's invitation to a "working" dinner didn't mean he wasn't coming.

Connor moved me between him and Ryan. "He'll recognize you."

"He won't," I denied.

"He will."

"He never looked at my face. Trust me on this, Connor. He can't pick me out of a lineup."

"Who?"

"Jack," Connor muttered.

"You know Jack?"

"I wouldn't say I know him. We've met. Sort of," I said.

"It'll screw the pooch. I thought since he asked you out, he wasn't going to be here. That was stupid." Connor looked disgusted. "He'll take one look and that'll be the end of it. He'll go straight to Gretchen. She's practically his mother."

That could be a problem. I bit my lip.

"Jack asked you out?" Ryan huffed. "When? How? Why is he still upright?"

"It's a long story," I said, shuffling deeper into their protective cocoon.

"Looks like you're not going to have time to tell it," Connor whispered. "He's headed this way."

"This is a problem?" Ryan asked. "Allow me."

With that Ryan steamed off, people parting before him like the Red Sea. He headed straight toward Jack. Ryan grabbed a glass of red wine off a waiter's tray and dumped it down Jack's front without any attempt to make it look like an accident. Postdousing, his contrition was so over-the-top I could hear it above the din of conversation. I swallowed a laugh.

I tried to tiptoe in my high heels, grabbing Connor's arm for support. "Bull's-eye. You know who Ryan reminds me of?"

"Jerry Lewis?"

"Close, but no. Russ." At that moment I missed my best friend more than I knew was possible.

"Talk about your lethal combination," Connor remarked.

"I shudder to think. You know, I did that to a guy who sat next to me at a wedding once. One second we were eating hors d'oeuvres, the next his powder blue tuxedo went tie-dye."

"It could only improve powder blue."

Ryan came toward me, winking. "White is really an impractical color, don't you think?"

We looked at Connor.

"Makes guys look"—Ryan rolled his eyes at Connor's uniform—"like ice-cream vendors."

"I like chocolate—chocolate chip."

We laughed.

"He'll be back, you know," Connor said. "We'll need to get to Gretchen before then. Just to be on the safe side. She clearly expects him to be here, and he won't disappoint. She intimidates the hell out of him."

A ship's bell sounded. "First bell for dinner," Connor said.

"So we should do this now. Can you see her?" I couldn't see anything through the elegantly clad Amazon contingent surrounding us.

"Relax. Let's go to the table. She'll find us."

"Are you sure?"

"He's sure," Ryan said, taking my arm. "She'll stop by long enough to condescend to us. If she didn't, her head would probably explode."

People began moving toward tables, pulling out chairs, and sitting down. We followed Ryan to a table in the middle of the room where his parents sat. Dougal rose as we approached.

"Hello, Sara." He moved over and kissed my cheek. If he was just tolerating me, I couldn't tell. "We're so glad you could join us."

"Yes, we are. That's a lovely dress, dear," Alyssa said, smiling from across the table. Okay so the father's tux might be rented, probably not, but maybe. Her dress was not. The gold flattered her coloring. Her hair was smooth and shiny. No frizzy curls for her. And the diamond-and-emerald necklace probably didn't come from a Cracker Jack box.

"Thank you, Mrs. McNamara."

"Please call me Alyssa."

"Or Duchess. She'll even respond to Your Gracious Majesty," Ryan said, kissing his mother with a loud smack. "But never to 'hey, Ma.' Gotta maintain those standards."

"Please excuse my youngest, Sara. We dropped him often as a child." Alyssa moved her gilt-edged program and pulled her napkin from its ceramic ring. She placed it on her lap, exchanging a look with Ryan.

He clutched at his chest and staggered a little. I looked back and forth like it was a tennis match. The diamonds were real, but so was the affection. The clothes might cost a fortune but they wore them like jeans. I watched Connor grinning and shaking his head. Whatever our differences, he'd chosen me.

Connor reached for my chair, but Ryan raced around the table to pull it out for me with a big show.

"Excuse me," Connor said pointedly.

"There's no excuse for him," Ryan stage-whispered to me. "There isn't even a reason for him."

"You're in a good mood," Dougal remarked as I slid into my chair. Ryan took his seat on one side of me and Connor on the other.

"It's my sunny personality shining through," Ryan offered.

"It's too much caffeine," Alyssa replied. "In addition to making it impossible to take you out in public, it will probably stunt your growth."

"I'm sorry I'm late," Siobhan said, coming up to the table breathlessly.

This wasn't good. I exchanged a look with Ryan. Jack was probably coming back.

"Sib, I thought you were giving this a miss." Ryan kissed her cheek.

"It's the social event of the year. I couldn't possibly miss this."

"Honey—" Connor began, so I stomped his foot discreetly.

"You look great, Siobhan." She did, too. She had a little color in her cheeks, although that could be the glass of wine in her hand. She was dressed in a pale green dress that suited her. The rubies were probably real. If she was upset, she was hiding it well. If it was a facade, I was buying it. Maybe Jack would, too. It would serve the bastard right to see her beautiful and poised among his peers.

The men stood as Siobhan went around the table exchanging hugs. She stopped and whispered into my ear, "I did it."

"Did what?"

"Took your advice and empowered myself."

I looked around the room. The cream of society. Probably a bunch of press types. Oh, no. "Good for you."

"What?" Ryan asked.

"Nothing for you to worry about, little brother." Siobhan swept into a chair and grinned at me. "You were absolutely right."

"It's always worked for me." I fanned my suddenly hot face with the program. What we needed was a nice, quiet evening. No drama. I hid my face with the heavy parchment. Oh, brother. Literally.

"What?" Ryan asked, louder.

"Mind your own business," Siobhan told him, shaking out her napkin and putting it in her lap.

Connor exchanged a look with his parents, then shrugged. Better not to tell him. At least not now. There were things brothers shouldn't hear in crowded rooms. I might be an only child, but even I knew that. Siobhan winked at me. What the hell? If it was making her feel better, it was worth it.

"Do you know?" Ryan questioned Connor.

"I've got no idea."

"You know, though, don't you?" Ryan leaned close to me, and I met him halfway, trying to keep a straight face.

"I might. But if I told you, I'd have to kill you."

Everyone laughed. Ryan tried to fight it, but had to give in. Dougal smiled at me, his eyebrows lifted. I thought I might see actual approval on his patrician features. Alyssa was a tougher nut. She'd laughed, but her eyes were still assessing. Not that it mattered. When they realized I'd corrupted their vulnerable daughter, I was dead meat.

"I'll tell my mother on you."

"Very evolved, dear," Alyssa offered as the waiter came to fill our wineglasses.

Dougal stood, lifting his glass and clearing his throat. "I would like to propose a toast."

We lifted our glasses.

"To Sara, for courage in the face of family, we're proud to welcome you into the fold."

"To Sara," they chorused, clinking glasses.

I was touched. I felt stupid for thinking of them as elitists. Dismissing their niceness as superficial social convention. Connor didn't care about that stuff or he'd have told me about the money long ago. Hell, if I were rich, I'd probably tell everyone I met. But he hadn't. Maybe he really didn't care about the externals. And maybe he'd learned that at home.

I hid my embarrassment by concentrating on the print. The name jumped off the page and smacked me in the head. I leaned close to Connor.

"Uh, Con?"

The corner of his mouth twitched. "Uh, Sara?"

"Check out who's doing the introduction of tonight's guest of honor." I pointed. "That's got to be the same Charles Smiths, right?"

"Shit," he said, too loudly.

"Am I interrupting?" a female voice asked behind me. It wasn't a question, and it didn't sound like she cared if she was.

I turned to see Dr. Gretchen Dreznik standing behind me. I recognized her from the photo in the hall. She was dressed in a silver two-piece outfit that reminded me of aluminum foil. She was in her sixties, fit in the way that only a personal trainer and a health club membership can achieve. Trailing behind her were two bland guys in nearly identical, poorly fitting tuxedoes. A regular entourage, grad-student types who followed her around and salaamed twice a day in the hopes of catching some of her grant money. Now she fit the mold of harridan mother-in-law with money.

"No, ma'am," Connor said.

"I was looking for Jackson. He seems to have disappeared."

"Haven't seen him," Ryan said. "Have you seen him, Connor?"

"May I introduce my wife, Doctor?"

If she was related to Lily, she probably always insisted on being addressed by her title. If Connor was a product of his upbringing, so was Lily. Connor's parents were nice and open-minded. Judging by her niece, Gretchen was a smug, class-conscious snob.

"This is Sara Townley. Sara, meet Dr. Gretchen Dreznik. She's the guest of honor here tonight."

I offered my hand. I'd bet she was a dead-fish shaker. "How do you do?"

"Ah, yes. My niece mentioned something about a marriage." And I was dismissed, my hand ignored. I was so glad I wasn't going to have to stick to the make-nice-and-pump-for-information approach.

"Of course." I gave a big smile and continued to hold my hand out. I stood up and stepped closer, grasping her hand and pumping vigorously. "I'm so sorry. Connor didn't mention that you were vision impaired."

Ryan gave a strangled laugh.

"I'm not."

"Oops. Sorry again. It's just . . . Well . . . isn't that a lovely outfit. So, um, vibrant."

Connor's hand touched my back. I couldn't tell if he was trying to get me to behave or showing support. His fingers slid beneath the fabric. Not behave. Definitely not.

"And the earrings. I'm sure they're some sort of family heirloom."

Siobhan squeaked. Gretchen gave me a look to harden stone, then turned to Alyssa.

"Have you seen Jackson?"

"I haven't, Gretchen." Alyssa waved a hand toward the two empty chairs. "Perhaps you would care to join us while you wait for him."

Now all the knives were out. His mother might sound perfectly civil, but only a fool would invite Gretchen to the table with me after I'd sliced and diced Lily at lunch. No, she must be doing it deliberately. She might not welcome a scene, but she wasn't avoiding one either.

"I am seated on the dais," Gretchen informed us. "Lily will be joining us in time for dessert. I'll be sure to send her over to say hello."

"Oh, goody," Ryan muttered.

"Yes," bumbling attendant number one said in a high-pitched voice. "Dr. Dreznik is receiving the Mental Health Institute's Person of the Year honor tonight. Her talent is simply inspiring. Her family is very proud."

"Her commitment to statistical research is legendary," added bumbler number two.

"Do you have a specialty?" I asked.

"I am expert in delusional disorders, although naturally my work brings me into close contact with a broad spectrum of illnesses. I have recently written a paper on the growing need for social acceptance of pharmacological intervention to treat disorders evidenced by adolescents."

"You drug kids?" I asked.

Connor had prepped me with everything he knew about Gretchen, which wasn't very much. What he had known, he'd gotten mostly from Jack. Since we'd opted to spend our few hours before the party playing a very adult version of I Spy, we didn't get a chance to run even a cursory search on Gretchen.

"I provide parents and society with the tools necessary to modify the behavior of their uncontrollable offspring."

"That's sporting of you," I said.

Two spots of color appeared along Gretchen's cheekbones. A woman not used to being challenged.

"Please advise Jackson, should you see him, to join us directly," Gretchen addressed Connor.

"Yes, ma'am."

"Alyssa. Dougal." Gretchen gave them bare nods. "Miss Townley." Frost dripped from each syllable.

"It's missus," I told her.

Without another word, Gretchen strode off with the bookends trailing behind.

"You really hit it off with her," Ryan said. "I've never seen old Wretch take to anybody with so much enthusiasm. You're practically like this." Ryan held up his hand with the first two fingers entwined.

"I can't believe you talked to her like that," Siobhan whispered, her face once again pale.

I looked around the table. "I apologize. I don't know what got into me." Other than me, of course.

"Discernment," Alyssa suggested, lifting her glass of wine.

"She's going to be so mad." Siobhan gulped at her wine.

"I'm sorry, Siobhan." I did feel bad. Siobhan was no match for that hag. "I got carried away. I shouldn't have been rude."

"She could give you lessons, Sara," Ryan objected. "Gretchen didn't get anything she didn't have coming."

I looked at Connor, then at Siobhan.

He put an arm around her. "It's no big deal."

Siobhan looked up, then straightened, her shoulders going back.

"You have nothing to apologize for, Sara. She's an old battle-ax. Acts like she's God's gift or something. Since Jack and I are getting a divorce, she is no longer my problem. The great Dr. Gretchen Dreznik is one thing I will definitely let him keep in the settlement. That and that horrible china his mother gave us for our wedding."

It was the first time I'd heard Siobhan actually use the D word. Siobhan had said "Jack and I will," "my husband and I are planning," and on and on.

"There is nothing worse than ugly dinnerware," Alyssa said. "We should go shopping, darling. We'll box up all that old stuff and buy something truly stunning."

"There go the credit cards." Doug moaned. He winked at his daughter.

"We'll get some new glassware while we're at it. There's a glassblower near Balboa Park who's doing marvelous things with color. You remember, Doug, the champagne flutes we got the Campbells for their anniversary last month?"

"Of course," Dougal said, clearly not remembering any such thing. "Beautiful."

"What did you do to Siobhan?" Connor asked me, leaning close to my ear.

"Nothing."

"Sara . . ."

"Nothing." I held up one hand. "I swear." *Liar, liar, pants on fire.*

"I have ways of making you talk," he said, sliding a hand under the table and onto my thigh.

"Stop that." I moved his hand to the top of the table. "Your parents already think I'm a nymphomaniac, and rude to boot. Could we wait until tomorrow to drop my stock further?"

"I think Mom was impressed with your handling of Gretchen."

"Don't be ridiculous. I was a verbal Shaquille O'Neal. All elbows and body English. That woman sets my teeth on edge. I'm glad we're not going to need her for anything. If Smiths is here, we can go direct."

"True. All we have to do is isolate Smiths and have a quiet word."

I nodded. "No one will even know I'm asking him if he stole a quarter of a million bucks from his own bank."

"You might think about how you want to put that."

"What are you two whispering about?" Ryan asked. "You can tell me. I'm the sole of discretion."

"I've only known you a few days, but I have doubts."

"Really." Ryan held up three fingers. "Boy Scout's honor."

"He was never a Boy Scout." Connor turned him in. "Excuse us for a second. We've got to make a call."

Connor took me by the hand and led me to the vestibule. We moved into a side hallway. Connor dialed his cell phone and hit speaker, turning the volume low.

"Go."

"Plan A's a bust," Blue said.

"Doesn't matter," Connor said. "Smiths is on the dais. Or he will be. We need art."

"Art?" I asked.

"Sara?"

"Hello, Blue."

"We on a party line?"

"With her, it's always a party line."

"Thanks, honey. That's sweet."

"Yeah, honey," Blue drawled. "Sweet. He means pictures of the target."

"Target. Ew. I can use my phone," I suggested.

"That's a backup," Connor said. "It's obvious, and the resolution tends to be bad. We want to stay below the radar for now."

"What about grandma?"

"Stay with Plan A. Sara took one look at Gretchen and couldn't play nice," Connor said. "I'm thinking we might be able to work on my other problem."

"I gotta tell you, I love that woman."

"Back at ya," I said.

"He meant Gretchen," Connor corrected.

"Let him think that, Sara. We know," Blue said. "Okay, Rock, DefCon3. I'm on mark. Tex is intel. Troj is perimeter. You've got Trouble."

"Trouble?" I asked.

He kissed my earlobe. "I don't have trouble. But I could."

"Having fun, are we?"

He kissed the corner of my mouth. "I could be having that, too."

I felt a shiver down my spine. "Uh, public place. Parental supervision."

"Ahem!"

"Get lost, Ry."

"Later. You two had better come."

I pulled away from Connor and tried to turn, but he caught my face in his hands and put his lips on mine.

"Jack's back," Ryan said.

Chapter Twenty-six

"Is that Charles Smiths?"

I nudged Ryan, pointing surreptitiously at the middle-aged blond man seated next to Jack on the dais. Jack had returned in a black dinner jacket. He still looked like an overblown Ken doll, albeit one without red wine stains.

"I guess." Ryan grabbed my elbow. "What's going on?"

"Nothing," I said.

"Nothing," Connor said in stereo.

"John and Charles do sort of look the same. Light hair, light eyes. Medium build, medium height, middle-aged white guys. They all look alike. Either could have done the interview. Either could have opened the accounts. Will the real embezzler please stand up?"

"It's not embezzlement if the bank never asked for its money back."

"Ironic, huh? If the poor, crazy guy figured out how to get a quarter of a million dollars out of them, then they want to strong-arm him into paying it back, threaten him with jail and lawsuits, and bully him into shutting up about the whole thing. If the rich, tuxedoed guy ended up with the cash, well, 'Thanks for playing and we'll never mention this again.' "

"What are you two whispering about?" Ryan asked loud enough for the whole family to play along.

"Sex." Connor shut him up in his usual volume.

"Oh, God." I dug my nails into his thigh.

"Yes, well, it is a good filet," Dougal offered with too much sincerity.

"The wine's nice, too." Siobhan lifted her glass for a refill.

"Oh, brother," Ryan said.

I turned and looked at Connor. "Other problem."

"What?"

"You said it on the phone. Then you distracted me. What other problem?"

"Nothing."

"Liar, liar, pants on fire."

He smiled slowly. I felt it slide into my bloodstream like cognac.

"It's an expression. What other problem?"

He nodded toward Siobhan, then looked toward the dais. I followed his gaze.

"Oh, absolutely." I patted his leg. "How may I be of assistance?"

"We're on silent running. The team is going to be doing a little fact gathering for me. Then we'll see what we've got. For now, let's just let things lie quiet."

I stared at Jack. He was too far away to notice me, and anyway, he was practically kissing the ground at Gretchen's feet. "I'm not that good at that part."

He leaned down and kissed me. "I don't want to mess with you," he said.

"Just you remember that."

Chapter Twenty-seven

Dinner seemed to last forever, although the chicken wasn't that bad. Then again, it might have been fish. Gretchen finally finished her I-am-the-world speech, and the audience clapped politely. She smiled and waved. Very Queen of England. I watched as Charles Smiths shook her hand and kissed her cheek. The guy looked miserable. He had either a serious head cold or the mother of all allergies. I'd started counting every time he sneezed. Thirty-eight during the entrée. Seventeen during dessert alone.

"Okay, Ryan, put on your thinking cap. We need to separate Gretchen from the guy who introduced her."

"She's a social climber. He's a bazillionaire. You'll need the Jaws of Life."

"Try to do it without making her mad," I said, sneaking a glance at Siobhan. She raised her empty wineglass and winked at me. "We're low-key on this one."

"You're taking all the fun out of it."

Ryan stared past me. People were moving around. The networking had begun. The clatter of silverware and the hum of conversation built a cocoon around our table. We needed to move fast, before Smiths or Dreznik left.

Ryan leaned back in his chair and crossed his legs, stuffing his hands into his pockets. "We need a distraction. What does Gretchen need more than money?"

"A fashion intervention?" I guessed.

"Exposure."

"That's too visual for me, Ry," Connor said.

"Check it. At Gretchen's four o'clock. See the guy? Sixties, hair plugs, bow tie?" Ryan pointed.

I put a hand on Connor's shoulder and lifted myself half out of my chair. "Got him."

"His name is Arthur Kleinschmidt. A power broker of the first order. His museum sponsored one of Mom's exhibits a couple of years ago. He made his money in television."

"So?"

"Think syndication."

"I still don't get it."

"Gretchen loves an audience. She's been shopping a talk show for a year. Who could make that happen with a phone call? Arthur Kleinschmidt."

"Why hasn't she hit him up already?"

"He won't take her call," Ryan offered. He leaned across me.

"Duchess?"

She turned away from her conversation with Dougal and Siobhan. "Yes, darling."

"I need a solid."

"Of course. What's a solid?"

"Can you get Uncle Artie to go talk to Gretchen? Maybe outside?"

Alyssa's eyes moved from Ryan's face to Connor's to mine and back again.

"Do I want to know why?"

I looked down. Beautiful. Now Connor's mom would know we were up to something.

"Not so much," Ryan replied.

"Okay, then." Alyssa rose. "But it will have to wait a few minutes. Your sister has had too much wine and I'd like to put her in a cab first."

All I needed was for Siobhan to flash some society-set camera guy while getting into a taxi drunk.

"Let me." I stood up and moved over to Siobhan's side.

"I need to go to the ladies' room first," she said, swaying a little.

I took her arm. "Okay, but then you need to go home."

"I'm not drunk."

"Of course not."

She straightened and looked straight at me. "I'm not. I've had a couple of glasses of wine, but I'm not drunk."

"I believe you, but the combination of alcohol and commando is really the advanced course. I wouldn't want you to try too much too soon."

She laughed, then snorted. I was turning his sister into a lush. Of course, if I were married to Jack, I'd pickle myself, too.

"It's hard." Tears filled her eyes. She shook her head roughly and they went away. "But I'm handling it. Hundreds of thousands. I can't believe I was so stupid."

"You're not stupid."

"Where did I think it was going? Joint accounts. The lawyers told me. But no, I knew he loved me. My mother never signed one. Connor would never have made Lily sign one. I bet he didn't even ask you. Jack loved me. I didn't need a prenup."

I stopped and turned her to face me. "Oh, my God, Siobhan, are you saying Jack's cleaned out your accounts?" Probably to keep Lily in sables. The worthless bastard. The first chance I got, I was going to skim him from the gene pool.

Siobhan put her hand over my mouth, her eyes huge. "You can't tell them. Promise."

"Siobhan, they'll want—"

"They'll want to save me. They'll never say, 'I told you so,' but I'll hear it every time I see them. It's my problem. I will fix this."

"You don't have to do it by yourself. They love you. We'll help you."

She blinked and her eyes hardened. "I will take care of Jack. I need to pee."

We pushed our way into the women's lounge area. The rich were different. They didn't have lines in the women's restroom.

Siobhan and I took stalls.

"I am taking a stand," Siobhan called from the end of the hall.

"Uh, that's good."

I flushed and left the stall.

"Well, if it isn't the little wife," Lily said, meeting my eyes in the mirror. I lifted my chin and took the sink next to hers. Her blond hair was pulled back, sleek and stylish. The diamond necklace was undoubtedly real. It matched the ring. Not as well as her dress matched mine. Actually, standing this close, we clashed. Go figure.

"Nice dress," I commented.

She looked down her nose at me. "You don't think Connor is going to confuse us, do you?" She put a hand on her hip and gave me a toothpaste smile. "I'm surprised you didn't go home to change. Not that it would matter, but perhaps you wouldn't seem so—"

"Happily married?" I offered, turning off the sink.

"Pathetic." Her smile didn't dim.

"Because we're wearing the same dress?"

Her gray eyes hardened. "It's not the same. This is an original."

"Not that original." I dried my hands. Two women walked into the bathroom. They looked at us and then at each other before heading to the facilities.

"An experienced eye knows the difference, and believe me, the women at this event, those who are here by rights and not as the plus-one, know the difference."

"I'm guessing they know the difference between an engagement ring and a wedding ring, too." I took a step closer to her, forcing her to back up. "Or between a wife and a can't-let-go ex-girlfriend."

"I know you won't believe this, Sara, but I haven't resumed my sexual relationship with Connor"—she raised one perfectly arched eyebrow—"yet."

"I do believe it. He wouldn't have you as a gift."

I shouldn't. I knew I shouldn't. I was getting drawn in. I could feel it. I wanted to reach out and wring her scrawny neck. I was letting her get to me. I glanced over my shoulder. Siobhan had slipped past me. Probably trying to get away from the claws. Couldn't blame her.

"I wouldn't count on that if I were you, Shelly."

I leaned very close to her. "And yet I will. Don't worry about it, Leslie. Miss Manners says you have a year to send the wedding gift."

I left her standing with her mouth open and her eyes on fire. Connor and Ryan were waiting for me in the lobby.

"Have you seen Siobhan?" I asked.

"I thought she was with you," Connor replied.

"She was, but then I ran into Lily, and when I turned around she'd bailed."

"Probably just went home," Ryan offered. "Sib's never been big on confrontation."

"You think?" I asked.

Connor kissed my temple. "I'm sure she's fine. She's a big girl."

Alyssa and Dougal stepped out of the shadows behind them. They were holding hands. Her hair was mussed.

"We're caught, Liss," Dougal said.

"We weren't until you said something," Alyssa responded, smoothing her hair and discreetly checking her lipstick in a compact mirror.

"Oh, jeez. Get a room, people." Ryan moaned. He put an arm across his face, staggering in the little hallway. "You'll scar me for life."

"One can only hope," Alyssa drawled. "Art told me to tell you ten minutes. He has some radio network to buy first. The music has started. Your father has promised me a waltz." She looked from Ryan to Connor to me. "What are you three up to?"

"Us?" Ryan placed a hand on his heart. Overplaying it.

"Me?" Connor placed a hand on his heart.

"Them?" I pointed at her sons. I was just an in-law, after all.

Their parents laughed.

"Terrible influence," Dougal suggested. "They take after their mother. Never boring, but you should always keep bail money at the ready. Just in case."

"Oh, hush, you." Alyssa swatted at him. "He exaggerates. Come on. Join us in the ballroom. If you're very good boys, I'll embarrass each of you with only a single dance."

"Maybe later, Mom," Ryan demurred.

"I knew you were up to no good."

"We're on the side of the angels. I swear. Besides, if we were misbehaving, I'm the youngest. I've been corrupted."

Alyssa took a long time assessing us. She exchanged a glance with her husband. With a half smile and a helpless shrug, he chose not to participate in her interrogation.

"Ready for that spin around the floor, honey?" Dougal asked. "I'm feeling particularly light on my feet tonight."

"As long as you're light on mine," she muttered, letting him lead her away.

We followed them toward the vestibule. Kleinschmidt was in a cluster inside the ballroom, Gretchen, Jack, and Smiths a few feet beyond. The band was playing something waltzy. Couples swirled around the floor.

"We need to get rid of Jack," Connor said loudly above the din.

"Oh, please, please, can I?" Ryan asked. He grinned. Not a happy grin. "I promise to leave a mark."

"I've got it." Connor took his BlackBerry out of his pocket and turned his back.

"I like my idea better," Ryan said.

"Me, too."

Connor turned back to us. "Five, four, three, two . . ."

Jack abandoned his position and stormed past us, toward the front doors.

"What did you do?" I asked.

"Called Blue. He called Jack to ask if there was a reason the Lojack on his Benz was disabled."

"Nice." I was impressed. "Why didn't you just call him?"

Ryan bonked me on the head. "Caller ID. Don't you watch *CSI*?"

"What was I thinking?"

"I'm going to go and isolate Smiths. I know the couple he's talking to right now. I'll move them out of the way to give you some privacy. It's better if he doesn't immediately connect us, just in case he runs to Jack. Give me a sixty-second head start."

Ryan and I checked our watches. I looked at his. He

looked at mine. Then we gave thumbs-up signs. I laughed.

"Nothing like getting on somebody's wavelength from the start," he muttered, heading off.

"One, one thousand. Two, one thousand," Ryan sing-songed in my ear.

I rolled my eyes. Connor moved to Smiths's side, then said something to a middle-aged woman who'd been holding court. He let himself get led away toward the far end of the room.

"Here's our chance." Ryan put his hand on my back just as raised voices came through the open front doors from the parking lot. Raised familiar voices.

Chapter Twenty-eight

"You worthless bastard," Siobhan shouted, a weird smile on her face.

People headed for their cars stopped to watch the show. I pushed my way forward beside Ryan. Siobhan was standing tall, her hands on her hips, facing her husband.

"Get him, sis," Ryan muttered.

Lily popped up on the right of the circle that had formed around the couple. Shit. So much for under the radar. She was smiling. A smug smile. Having a good time. Bully for her. Connor emerged from the pack and moved forward, putting a hand on Siobhan's shoulder. I edged closer.

Jack was flushed but kept his voice low. "Connor," Jack said quietly. "Siobhan is very upset. I honestly believe you should consider calling in a professional to help. Given my relationship with her, it would be inappropriate for me to prescribe."

The jerk thought he could co-opt her own brother. Ryan took a step toward Jack, his hands clenched. I held him back.

"Now would be a good time to leave, Reed."

"Not now, Connor," Siobhan challenged. She didn't seem drunk. Her tone was conversational, maybe a little too loud. Just enough to hold the audience. "Not when Jack and I have finally discovered honesty. Jack honestly believes I need a shrink. I honestly believe that I have had enough shrinks to last me a lifetime. There's you."

Siobhan pointed at Jack. "There's your penis." Her finger pointed lower.

A woman behind me gasped. I looked at Ryan. Past the point of no return. I stepped back and let Siobhan have him. Too late to fix this now.

"I'm sure you already know this, Lily, but that impotence thing is a real drag. Nothing worse than a small dog who's a legend *strictly* in his own mind."

Well, that was one cat out of the bag. I wondered how long she'd known that Lily was one of Jack's little distractions. Lily's picture-perfect image had started to smear around the edges. Smug had become frozen as she looked around the crowd. Not enjoying it so much now.

"Technically, I suppose that's a delusion," Siobhan said. "You should get some help with that, Jack. Based on our relationship, it would be inappropriate for me to suggest you get help from someone other than your oedipal partner, Gretchen, but, frankly, I think you need someone to prescribe. Well, look who's decided to join us."

Gretchen stormed into the crowd. People jumped to get out of her path.

"Jackson, bring the car around," Gretchen ordered.

"Oedipal. That's the right term, isn't it, Gretch?" Siobhan asked. "All those years married to your little"—Siobhan winked at a man near her elbow—"and I mean little—protégé, I was bound to learn something."

"Dignity clearly wasn't it," Gretchen said frostily.

"Hey," I began, but stopped when Siobhan held up a hand. Ryan moved to stand behind her but stayed silent. I caught Connor's eye behind Gretchen.

"There's no dignity in letting people walk all over you. Jack abused my trust. He lied. He cheated. He stole. I'm not letting him do it anymore." Siobhan moved to stand inches from Gretchen. Siobhan's face was flushed and her voice was even. "I'm not letting you do it anymore, either. I'm not afraid for my friends to know. I haven't done anything wrong and I'm not going to hide in corners like I have. Not for him, and not for you."

"You go, girl," a woman's voice called from near the doors.

"Amen," Ryan shouted.

"I'm sure your parents won't be pleased that you've made such a scene." Gretchen signaled to the bookends and made to leave.

"I can't speak for my parents, but I'm damned proud of her," Connor said, putting an arm around Siobhan's shoulders and hugging her close.

"Me, too," Ryan said, putting his arm around Siobhan's waist.

"I haven't known her long enough to be entitled to pride," I said, stepping forward. Gretchen spun to face me. "But I wouldn't mess with her if I were you. She's tough. And she's got friends."

Gretchen was nearly purple. She snapped her fingers at the grad students and left. I glimpsed movement in the gloom of the parking lot. Yep. Applause, more enthusiastic than the polite bit Gretchen's speech had generated, followed her into the night. Siobhan wavered for an instant.

Lily stormed forward. "I can't believe you just let her humiliate herself in that way, Connor."

It took a second for the dresses side by side to capture the crowd's attention. Once they did, the hum grew loud.

"That color doesn't do a thing for you," Ryan said a little loudly. "And it's downright pathetic the way you keep trying to upstage Sara. Connor married her. Pretend all you want, you can't be her."

Lily gaped at me, her face drained of color.

"Maybe you could take it back," I suggested.

Lily's eyes nearly bugged out of her head. She glared at all of us, turned on her heel, and stormed off.

"Gretchen might do good work, but that woman is a real harridan," an old woman said next to me. She held out a hand. "Gerta. Gerta Hoffner. I'm an old friend of their grandmother's."

"Sara."

"Siobhan will bring you to tea." She walked to Siobhan and patted her cheek. "And you can do better than the small dog."

"Yes, Grandma Gertie."

"She's right," another woman said. Twenty years

younger but probably still seventy, she was a carbon copy of Grandma Gertie.

"I'm Lydia Golan." We shook hands. Lydia moved forward and offered her older look-alike an arm. "Life is too short to waste on a man who doesn't know what he's doing in the bedroom."

The crowd swelled and surged. Women surrounded Siobhan, congratulating her on her public emasculation of Jack. No one mentioned Lily or the dress. The men hovered at the edges. They didn't make eye contact. They might agree that Jack was a scumball who shouldn't be married to their sisters or cousins, but being called impotent in public was a nightmare no guy wished on another. I felt a hand slide into mine. I smiled up at Connor.

"Wow," I said. "I know this is going to sound crazy, but wearing the same dress as your ex-fiancée was the most normal thing that happened all night."

"Yeah."

"You were good, too. You and Ryan."

"You weren't half-bad, either." He put his arm around me and steered me away from the gawkers. "Unfortunately, Smiths seems to have left the building."

"Oh, no." I looked around. "Damn."

"Sorry about that. We'll figure something else out."

"Don't worry about it. It was worth it to watch Siobhan do the measure gesture."

"Measure gesture?" Ryan asked.

I held up my hand, my bent forefinger indicating the nub of my thumb. "If I hadn't met him, I might feel sorry for Jack. As it is, I think she was probably generous."

"What did you say to Siobhan, anyway?" Connor asked.

"I just gave her a little advice."

I met Ryan's eyes. He pointed to Siobhan, still in the middle of laughing women, then to himself before raising a thumbs-up. I waved good-bye. He blew me a kiss and I made a big show of catching it.

"What kind of advice?" Connor just wasn't going to let this go.

"No underwear."

He stopped. "What?"

"I told her not to wear underwear."

"Information overload, Sara."

"Big, bad Navy SEAL can't stand to think of his little sister without her britches?"

"Sara."

"It helped her. Before, she was letting him push her around. Tonight she took charge."

"She was out of control."

"Well, that can happen. It's hard to harness that kind of power."

He laughed, opening the door to the BMW.

"You're crazy." He kissed my nose.

"History supports me on this, Connor. Cleopatra. Elizabeth the First. Joan of Arc. Powerful women. No underwear."

Chapter Twenty-nine

We didn't talk about it all the way home. Not much to be said after you watched your panty-eschewing baby sister emasculate her husband in front of your friends.

Pavarotti emerged from the dark like smoke. She separated herself from the bushes near the edge of the condo, sliding toward me. When a rough tongue touched my hand, I nearly popped out of my own skin.

"Hold still, Sara."

"Holding."

Connor moved as silkily as the dog. He reached out a hand but didn't flinch when she growled softly.

"Hey," I protested.

Connor moved lightning-fast and scooped up the dog, moving her ten feet toward the street and putting her on the ground before he backed away. The dog feinted left, right, then ran through Connor's legs straight back at me. I held my ground. Connor whirled and the dog took a position between us, growling low and moving in parallel with Connor, staying between us.

"Sara, go inside."

"I don't think she's dangerous." Connor took a step toward me, and the dog's growl deepened. He crouched lower.

"Inside."

I moved toward the dog. She kept her eyes fixed on Connor. "That's a good dog. That's a pretty dog." I reached out and touched her fur, ready to jerk my hand out of reach. Soft. Silky. The dog tightened but didn't turn.

"You're a sweet girl, aren't you? A good girl."

"Sara . . ." More low-voiced menace. Testosterone overload. They should all give peace a chance.

"Don't be afraid, puppy." I rubbed the back of her neck. "We're going to be friends. You rescued me. Just like Lassie." The dog's body eased. "Well, not Lassie, obviously. Not even distantly related, unless your dad had an interesting life."

Connor stood straight. Staring. Poised to strike.

"She likes me." I leaned down and hugged her body. She was the perfect hugging-size dog. Fifty pounds, maybe. "You haven't had your shots, and I'm not holding it against you."

The dog leaned into me, closing her eyes for a second while I stroked her neck.

"Why didn't you tell them?"

I flinched. Connor moved, and the dog jumped. I grabbed her and held on. She strained against my hold but didn't try to bite me.

John Doe. His face dirty. His clothing rumpled. His green eyes wild. He moved into the light.

"Why?"

"John—" I began.

"Charles," he screamed, stumbling forward. Connor put a hand up and John stopped. The dog squirmed. I let her go. She ran past Connor to John's side, turning and protecting her master. Growling and drooling.

"Stay calm, man. No one wants to hurt you." Connor had his hands up, placating.

"It's my fault, Charles," I confessed. "I want to tell them."

"Don't steal me."

"We won't steal you."

John deflated. Connor eased back. I reached out to touch him at his waist. He stopped moving. I patted gently. We all needed to take a deep breath.

"Please," John said, tears falling down. He was broken. Terrified. I stepped to Connor's left and he moved to stay in front of me. Pavarotti barked.

"We want to tell them." Who and what remained a little obscure to me, but the guy was really scared. Maybe it was his delusions talking, but I wanted him to feel better.

"Really?"

"Really. But they won't believe us."

He dropped to his knees. John lay his head against the dog's neck, his tears glistening on the dark fur. "I know."

Chapter Thirty

We huddled with Blue in the living room doorway, keeping John in sight at the kitchen table. Connor called Blue as soon as we got John into the apartment. It took longer for us to get John in the apartment than it had for Blue to show up. With Blue, it took a phone call. For John, he'd committed only when Pavarotti strolled in as if she owned the place.

"There's got to be some way to prove it. One way or the other."

Neither Connor nor Blue looked away from John Doe as he paced and twitched in the entryway. He wasn't dangerous, but they couldn't see it. Or maybe their training made it impossible for them to think of anyone as innocent. He was just scared. A little paranoid. He wanted to run, not strike. Anyone could see that.

"Like what?" Blue asked.

"Fingerprints, DNA, something."

Blue shook his head. "DNA won't fly. Nothing to compare it to. The murder happened in 1981. Pre-DNA everything at a crime scene."

"Fingerprints won't work either," Connor offered unhelpfully. "As far as we know, Charles Smiths was never printed. No military time, no police record. It's a dead end."

"What about a lie-detector test?" I suggested. "We could rent equipment, probably. I mean, somebody's got to have some they'd loan us for cash. Or maybe even a service that will run the test for us."

Blue shrugged. "We could use the field gear."

"That wouldn't prove anything." Connor stayed with pessimism.

"Sure it would." I grabbed his arm. I wanted to shake him. "You've got this stuff? You've done it before? What are we waiting for?"

Blue raised his eyebrows and leaned back against the refrigerator, his arms crossed. His eyes never left John Doe. Or Charles Smiths, or whoever the heck he was.

"Sara, the reason lie detectors can't be used in court is because they don't actually test for truth. They test belief. It's the reason that psychotics pass. They believe their own bull. He'll probably pass regardless."

Pavarotti growled softly. I knew how she felt. I petted her head and she stopped. "Okay, so maybe it wouldn't hold up in a court of law. Right now the only person he has to convince is you, Connor. Admit it. Half of you still thinks he's a scam artist playing 'poor little naive me.'"

Blue moved over to John, distancing himself from the greater threat. His training did him proud. Pavarotti left me and moved to stand between John and Blue. Her training was pretty good, too.

"I don't think that."

"You don't believe him, either." I kept my voice low. I didn't want John to know Connor didn't believe him. He had enough demons.

"It doesn't matter if I believe him or not. You want to help him. That's fine with me. I'll back you."

"That's not the same as actually believing, Con. He's scared and he's alone. Somebody's trying to kill him. He needs someone to believe in him."

"You believe enough for both of us."

"Might still be useful, Rock." Blue came back into the conversation with his back still turned to us.

I waited.

"Say she's right. This guy is the real Charles Smiths. If that's true, why hasn't Reed told anyone that guy at the benefit isn't the real deal? Even if he could explain it—call it a security precaution, maybe—if this guy is a patient of your brother-in-law's, might be he knows help-

ful. And if he isn't Charles Smiths, we're out nothing,"
Blue pressed.

"Wait a minute," I protested. "You don't believe him,
but just in case you're wrong you want to use him? I
don't think we ought to ask him about that. What about
doctor–patient privilege? Privacy? If he is Jack's patient,
he needs help. Hell, he needs help anyway."

It wasn't that I didn't sympathize with Connor's position. John Doe might give him the ammunition he
needed to get rid of Jack permanently. As patronizing
as Jack was, he might brag to a patient. After all, Jack
was the semifamous doctor, and a patient would be just
some head case. Plausible deniability. If Connor earned
helpful-husband points at the same time, that was just
efficient. Except I didn't want him to do it to humor me.
I wanted him to listen. To believe. To have a little faith
in my belief.

"I think we should do the test." Connor agreed. Hu-
moring me. Definitely.

"Fine. But you promise to keep an open mind. And
we agree, whatever we find, we don't leave John hanging
out to dry," I insisted. "We find a doctor, a real one, to
help him. Even if he can't help us."

"Let's do it," Connor said.

"Not us, Rock. Her." Blue looked over his shoulder
at me just for a second before turning back to John.

"She's never done it before."

"Only way, man. He ain't gonna go candid with me,
and you've already got his blood pressure in the red
zone. We won't be able to tell if he's lying or having a
stroke with you at the helm."

"Blue's right. You haven't stopped glaring at him
since we brought him back. I should do it."

"I haven't been glaring."

"You've done everything short of sticking pins in a
John Doe doll."

Blue stepped back and leaned against the kitchen wall.
He could see all of us from that vantage point. He must
think the fireworks between Connor and me were over
for the evening. It would explain the three divorces.

"He's gotta keep something for his grand finale." Blue grinned at me.

"Get the gear," Connor told Blue.

"I'm out," Blue said, heading for the door. John flinched when Blue took the first step, and backed up against the front door. Blue put up his hands in supplication, trying to ease John, but one look at his panicked face said that wasn't going to happen.

"It's okay," I said, stepping around Blue. "He's just going to go pick something up. Something we need to help you prove they're trying to steal you."

I reached out a hand to him. Connor stopped breathing. Pavarotti's tail thumped against my leg.

"Don't touch him, Sara." Connor eased a step closer.

"It's fine. Everything's all right." I looked at Connor over my shoulder, trying to freeze him with a stare. The dog whined.

"Charles. Please." I ignored Connor, sliding another inch closer. When he didn't flinch I moved closer, touching his shoulder, then sliding my hand down his arm, patting his hand. He was stiff. The dog head-butted him. John reached out and touched her fur. John slowly slid to a sitting position against the door, covering his head with his arms. I sat beside him and made shushing sounds. Pavarotti crawled across us, lying on our legs and pinning us down.

I laughed. "I think someone is looking for attention."

John Doe hugged the dog's neck, earning a lick across the face.

I exchanged a long look with Connor. He shrugged, then glanced at the sliding glass door.

Blue looked behind him. "What the hell? It's only the tenth floor."

He walked over to the door, stepped onto the patio, and climbed over the side.

By the time Blue returned with the lie-detector unit, I'd sweet-talked John into sitting in the kitchen with Pavarotti at his feet. Connor kept John in his line of sight but stayed quiet, blending into the background. I was grateful. John seemed to be relaxing. He'd even eaten the sandwich I'd fixed for him. Half of it, anyway. The other half went to the dog.

Blue talked me through putting the strap around John's chest and hooking up the machine. Connor set up the video camera in the doorway to the living room. He moved behind the camera, silent. Like he'd been for the last hour. That could not be good.

Blue stayed behind John, hunkered down, trying to look as nonthreatening as a six-foot-seven badass SEAL could look. John seemed to have forgotten all about him. Even Pavarotti had stopped growling. I chatted quietly with John, smiling as I connected his finger to the indicator. His hands were dirty but the skin was soft. Not calloused. Huh.

"Ready?" I asked.

"Okay," John said, never looking away from me.

"It'll be just like Blue said. I'll ask you some questions. Answer yes or no. I'll start with some easy ones while we get the hang of it. They'll be your base. Then we'll ask some other ones. Yes/no, like before."

"And then you can tell them I'm me?"

"Right."

"And that they're after me." John showed some signs of agitation, his breath louder, fidgeting in his chair, as if saying it out loud brought his pursuers, real or imagined, closer to him.

"He's got to calm down, Sara," Blue said.

"We're calm. Nice and easy. No one can get us here, right?" I patted his hand. He nodded. Connor was radiating energy, and I wished he'd knock it off. This was already hard enough.

I moved back away from John. Sitting in the chair opposite him, I took a deep breath. "Let's start with something easy. Is today Friday?"

"No."

Blue put his watch on the table and backed out of my range of vision. One fourteen a.m.

"Saturday?" I asked.

We hadn't discussed what I would ask him, and it suddenly occurred to me how hard even the easy questions were. He was disoriented. He thought he was Charles Smiths, but was he? His truth could be—probably was—just delusion. Why was he in San Diego? Who was after him? He really didn't have a point of reference. There wasn't a single detail about his life that was black-and-white. To someone as confused about his identity as John Doe was, everything was a variation of gray. I'd be crazy, too, if that much of my world were askew. I wondered what I would do if someone convinced me that everything I thought was real was a lie.

"Yes," John answered.

"Is it nighttime?"

"Yes."

"Are you wearing a blue shirt?"

He looked down and nodded.

"You have to say it out loud, John."

"Charles. My name is Charles." His voice hit a high note.

Mistake. That was a mistake. Calm. You need to calm him down.

"You're right. I'm sorry, Charles."

"It's okay," he mumbled.

"Can we start over?"

"I guess." His head was lowered.

"Is the sky blue?"

"Yes."

"Is the grass green?"

"Yes."

"Do you speak English?"

"Yes."

"Is your name Charles Smiths?" His eyes welled, and for a second I thought he might cry. I wanted to cry for him.

"Yes."

"Were your parents Martin and Andrea Smiths?"

"Yes."

Blue eased himself to a standing position behind John. He pulled his pager off his belt and looked at the readout. He made a telephone with his hand.

I nodded and reached for John's hand. "You're doing really well. These are hard questions. I'm not trying to upset you." Blue eased from the room like smoke. "Are you okay to go on?"

He nodded. Pavarotti put his head on John's lap.

"Were your parents murdered?"

John sucked in a breath. Probably no way to sneak up on that one. I thought about Connor and how close he was to his parents. Connor, my best friend, Russ. If someone had killed them in front of me, would I stay sane? I honestly didn't know. I never wanted to find out.

"Yes," he whispered.

"Were you there when it happened?"

"Yes." Quieter, his eyes down, picking at the tablecloth.

"Did you speak to the police about it?"

John didn't answer. Blinking back tears, I looked at Connor. He mouthed, *Move on.* Swallowing, I turned back to John.

"Did you open a bank account in San Diego?"

John wiped at his eyes and sat up a little straighter, swallowing hard. He gave me a whisper of a smile. His first smile. Past the worst.

"Yes, I did."

"Did you transfer money from Seattle?"

"No."

"Did you"—I glanced at Connor—"I'm sorry. Did you say no?"'

"Yes."

"Yes, you said no?"

His smile grew. "Yes, I said no."

"Did you meet with Henry DeVries?"

John bit his lip. The payoff.

"Who's he?"

"He was the radio host. You gave him an interview." I shook my head. That question wasn't going to do us any good. It wasn't yes or no, and I'd as much as told him the answer. He could be blocking or lying or just following my lead. I was making a mess of this.

"He's dead now," John said.

I froze.

"Go on, Sara," Connor said.

I took a deep breath. "Do you know Officer Esteban?"

John looked confused. He was fading. Fatigue or drugs, I couldn't be sure. I needed to wrap this up while he was still all there. John's responses had to be sharp or the results would be harder to figure out. Connor made a hurry-up gesture, which caught John's eye. He froze.

"Are you under a doctor's care?" I pulled his gaze back to mine.

"She said."

"Who said?"

"Yes."

Boom. The explosion rocked the building, rattling the glass. Connor dove into me, knocking me to the floor and tipping the table over. The camera and lie-detector equipment crashed, and John leaped back out of the way. Pavarotti was singing frenetically. Connor tucked me under him. He was heavy. I coughed. The room was filling with smoke. Oh, God. Fire. We were on fire. I struggled beneath Connor. He wouldn't let go.

"Stay," Connor yelled. He turned his back and crawled on his belly toward the living room. I got on all fours and followed him. A huge plume of smoke billowed up past the open patio doors. It was close. Probably right in front of the building. Blue was on his belly in the bedroom doorway, a gun in each hand. He tossed one to Connor. Connor made a hand sign and the two men started moving toward the patio. I reached out and yanked on his leg.

"Don't go out there."

He turned to look at me. Blue slid past him. He tried to push me back behind the table but I balked.

"Stay behind there, out of range," Connor yelled.

"She okay?" Blue called.

"Yeah."

There was a second explosion and I threw myself on top of Connor. I wrapped my arms around his head. He untangled me and shoved me into the kitchen. He put a finger against my lips. I froze.

"I need you to stay here."

I stared. I couldn't. Not if he was out there.

"Promise."

Biting my lip hard enough to draw blood, I nodded. Connor turned and dropped back onto his stomach. He knew what he was doing. He was going to be fine. They both were. They were going to be fine. I fought against hysteria.

I moved to the far opening of the kitchen so I could keep them both in sight. Connor slithered to the front door and put the key in the lock. He whistled. Blue moved onto the patio. Connor went into the bedroom. I chanced it. I crawled out of the kitchen and into the hallway in front of the door. Connor moved fast. He was already at the bedroom window, gun in hand, by the time I got into position. Blue was hunched behind a potted palm. His weapon was pointed at the street.

I huddled against the door. The smoke burned my eyes. I dropped lower, wiping at them. The tears were making it hard to see. I crawled toward Connor. At the bedroom door I peeked at Blue. He was still down, his weapon moving up and back, up and back along the bottom edge of the railing. I went into the bedroom.

"I'm clear," Blue called.

"I'm clear," Connor yelled back.

"Sara? Shit. Do you ever follow orders?"

"I assume that's rhetorical." I slid my hand into his. He squeezed my fingers. We looked out the window.

"Oh," I said.

"Yeah."

"That's too bad. That was a nice car."

He sighed. "I liked it, too."

"That one behind it . . . oh, no, that's not . . ." I leaned against him, trying to get a better view.

"I knew that parking place was too good to be true," Blue commented, joining us. "Damn. It was practically new."

"It's not new now," I said.

"Nope," Connor agreed.

Sirens sounded in the distance. Well, we were certainly getting our tax dollars' worth. Hopefully the cops would invite a couple of fire trucks. With the way Connor's and Blue's cars were roasting, we'd need all the water we could get.

"I'm really sorry about your SUV, Blue." I rubbed his arm.

"It's insured." Blue shrugged. "Suppose we ought to go down."

"Probably," I said. I led the men toward the open front door.

"I've got just one question before we dive into paperwork hell," Connor said.

"What's that?" I asked.

"What happened to John Doe?"

I stared at the open door. Dropping Connor's hand, I peered into the kitchen. The table was turned over. The floor was littered with equipment, and a glass of water had spilled. The only thing missing was John Doe. And the dog.

"He's in the wind," Blue said. "Him and his little dog, too."

Chapter Thirty-one

We watched the cars burn. The fire department arrived fast, but it was too late. The cops asked a few questions. We played blonder than the Andrews Sisters. If the police suspected anything other than a fraternity prank gone bad, they didn't say so. No one made a connection to the previous night. Sometimes it was better to be lucky than good.

Connor and Blue had a whispered conversation at the door while I cleaned the kitchen. I was too strung out to eavesdrop. Let them have their little secrets. I'd grill Connor tomorrow, for tomorrow was another day. I'd already packed too much into this one. Luckily, none of the high-tech stuff was broken, just banged up. I wouldn't want to think how much it would cost us to replace that stuff. The videotape was unharmed. We'd scanned through the beginning, to make sure, but hadn't really watched it. Anything useful on that tape would require brain cells to analyze. I was packing the video case when I saw it. A single sheet of paper.

Don't let them steal me. Charles Martin Smiths.

"Bed," Connor said.

I jumped. Folding the note, I slid it behind a canister. "Shower," I corrected.

He hugged me from behind. "Bed."

"I smell like a chimney sweep."

He breathed in my hair. "Nah."

I looked at him over my shoulder.

"Well, maybe a little."

I stripped on my way to the bathroom. I adjusted the water. Six showerheads. Money had its perks.

"Looking for company?" he asked, already naked.

"Well, I wouldn't want you to catch cold."

He grinned and joined me.

After the shower, we lay tucked together, damp and drained.

"I've got something for you," Connor said, holding me closer.

"You are insatiable."

"The bedside table."

I stared at the polished oak dresser. "And I didn't get anything for you."

"Open it."

I reached across and opened the drawer, pulling a remote control from its depths.

"That is sweet, honey."

"Keep digging."

LifeSavers. I held them up.

"That's not it, either."

"They're not for me?" I helped myself to a red one.

"Try again," he said into my ear.

"Connor, you didn't have to . . ." I said as I pulled a square gray box from the drawer in the bedside table. "Oh," I said sheepishly, sitting up with the sheet tucked under my arms. The box was too big for a ring. That was stupid. I don't know why I thought he'd . . . Well, it was ridiculous. I didn't even want a ring.

"What?"

"Nothing."

"That wasn't a nothing 'oh.' "

"I just thought you meant something different. I mean, I didn't know what you meant, but you don't have to buy me presents. You got me a . . ." I opened the box.

"Sara, wait."

"Gun. You bought me a gun." I stared at the shiny metal gun in the box. "You bought me a gun."

"It's not exactly a present."

"No, really, Connor. It's just what every girl wants. It's what she dreams most about getting from the man

she just made love with. Maybe I'm not doing it right."
I shifted around until I was looking at him, the box held
like a tray in both hands.

"My timing could have been better."

"So it's not a critique. That's heartening, anyway."

"Let me out of the doghouse, okay? This is important.
Hell, no, it's not a critique. God, you didn't actually
think—"

I laughed, shaking my head. "You are so easy. And I
mean that in the teasing sense and not as a commentary
on the frequency with which you abandon both clothes
and decorum."

He groaned. "Generous of you."

"I'm that way." I held the box out to him. "I can't
take this."

"Those bullets were real. That car did not explode by
accident. You need protection."

"You're protecting me."

"Which would work great if you actually told me
where you were going twenty-four-seven. You don't. I
doubt you ever will. I'm not risking your life by pretending otherwise."

"I'm more likely to shoot you."

"I'll teach you. No one should own a gun if they don't
know how to use it."

"I wasn't actually thinking about an accidental shooting."

His eyes widened. "You're planning on killing me?"

"I wasn't, but that was before I knew you were a trust-
fund baby. Now I'm weighing my options."

He shook his head. "Be serious."

"I am seriously weighing my options."

"Sara."

"Con-nor."

I set the box on the bedside table and got out of bed.
I picked up his T-shirt, pulling it over my head. I was
going to have to tell him. He had that mutinous look that
told me he was going to dig his heels in, but I couldn't
take a gun. I couldn't have one around me. Ever. He sat
back against the headboard and folded his arms across his
chest. Planning on having his way. Oh, God.

"No," I said quietly, sitting on the end of the bed, keeping my face turned away from him.

"Yes."

"I have my reasons."

"I'm sure you do. Whatever they are, they're not good enough. Not with your life at stake."

"The risks are higher than you know."

My hands were shaking. This was so hard. I thought I was over it. The past was the past. It was years ago. Lifetimes. Then, in a moment, here it was again. Still clouding my horizons. Would I never be free? I pulled at the sheet, twisting it into knots.

"You have a nice family," I said, trying to give him context.

"Don't change the subject."

"I'm not." I shrugged. "I'm just trying to figure out how to sneak up on it."

"Straight ahead always works for me."

"That's because you grew up with Ozzie and Harriet."

"We had our problems."

"I'm sure you did. I guess everyone's got a story to tell. I'm no different."

"Tell me. I'd like to help."

I turned my back to him. I rolled my shoulders, trying to ease the tension. My head was pounding. I closed the gun box and set it on the bedside table. This was going to be bad.

"My father had a gun."

"Lots of parents do."

"He liked beer. He liked it every day. He liked it a lot."

"Go on." Connor's hands began kneading the tight muscles of my shoulders. His touch was gentle, soothing.

"It made him stupid. And mean."

His hands hesitated, then stopped. It wasn't a new story. He'd probably heard it before. He was a soldier. He'd known enemies. Threats. He'd used force. He'd had to to survive. He'd understand. He kissed my hair.

"What did he do?"

"I'm sure you can fill in the blanks."

"Where was your mom?"

"I don't know. I never met her. Or at least, I don't remember her. My father never talked about it other than to say she'd died."

"So it was just you and him."

"Yes."

"He hit you."

"Yes."

His arms came around me. He pulled me back into him, and I felt his warmth along my back. His face rested against my hair. If he was disappointed in me I couldn't tell. I leaned back into him.

"And the gun?"

"He bought it when I was in high school. Or maybe he stole it. One day he brought it home. Then he had a beer. And another. One thing led to another, and he was passed out while I was bleeding. Magically, there was the gun."

He stiffened. I felt tears on my face.

"I thought how easy it would be." I could still see his face. Flushed and bloated with drink. Snoring. Sleeping like the dead. The dead. "Then I started to think that maybe I could get away with it."

"It was self-defense, Sara. There was no 'getting away' about it." His arms tightened around me.

"I thought maybe the police would believe me. Maybe they would just look the other way."

"What happened?"

"I had it in my hands. I pointed it at his head."

I was shaking now, small tremors running through me. I wanted him to tell me it was okay to stop. I wanted him to say it didn't matter.

"It wasn't your fault," Connor whispered.

"Then I ran away."

He moved back on the bed and took my shoulders, turning me. I couldn't look at him, but he lifted my chin. His eyes, his beautiful green eyes, were full of compassion. I didn't see any condemnation, any judgment. I took a breath that caught on a sob. He stroked my cheek, brushing my tears away.

"You ran away?"

"I wasn't going to let him take anything else from me.

I knew that if I used that gun, if I shot another person, I'd never be okay again. And I wanted to be okay."

"You are more than okay."

"I can't take the gun, Connor."

He reached over without looking away from me, putting the gun box back in the drawer. "You stick to me like glue, okay?"

I got to my knees and wrapped my arms around him. "You won't be able to tell where you stop and I start."

"You promise?"

"I promise."

Chapter Thirty-two

I tossed and turned. I kept dozing, only to wake up and look at the clock ten minutes after the last time. Connor slept like the dead. He tried to hold me, but I'd twisted away. He rolled over and went back to sleep. Men. I got out of bed and went into the kitchen, pouring myself a glass of orange juice and going into the living room. I took the videotape of John's polygraph and slid it into the VCR. I kept the sound low and watched the tape once through. Then I rewound it and watched again. There had to be something here. None of it made any sense. John didn't seem to have enough on the ball to pull off a swindle. He barely seemed to be holding himself together. Smiths seemed like a nonfactor, too. He hadn't missed the money. Even if he had, the bank got it back. So it couldn't be about the money.

What was it about? The interview? Slipping into the bedroom, I picked up the files. I dug for the transcript. Line by line I read it through. Except for the description of the murder of his parents, it was all white noise. No specifics, just lots of conspiracy theories about the government. People out to get him. Delusion or reality?

It wasn't so much that all the victims were tied to Charles Smiths. It was more than that. They were all tied to the murder of Charles's parents. The maid who witnessed it. The cop who took the report. The kid left an orphan. The interviewer who heard the story. One missing, one shut out of the case, one crazy, and one dead. Why?

"Why what?" Connor asked from the doorway, rubbing his eyes. He was wearing boxer briefs and nothing else.

"I must've been talking to myself. I didn't mean to wake you."

"You didn't." He sank into the chair opposite me. "Why what?"

"I was just thinking about things."

"Me, too."

"Something happened, Con. It's been fifteen years since the Smithses were murdered. Fifteen years of silence and nothing. But ever since John Doe gave that first interview, there've been machine guns and dead guys and bombs. That interview changed something for somebody and people are getting hurt."

"What does that tell you?" he asked.

"If John's really gone and Charles Smiths is a dead end . . . or a fake, there're still three people who might know what happened the night the Smithses were killed."

Connor nodded.

"John Doe and Maria the maid," I offered.

"Who're in the wind."

"That means missing, right?"

He kissed my hand and rubbed it against his stubbled cheek.

"Which just leaves Dr. Jack. The only problem is, I don't know how to get to him. If tonight didn't work . . ."

"Have you ever been fishing?"

"What?"

"Fishing."

I shook my head.

"Sometimes you have to bait the hook and wait."

"I've got a feeling fishing isn't my game."

"Technically, I think it's a sport."

"Whatever."

"Well, the thing about sports is, it's better to do them rested. If you're not rested, you might lose to a weaker opponent."

"That would be bad."

He stood up and took my hand. "I wouldn't want you to be bad."

Chapter Thirty-three

"**D**o you ever actually sleep?" I asked groggily without opening my eyes.

"Not so you'd notice." He pulled me closer.

"Can we put that in the prenup? I mean, since we're doing one anyway?" I shifted against him, my cheek rubbing against his chest.

"What?"

"I get any sleep hours you don't use while we're married."

"Sure. If I get to keep you."

"The concept of divorce seems to elude you, Connor." I pulled back, opening my eyes and looking up at him. The light hurt. "Are we fighting?"

He propped his head on his hand and brushed my curls back from my face. "You missed making up? I must be losing my touch."

"So if we're not fighting, why aren't we sleeping?"

"I don't need much."

I moved farther back, tucking the sheet under my arms and propping my head up in a mirror of his body position.

"Lucky you. What do you need?"

"I need you to be safe."

"Even if I'm not a cookie-baking, charity-matron sort of wife?"

"Especially if you're not a cookie-baking kind of wife." He took my hand and held it against his chest. "You've got a dangerous job. There are ways to make it less dangerous. Skills you can develop. Since you're sticking with it, it makes sense to learn to minimize the risks."

"Believe me, the kitchen is the most dangerous place I could be. Everywhere other than that is much safer."

Last night this had seemed resolved. I thought he'd been planning something. Today he seemed less sure. More the old protect-the-little-woman Connor and less the if-you-can't-beat-her-join-her coconspirator. I watched him but he didn't go with the joke. *Bright light of day, Sara, regrets. Probably running through the whole debacle in his mind. Machine guns. Car explosions. Commando siblings.* "I was thinking—" I began.

"Dangerous," he said.

"Smart aleck." I leaned in and kissed him. He put his arm around me and moved closer.

"You were thinking . . ." he prompted.

"We've kind of been working against each other."

"You mean I've been working against you."

"We've already fought about it. It's done."

I wanted to get past the rough part. Move on to the accomplice phase. I wasn't going to be Lily, throwing his choices in his face years after the fact. I wasn't going to be Siobhan, waiting at home. I wasn't even going to be Blue, playing second banana to him. We needed new rules of engagement.

"Roger that." He smiled, slow and sweet. I could feel it slide inside me, warming me all the way down.

"Roger wilco." I smiled back.

He inched closer. I put a hand against his chest and pushed him back. "Since we're not trying to one-up each other anymore, I thought maybe we could work together on this case."

"Partners, huh?"

"With you being the junior partner."

"Naturally," Connor drawled.

"I thought we should play to our strengths."

"Okay."

I know you don't think John is worth helping."

"I never said that."

"My cases aren't the same as your missions, Connor.

It's not a question of who has the biggest guns or the best strategy. Cases get messy. Complicated."

He started to protest, but I shushed him with a finger against his lips. "I'm not saying your missions don't get that way, too, but it's different. You can always tell the good guys from the bad guys. You know you're in the white hat. I'm not so sure about me. I don't want to wake up and realize I'm one of the bad guys."

"That could never happen, Sara."

"It could. It might be happening with John Doe. Maybe he's a slick con artist and I've been totally scammed. And maybe he's the one who's been shafted. Maybe I helped that happen. My boss, that cop Montoya, those bank guys, they could all have agendas. I know you don't believe in intuition, Connor."

"Sara—"

"Shhh. It's okay. I know you're a concrete sort of guy, logic and reason and all that, but I'm not. I just need you to hang in with me until I know that I've done the best I can. If you can keep us both in the same number of pieces we started in, more power to you."

"Your gut, my gun. It's a plan," he said.

My smile felt a little wobbly. He pulled me into him and lay back, my head on his chest. I snuggled closer and his arms tightened.

"I may not believe in intuition, babe," he whispered into my hair, "but I believe in you."

Chapter Thirty-four

Blue and I were laughing over coffee at the kitchen table when Connor got out of the shower. I was wearing one of his T-shirts like a dress. As he came into the room, his eyes traveled the length of my legs. His green eyes narrowed. After the no-underwear speech I wasn't surprised he was wondering.

"Hey," I said.

"Morning." He kissed my head and moved to the coffeemaker. He held up the pot. I pointed at Blue and Connor poured himself a cup.

"Sorry I missed the other fireworks last night," Blue said. "Sounds like Siobhan's coming into her own."

"You got to see your SUV explode. That was exciting."

"Yeah. Exciting," Blue deadpanned.

Connor and Blue did the telepathy thing. I looked from one to the other. "Since I waited so patiently, will you tell me what we've got already?" I asked.

"That was patient?" Blue asked.

"For her." Connor sipped.

"Okay, then." Blue pulled an athletic bag off a kitchen chair. He took a CD out of the bag and handed it to Connor. "I burned that for you. I listened to everything. It's last night's action—everything we got from the bugs and the directional mic. Dreznik read Reed the riot act in the parking lot, then used her car phone to beat him up some more. Kept asking him what the hell he was thinking. She likes the guilt card."

"Bugs and directional mics. Very cool," I said, genuinely impressed.

"Reed made two calls when he got home. One to your ex. She does not play the guilt card. She prefers the I'm-gonna-cut-your-balls-off approach."

"She was mad about the dress?" I smiled. Bummer for her. I, in contrast, was over the trauma.

"Well"—Blue drank—"your name did come up. But her bigger gripe had something to do with Gretchen finding out about what they'd done."

"No details, please," I begged. "Total information overload."

Connor winked at me.

"They don't care if Siobhan finds out, but if Gretchen does there will be hell to pay?" That didn't seem right. "Who is this woman?"

"Gretchen trades on family connections," Connor volunteered.

"That's funny. I didn't get the impression you were her favorite person, even before I mentioned her fashion felony."

"She's a theorist. She likes the idea of connection more than the actual connecting," Connor offered.

"She gives me the warm fuzzies, too," Blue said, rolling his eyes.

I gulped, breathed coffee into my lungs, and coughed. Connor patted me on the back.

"The second call?" he asked.

"Siobhan."

"Oh, no." I covered my mouth. The coffee burned in my gut. Poor kid.

"She either wasn't home or she didn't pick up."

I stared at Connor. Oh, no. Oh, please. Please, please, please . . .

Connor was already on the phone. "Sib? No, wait. Slow down." He listened. "Sure." He handed the phone to me.

"Siobhan?"

"Sara?" Daisy Duck's voice. Adrenaline, I hoped.

"Are you okay?" She gulped. Crying? No, laughing. No laughing and crying.

"I'm fine."

"You don't sound fine."

"Want to come over for s'mores?"

"For what?"

"S'mores." Siobhan coughed, hacking. "That's blowing inside, Dad. Yeah. Could you close the window?"

"Dad? Is your dad there, Siobhan?"

"He's playing fire marshal. I think it's totally unnecessary. I mean, it's not like the house was on fire or anything."

"Oh, Jesus, what did you do?"

"It's a ritual."

I saw live chickens and dead husbands surrounded by pentagrams.

"It was Mom's idea. A cleanse. She said I needed a cleanse. For my soul."

Alyssa McNamara hadn't struck me as a New Ager. Then again, watching her kid meltdown at a four-star hotel in their hometown might have called for the scientific spectrum.

"Now I guess I'll need one for this dress. It's covered in soot."

"Do you feel better?" Connor refilled my cup. He and Blue stepped into the living room whispering. I tried to read their lips and listen to Siobhan at the same time. It was too much for my poor sleep-deprived brain to handle. I got up and left the kitchen, taking the portable phone with me.

"You should bring your dress. We'll add it to the pile. A two-for-the-price-of-one barbecue."

I sat up straighter. "What pile?"

"His clothes. His shoes. His thousand-dollar neckties. All of it."

"Nice."

"Really, you and Con should come over. We'll burn the dress—did you know I never even noticed it last night? Talk about blind—Mom said something this morning or I'd never even have realized. . . ."

Connor and Blue continued the exchange. I had to break that up or I wouldn't know anything that was going on in my own case. Sneaky. Sexy, too. Real men.

"I'm sorry, Siobhan, but I've got to work today. Later?"

"Great."

"You're okay? And your parents are there?"

"Yeah. Well, not Mom. She went to get more graham crackers. S'mores aren't the same with saltines."

"You have to maintain standards," I told her.

"I intend to."

I hung up.

"She okay?" Blue asked when I joined them in the living room.

"Hard to tell. What did you tell Connor that he isn't going to share with me?"

Connor leaned back on the couch and I went to sit beside him. I tucked my legs under me and leaned against him. He put an arm around me.

"Might as well tell her," Connor said.

Blue just looked at him, his brown eyes placid.

"All of it," Connor confirmed.

"All of it." I turned my head and kissed his chest. "But in English. For us non-navy types."

"Yes, ma'am. Troj got curious."

"About?"

"He was on tech last night. He gets bored hanging on audio."

Connor nodded.

"Troj did some more checking into the players. The father, the one who was killed, had active TS clearance."

"Hello . . . ?"

"Top-secret security clearance," Connor translated.

"Oh," I said. "And?"

"It was under review."

"Regular requalification?" Connor asked. Apparently Blue hadn't had time to tell Connor everything before I joined the party.

"Nothing regular about it."

It was like watching tennis.

"Which agency?" Connor asked.

"NSA."

"Which one is that?" I jumped in. They ignored me.

"Damn," Connor said.

"It gets worse. Your dead guy, DeVries? It turns out he was working with the feds."

I wasn't sure how Blue had gotten the information, but I really, really wanted him to show me.

"Let me guess. Not DEA. Not FBI. NSA."

"Roger that."

"What is NSA?"

"National Security Administration. Think CIA without the social graces."

"Uggggh." That did not sound good. "What were they working on?"

"No way to get that. We're already beyond the target range on this."

"Are we on anybody's radar?"

Blue shrugged. He reached into the athletic bag and pulled out a box. He handed it to Connor while watching me. I moved my feet to the floor. Connor kissed my temple. I wasn't sure I wanted to know what was in the box. My breath came faster. Well, at least I couldn't hear the box ticking. Without another word, Blue headed toward the door.

"We need to find that maid," Connor called after him.

"Tex is working it. Troj has sent the stills from last night to your PDA already."

"Good. And, Blue?"

He turned. "Yeah."

"Watch your back."

"Roger that."

"Where's he going?" I asked, too restless to sit. I got up and paced, trying not to look at the box. It wasn't the box itself. It was just an ordinary square black box. The size of a handkerchief. It was the look. On Blue's face. In Connor's eyes. The box was bad.

"He had errands."

I gave him a long look. I took my cup into the kitchen and poured more coffee. I didn't need the caffeine but Blue's coffee was better than mine. A shame to waste it. Connor lounged against the doorjamb. "Dry cleaning, post office, that kind of thing?"

"Yeah. What did Siobhan want to tell you? Is she okay?"

I grinned, picturing the scene. Relaxed. If nothing else ever came from this case, thinking about Siobhan and

Connor's parents piling up the "firewood" was going to remain a good memory. "She's going to be. At least, I think she will after the fire goes out."

Connor stiffened. "Fire?"

"Seems Jack only took an overnight bag when he moved out. Left most of his clothes. They're toasting marshmallows."

"They?"

"I got the impression it was your mother's idea. Ritual cleansing through fire or something like that."

"Oh, shit. She's liable to burn the house down."

"Your dad is manning the hose. From what Siobhan said, I wouldn't be surprised if half the block showed up and it turned into a real party."

"What's our plan for today?" Connor asked.

"The banking pooh-bahs. The guy I originally talked to in Seattle has handed it off to a local guy. A vice president at the La Jolla branch named Carson. I'm supposed to update them today. I think we ought to do that."

Connor pulled out a chair and sat down. He laced his fingers behind his head and tipped his chair back. "We've got nothing to update them about, do we?"

"I was thinking maybe they could update us on exactly how the line of credit got repaid."

His chair hit the floor. Hard. "How did the money get repaid?"

I took the chair across from him. "Sorry. Thought I told you. Singh, the Seattle guy, told me the money had been repaid, but he wanted me to keep looking for John. Some BS about procedures and recommending changes. I think there's something hinky with the bank, beyond whatever identity theft might have happened. And I think it has something to do with how the account was originally set up. That's not the only social engagement we have, either." I leaned my chin on my hand.

"Who?"

"Detective Montoya left another message."

"He either wants to ogle you or arrest you." Connor's voice was flat.

"Not so much," I denied. "You know how I know?"

He shook his head, more in denial than disagreement.

"He asked me if I wanted to bring my lawyer. Apparently he thinks some former attorney general is representing me. Now, I don't know anybody like that. Then I started thinking, Who do I know who might know somebody like that? Gee, I wonder."

"Oh, man. Don't suppose you'll believe it slipped my mind?"

"Sure. Why not? I'm having one of those weeks myself." I shrugged. "I vote for Carson, Esteban, then Montoya."

"Alphabetical works for me."

Chapter Thirty-five

Half an hour later we were waiting in a private office of the bank's La Jolla branch. The office didn't have a name on it, but we'd apparently been expected, because a secretary had immediately ushered us back upon our arrival. I sat in a chair and fidgeted in my suit. It was my best suit. Okay, it was my only real suit. Usually for work I made do with dress pants and a blouse or sweater. The only perk of living the cubicle life on the lowest level of a five-floor law firm fiefdom was that the dress code standards dropped the farther away you got from the anal-retentive grand office suites. But here, sitting in the overstuffed leather chair, I felt like I should be wearing Ivy League school colors in a suit that cost more than the red dress.

I got up and started to pace on the thick carpet. The room was muted, a gauzy shade keeping out the harsh afternoon sun. Connor appeared to be taking a nap.

"How come you never get frustrated?"

He opened one green eye.

"Or impatient. Or just plain snarky."

He closed his eye and smiled. "Hurry up and wait."

"What?"

"A time-honored military tradition."

"Well, do you have to be so calm about it? You make it look easy, and that's getting on my nerves." I walked over to the desk, keeping an eye on the closed door.

"I know what we can do to pass the time."

"No."

"You don't even know what it is yet."

"No."

"He'll never even know." I moved the chair.

"No point."

"Why not?" I pulled open the drawer. Pencils, paper clips, Post-its. No clues.

"It's not his office."

I tried the side drawer. Staple puller, more pencils, manual for the phone. Underneath, file drawer. Lots of hanging folders, no paper. Damn.

"How did you know?"

"Carpet."

I looked down. Footprints from the door to the guest chairs. Vacuum streaks down the rest. "They've got a janitor who actually cleans. So what?"

"Bookshelf."

I looked at the oak top. Dust.

"Half cleans," I corrected.

He shook his head. I looked around the room. Sniffed. Musty.

"If the room stayed closed . . ." he prompted.

"There'd be dust but the carpet would still look vacuumed. And it would smell stale. Damn." He was so irritating. How long had it taken him to read the place? Ten seconds? Five? Who was the detective here? I walked over and dropped into the guest chair.

"Is there anything you aren't good at?"

He smiled. His eyes opened and he sat up. The door opened. I checked my watch. Sixteen minutes he'd kept us waiting. Philip was about fifty years old, big and broad, with a watchful expression. Connor looked like that sometimes. Blue, too. I looked from one man to the other. If this was a desk jockey, I was RuPaul.

The dweebie little guy behind him was another story. He wore a slick suit, cut to fit his one-of-the-seven-dwarves frame and quivered with self-importance. If the bank thing didn't work out, he could go to law school.

"Hello. I'm Derek Evans. This is my colleague, Mr. Carson. You must be Ms. Townley."

He offered a hand to me. I shook. Dead fish. Figured. Derek Evans never looked at Connor. Philip Carson never looked away. The room hummed with testosterone. Two alphas, a wife, and a gnome. Quite the tableau. Carson moved out of my line of vision and Connor shifted, keeping between me and the interesting guy on my right. Evans took a seat in one of the club chairs and waved a hand for me to sit down.

"We'd like to speak with you alone, Ms. Townley." Evans smirked with perfect capped teeth.

"No," Connor said.

"Morris Hamilton didn't tell us you were working with a colleague. We were under the impression that you were exercising utmost discretion in this matter."

Evans was doing all the talking. I couldn't help wondering if the other guy's lips moved. Connor shook his head almost imperceptibly. I resisted the urge to turn around to see Carson. The hair on the back of my neck stood up.

"Of course," I soothed. "Mr. Hamilton doesn't always know the details of any particular investigation. Mr. McNamara is a local associate of mine. You can rely on our discretion, Mr. Evans."

Local associate. A nice euphemism.

"Have you made contact with the subject yet?" Evans asked.

Subject. Not a person. Enough said about what Evans thought about John.

"No, sir, but I understand the money was paid back. I'm not sure what you want me to do at this point."

Evans's eyes darted to Carson. *That's it, Charlie McCarthy, look like you're the one doing the talking.*

"I can't comment on that, Ms. Townley," Evans said coolly. "I can say that the bank is still interested in determining the manner in which the money may have been diverted. To that end, we would like to talk to this man. It's important for us to follow up to improve our internal processes, you understand."

That was a whole lot of hooey. Ivy League quality, but a bunch of bull, nonetheless. Why would they care? They got their money back.

"The bank is the client, of course. However, I think I should tell you that there may not be an identity thief in this case."

Connor's expression was completely blank. Did I screw it up? Maybe I shouldn't have mentioned it. It was hard. No matter how much you talked about what to do, until you were actually in the moment, it was impossible to decide how to play something, or someone. Evans seemed like an empty shirt. Carson seemed like a real threat.

"What do you mean?" Evans asked.

"Well, for one thing, repayment of the money might be construed as Charles Smiths recognizing a legal obligation because he opened the line of credit himself. Maybe he just didn't notice or react immediately when the line was cut off. When he realized, he paid it off. Since the bank didn't contact him when they suspected fraud, he'd have no reason to think anything was out of the ordinary."

"That's irrelevant," Carson spoke behind me. "We want to talk to the man calling himself Charles Smiths. That's your job."

"That's the other problem," I said.

"What do you mean?" Evans asked.

"There were only two things connected to the so-called identity thief. One was the line of credit. As I've just explained, in retrospect that means nothing. The other was an interview the alleged thief gave to a local radio deejay. It was, after all, the potential for adverse publicity more than the loss of money that got the bank involved."

"I wouldn't hazard to ascribe motivations, Ms. Townley," Evans said. Hazard? Who taught this guy to talk?

"Fine," I allowed. "Whatever your reasons, you want to talk to the man who gave the interview, correct?"

"Yes," Evans said.

"Then you'll need to talk to Charles Smiths. He gave the interview."

"He didn't," Evans began.

"He did," I contradicted.

"How do you know?" Evans leaned back, crossing one leg over the other.

"I asked him."

Chapter Thirty-six

"Connor?"

"I see him."

I stared across the street. The dog stared back. She was either our serenader or her doppelgänger. "She's definitely following us, but I don't see how."

I looked at Connor. His head was moving slowly, up the street and down. "See anyone familiar?"

The people on the street looked innocuous to me. Tourists with sunburned noses. Surfers with bleached hair and hanging shorts. Workaholic businesspeople catching a little weekend sun at lunch. "Not really, no."

We walked from the bank. Pavarotti followed us for a block, then disappeared into the crowd. We stopped in a fast-food place, and I got a milk shake while Connor chose a virtuous bottled water.

"They seemed pretty surprised," I said.

"I don't know about that."

"Okay, so maybe Carson isn't that easy to read, but that younger guy, he seemed shocked we'd talked to Charles Smiths. I thought he might have a coronary right there."

Connor unlocked the car and opened my door. I slid in and he went around to the driver's side. He put the top down before we pulled out of the lot.

"What's the game?"

"What do you mean?"

"Why is the bank still spending money to have me chase John Doe? They got their money back. So what if a crazy guy tells his story to some equally nuts public-access radio guy? It's not like anyone would believe either one of them. I don't really think there's much chance that some society matron is going to move her account because John says aliens have invaded the vault." I ran my hand through my hair.

"Especially now that the radio guy is dead."

"I know why I'm still looking."

"Why?"

"The dog."

"You're looking because of the dog?"

"If John were that crazy, why would Pavarotti stay? Aren't dogs supposed to sense stuff like this?"

"You're kidding."

"Didn't you ever have a dog as a kid?"

"We were in the navy. Too much moving. Did you?" I slouched in my seat. "No, but I always wanted to."

She reached over and petted the dog's head. "I think this one is yours for the taking."

"She already belongs to someone."

Connor leaned over and kissed me. "So do you."

Connor's cell phone rang. He hit speaker. "Go."

"Hey, Rock. You got a weird one. Some woman. Mary, I think. It was hard to tell through the crying. She said you visited with her dad yesterday."

It took a minute to figure it out. "Pablo Esteban."

"Please identify," the voice drawled.

"Sara, Tex. Tex, Sara," Connor said, doing the introductions.

"Another one of the merry men," I said. "Nice to meet you, Tex."

"Hey, Sara. How're you doin'?"

"I'm good."

"What did she want?" Connor asked.

"She came back from church this morning—guess the father didn't go with her—anyway, somebody beat the old man up. Bad. Tore up the place. Had your card."

Guilt flooded me. We must have led them, whoever they were, straight to him. To an old man who couldn't defend himself.

"Did she say how badly he was hurt?" I croaked.

"What?"

I cleared my throat.

"How bad?" Connor asked. The car accelerated.

"Didn't sound great," Tex replied. "Didn't sould like he'd die either."

"Did she say where they took him?"

"Alvarado."

"Thanks, Tex."

"You need me, I'm on the radio." He hung up.

I looked out the window and blinked back tears. He was a nice man. He was only trying to help us. To help me.

"It's my fault."

"The only person responsible for what happened to Esteban is the person who broke into his house. You didn't do anything wrong. There was no way to know that he was at risk."

"I made him part of this."

"He was already part of it, hon. He made his own choices."

His choices. A retired cop whiling away the boredom of suburban life. I'd offered him a chance to get back in the game, if only peripherally. Except he hadn't been on the sidelines. He was hurt. Someone hit that nice old man. He couldn't pose a threat to anyone. I pulled at the seat belt.

"They need to be stopped."

"Anger isn't the right mind-set for this, Sara."

He didn't look angry. His hands were loose on the wheel. His expression bland. His eyes, hidden behind his dark glasses, told nothing.

"Aren't you mad?"

"No."

I believed him. He wasn't mad. He was cold. Ready. Scary.

"I'm really getting sick of feeling like everyone's three steps ahead of us," I declared.

He changed lanes and we roared down the highway. The speedometer showed eighty-five. "Roger that."

"So what are we going to do about it?"

"First, we're going to see if Pablo Esteban saw anything. If he's up to it we're going to see if he can ID the pictures Troj took last night of Charles Smiths. Find out if it's the same kid Esteban helped all those years ago. Then we're going to meet Blue and see what he has to say."

"I still didn't pick him out. What does he look like? The troops were out in force last night. Troj, Blue, you, me, Ryan, and let's not forget Siobhan without her knickers."

"On second thought, let's."

"And after Blue?"

"We're going to find an independent source to corroborate the identity of Charles Smiths."

"Jack?" I guessed. Who else?

Connor smiled.

"No," I said.

He looked at me. "What?"

"You can't beat him up."

"What makes you think—"

"Please, Connor." I folded my arms, shaking my head. "We need him. Besides, how would you explain it to Siobhan?"

"She's charbroiling his clothes as we speak."

"*She's* doing it. As long as it's her decision, her action, it's okay. But you've got to give her a chance to work this out for herself. No swooping in and playing fairy godmother. She needs to do it for herself. Otherwise you'll have to admit to beating him up and treating her like a child. She won't blame him; she'll blame you."

I had a point, as much as he hated to admit it. Brutality wasn't always the right approach. In this case, it just felt right.

"I didn't mean Jack, anyway," he said.

"Then who?"

"The maid. The one who was there the night that the Smithses were murdered."

"How do we find her?"

"We'll figure something out."

"Okay. Connor, did you ever see *The Thomas Crown Affair*?"

"The movie?"

"Yeah."

"What do you remember about it?"

"Rene Russo in a hot dress."

Figured. I pinched him.

"Hey."

"Enough with the dresses already."

"Fine. What about it?"

"What I remember is the scene when Pierce Brosnan puts the painting back. He hires a bunch of guys and dresses them all the same, and pretty soon there's a whole museum full of look-alikes. No one can tell one from another."

"So?"

"That's what this is like. Everybody's the same. Caucasian. Male. Thirty-five to forty-five. Light hair. Light eyes. That description matches everyone. John Doe. Charles Smiths. Henry DeVries. Even you. It's like the world is suddenly full of bowlers and briefcases and they all look alike to me."

I was winding myself up. I shouldn't but I couldn't help it. Who knew anyone? If I needed someone to swear on a stack of Bibles that I was Sara Townley, who could do it? Russ and Connor. Joe from work? What did he know about me, really? No family. A best friend with a penchant for lying. A husband who had a dangerous job that took him away for long periods of time. If I had to prove I was me, how would I do it?

"History favors the bold," Connor said.

"What?"

"When I was at the academy we had a field training exercise. War games."

"Okay," I said, not following.

"I got cut off from my team. It was hot. I was running out of supplies. One morning I swapped armbands with a guy who'd been DQd and walked through the other team's chow line." Connor pulled into a parking place and cut the engine.

"So?"

"They served rubber chicken."

"Tell that to Pablo Esteban. He's eating hospital food."

* * *

The old man was in intensive care. The doctor wouldn't tell us anything. I gave Connor a little space, and he charmed a nurse into telling us Esteban was in a coma. He wouldn't be talking to anyone for a while. I scrolled through the pictures on Connor's phone. John Doe. Charles Smiths. Jack Reed. If one of them was the bad guy, Pablo couldn't tell us. We went to the waiting room.

"I'm so sorry about your father, Mercedes." I told the other woman, sitting next to her on an ugly green couch. She was crying, clutching Kleenex.

"Who would do that? He's an old man. He couldn't defend himself."

There ought to be a special place in hell for people who beat the defenseless. I'd like to help whoever pounded Pablo find that place.

"Is there anything we can do? Do you need help?"

She shook her head. "No. Thanks. My cousin is coming to help." She teared up. "He's was so happy, working on your case. It's . . . he's been so excited about it. I can't remember the last time he raced around like he has since he talked to you. He said he felt like a young man again. Then"—she blew her nose—"this."

"We're so sorry."

"Did it help? The things he found?"

"What things?"

"He found something— Oh, *Madre de Dios*, I'm so stupid." Mercedes took her handbag from next to her chair and started to dig through it. She pulled out a crumpled envelope. "I forgot. I told him I'd mail it but I forgot."

I patted her back as Connor took the envelope. "It's okay."

She nodded. "I'm sorry."

"So are we."

A woman raced into the waiting room and swallowed Mercedes up in a hug. They exchanged rapid-fire Spanish and tears. Connor and I slipped from the room. He walked to the end of the hall and opened the envelope. He pulled a spiral notebook out. He flipped through the pages, then handed it to me.

I read. "Nothing. There's nothing here. They interviewed the maid. She'd written a statment and signed it. They interviewed Charles. There was a draft statement, in block letters, unsighed. A picture of the scene. The red eyes. More notes. Time, date, description of the scene. Nothing we didn't already know."

"Read it again."

I did. Then I read it a third time. I looked up.

"Green."

"Roger that."

"His eyes were green." I ran my finger down the page. "Charles Martin Smiths. Adolescent male. Fifteen years. Five foot, seven inches. One hundred eight pounds. Blond and green."

Connor pulled out his BlackBerry and scrolled. He put Charles Smiths's picture on the screen and held it up.

"So?"

He peered closer. "This is why we need to confirm with the pictures Blue took the night of the banquet. You didn't get a close look. I did. His eyes are blue."

"Charles Smiths isn't Charles Smiths," I said.

Chapter Thirty-seven

"I've got good news and bad news," Blue said, striding toward us.

"John Doe is the real Charles Smiths." I hit him with it. "We need a copy of the pictures you took the night of the party. Are they at the condo? We should go there. Can we enhance them? Make them really clear?"

"Slow down," Connor said. "We'll confirm. Right now, we've got other fish to fry. Let's take this outside." He pointed to the exit sign.

We walked out into the bright sunshine. Pavarotti was sitting next to a picnic table. I put on my sunglasses and joined her, Connor and Blue following close behind.

"Doe is Smiths?" Blue asked, patting the dog's head.

"Yeah. Charles Smiths—or the guy pretending to be him, anyway—his eyes are wrong. The wrong color."

"Which makes my bad-news coincidence easier to grasp," Blue said. "I found the maid."

That got my attention. Finally, a break. It was about time.

"That's great." I jumped up from the bench, needing somewhere to put my nervous energy. "It's better than the picture. She worked for the Smithses for three years. She knows John. I mean Charles. I'm never going to get used to calling him that. She'll be able to confirm. . . ."

Blue didn't say a word.

Connor stood up and moved over to me. He put his hand on my back, bracing me. Blue's face gave nothing away. A rough tongue bathed my hand. He'd said bad news. Bad must be terrible.

"What?" I didn't think I could take any more terrible today. I looked over at Blue.

"She's dead," Blue said.

"What?" Connor led me to the table. I dropped onto the wooden bench. It felt like it was raining anvils. Pouring. Connor put an arm around me.

"How?" I whispered.

"When?" Connor asked.

"Gunshot. Shotgun, actually."

That was horrible. The poor woman. Her family. Like Henry DeVries. Or that hadn't been a shotgun really. A different kind of gun. Machine gun. Shotguns, they were more like hunting guns. That wasn't a good image. Now I was thinking about some poor woman being hunted and killed.

"When?" Connor repeated.

"Thursday night, more or less. My buddy at the medical examiner's office didn't think the time had been confirmed yet."

"That's the day after Henry DeVries was killed," I said. Somehow when Blue said *dead*, I'd assumed it was years ago. It was twenty-seven years since the Smithses were killed. The night after DeVries died was no coincidence.

"What are the cops calling it?"

"Not the elimination of a witness, that's for sure. Interesting all the same, though. Your buddy Montoya? He was assigned."

"That makes sense," I said. "DeVries and the maid are both connected to the elusive Charles Smiths. Assigning the same detective is the obvious answer."

"Sure." Connor didn't sound convinced. "If you knew that DeVries and the maid were the only two people who could identify John Doe as the real Charles Smiths. If you don't know that, the link is pretty damn weak and the assignment is a reach."

"Roger that," Blue conceded.

"Any way you could find out if Montoya was assigned on rotation or if he fired out of sequence?" Connor asked Blue.

"On it. It's not straight duty, Rock. It's a liaison. Montoya and the *federales*."

"Why?" I interrupted.

"Maria washed ashore a few miles north of Ensenada. Somebody sent a bulletin looking for her. When they ID'd her, locals were notified."

I looked at Connor. I felt sick. "That had to be Montoya."

Blue shrugged. "Don't know what their thinkin' is yet, but there's somethin' else."

"What?" Connor asked.

"Montoya is connected. Talk is he'll jump to the hall."

Great. A political wannabe. A hundred agendas behind every operation, most of them making no logical sense.

"Wait a minute. You think Montoya is up to something? That someone made sure he was assigned both cases so he could cover something up for them?"

"Could just be lookin' to make his bones, Sara," Blue suggested. "Famous family might attract the wrong sort of publicity, even if it hasn't got anything to do with them. You know." Blue pointed at Connor. "I'm sure your family's been there a time or ten."

"Yeah."

"Your family? Why? Oh," I said. "Of course. For a second I forgot about the silver spoon."

"His tag ain't Rockefeller for nothin'."

"Rockefeller. Right. Rock as in Rockefeller." I looked at Connor and shook my head, rolling my eyes. Pavarotti rested her head on my lap. "Here I was thinking you called him Rock because of his conversational style. It's about how much information he shares."

There was the damn money again. I don't know why I was still letting it bother me. It wasn't like he'd kept a prison record secret. He hadn't actually kept anything from me. I hadn't asked. Next husband.

"Or dumb as a . . ." Blue said, rising from the bench. He clapped Connor on the shoulder and left.

Connor switched sides so he was facing me across the picnic table. "You never asked."

"You're right. I never asked. My fault entirely." I looked up and stared at him. "Why now?"

"Why what now?"

"Maria. Why kill her now? Because the real Charles Smiths turned up? So what? That didn't have anything to do with her. She hasn't seen him for years. Even if she could identify him, it's hardly a slam dunk. It would be her word against this impostor, and he has cash to burn. Makes for a lot of corroboration."

"It's not the ID," Connor said quietly.

"Then what is it? You're not trying coincidence again?"

"Maria Gonzales could only know one thing that could get her killed now."

I couldn't see his eyes through his sunglasses, but I could feel his gaze burning into me. "Charles Smiths— the real Charles Smiths—killed his parents. And he started talking about it."

That broken man. A broken boy. His parents lying in their own blood. "Are you saying Pablo Esteban covered it up?"

Connor shook his head. "He might have missed it. We know the kid was already being treated by Gretchen."

"Pharmaceuticals for teens," I spat. She'd told me herself. I didn't know much about drugs, but I'd read enough to know they could make you crazy, even if you weren't already. He'd asked us for help. We'd helped him, all right. We'd helped find out he was a murderer.

"Are you going to call the bank?" Connor asked.

"Why? They don't want John. They never did. The bank won't care if he killed his parents. They want the new, improved Charles Smiths. It's all about the money. It's like the art forger who was asked to authenticate a painting he forged. The bank spotted the missing quarter million and went to the identity thief to assure themselves the accounts were legitimate. He's probably the one who paid it back. Maybe even helped himself to another account to do it. God, the banquet guy could have been in place for a really long time. Who knows?"

"Somebody knows." Connor was grim.

I covered my mouth with my hand. "Jack," I whispered. "He'd have to know."

Pavarotti barked.

Chapter Thirty-eight

We were driving back toward the city when the car phone buzzed. I jumped, giving Connor a sheepish grin. Hard-boiled I wasn't. I pushed the speaker button.

"Yeah?"

"You're a go," a voice said.

"Who is this?" I asked.

"Trojan, ma'am."

"Another as-yet-unmet Musketeer. I'm Sara."

"Yes, ma'am."

"I didn't spot you."

"That's good to hear, ma'am."

"Stop flirting," Connor said. "Where's our bogie?"

"On foot headed west on Pike. We confirmed Doe is living there. Spotted him in and out. No canine on site."

They'd spotted John. I breathed a sigh of relief. We hadn't seen him since the explosion. Maybe he killed his parents. Well, probably, but I couldn't help worrying about him. Just a little. He needed help. Definitely needed a better psychiatrist. But even knowing what I did now, I didn't want him hurt. The man had a dog to take care of.

"Charles," I said. "His name isn't John Doe. It's Charles Martin Smiths. And the dog is Pavarotti."

"Yes, ma'am."

"And our dead zone?" Connor asked.

A lovely euphemism for Jack.

"Still tracking. We've got his office, his apartment, his house all covered."

"His boat?"

"Checking marinas. It'll take a bit, but we'll get him, sir."

"Roger that."

Connor clicked off. We drove for a couple more minutes. When Connor pulled to the curb, I was reaching for the car door before the engine was turned off. I waited for him to tell me to stay in the car. He surprised me.

"C'mon," he whispered. "I don't want him coming back and catching us."

I followed Connor across the street to the front door of the little apartment building. It wasn't the the big house in the nice neighborhood, but it wasn't the worst either. And this one had the added bonus of actually being paid for by the real Charles Smiths. I'd bet my last dollar that the house Blue and I searched was part of Mr. Guest-of-Honor's-Special-Friend's bank fraud investment portfolio.

The owner of this building still took a little pride in it. The grass was cut and the shutters freshly painted a bright blue. Charles Smiths, aka John Doe lived here. I thought it would be worse. More depressing. More squat than home. Wrong again.

I hovered as Connor picked the lock on the glass door, then the one on the apartment door. I was definitely going to get him to show me how to do that. Connor pushed me to one side of the door, entered the hall, then went into the apartment and closed the door. He was back in a minute, holding open the door for me.

There was enough of the late-evening sun coming in the big front windows to see the room. Sleeping bag, shadeless lamp, crate of clothes, and stack of books and magazines in the living room. Bowl, spoon, and glass in the kitchen sink. Ketchup and half a loaf of bread in the refrigerator. Toothbrush and razor on the ledge above the bathroom sink. One towel, damp, hung over the rod. Basics only. Dog bowls. No separate bed. They probably shared. Still, it had a roof and required rent. I stood in the middle of the nearly empty living/dining room with my hands on my hips, thinking.

"Would you live like this?" I asked.

"It keeps the rain off."

"He's got more than a quarter of a million dollars, but he's sleeping in a sleeping bag"—I toed the cloth—"reading"—I knelt next to the small stack of paperbacks—"half-priced books, and living on ketchup sandwiches. I mean, would you live like this if you had that much money? Jesus, who am I talking to? You've probably got tons more than him, and you live in that swanky place on the water."

"*We* live there, and you never asked about the money."

"Would it kill you to volunteer information once in a while?"

"Probably. I'm a guy."

I sighed and rolled my eyes. I didn't know how to feel. All that money. Endless opportunity and this was what he had. This was subsistence only. I guess money hadn't even been enough for a down payment on the good life for John Doe.

"Well, stop being such a guy, then. Let's argue about that later."

"Works for me," he said.

"I'm sure it does."

Connor gestured toward the room. "What does this tell us?"

I eyed him suspiciously. He wanted me to free-associate our next, probably wrong conclusion? "He's neat."

"So? So am I."

"But you're military. They probably drill neatness into you. John Doe makes me look like a slob." Everything was shipshape.

"Institutional living, maybe. If he's been in and out of hospitals, he would have learned to control his quarters."

"Maybe." I went into the kitchen and started opening cabinets. "But if he grew up with servants and stuff, wouldn't he naturally leave things out? And he wouldn't have a pet."

Connor checked the knives in the silverware drawer.

He touched a blade and pulled back a bloody thumb. Honed or new? "He might have had to make his own bed, servants or not."

"Did you?"

"Yes."

"Oh, my God. You had servants?"

"I thought we were going to argue about that later?"

"I forgot. I was suddenly picturing you with one of those cushy nanny types."

He leaned over and kissed me. "We could get you a uniform."

I pushed him away. "Pervert. Do you ever think about anything but sex?"

"Not with you in the room."

"There's nothing in here." I closed the cabinet.

Back in the living room I flipped through the books. Connor took the clothes out of a crate and flipped it, using it as a chair.

"Don't do that," I said.

"I'm just going to check the pockets."

"It's creeping me out. It's too, well, personal. It feels like a violation."

"We already broke in."

There were limits, for Pete's sake. "I know, but let's not."

"Sara, we've got to find out more about this guy than what kind of toothbrush he uses."

I sank back onto my butt. It felt wrong. He had to see that.

"We're not out to hurt him, Sara. We just need to know what's going on."

"I know." I sighed, flipping pages, setting the book down, and picking up another.

"John Doe really got to you."

"He was so scared, Connor."

Connor lifted a shirt, checked the pockets, and re-folded it.

"How much do you think the rent on this place is?" I asked, leafing through another volume.

"Eight, nine hundred maybe."

I watched Connor from the corner of my eye. He

wasn't saying anything, judging anything.   That was good. "So why not get a better place? Or furniture?"

"He's keeping a low profile. The best way not to get caught is not to draw attention. He picks a nondescript place like this, no one asks questions. And the money lasts longer," Connor guessed.

"If he's keeping a low profile, why do an interview? What's the upside?"

"Maybe he couldn't resist. Like a pyromaniac watching a blaze."

Connor pulled a card from the pocket of a T-shirt. Glancing at it, he read. Then he handed it over. My business card. In the corner, a hole and a twist tie.

"Now we know how John found you," Connor said.

I glanced at a magazine cover, then tossed it on the pile. A piece of paper fluttered. Picking up the magazine, I turned pages until I found it. It was a loose Xerox copy. The ink was blurred, but I could read the police report. It was a copy of the report Pablo Esteban had given us. The Smiths murder report. I handed it to Connor without a word.

"And that's how John Doe knew about the Smithses murders," I muttered, not meeting his eyes. "I was so sure . . .

"It doesn't explain how John knew all about Charles Smiths's medical history, babe. So he kept a copy of the police report about his parents' murders. That's grim, but understandable." He still knows more than a stranger would. And his mental state, well, it would take a lot to make that up. It's not like Charles Smiths was mainstream crazy.

I stared at the article. The one bookmarked by the police report. Scanning, I felt my heart drop. " 'Capgras syndrome,' " I read aloud, " 'a case study by Gretchen Dreznik.' "

Chapter Thirty-nine

I was quiet on the ride back. Pavarotti's head rested between the seats. She'd been waiting for us when we came out of the apartment. Slipping past us when we'd opened the door, she checked the apartment, slurped a little water, and came back to stand next to me. I couldn't leave her locked up in the apartment by herself. When we got to the car, she got in.

Connor left me with my own thoughts. I kept circling around. There were still a lot of loose ends. Nothing was matching up. John's apartment, for one. He had an apartment. I'd missed it. His clothes, his hair. They'd said homeless. His hands. Hindsight really was twenty-twenty. They'd been soft. Not calloused. Not used to living hard. Pavarotti, too. She was well fed. Not skittish. There'd been plenty of clues and I'd missed them all. John had to be living somewhere, with those hands. I don't know why I was so mad at him. It wasn't like he told me he was homeless. It wasn't his fault that I'd assumed. I hated feeling stupid.

Pavarotti laid her head on my shoulder. I met her eyes in the rearview mirror and reached up to scratch her chin. An apartment. Dog bowls full of food and water. The perfect picture. So why did John leave the dog now? Every time I'd seen John, and at least a half dozen other times, the dog was free. Roaming. Now she was riding in the car with us and John was nowhere. It was like his hands—nothing fit.

"Why did he leave the dog?" I asked Connor.

"Maybe he didn't. It's possible the dog comes and goes as she pleases."

"Does it feel right to you?"

"We don't know this guy, babe. We don't know what makes him tick."

He seemed satisfied with that. We weren't alike in that way. SEALs apparently didn't need to know why. Just do. Handle the task and move on. I couldn't stop asking the question. I couldn't help digging. Connor might not need it, but I needed some reason for things.

When we got to the condo, Connor checked in. If his mood was anything to go by, his team still hadn't found Jack. I went to the patio, sliding open the door and moving over to the railing. Pavarotti sat down next to me and we watched the boats in the distance. The dog chatted with me. She didn't seem to require a response. Connor handed me a cold bottle. Water. How very abstemious of him. He leaned against the railing with his back to the setting sun.

"John passed the polygraph," I said. "He didn't lie."

"No, he didn't."

"A measure of belief. Isn't that how you put it? John believes he is Charles Smiths."

"He does."

"It could still be the truth."

"Sure."

"Just because his knowledge about the deaths of the Smithses and Capgras syndrome can be explained by the papers we found at his apartment, it doesn't necessarily follow that he didn't know that stuff anyway."

All of which was true but didn't seem make me feel better. Even I could hear the rationalization.

"Do you think John beat up Pablo Esteban to get the police report?" We'd seen the dog. Maybe John had been there, too. Maybe, hell. Probably.

"Maybe, but there were other ways. The reporter might have had a copy. Researched the subject. Esteban's partner, their lieutenant at the time, or anyone else in the police or the brass could have ended up with the statements. DeVries was a journalist. He'd have had his own sources."

"Maybe he handed a copy to John before the interview," I added, warming to the idea. "Especially if he was genuinely convinced that he was going to get the first real sit-down with the elusive Charles Smiths. Getting him to open up about his parents, priming the pump for dramatic revelations, etc. Yeah. Okay. That works. For the article, too, if DeVries found out John was being treated by the great Gretchen at the time of the murders. It's possible Henry put two and two together and figured out Charles was the killer."

Connor drank and thought. "Probably not."

I stared. This theory fit as well as anything and meant I hadn't led an old man into a brutal beating. I liked it better than our previous analysis and I wasn't ready to give up on it yet.

"Why not?" I asked with a bit too much unwarranted hostility.

"DeVries didn't ask him questions about Gretchen. DeVries would have raged on about violations of patient confidentiality and how the government and its chosen ones hide behind their medical licenses and the AMA to get away with murder."

I nodded. "It's not the crime that kills you. It's the cover-up. Call Michael Moore. I can sell the film rights."

Connor saluted me with his water bottle.

"If it wasn't John, who attacked Pablo? My money is on Jack. Not personally, of course. He'd never get his hands dirty."

"You changed your mind pretty fast."

"What do you mean?"

"It was only a couple of days ago you were telling me that Jack didn't have the stomach for anything really bad."

"That was a couple of days ago. Before the maid. Before Esteban. Before we knew that the only way that suit at the banquet could get away with pretending to be Charles Smiths was if the doctor went along with it."

"Or killing John Doe. They killed plenty of others. Why not just kill him and be done with it?"

"We found him."

"He found you. He's been missing since the explosion,

and my team has been looking. We haven't spotted him yet. This guy is not easily found."

"Which explains the banquet guy. The impostor is plan B."

"So he went along. Jack was screwing with the insurance. We figured it out. Someone else might have, too. Maybe he was being blackmailed."

"If he was, we'd know. He couldn't get that kind of money without Siobhan's help. Unlike you, he married for money." Connor paced toward the kitchen. I heard the refrigerator open and a bottle cap hit the garbage can.

Oh, no. What did she say? Hundreds of thousands. I'd promised. I told Siobhan I wouldn't tell him. Wouldn't it just make him madder? He came back and handed me a beer. I took a sip. Then another.

"He's a liar and an adulterer, Con. Assaulter of old men doesn't fit. Not to mention murderer."

"Esteban is weak. Reed preys on the weak."

He was thinking about his sister. I didn't blame him. Jackson Reed had a lot to answer for no matter how you looked at it.

"How would Jack know about Pablo Esteban? Do you think he followed us?"

"Yes."

"We didn't see him." I stared at Connor. "Did you see him?"

"No." It sounded grudging.

I hated imagining Pablo all bruised and battered. But Jack? A bribe, sure. He probably paid off the bank. Get them to stop looking. Used his joint account with Siobhan to do it, but if he were going to do that, he wouldn't need to eliminate witnesses. I wanted to tell Connor. I didn't want to betray Siobhan.

"The only reason to go after that old man was to keep him from talking, from helping us." I played devil's advocate. "Maybe John was afraid that Esteban wasn't going to stay silent about that night. That the Smithses' family secret would come to light."

Connor took the chair next to me. "Esteban's been protecting him for twenty-seven years. We're talking about a documented teenage mental patient and a cold case that was never really investigated. Add in Charles Smiths's assets and no prosecutor in his right mind files a case. I don't think the assault was the point. I think the theft was."

"Jack broke in to steal the police report? Why? How would he know it even existed?"

"If he followed us, he knew we thought the old man knew something. Twenty-seven years? No one has that kind of memory. Details that old would require checking a file."

I drank and thought. It made sense. "You've got a big hole in your theory. Even if Jack suspected there was a personal file, getting rid of Pablo doesn't get close to getting rid of the information. It's easier to assume there's an official file."

"An official file held by a police officer with political ambitions? One who'd need money for his next campaign, maybe? Or support with the party from a society doctor? Believe me, Jack could make an official record disappear a lot easier than he could get an honorable old man to give it up."

"Maybe we should go back to the insurance thing. Try to make a case that way. At least it would be something," I suggested.

"White-collar crime? He wouldn't even get a slap on the wrist."

"He might get more than that. We know about the billing thing with Smiths. Thieves never steal once, right?"

"Where are you going with this?"

"Gretchen. She'd never get her talk show if her partner was outted for his role in scamming the cream of San Diego society into thinking a fake was Charles Smiths, right?"

"You expect her to silence him?"

"I expect her to be the Unabomber's brother and sacrifice those she loves for the greater good."

"The greater good being her reputation."

"Exactly. Now all we need to do is prove that John Doe is Charles Smiths. The eye color won't be enough.

We need tangible proof. Then we've got a hundred witnesses who saw Jack sing the school song with Smiths at the Yacht Club the night of the charity benefit."

"Wait a minute." Connor got up and disappeared into the condo. He came back carrying the file with my notes in it. "It's a long shot."

"What is?" I asked.

He flipped pages.

"We don't have base prints, Con. If we could find fingerprints at all, we couldn't match them up to anyone. Oh, I'm so stupid." I jumped up and raced into the kitchen. Spotless. I pulled open the dishwasher. It smelled clean. The glasses shone. I slammed the appliance shut and returned to the patio.

"We had them. The night he was here. He drank from the glass. Probably touched the plate."

Connor looked up. He nodded. "It's the maid's day."

I sat down. "We have a maid?"

"Still hate the money?"

"I'm adjusting. It doesn't matter anyway. There's no way we'd be able to get prints off that statement from 1981."

"It was in a file cabinet in an attic. They got pulled before it was in an official file. Before it was accessible anywhere. That leaves your prints, mine, his, maybe his partner's, and at least one other set."

"From the Charles Smiths who wrote it," I said.

Chapter Forty

"**J**ust don't kill the messenger, okay?" Ryan spoke without so much as a hello.

I switched the phone to my other ear.

"What did he do now?" I sighed.

"I don't want you to tell him it was me, either. I mean, he'll probably know but he won't really know, get it?"

"Fine. What is it?" No doubt Ryan would come up untarnished while I got to play the recalcitrant wife. Partners. My suggestion. Of course, that was before duty called Connor and I was stuck twiddling my thumbs. No sense losing the whole day, and I'd have Ryan with me.

"Siobhan's planning to see Jack."

"What?" I exploded. I never thought she'd do something that dumb.

"She figures that even if he catches her, he probably won't hurt her."

"Catch her doing what?"

"Finding dirt."

"Oh, God, didn't you try to talk her out of it?"

"Of course I did. She won't listen. She's a woman."

"I'll try. What's her number?"

"Her cell phone is out of range."

"That's good, though. It means she didn't go to his office. Or that apartment Lily mentioned. Right?" I took a couple of deep breaths. Ryan had scared me to death.

"Not good."

"Why?"

"His boat."

"What about his boat?"

"His boat is definitely out of range. It's in Mexico. Ensenada."

"Goddamn it."

"I told her she should talk to you first. You'd have a much better chance of sneaking onto the thing than she would. Besides, she was already hagged out from Friday night."

"Ryan, in two seconds I'm coming through the phone. Where in the hell is she?"

"Tijuana."

"Christ. If she calls you, tell her to get back over the border. Tell her I said so."

"Somehow I don't think that's gonna work."

"Don't I know it," I muttered, and hung up. I dialed Connor's office.

"Chief Petty Officer Todd. May I help you?"

"Thank God it's you."

"Sara?"

"Is Connor there?"

"No. What's the matter?"

"Where is he? Can you get a message to him?"

"Unlikely. One of the tads got hurt. He's in surgery and Rock's at the hospital. Probably out of range. What's up?"

"Tad?"

"Tadpole. New guy. What do you need?"

"I've got to go to Mexico. Ensenada via Tijuana." I tucked the phone on my shoulder and started pulling on my clothes. I stepped into the bathroom. Yikes. Bad hair.

"No. Wait there."

"I can't. This is an emergency. Where is Connor?"

"Unavailable."

"What does that mean?" I put toothpaste onto my toothbrush.

"It means stay there. I'll let him know as soon as he's free." Blue sounded a little perturbed. Welcome to my world, buddy.

"Tell him to meet me there."

"No, Sara—"

I hung up. One of them was bound to show.

* * *

My phone rang as I merged onto I-5.

"Sara?"

"Hi, honey. How's work?"

"Are you under arrest?"

"Not yet."

"That's good, because you know the Mexican jails aren't generous with conjugal visits."

"That'll suck."

"You need backup."

"I need my head checked. Yeah. Backup would be good. I'm going to Ensenada. Juanito's Docks. The *Hippocratic Oath*. Slip A-thirty-one." I accelerated past a truck, the speedometer hovering near ninety.

"Jack's sloop's in Ensenada?"

"Yeah."

"We were supposed to go together when I got home." Now he sounded mad. Besides, I didn't remember anything about going to Mexico. I couldn't tell him Siobhan was already en route. I didn't know how much of a head start she had on me, and he'd blow a gasket. Probably do something dangerous, like speed. No, better just to wait until I couldn't avoid it any longer.

"How's the guppy?"

"What?"

"The one who got hurt."

"Tadpole," he corrected. "He's gonna be okay."

"I'm glad." I slammed on the brakes and pounded the horn, dropping the phone. At this speed I had to use feel to find the darn thing again. Taking my eyes off the road could prove hazardous. "Connor? You still there?"

Silence.

"Connor?"

"I'm on my way. What else?" That was too quiet. He was definitely going to be yelling later to even things out.

"Put together a plan B. If this goes bad, we're going to need someone to get us out of Mexico."

"Sure. I'll do that." He clicked the phone off. With that head of steam, he might beat me to Old Mexico.

I paid twenty bucks to park close to the border. I didn't have the patience to wait while cars crept toward the border patrol. The guard barely looked up when I showed him my passport.

"Reason for going to Mexico, *señorita*?"

"Pleasure." A misnomer, for sure.

"How long are you staying?"

"I'll be back tonight."

"Gracias."

"Thanks."

I passed through the turnstile and into the Mexican sunshine. I took the first cab at the curb without even haggling about the price.

"Juanito's Docks."

"Sí, señorita."

The taxi rocketed away from the curb and screeched to a halt ten feet away as the driver waited for the river of humanity to part. I tapped my fingers on the armrest. Siobhan couldn't have had that much of a head start on me. I should have asked Ryan when I had him on the phone. Naive to think that she could handle Jack. One alfresco altercation did not a heavyweight make. Without the audience, who knew what he'd do? Put her down? Rip her confidence away? I wouldn't put it past the guy to take a swing at her. No. Connor would rip his heart out. Ryan, too. Jack wasn't that stupid. Then again, I was just a stranger. "Twenty more if you step on it."

"Sí, señorita."

The cabbie earned his twenty bucks and then some. Riding with Russ, who'd passed his driver's test only on the fifth try, hadn't been that life threatening. At the marina I had the cabbie stop at the entrance. I tossed forty dollars to him and got out.

I should have brought binoculars. There were at least thirty boats tied up at the marina, large boats shielding smaller ones from view. I didn't even know what a sloop looked like. They all looked like boats to me. I hesitated for a minute. I could work my way toward the end of the pier. If I stayed close to the boats and Jack was on one of them, he might not see me until I was pretty close. Then again, Siobhan wouldn't think twice about walking straight up to him. Better to go in guns blazing. Knock him back long enough for Connor to get there. Jack might call the cops. No. First real perk in the family lotto. Jack couldn't outbribe the *federales*. That could be handy.

The *Oath* was near the end of the pier. I did a quick scan of the deck. No signs of activity. I walked down the dock, crossed the short walkway, and jumped onto the deck.

"What did you find?"

"Eeyugh," I squeaked, slapping a hand over my mouth. "You ought to wear a bell or something." I patted my chest. Connor's eyes followed the movement.

"Forget flirting. I'm mad. If you're done with this particular felony, I suggest we get out of here."

"You made good time."

"I broke the land speed record."

"I thought you were unavailable."

He glared. "Blue covered me."

"Are you in trouble?"

"Not yet. Let's get out of here before that changes."

"I haven't finished looking yet." And I hadn't found Siobhan.

"Yes, you have."

Maybe I had beaten her down. More likely Ryan got it wrong. I was going to brain him the next time I saw him. Then again, since I was already here . . . "No, I haven't. This thing's got all these little cupboards everywhere. All built-in. It's amazing, really. I bet he's got more storage space than I have in my whole apartment."

"As interesting as this is, we do not want to get caught. Not here. The locals take American lawbreakers pretty seriously. They'd throw even your cute butt in jail."

"Didn't you say we were going sailing? Here we are."

"The plan was for you to wait for me and for us to do this without causing an international incident. That plan has gone to hell. Now we're going to get out of this without making it worse."

I bent down to reach a lower drawer. "I was trying to save time. I know about the Mexican jails. I've seen *Tequila Sunrise*."

"What?"

"It's a movie. Mel Gibson gets sent to a Mexican prison for a really long time for smoking pot on the beach." I closed the drawer and moved to another.

Connor took my left arm and hoisted me over his shoulders.

"Hey."

He moved toward the door.

"Hey. Stop it."

He kept moving. I went stiff at the stairs, spreading my arms and legs so I wouldn't fit through the little opening. He reached up and grabbed my arm with his free hand and tried to force my arms together. I swung my arms and kept my legs wide.

"Babu," I shouted. "Knock it off."

"Stop fighting, Sara." Turning sideways, he tried to maneuver me through the door. "It's not the U.S., you know. There'd be real consequences if the cops caught you."

"Which is exactly why I asked the police before I boarded. We talked to them at the station and a very nice officer made a call."

"What?"

"They told the dockmaster to let me on board."

"Why?"

"What do you mean, 'why'?" I punched his shoulder and he set me on my feet. "I can be very persuasive." I poked him and went back to rummaging.

I'd lied through my teeth to the cops of course, but I wanted them around in case Jack went ballistic. Or Siobhan got crazy. Since neither one of them was on the boat, I supposed getting the police involved might have been a little over-the-top on my part.

"They just let you on?" Connor asked.

" '*Con mi favor, señorita.*' "

" 'With my favor?' "

"My Spanish isn't very good. I think that's what the

guy said when he told the other guy to let me look
around."

"You are full of surprises, Mrs. McNamara. Which is
señora, for the record. Find anything?" Connor asked.

"No. He's got tons of charts and papers, but none of
it seems important."

I thought about John Doe. As long as neither marital
discord nor arrest was imminent, we should look around
for anything that might indicate he'd been on board.
Blood. A body. Medical records stating, *Today I, Jackson Reed, quack psychiatrist, renamed my patient Charles
Smiths John Doe.* I glanced at Connor. He was already
going through the drawers. Great minds . . .

"You look topside?" he asked.

"No. All the storage stuff is down here."

"Keep an eye out for anything that looks like a log-
book."

I snapped my fingers. "Safe."

"For now, yeah. Get the lead out."

"No, I meant, does he have a safe?"

Connor straightened. "Right. Why quit a winner?"

He moved to the middle of the room and started a
slow spin. His eyes went from ceiling to floor, then
moved on to the next section of cabinetry. I watched
him. It was like his radar was on fine-tune. Searching.
For what? If it was obvious, I'd have found it. Or at
least I hoped I would.

"Sonar," he said.

"That's weird. I was just thinking it was like you
had—"

"No. I meant the sonar is wrong." Connor climbed
the stairs. I followed him up on deck. He walked to
midships and stepped into the enclosed area housing the
high-tech equipment.

"It looks okay to me."

Connor shook his head. He pulled a pocketknife out
of his uniform and twisted the screws off the casing. He
lifted it and stepped back for me to see. The guy did
prefer cash.

"How could you possibly know that?"

"I glanced around on my way in. The jib is frayed but the sonar is new."

"Maybe he's just got the sails for show? Maybe he only needs the mechanical stuff."

"In which case he'd have a new engine, GPS, something like that. Sonar on a boat like this is for finding fish. Maybe diving."

"So?"

"Did Jack strike you as the get-out-and-do type?"

I thought about that for a millisecond. "No. That's a McNamara trait. And he's just an in-law."

Connor smiled at me.

I reached into the hole and pulled out the money. Underneath were two file folders, one thick, one thin. I took them and Connor set the fake sonar housing down.

I started with the thicker folder. It was marked, SMITHS, CHARLES, and included a picture. The picture was new and did Gretchen's philanthropist proud. Mental instability didn't necessarily show from the outside. Pages in reverse chronological order. Faded near the back, the copies marked with dark streaks near the upper left corner. They went back to the late seventies. Must have been stripped for just the meat or it would come with volume numbers. Diagnosis was Capgras syndrome, just like Jack's hypothetical case. Maybe John had mimicked it. Man, I'd bought hook, line, and sinker. I kept flipping papers. Enough medications to fill a pharmacy. Most with fifteen letters and no vowels. Page after page after page.

I handed the file to Connor and opened the other. John Doe. Real name Edward Abernathy. He looked so young in the picture. Maybe late teens. Three years of crammed penmanship. Medications, diagnosis. Sociopathy. Three dozen pages of background, including references to increasing violence. A sister drowned, ruled accidental. A neighbor shot, ruled accidental but resulting in the first court-ordered psychiatric visit. Bomb threats to the local school. Arson at a nearby church. More doctors. Age twelve. Juvenile detention. Involuntary commitment. Age fifteen. Poor John. He hadn't seemed like that. Crazy, sure, but not crazy-crazy. Just . . . lost.

"Jack's not a very good doctor," I said.

Connor looked up from his reading. "This surprises you?"

"Well, no, not really, I guess. It's just that he got John wrong."

"You're not a doctor but you play one on TV?" he quipped.

I stared. "That was a joke."

"I know."

"You don't tell jokes."

"I'm in a good mood."

I eyed him. "Why?"

"We've got him."

"What do you mean?"

"Look." he pointed to a line in the Smiths file. "Jack's notes say that Charles Smiths was in the hospital up until two weeks ago. There's a notation about charging the SDCF for in-patient treatment."

"So?" Light dawned. I looked back at the file and returned to the first page, running my hand down the notes. "He couldn't be. Charles Smiths was in Seattle. Not in San Diego. You were right all along. Jack is committing fraud. SDCF must be the billing agency or something, but it doesn't matter. Jack charged Charles Smiths for in-patient treatment that couldn't possibly have happened unless Banquet Guy has mastered the art of being in two places at once."

"Exactly." Connor reached for the file. "Let's go."

"No, Connor, wait." I reread the passage. "We've got more than that. I knew it. I knew I was right."

"What?"

Flipping the file, I held it up to him. "Two-thirds of the way down the page. Hospital admission last January."

I turned the file around and flipped pages until I found it, flashing it at him in triumph.

"'Acute canine dander reaction,'" he read aloud. "Anaphylactic shock due to exposure. Epinephrine administered. Emergency room visit." His head lifted. We stared at each other. Connor reached out and took the file from my hand, setting it next to his on the console, both open to the inside flap.

"Maybe it's just the miracle of modern medicine, but what are the chances Edward Abernathy was cured from his allergy to dogs?"

Connor turned a couple of pages. "No allergy meds on the list."

"It's a miracle."

"Why would Jack have both files? Why would he be hiding them here?" Connor pulled the photos from underneath the paper clips holding them. He crossed his hands and slid the photos into the opposite folders.

I helped him push them under the clips. A young boy's picture from the seventies with the decades of medical jargon and history of violence. The crisp color print matching the laser print of the thinner file.

"He switched them," Connor said.

Chapter Forty-one

"**F**ind anything?"

I jumped. "Maybe we ought to get bells for the whole team."

Blue smiled. "Hi, Sara."

"Hello, Blue. So glad you could join us."

"Wouldn't miss it. Find anything interesting?"

"You'll never guess," I said. "John Doe is the real Charles Smiths. Jack switched them."

Connor took my arm and helped me jump to the dock. He landed behind me; then Blue touched down. They were like cats.

"Why?" Blue asked, leading us down the dock toward the marina.

"Why what?"

"Why did Jack switch Smiths?"

I stopped. Connor reached back and took my hand, towing me along.

"I don't know. Our best guess is still that John ran away and Jack couldn't afford to have John out there as Charles Smiths."

"Why? Who'd believe him? I mean, he's crazy, right? Whether he's Smiths or Doe or somebody else, he's nuts. He could say the sky was blue and no one would buy it."

"You're right. No one would believe John Doe alias Charles Smiths. But someone might believe Henry DeVries."

The lunatic who'd driven me to the dock was still parked at the end. He stood outside his cab smoking a cigarette and smiling. Probably waiting for the return fare. Given how much I'd paid him to get me here, I couldn't blame him.

"Conducirnos al paso de frontera, por favor," Blue said, sounding like a native.

"Sí, señores, señora," the little man said, grinning and bowing.

"Please tell me you didn't just ask him to throw me in the bay?"

Blue held open the door for me. "Not you. Rock. You"—he kissed my cheek—"are a genius."

Connor got in beside me, and Blue took the passenger seat. The few miles to the border went a lot slower on the return trip. Blue chatted with the driver. I couldn't understand a word.

"Abu?" Connor asked.

I giggled. "Well, it was part 'baboon' and part 'hey you.' " I took his hand, winking. "Somehow in the translation you became the monkey in *Aladdin*."

"A monkey, huh?"

"Hey, don't knock it. He was cute."

"Cute. Great." He nodded toward Blue. Connor checked his cell phone. "No service. We've got to get to the cops. Tell them what we know."

"Oh, my God." I slapped my hand to my forehead. "I totally forgot."

"Forgot what?"

"Why I raced down here."

"It wasn't to make me crazy?" Connor asked.

"Ryan told me Siobhan was on her way to Jack's boat. To confront him. But she wasn't on the boat."

Connor checked his phone again. He slapped it against his leg and gritted his teeth. We waited in silence, Connor checking his phone every five seconds. When we hit a spot with cell service, he speed dialed.

"Sib? Where are you?"

I wondered if he realized he was snapping at her.

"No. Nothing. I just wanted to know if you were okay."

He gave me an "okay" sign. I started breathing again.

"We're on our way back now. Why don't you meet us at the condo and we'll catch dinner? Okay. Bye."

"I take it she's not beating Jack with a stick," I said.

"That's too bad," Blue said without turning around.

"Not right now. You must have gotten it wrong. Or Ryan did."

I narrowed my eyes at him. "So, making you crazy was the only part I got right."

He laughed.

I held out my hand. "Can I borrow your phone?"

He handed it over.

"I've got to call the office," I told him.

"Why?"

"I solved the case. I found Charles Smiths." I linked hands with Connor. Find the guy. That's what my boss had demanded. That was what the bigwig client, the bank, wanted. They'd all been fooled. I found the guy, all right. And I saw what they hadn't seen. I was definitely getting better at this job.

"You figured out that John Doe was Smiths. And you did find him. But in case you forgot, we lost him again. After we talk to the cops, we'll go looking."

"We don't have to. He'll find us."

"Maybe. Once he knows Jack's behind bars and it's safe to come out."

"He wasn't worried about Jack. He's so confused he . . ." I trailed off. Something was nagging just out of reach.

"He what?"

"He'll find us."

"What makes you think so?"

"We have his dog."

Chapter Forty-two

"**S**ara?"

I was half asleep, dozing on the couch. Connor'd been called back into the office. When the phone rang, I'd picked it up automatically, but my brain wasn't functioning properly.

"Who's this?" I shook my head to clear some of the cobwebs.

"Siobhan," she yelled, freeway traffic loud in the background. "Connor's sister?" A little tentative.

"Of course. Sorry, Siobhan." I sat up, rubbing at my eyes. "I'm dead on my feet. What's up?"

"I'm going to do it."

"Do what?"

"Confront him."

My stomach plunged. I was wide-awake now.

"Confront who?" As if I didn't know.

"Jack. I was going to do it earlier but I lost my nerve. But I've been thinking about it all afternoon. I have to do it. I have to. He took two hundred forty-one thousand, seven hundred and sixty-one dollars out of our accounts. Practically cleaned them all out. Including the home-equity line. Everything in both our names. Our names," she sputtered. "It was my money. All of it. I'm not taking it anymore. I'm taking control of my life."

"This is a bad idea, Siobhan. Why don't you meet me? We'll talk about it. Come up with a plan." I searched under the coffee table for my shoes.

"Someone stole my purse."

"Are you okay?"

"Everyone thinks they can just do anything they want. Take things. Destroy things. Without a note or an apology or anything. And no one stops them."

"Are you hurt?"

"Yes. I'm hurt. I turn my back for a minute and some lowlife takes my handbag right out of my shopping bag. In my favorite store. In the middle of the day. Like it's nothing, and no one will say anything because you can't just have a meltdown in a public place like that with everyone watching. Like I've just got to stay quiet forever."

We probably weren't talking about driver's licenses needing to be renewed.

"I'm not taking it anymore," Siobhan was yelling. "Not from thieves or liars or husbands or anyone."

"Siobhan, are you okay?"

"I have a plan." On the edge of hysteria. So not good. Why the hell couldn't Connor be here to handle this?

"What plan?"

Finding one shoe, I dug under the couch. Where the heck could the stupid thing be?

"I'm taking it all back. The practice. Did you know I gave him the money to join it? It was my wedding gift to him." She coughed or maybe sobbed, I couldn't be sure. Probably both. "My fucking wedding gift."

A new word for his sister's vocabulary. A nice complement to my fashion advice. Oh, brother.

"Gretchen was already established. Making a reputation with her books. On the pundit circuit. Jack would never have been asked to join the practice if I hadn't written the check. That means it's mine. His precious career. I'm taking it back."

Jack was going to blow a gasket.

"The house. The cars. The boat. The clothes. Everything. He barely makes a living. Did you know that? Oh, he gets invited to the right panels and the right seminars. Gets his name in the program. Gretchen Dreznik and Jackson Reed, partners in a prestigious San Diego private practice.

I unearthed the shoe. Keys. I needed keys. Oh, no. No car. I needed a car. I tripped into the kitchen. Phone book. *Cab. Cab. Damn. Try taxi.*

"Come here, Siobhan. We'll talk about it."

The background noise stopped abruptly. A car door slammed.

"Don't worry. I'll call you after. Thanks, Sara. Without you I couldn't have done this."

Oh, dear Lord.

Chapter Forty-three

The cab showed up in less than five minutes. A week of my salary had him driving like he lived south of the border. Thank God he accepted plastic. Money did make the world go around. Fast. Very, very fast. I prayed Siobhan had gone to Jack's office. I didn't know where else to go and she wasn't answering her cell phone. Not a good sign. Connor was also not picking up when I called. Much as I'd like to handle his sister's sudden burst of castration frenzy without getting him involved, if Siobhan was meeting Jack somewhere else, I'd need his help figuring it out. It wasn't their house. She'd been in the car. If it was Jack's new bachelor pad, I was out of luck.

The cab squealed to a stop and the driver grinned wickedly. "Quick enough, missus?"

"Like a bat out of hell." I signed the charge slip and he handed me my credit card.

"You want another ride, ask for Enrique."

"Thanks. I'll do that." After I bought more life insurance.

I could hear an angry voice through the closed door. The receptionist jumped when I entered. Finally, a break.

"I have an appointment." I headed straight for his door.

"Wait. You can't go in there."

"You need a coffee break." I dug into my pocket and handed the startled woman a twenty. She stared. Probably trying to place me. I handed her my last twenty. "Get some lunch, too. You deserve it, working here."

"I sure do." She took a purse from the bottom drawer of her desk and left without looking back. I wished I could join her.

The volume in the office went up a decibel. I opened the door.

"You bitch. You stupid, useless bitch." Jack's face was mottled. The flush on his skin ran all the way down his neck.

Siobhan was crying. Her face was blotched. I stepped closer. Not blotched. Bruised. Black and blue along her cheek. Her eye was swollen.

Jack raised his hands.

I charged, hitting him straight on. Pushing him back over a chair. "You son of a bitch."

Jack jumped up. Used the chair as a shield. "What the hell?"

"How dare you hit her? You worthless piece of—"

"I didn't hit her. I never hit her. She's crazy."

"You beat up on me every time you see me. You make me feel stupid," she screamed.

"You are stupid."

"You make me feel incompetent."

"You are incompetent."

I grabbed the arms of the chair and jammed Jack back against the file cabinet. "Siobhan, let's go."

She grabbed me and tried to climb over the chair to get to him.

"Let's just go."

"You!" Jack said, staring at me.

"Siobhan . . ." I pleaded.

"You sent her to spy on me?"

Uh-oh. Oh, well. So my cover was blown. I had bigger trouble. Jack reached down and shoved the chair hard. Siobhan fell into me, and we both went head over heels. Tangled on the floor, I was grabbed and jerked upright.

"Get your hands off me."

He shook me. My head flopped back and forth. He shook harder, his hands sliding to my neck. His nails dug into the skin above my collarbone. Back and forth, my head slammed against the arm of the chair.

I heard a banshee scream. My vision blurred. The

pressure slackened and I heard a crash, something hitting the bookcase hard. Then he was gone and I was on my hands and knees, choking. I rubbed at the sore skin of my throat. Siobhan lay dazed, splayed like a rag doll against the bookcase.

I looked up, blinking as the sunshine lit the angel who'd saved me. The one who had Jack by the shirt and was hitting him again and again.

Connor.

Chapter Forty-four

"You're going to kill him. Connor," I screamed. "Stop. You've got to stop."

I dragged at his arm. Jack slumped to the floor. My left hand gripped Connor's bloodstained shirt. Oh, God, this was so bad. "Please, Connor. He's not worth it."

I dropped to my knees next to Jack. I stared at his face. His nose looked broken and blood gushed from his gap-toothed mouth. His left eye was already swollen shut. He was conscious, but barely.

"Please, Connor, check Siobhan. Make sure she's okay."

I looked at him. He was scaring me. I wasn't afraid of him. He'd never hurt me. Or Siobhan. But Jack . . . Connor didn't look mad, and yet . . . I looked down at Jack. That was the scariest part. Connor had looked calm the whole time he was pounding Jack. Normal. Connor stared at me. I waited, leaning over Jack, keeping my body between him and Connor.

Connor strode over to his sister, his fingers touching a trail of blood that ran down her chin. He gathered her close.

"Connor?" she sobbed.

"I'm sorry, Sib." He held her tighter.

I reached for my cell phone. This was going to be bad. They'd probably blame Connor. Maybe arrest him. They'd grill Siobhan. They'd question me about the case and Jack and everything. I didn't want Siobhan to have to face that, but I couldn't see a way around it. I called for an ambulance. Then I called the police. If we didn't, they'd wonder. We'd look guilty.

"He's not a bad person," Siobhan cried. "He's not. Really."

I met Connor's eyes. His were so cold I felt the chill. I checked Jack's pulse. Not dead. That was good for us. Sort of. He was breathing okay. His color was bad, except for the bruises that were blooming and the blood coming from his nose.

"The police are on their way," I told them. "An ambulance, too."

"Okay," Connor said.

"Jack?" Siobhan tried to pull away from him, but Connor held on.

"He'll live."

"What?" Siobhan pushed away. She stepped around me and stared down at Jack. I patted her on the back. He was moaning and moving around. Better that she didn't feel guilty about him dying. Something told me she was going to try to take responsibility for the rest.

"Jack," Siobhan cried, rushing to his side. She knelt beside him and held out a hand, stopping just short of touching him. I wanted to pull her away, to get her out of his reach forever. Connor stepped forward, his hands reaching for her, but I held him back.

"Siobhan?" I tried to make my voice gentle. Nonjudgmental. *Get away. Run away. Stay away. He's a bastard and it's not your fault.*

"He was going to hit you." Siobhan's voice quavered. "He was going to hurt you." She started to cry.

"You saved me," I told her.

"I didn't."

"You did. You stood up to him and you saved me. That took real courage, Siobhan." I knelt next to her, putting an arm around Sib's shoulders.

"I'm a coward. I let him." She shuddered.

"You didn't let him do anything. He did it. Him. He's the one responsible. Not you. And when it came down to protecting someone else from him, you came through with flying colors. Didn't she, Connor?"

Connor cleared his throat. "She sure did."

I looked at him and smiled. He hated it. The whole thing. I knew that. But whatever he thought, felt about Jack, he was putting it aside to help his sister.

"He never pushed me before." Siobhan said it quietly, without accusation. Guilt ripped through me.

"Okay." I put my other arm around Siobhan and held her, rocking gently. It might be true. Maybe he'd never physically hurt her until today, but he sure as hell had put plenty of energy into undermining her. Belittling. Demeaning. Hurting her.

"You weren't afraid of him like I was," Siobhan choked.

I wondered if she knew how much that said. He'd never hit her before but she was afraid of him? He'd never hurt her, and she flinched when he was mad or upset? Connor moved away, turning his back to us and staring out the window.

"I was afraid. He had me in a choke hold. If you hadn't pulled him off when you did . . . well, thanks."

"I didn't. I couldn't. He was too strong. He was always too strong."

"You did enough, Siobhan. I was blacking out. You distracted him long enough for me to crawl away. You got injured helping me. I know how hard that was for you."

"It was my fault."

Siobhan's whole body shook, leaning against me. A siren wailed in the distance. Connor's hands clenched and unclenched. If I had to stay in this room for one more minute, I'd grab Jack and finish the job. I had to move. I lifted Siobhan to her feet. Jack moaned and we froze. Connor turned and stepped toward us. I shook my head.

"Connor, we should go outside and wait for the ambulance. Siobhan will need some medical attention. And him." I nodded toward Jack. I didn't look in his direction. The urge to kick him was so strong.

"Yeah." Connor led us out of the room and through the reception area, opening the door and stepping out. I took deep breaths. Siobhan sobbed in my arms.

All those years they'd been treating him like family.

He stole from her. He cheated on her. Then, after he'd taken everything else from her, he hit her. I had to will my feet not to take me back into that room. I stayed between Connor and the door. If I felt like this, I couldn't imagine the control it took for him to keep his hands off Jack.

Red flashing lights strobed across the hedge before a black-and-white pulled into the parking lot. The ambulance was right behind it. The vehicles stopped and a uniformed officer got out, sliding his baton into a holder on his belt. We waited for them to reach the porch.

"Thanks for coming. I'm Commander Connor McNamara. The guy you want is inside." He gestured toward the office.

"I'm Officer Denallo." The cop preceded the paramedics into the office and returned a minute later.

"Do you want to tell me what happened here, sir?" The cop directed the question to Connor but was staring at my neck. His brown eyes moved to the blood on Siobhan's collar.

"His name is Jackson Reed." Connor said. "When I came in he had his hands around my wife's throat, and my sister was slumped against the door. I took him out and then we called the police."

"You took him out, sir?"

"A figure of speech, Officer."

"Which one of you is the wife?"

"I am." I raised my hand. Siobhan clung to me. One of the paramedics emerged from the office and moved toward Siobhan. She clung to me. I patted her back and turned her so the guy could get a good look at the gash on her chin. He smiled at me.

"It's okay, ma'am. I just need to see."

"Go ahead, Sib," Connor soothed, coming up behind her. "He just needs to take a look at you."

"I'm Sara Townley, Officer."

"What happened here, ma'am?"

"That man"—I pointed to Jack, who was being led out of the office by the other paramedic; he glowered—"assaulted me. And his wife. He was choking me to death when my husband showed up."

"He"—the cop pointed toward Jack—"did that to your throat?"

I put a hand up. Just touching the skin made the bruises pulse.

"Yes."

"And he made his wife bleed?"

"Yes."

The cop met Connor's eyes. "Next time we'll be late."

"I'd appreciate that."

Chapter Forty-five

"He didn't do it."

"Goddamn it, Sara. Leave it alone."

I shouldn't have been so direct, I guess. I could understand Connor not wanting to believe it. His sister was in the next room getting stitches and being treated for shock because of what Jack did to her. Her eye was already black from the earlier assault. I was sporting my own bruises. That couldn't be easy for him to see, either. Jack was a bastard. He was a philandering thief and a bully. But he wasn't a murderer.

"Just listen," I implored.

"No," he shouted. "Enough." He raked his hands through his hair. Pacing, he went to the end of the waiting room and back. Good thing the room was empty. Someone might call the cops. We'd had enough of them for one day.

"I know you're upset, but if you just thought about it . . ." I took a step closer, holding my hands out.

"There's nothing to think about." He turned away.

Siobhan was lying in that hospital bed because I'd been blind. Now the blinders were off. I couldn't let Connor keep wearing his. "There is." I pulled at his arm, but he resisted. "Connor, please."

"He hit her. He hit you." The words escaped in a whisper.

Guilt. It killed. I was feeling plenty of my own. I'd as much as drawn a target around Jack. I put my hand on Connor's cheek. It felt hot. I turned his face to me. He closed his eyes.

"Look at me."

"He beat her."

"Connor, look at me."

Tears ran down my cheeks. He opened his eyes and flinched.

"We don't know that. She says he didn't and I believe her. He was mean to her. He yelled and called her names and made her feel bad about herself. All of that is true." Connor tried to pull away but I held on. "Jackson did that. Not you. It's horrible, and we should get him out of her life forever for it."

"She's protecting him."

I shook my head. "I don't think she is. Whatever hold he had on her, she's past it. She freed herself when she tried to save me. She sees him clearly now."

"Then why is she being treated for shock?"

"It *was* a shock. A huge shock. She'd been lying to herself for so long it was hard to face the truth. Especially like that. But if he'd been hitting her before today, she'd have said so. The black eye probably had come from hitting an open medicine cabinet door. Siobhan had been a little free with the mojitos since reality set in. But if Jack had been physical before today, she'd have faced it. There. Right then. Don't get me wrong. He deserves jail. He deserves worse. But because of what he did to Siobhan during their marriage. Not because he hit her this afternoon, and not because he killed Henry DeVries." I reached down and took his hands. "You have to have a little faith in her."

"Faith in her." He jerked away. "Faith in her? She didn't do anything wrong."

"I know. I didn't mean that she did. I said it wrong. She was a victim. I know that. But she's standing up for herself now. She told me Jack didn't. She said it this morning and she said it again to the cops just now. When she called me I jumped to the conclusion. I sold it to her. That was all me. She said she didn't see him. She didn't know who hit her. You've got to believe in her."

"She's making excuses for him. Protecting him. Even after . . ." Connor turned away.

"I know it seems like that, but I don't think that's

what she's doing. She knows him. Really knows him.
She knows he's an arrogant ass who feeds his own ego
by putting other people down. She also knows that he
wouldn't do anything to tarnish his public perception.
Siobhan doesn't think Jack had anything to do with
DeVries. I believe it. You told me he didn't have the
stomach. Everything he's done supports that."

"He could have hired—"

"Yeah. He could have used your family connections
to hire someone. Keep his hands clean. Then how do
you explain this afternoon?"

"He's unraveling."

"Then he goes back to his office and sees patients?"

Connor slumped onto a sofa, his head in his hands. I
sat next to him. "Whoever hurt Siobhan tried to knock
her out first. Jack wouldn't have done that. He couldn't
watch her shrivel that way. That's what turns him on,
Connor. The private demoralization. DeVries was different, too. Impersonal. In public. Neither of those things
fits with what we know about Jack."

"DeVries met John Doe. DeVries was a reporter.
He'd follow up. He'd check out Charles Smiths. He'd
check out Smiths's doctor. It was only a matter of time
before Jack was exposed. For fraud. For being a hack.
What difference would it make? Jack's life would get
flushed. That's plenty of motive. Add means. We certainly
had the money to hire someone. He could use some military connection he met through us. Even dropped the
McNamara name. There are plenty of guys we've served
with who would think it was their duty to help us if they
were convinced we needed it. They'd do it without question and without checking first. Give us plausible deniability. Or Gretchen is big in the prison reform world. Jack
could have met a hundred guys who'd kill their own
mother for cash. Either way, Jack had means."

I was exhausted. I didn't remember ever feeling so
tired. I knelt in front of him. "You're right. Henry De-
Vries was a threat—if he knew about the fraud. A big
if. Even then, I think Jack tried to pay it off. Without
any money missing, what's the worst that could happen
to him? A slap on the wrist? Maybe?"

"He could lose his license. His reputation. Hell, Drez-nik would kill him for that alone. Jack would have to get rid of DeVries."

I couldn't fight him anymore. "Maybe Jack did hire someone to kill him."

"That's a no-go," Blue said from the doorway.

"What?" Connor snapped.

"How's Sib?"

"She's going to be okay." I tried to smile. It hurt. "They're keeping her in overnight. Just to be sure."

"Why a no-go?" Connor asked.

"The money in Reed's office."

I shook my head. "That's not it. Siobhan said Jack cleaned them out. He took a lot more than we found. He could have used it to repay what he overbilled Charles Smiths. It would be simpler than murder."

"Unless there are other patients we don't know about," Connor bit out. "He's a thief. Charles Smiths probably wasn't his only victim. An investigation would have others asking questions. The medical licensing board, the IRS, insurance companies, patients. All wanting to audit his records. Who knows how much he took over the years? It could be millions. Two hundred thou might not be nearly enough for Jack to buy his way out of trouble."

I shrugged. "And DeVries had proof. Okay, maybe it was extortion, not restitution. That's what the money was for." I stood up. It made complete sense.

"That's a negative." Blue killed my flow.

"It makes sense."

"Maybe, but it's still wrong."

"Spit it out, Blue."

"Fingerprints."

"What?" I asked.

"A little bird told a guy who told me that the cops found Reed's stash in the office. It's technically a crime scene, so they did an inventory. Ran a few tests."

"And found?" Connor snapped.

"Fingerprints on the money."

"Whose?" I asked.

"None other than Henry DeVries."

Chapter Forty-six

"**H**e could have bribed him, then taken the money back after the hit."

"Give it up, man. The pieces just don't fit. The brothers in blue swarmed the station after the attack. No way Reed went back. He's an asshole but he's not stupid." Blue leaned back against the ugly green upholstery.

"He wouldn't have kept that much cash in that neighborhood."

"Troj went in the morning after. High-end security. Took him nearly twenty minutes to compromise it. Reed doesn't have those skills."

"Why did Troj go in?"

Blue looked at Connor.

"Right. Of course." Connor told him to. "Deep cache?"

"What?" I asked.

"DeVries was a security nut," Conner began. "Big on government evil and the likelihood that one day Big Brother would be knocking on his door. He was the kind of guy who might have a rainy day fund off the radar for that eventuality. Or something other than cash. Diamonds, guns, whatever. We thought it prudent to get a little background on DeVries after the shooting. Troj went fishing."

"It was a theory. But how would Reed know?" Blue asked. "And it doesn't matter since we didn't find one."

"So if that's the case, how did Henry DeVries's prints end up on the money?" I asked.

"Only one explanation," Connor said.

"Well, don't keep it to yourself." They looked at each other. Men. "Tell me."

"The deejay gave the money to Jack," Connor said.

"Why?"

"Bigger fish."

"I don't . . . Oh. You were right. DeVries was checking it out. He thought he had something big. Valuable. Not on Jack. On Charles Smiths. The money was a bribe. But to Jack, not from him. Whatever DeVries knew, Jack could corroborate. He's probably not that big on doctor-patient confidentiality."

Blue nodded. Connor said nothing.

Connor's parents rushed into the waiting room.

"Where is she? Where's my little girl?" Alyssa asked with wide, scared eyes.

We rose to greet them. "She's in the procedure room. She needs stitches. They'll come tell us when they've put her in a regular room," Connor said. Dougal was ashen. Connor went over and hugged his mother. Blue moved and stood behind Dougal, patting him on the back. I didn't know what to do.

"What did the doctor say?" Alyssa asked.

"She's going to be all right." Connor soothed. "She's got a cut on her chin. It's deep but not life threatening. She's got some other cuts and bruises. She was in shock. They want to keep her in overnight. Physically, she'll heal." No mention of two attacks. Probably just as well.

"Did they catch the bastard?" Dougal asked.

"They arrested Jack."

"Jack?" Alyssa swayed, and Dougal took one of her arms while Connor took the other. Blue disappeared.

"Jack?" Alyssa's voice was a squeak.

"Yes." I didn't know if I should say anything. Connor was letting them think it was all Jack. What did it matter? The cut and the shock were his fault. A second attacker wouldn't change that. He was their son-in-law, and his victim was their daughter. I doubted anything else would matter for a little while.

"I'll kill him," Dougal said.

"He's already in custody," Blue said, coming into the room with two cups of water. He nodded toward the couch, and Dougal took a seat next to his wife. Blue handed them the cups. "The police will deal with him. He won't get away with what he's done."

Dougal stared at Blue. Alyssa waited for Connor to offer confirmation. A muscle twitched along his jaw.

"He'll be punished," Connor said it gently. "Right now Siobhan needs you."

"She's right, Doug. Siobhan's needs have to come first." Alyssa pulled herself together. Her chin rose and she stood up. She pulled her husband to his feet. "No glum faces. No guilt. Just love and support."

Dougal nodded at me. "Is that Jack's work, too?"

Father and son wore matching grim expressions. I could tell they both wanted five minutes alone with Jack.

Dougal's eyes went blank for an instant, then cleared. He took a deep breath and his hands unclenched. He took his wife's arm. "Your mother's right. Siobhan is our first priority. Connor, call Ryan. We didn't want to worry him until we knew what was going on. He needs to be here."

"I'll do it," I offered. "There's the doctor. I know you'll want to talk to him." I pointed. Dougal turned to stare at Connor, then Blue. When he turned back, he looked normal.

Dougal led his wife toward the doctor. The men shook hands and they started moving down the hall.

"Your dad wants Jack dead."

Chapter Forty-seven

"If it's not Jack, who killed the radio star?" Ryan asked, sipping his coffee.

Connor, Ryan, and I walked a block to a nearby coffee shop. Ryan was not good with hospitals.

"I don't know. The mob. An angry advertiser. The liberal left. Pick 'em." I slumped in my chair. My fight with Connor weighed on my mind. I didn't like fighting with him.

"Why didn't he bail?" Ryan stared into his cup. "He had fifty grand in cash, plus whatever else he took from Siobhan. He had the boat. He knew we were gunning for him. Jack's a coward. Why didn't he just blow town?"

"He's not that smart?" I guessed, dipping a French fry in ketchup.

"No. He's smart. He fooled us for years. I didn't have any idea about Siobhan."

"You knew he was cheating on her."

"Yeah, but the rest. Hitting her?"

"You don't believe today was the first time?"

"God, no. Do you?"

It defied logic, but I did believe he'd never hit her before that morning. Even then, it was more of a push. He'd grabbed me, but he'd kept his hands off Siobhan. I chewed thoughtfully. "She says he didn't."

"She said he loved her for fifteen years. She's delusional."

"That's not funny."

"Not even a little bit."

Blue slid into the booth next to me, helping himself to my glass of water.

"I'm sorry about Sib."

"Thanks, man," Connor said.

I pushed the plate of fries toward him. "Whose prints were on the money?"

"I told you. Henry DeVries."

"Who else?"

"Jack. He got printed for his license. They match."

"And?"

"And nothing. Jack and the DB."

"Don't you think that's weird?"

"How?"

"No bank teller. No grocery clerk. No gas station attendant. Fifty thousand dollars and there are only two sets of prints on them?"

"Connor told me they were still bundled," Ryan said.

"Okay. So maybe some machine counts the bills and puts the little tape around them. Somebody handed the money to DeVries. Somebody with fingers. Who?"

Ryan stretched his arms along the back of the booth. "Gloves."

"Or they've been wiped." Blue ate another fry. "Who?"

"Better question is why," Connor said.

"Why what?" I asked.

"Why wipe your fingerprints off? You wouldn't if you were just some cog in the monetary system. No need. You'd have a perfectly reasonable explanation."

"The absence of any of those prints means someone thought they wouldn't have an explanation. They wiped the explainable prints when they wiped their own." Ryan leaned forward and put his arms on the table.

"Why would our mystery money launderer need to hide their connection to that cash?" I asked.

Silence. I could hear the wheels grinding.

"Who has access to the safe?" Blue asked.

"It's not Siobhan," Ryan protested.

"Of course not," I agreed.

"Confirm. If she wanted Jack wounded, she'd have teed him up for Rock. Or Trouble, here."

"Why do you keep calling me that?"

"It's your call sign."

"You gave me a call sign?"

"Connor did."

"He named me Trouble?"

Blue and Ryan exchanged a glance. Neither one of them met my eyes.

"Trouble. He thinks I'm trouble."

Ryan rolled his eyes.

"Who had access?" Blue brought us back to the point at hand. I'd have to discuss my moniker with Connor later.

"Jack and Siobhan. The receptionist maybe," Ryan guessed.

I shook my head. "No. She didn't seem close to the boss. Maybe the safe company?"

"Probably not," Blue said, then stopped.

The waitress came and refilled our water glasses. She left the check.

"You usually set your own code."

"It was obvious." Blue turned to look at me. Ryan kept his head down. I held my hands up. "If someone wanted in to the safe and knew Jack well enough, he could do what we did and figure out the code."

"Did he lock his door? Not the one to the street. The one to his actual office?"

Blue looked from me to Ryan and back.

"Probably." I sighed. "Yes. Okay. He did."

Blue shook his head. He laughed softly. "Rock and the Troublemakers. You should take your act on the road."

"He didn't tell you we were there?"

"I was not in that office. No one saw me in that office. No one can testify that I was in that office." Ryan was all innocent.

"He was the lookout." I outed Ryan.

"Figured."

"So it's just Jack and Siobhan, and we know my sister didn't have anything to do with it."

"I'm thinking girlfriend," Blue said.

I took a bite of French fry. It was cold and rubbery. I put the other half back on the plate and pushed it away.

Ryan's face went stormy. "Yeah," he snarled. "That fits."

"And if Siobhan hadn't picked that moment to get her dander up? What if we hadn't followed through right away?"

No one spoke.

"It plays out nearly the same," Blue said. "If Jack doesn't run, he becomes the next Pablo or Maria." He looked at me. "Careful planning yields no provocation. No witnesses. Every male McNamara a viable suspect." Blue stared into my eyes. "Your case, your fault."

"Jack gets beaten up or killed. Siobhan takes sides. The family is caught in the cross fire. I bring death and destruction and ruin to all things McNamara. Lily gets revenge in capital letters. Against everyone."

"Well, if Jack and Lily are really hitting the sheets," Blue said, "the honeymoon is definitely over."

Chapter Forty-eight

"**I**t's not jealousy."

"Lily is not out there plotting against me. Or you."

Connor looked tired. Exhausted. He'd spent the night at the hospital, sending me home after midnight. With an escort, naturally. The mysterious Trojan turned out to be a dark-haired, dark-eyed, quiet guy very big on *ma'am*. He felt like the Secret Service, except I wasn't Jackie O.

"I know you don't want to believe it."

"Sara," he warned. He went into the bathroom and closed the door. I could hear the shower run. I guess I wasn't invited.

I went to make coffee. When Connor came into the kitchen, I handed him a mug. He grimaced but took it. He set it on the counter and put his arms around me, resting his head on top of mine.

"I'm sorry."

"Tough night," I said. "Don't worry about it."

He kissed my forehead and let go, saluting me with the coffee cup.

"Are they going to let her go home today?"

"Yeah."

"Did you get any sleep?"

"Not much. You?"

"Me either." We leaned back against the counter, side by side. The silence dragged. It was uncomfortable. Maybe our first really uncomfortable silence since we'd gotten married. A milestone. Hurray.

"I know you don't want to hear this, Connor. . . ."

He shook his head, closing his eyes. "Not now."

"He had to have help. He doesn't have what it takes to kill someone. He'd need to import a spine. Who has that degree of commitment? Of malice?"

"Lily may be a bitch, but she'd never sink that low."

"Connor, just listen—"

"Goddamn it, Sara," he exploded.

I stepped back. I'd seen him annoyed, frustrated, and scared. He'd never shouted. Not really.

"Jack couldn't—"

"No more," he yelled.

I stopped. Held my breath. I wanted to stop. I wanted to forget about all of it. Henry DeVries on the sidewalk leaking blood. Pablo Esteban in a hospital bed with his daughter crying beside him. Maria with her shotgun wounds. John Doe, desperate and scared. But I couldn't. Just because I couldn't let it go didn't mean I had to drag Connor along with me. His sister was hurt, inside and out. His family needed him. He needed to be there.

"You're right," I said. "I'm sorry."

He froze. I didn't blame him. Everywhere we turned, more drama. "I shouldn't have yelled at you."

"It's okay."

"It's not." He put an arm around me and kissed me on the forehead. I swallowed back the tears. "I love you."

"I love you, too." I hugged him hard, then stepped away. "Are you headed back to the hospital? Ryan is picking me up, so you'll have the car if you need it."

"Yeah, I want to be there when they release her."

What he really meant was that he wanted to make sure Jack wasn't home when Siobhan got there. Who knew how fast he could get bail? "Give her my love."

"Come with me."

I shook my head. "I don't want her to feel even a little uncomfortable. She'll want just family."

"You're family."

I gripped my hands behind my back, squeezing until the pain freed my breath. "Not yet, but I'm getting there."

Chapter Forty-nine

I tossed on the couch. I couldn't bring myself to go into the bedroom to try to sleep. Connor was right. Lily. Ridiculous to think of her killing people. Cutting with sarcasm, of course, but not killing. Not her. It was even crazier to think of her as a bomb maker. Connor was where he needed to be and it wasn't like I had concrete proof. He'd leave his family to ride to my rescue and I might once again be wrong. I hated her. I wanted her to be the source of all evil, so I was seeing it. She couldn't shoot a guy from a moving car. Or blow up a car. That kind of expertise did not come at the Junior League.

I sat up. She told me. Sitting in this room, Lily said it. Burglars, arsonists, and killers. I left a message. Twenty minutes later, I got a return text. One line. Time and address. No cute emoticons or incomprehensible acronyms. I started to sweat. Not calling Connor, okay. Meeting possible killers without backup—really, really stupid. I dialed but had to leave a message. Didn't anyone answer their phone anymore?

I couldn't wait for a call back. I borrowed Connor's keys and took the BMW to the meet. Another warehouse. I wasn't lucky with warehouses.

"Where are you?" Blue sounded calm.

I gave him the address. "How long will it take you to get here?"

"Twenty minutes. Can you be seen from the windows?"

I looked up. The windows were high. Small. "Hurry," I told him.

"You need to wait outside, Sara."

I clicked off. He'd call Connor. I knew he would. Twenty minutes. I checked my watch. She'd be gone by then. I could feel it. I didn't have proof. I had gut. And now it was telling me if I wasn't on time for this, she'd realize coming into the open was a mistake. She'd go back into the shadows and let the chips fall. Too many people had paid too high a price for me to allow that. I got out of the car, touched the small of my back, and rubbed at the wetness pooling there. I moved toward the building.

One second I was in the bright sunshine; the next it seemed like I was in the dark. In the cold. My sweat froze. I kept my back toward the wall and moved deeper into the shadows. The click sounded like a shot.

"Hello, Gretchen."

She gestured with the gun off to my right. I couldn't see well in the gloom. I raised my hands and she grabbed me from the left side. Shocked at how fast she moved, I turned toward her and she hit me. Hard. I was dizzy and nauseated. The pain radiated in my head. She grabbed me by the hair and jerked me upright, pushing me hard toward the center of the space. I tried to keep my balance but fell onto my hands and knees in a shaft of light. The room spun around me. I gagged. I lurched toward her, and she kicked me in the ribs on my exposed side. The blow to my head was disorienting me. I rolled away.

"If you try that again, I'll shoot you."

"Shoot me? As in personally? Or are you just going to release another psychotic and point him in my direction?" Sagging and trying to catch my breath, I held my ribs. Damn, that hurt. I blinked at her. "The apple doesn't far fall from the tree."

"What the hell is that supposed to mean?"

"I thought it was Lily. The violent half of the team. One brain, one brute."

"Making Jackson the brain? I don't think so." She

moved closer. I could see her more clearly. The same smugness as her niece.

"Does he know you're in love with him?" Psychoanalyzing the shrink. Well, whatever bought me enough time for Blue to show.

"Quite the little amateur—and totally wrong. Who have you told?"

"Connor."

She shook her head and extended her arm, aiming. "Don't lie to me. If you'd told Connor he'd be here. You would have told someone. A failsafe. You're weak, not stupid."

"No matter what Lily thinks?" I guessed.

"Still trying to connect her? Don't bother. She's my sister's child. Not the deep end of the gene pool." She looked bored. Pointing a gun at my head, planning to kill me, not stimulated enough.

"She's deep enough to pique Jack's interest. I bet that really stung, huh, Gretchen? Him sleeping with her?"

"You don't have a clue, do you? Of course not. I don't care who Jackson sleeps with. Or doesn't sleep with. Lily either."

She smiled. I was dead. She stepped close enough to touch the muzzle of the gun to my head. "It doesn't matter if you told someone. You don't know anything."

I closed my eyes.

"I've really got to start listening to that woman's instincts." Connor stepped out from behind the pillar, his gun pointed at Gretchen's forehead. "Sorry, I'm late, babe. It won't happen again."

Gretchen yanked my head back by my hair, digging the muzzle of the gun into the underside of my chin hard enough to make me groan. I wouldn't give the bitch the satisfaction of crying. I wouldn't. She was pulling my hair out by the roots and I could taste blood in my mouth, but I wasn't going to be her victim. Connor's eyes flashed. For a second I thought I'd imagined it. He didn't react. Ever. He was Mr. Cool in a Crisis. He was here to save me. To save us. He'd do it. I knew he'd do it.

"Put the gun down," Gretchen ordered.

Gretchen moved behind me. Connor's gun moved a fraction of an inch.

"Shoot her," I moaned.

Gretchen yanked on my hair and pushed the gun into my throat. I gagged.

"No," Connor said. To me or to her, I wasn't sure. Why didn't he just shoot her? Gretchen shifted, dragging me with her. Connor moved slowly. They were dancing. He was waiting. He must have a plan. Or backup. Blue or one of the other guys. He must be waiting for them to be in place. It was going to be okay. My heart rate slowed. I tried to smile at him.

"I'll kill her." Gretchen twisted her hold, eliciting another feeble moan. I'd make her pay.

"Then you'll be begging me to kill you long before I do," Connor said.

Gretchen gave a short laugh. "No, you won't. You'll put the gun down. You'll put it down because if you don't, your precious Sara will be dead, and it will be your fault. The blood will be on your hands, Connor."

Her words were brash but her hand trembled faintly. She wasn't as sure as she wanted Connor to think. She could shoot me at any moment. Before Connor's plan had a chance. I had to help him somehow. I let my weight sag, dragging on her arms. She yanked me, her hand grabbing more hair near my scalp. It burned.

"Looks like we've got a standoff then." Connor shifted his weight, easing an inch farther right.

"I don't think so. I think there's nothing you won't do to save her. You're very predictable, Connor. You have a caretaker personality. You'll do anything you have to do to keep the people under your protection safe. You'll even give your own life."

"If I put the gun down, I'm giving her life, too. You said it yourself, Doctor," Connor mocked her with the title. "I'll never give you that."

"You won't have to. We'll just wait for the police. You did call the police, didn't you? Don't bother to lie. Like I said, you are so predictable. She didn't call them. You probably know that."

She was close, but wrong. I hadn't called the cops. I'd called Blue.

"I'm surprised you're looking forward to the police. They won't help you. They know everything. There's probably already a warrant for your arrest."

"Don't be ridiculous. Jackson was—is—an accomplished liar. A manipulator. He was a thief. You know that, Connor. A brute who was violent with his own wife. Why, just this morning I bailed him out of jail for domestic violence, of all things. I understand he blamed your wife. Of course, my relationship with him has all but dissolved over time. I've been very busy with my new career as an expert. I no longer actively participate with Jack in the practice. I barely know him at this stage in our careers." She yanked on my hair.

"Exactly my point. He wasn't the doctor of record when the Smithses were murdered. You were. That's what this whole thing was about from the beginning. What's that old saying? It's the coverup that will get you."

Gretchen squeezed and I gagged. My brain wasn't getting enough oxygen, and I couldn't seem to figure out what Connor was saying. What coverup?

"Shut up."

"It had to be the kid. Nothing else plays. When did Charles Smiths tell you he killed his parents?"

"If you repeat that slander—" Gretchen hissed.

"Repeat it? I'm taking out a billboard. The great Gretchen Dreznik's shining therapeutic example murders his parents in cold blood. What did you do? Clean him up and sedate him before you called the cops? Pay the maid to lie? There had to be some reason she could suddenly afford to go back to Mexico. Then you put pressure on the cops to close the case, write it off as random."

The gun twitched, moved off my face enough for me to see the barrel in my peripheral vision, then slammed back against my temple.

"Nice try, Connor. But I'm not distracted. You don't have any proof Charles Smiths killed his parents."

"I have proof Charles Smiths isn't Charles Smiths."

"Which can be laid at Jack's door. He was a thief,"

Gretchen continued. "He stole from his patients. That certainly didn't happen on my watch. He tried to cover it up. Do you know he killed a witness? Assaulted another? An old man. Isn't that terrible? Of course you do. Your family provided the military connections he needed to find an assassin. Why, you're as much to blame as he is, really."

"True. Neither one of us had Pablo Esteban beaten. Or orchestrated the murder of the maid or Henry DeVries. That was all you." Connor sidled a little to the right. I saw a flash above him on a catwalk. It might have been the sun, or maybe I was finally passing out.

"Are you accusing me of physically assaulting someone? Of gunning down that radio man or murdering some poor Mexican woman? I'm a sixty-year-old professional woman with an impeccable reputation. Now you're just being ridiculous." Gretchen tsked and yanked my head back. I saw stars.

"Edward Abernathy," I gasped. "You set loose. Not Jack."

She smacked the gun against my head and pain exploded. Connor took a step forward but stopped when Gretchen dug the gun into the side of my head.

"I don't set people loose. A board of medical experts does that. A board, I might add, of which I am not a member. I do have a passing acquaintanceship with several of the members. I am the leading psychiatrist in the area, after all, and I am familiar with the chairman, Dr. Jackson Reed."

I dragged my foot underneath me. Connor was buying time. He had to be. I didn't know what he was up to, but I wanted to be ready. I'd gotten the wrong bad guy, the wrong theory, and no proof once. I was pretty much out of mistakes.

"Jack was the one who introduced Edward Abernathy as Charles Smiths on the night of the banquet. I couldn't be expected to recognize him. After all, Jack's been his treating physician for fifteen years. I hadn't seen Charles since he was a very young man."

"You manipulated Jack," Connor said.

"If that were true, why would he pay it all back? The

money. You do know Jack paid the bank? What more proof do you need?"

"Jack was trying to stop the investigation into fraud. That's why he paid it back," Connor said.

"That is a motive for a lot of things, I suppose."

I coughed.

"You don't believe it, Sara? Well, maybe Jack will be able to convince a jury that Edward Abernathy was the manipulative one. Edward Abernathy is a sociopath with a long history of violence. Guns, explosives, knives. Jack could say, quite convincingly, that he was just a pawn. Edward threatened him. Made him share all the intimate details of Charles Smiths's life and background in the same way he scared Jack into using his chairmanship to secure Edward's release from the psychiatric hospital. Once released, Jack had to do anything he said or someone would get hurt. His wife perhaps?"

Connor's face looked grim. I couldn't tell if he thought Gretchen was just spinning the story Jack might try or if she was threatening Siobhan. Probably both. She was crazier than either John Doe or Edward Abernathy if she thought Connor wouldn't do everything in his power to make sure that didn't happen. Everything.

"Edward has been very efficient so far. Of course, one couldn't rely on such precision forever. Someone else might get hurt." She pulled my hair so hard I saw stars.

"Plan B is blame it all on Edward Abernathy," Connor stated.

Gretchen loosened her grip to get a better hold. I tipped my head. Her grip on my hair ended up a few inches from my scalp. Then I let my weight sag against her. *C'mon, Blue.*

"No one is going to buy that."

"Unfortunately, the mentally ill are often misunderstood. So, too, are adulterers and thieves. Once a criminal and all that. The police, the public, they're like you. Drones on little wheels, spinning their lives away without any perception of how insignificant they really are. Naturally, you wouldn't understand. You have so little personal understanding, don't you, Connor?"

If I could just tip my head forward, maybe I could

bite her. Hard. Would she shoot me right away? I
pushed back against her, trying to get my face behind
the barrel of the gun.

"You're just like Jackson," Gretchen continued.

"Siobhan is the only thing we ever had in common."

I caught a glint of light behind Connor. I was passing
out. I was seeing the light.

"Both you and Jackson are narcissistic personalities.
You are convinced that you are the central point of your
relationships," Gretchen said. "It is a delusion. Jackson
would say that he made all his own choices. He would
insist that he is in control of his career, his marriage, his
life. You think that also. But she knew."

Gretchen let go of my hair. She wrapped her arm
around my throat and jerked me upright. Air. I needed
air. I clawed at her arm. She jammed the gun into my
temple and I saw stars.

"It's okay, Sara. Just hold still," Connor said.

"Everything he ever had. His entire career. I gave it
to him. And I can take it away. I always knew one day
I would. That was the point, after all. Whenever, wherever. I would decide."

I stopped fighting. Let the darkness come. As soon as
my fingers stopped digging into her flesh, she loosened her
hold a little. I gulped air, leaning heavily against Gretchen.

"You're the same. Lily's the perfect example. Do you
think it was coincidence? Her sleeping with that idiot?
The wedding called off? I had Jackson. Siobhan was an
irrelevant mouse but you were a complication. Which is
why you couldn't be my family. I wouldn't allow it. You
think you're in control here, Connor? You're not. I am."
The barrel of the gun pushed upward. "I am in control."

In my peripheral vision I saw her finger tighten on the
trigger. *No. Please, God. I'll do anything.*

"Gretchen, please. Okay. I'll do whatever you want.
You don't have to hurt her."

"If you don't put your gun down right now, I will hurt
her and it will be your fault. You'll watch her die and
know you killed her. Can you live with that, Connor?
With knowing that you are the reason she's dead?"

Gretchen said it all very conversationally, like they

were chatting about the weather. Did she think he was stupid? She was going to kill me anyway. And if Connor put down his gun, she'd kill him, too. I let my head flop back. For a second I met Connor's eyes. Then I closed mine. I went limp.

"Okay, Gretchen. You win."

"Put it on the ground."

No. No. No. No. Keep the gun. She'll shoot you. She'll kill you. Keep the gun.

"I am in control."

I felt the barrel of the gun move off my cheek. With all my might I slammed my head back, trying to break her nose. Gretchen gave a strangled sound and then I was free. I rolled away. A gun went off. I flinched and scrambled toward the boxes. I was lifted off the ground and away from Gretchen. Connor. Thank God. I looked back. Blue had her arms pinned behind her back, her gun lying on the floor. Another guy had his weapon pointed at her head. Tex? Troj? Whoever it was, I wanted to kiss him.

"Sara?" Connor pushed my hair back from my face. Even that tension made my scalp sing. "Baby, can you hear me?"

I rubbed at the back of my head. "Man, that hurt. It looks so easy on *SmackDown*." I rested against his chest. His heart pounded. I kissed him over it. "That was scary. Let's not do that again."

"Roger that."

I looked up at Blue. He'd strapped Gretchen's hands together with something and had her on her knees. She spit and kicked. Blue and Tex kept out of hocking range, watching her like the circus sideshow she'd become.

"Stay here." Connor rose and stepped toward the woman.

"You have no idea what you've done. No jury will convict me. I've given them their guilty party. Their evil-doer. Any jury will see that. Everything you've done is for nothing."

"I don't know about that," he said. "There's always personal satisfaction."

Connor strode toward her, and Gretchen's head exploded.

Chapter Fifty

They split us up to question us. I got Montoya and Peter Christenson, former attorney general of the United States. My in-laws had juice.

"Turning into a regular little Typhoid Mary, aren't you, Sara?" Montoya asked. "Everywhere you go, people die."

He didn't say it meanly, and I couldn't really dispute it. I was turning San Diego into Cabot Cove.

"Refer to my client as Ms. Townley. Drop the sarcasm and ask real questions or this interview is over, Detective." Christenson was dressed like a golfer. He had the requisite silver hair and James Earl Jones baritone. He didn't have the same stick up his behind as my boss.

"What he said." I smiled at my lawyer. He smiled back, shaking his head slightly. "Although I'd like to take this opportunity to tell you I'm not convinced you didn't have a hand in the maid ending up a floater, so you might not want to throw stones."

Montoya looked shocked. "What?"

"There's a rumor going around that you've got political ambitions. Any chance you kept a certain prominent local doctor or a generous donor up-to-date on your current caseload? Ever mention the name Maria Gonzales? She's dead, you know. The only place to get her name was the police files."

"What the hell do you think you're talking about?"

"Sara," my lawyer warned with a twinkle in his eye, "technically he is the one doing the interviewing. Maybe we should let him get on with it so we can leave?"

"Maybe then he'll have time to teach you about libel, too?" Montoya spat.

"Slander," Peter Christenson corrected. "Alleged slander, at that."

"Why were you meeting with Henry DeVries, Sara?"

"She's not going to answer that."

"She already told me."

"Then why are you wasting our time?"

"Good one," I congratulated him. I looked at Montoya. "Your turn."

"What was the relationship between Gretchen Dreznik and Henry DeVries?"

"Beyond the scope," Christenson said.

I put my hands in the pockets of the orange jumpsuit. I wasn't under arrest. They'd taken my clothes as evidence. Just as well. I never wanted to see them again. It was funny. Funny strange, not funny ha-ha. Two hours ago I'd tossed my cookies because of a dead body. Now I was cracking jokes. Bad ones, but still. Good thing I had the expensive suit to do my talking. Who knew what I might say?

"Are you aware that hundreds of thousands of dollars were embezzled from the account of a patient of Dr. Dreznik?"

"Beyond the scope."

"You were at the bank branch where the bogus account was set up. You were seen in the company of the man accused of the crime."

"Accused?" I asked. Were they after John?

Christenson patted my hand. "Has a warrant been issued on this alleged crime?"

"I'm not at liberty to say." Montoya threw the cold shoulder back at my lawyer. He winked at me.

"Then we won't be speculating."

"You know, Sara, your husband played nicer. Then again, the navy doesn't have the same protections as we do in here. Connor isn't going to be able to take the Fifth. Not with his own people. If you don't get your story out, well, he's going to be left holding the bag. Or his friends will. Not everyone can afford Mr. Christenson's services. In fact, members of the armed services aren't always entitled to counsel at any price. Isn't that correct, Counselor?"

"They didn't—" I started.

"Are you arresting her?" The lawyer gripped my hand tighter.

I bit my lip. They couldn't have lawyers? They couldn't remain silent?

"Not at this time."

"Then we're leaving." Peter rose and held my chair.

"Up to you, Sara." Montoya rose. "If you're not willing to talk to me, I can't help you."

"Except for the snarkiness, Detective, I appreciate that you're just doing your job. You have to understand. That dead person everywhere I go thing is no joke. My husband's mad. His friends aren't thrilled, and the shrinks are loonier than the patients. The guy I was sent here to find by my tightwad of a boss is still missing, and I'm being stalked by a Labrador retriever. Don't take this the wrong way, but you're not even the scariest person I've met today."

"No." Peter clucked. "That would be me."

Chapter Fifty-one

"**Y**ou bitch!" Lily screamed, and charged me, claws extended.

The cops escorting me from the building stopped to arrest her. If I were having the day she was having, I'd be a little out there, too. Lily's married boyfriend was out on bail and facing the loss of his earning capacity when the medical board investigated his billing practices. Her boyfriend's wife, a scion of society, now knew about the affair and would probably have something to say as soon as she stopped burning her adulterous soon-to-be-former spouse's clothes. Her financially supportive but deeply antisocial aunt was looking at multiple counts of conspiracy to commit murder and murder for hire. To cap it off, the woman sleeping with the best thing that ever happened to her got to watch as she was taken away in silver handcuffs that clashed with the engagement ring she'd taunted me with. Connor, cleverly, said nothing.

I'd spent twice as long being questioned by the police as any of them. It paid to be a choirboy. It helped that none of their guns matched, the bullets and the blood-spray pattern made it clear that all of us had been standing too close to have shot Gretchen. The same could be said of me, of course, minus the weapon, but somehow my general demeanor had screamed *psycho killer on the loose*, whereas the naval contingent looked like angels. Tex and Blue were gone by the time Christenson walked me out.

"Let's get out of this sun." Peter Christenson moved

us down the stairs. Two limos stood at the curb. Drivers stood next to open passenger doors.

The driver at the front car touched the brim of his hat as I slid into the backseat. I'd seen smaller restaurants. It smelled new. Which was a nice change from me. I smelled old.

The lawyer leaned into the car. "The police know not to question you without me present, but don't talk to anyone about this, Sara. You and Connor can't be called to testify against each other, but don't speak on this subject with his family or the other members of his team. It will compromise them."

I offered him my hand. "The next time I'm arrested for something, I'm definitely calling you."

He smiled. "The next time I want to see a young woman under investigation for murder body-slam the cops in their own ring, I'll be sure to come. Technically, I'm retired, but it's nice to keep my hand in. Don't trust Montoya."

"I'm sticking with name, rank, and serial number from now on."

"Yeah, right," Connor muttered.

"Well, Gertie was right. You're a firecracker, and this has been a most interesting day."

"Thanks, Pete."

"Anytime. Oh, and she asked me to give this to you." He handed an envelope to Connor. "Said it belonged to you."

The door closed and the car pulled away. "Grandma Gertie sent him?"

"They're old, uh, friends."

Gertie had to be ninety. Peter a suave seventy, max. "Get 'em young, train 'em right. Go, Gertie."

"Yeah." He opened the envelope and tipped the contents into his palm. Round, shiny. More carats than Peter Rabbit needed, and it made Lily's look like a chip.

Connor held it out.

I shook my head. "Thanks, no, I'm trying to cut back."

He swallowed a laugh.

"Any word on John?" I asked.

He put an arm around me and I snuggled into him.
"No."

"Any luck finding the shooter?"

"Edward Abernathy, aka Charles Smiths, was found twenty minutes before Montoya let you go. Duct-taped hands and feet in a maintenance shed less than a mile from the warehouse."

"He didn't get far. Any evidence tying him to Gretchen's murder?"

"Murder weapon. Fingerprints. Gunpowder residue. Might get lucky with his house, too, now that the police know where to look."

I tipped my head back to look up at him. "What made the police look in that particular maintenance shed?"

"Anonymous tip." He kissed my nose.

"A team sport?"

"Something like that."

"I don't suppose anyone asked him why he blew up Blue's truck?"

"It might have come up. Officially, no comment. Unofficially, he's got a couple of nasty dog bites he might have acquired while trying to manhandle somebody who wasn't interested in going somewhere while we were distracted."

"Good for Pavarotti. Is there any chance Abernathy got to John after we were at his place? Charles, I mean. I suppose I can't keep calling him John."

"The guy's smoke. I've seen Rangers with brighter trails."

"Not SEALs?"

He kissed my head. "Never. Although we could use that dog."

I chuckled. After today, it felt odd. "How did Abernathy get the shot off? Or get away, for that matter?"

"Someone went in before her backup was in place. Blue and I got there first. Gretchen already had you. We didn't get the chance to look for secondary targets. Tex and Troj were just coming into the field when the scene went loud. Their primary mission was cover. As soon as we were secure, they cleaned up."

"Abernathy didn't get far."

"They know what they're doing."

I sighed. "I got her killed."

"No. She released that thing into the world. She brought him there to kill us." Connor tucked me closer against him.

"Why didn't he? I stood in the middle of that room. You, too. If he could kill Henry DeVries from a moving car, he could kill us."

He squeezed harder. "Any guy who could make the shot on DeVries didn't miss when he took out Gretchen. Whatever she thought, his target was her. We were lucky, not good."

"Any chance you'll be good and I'll get lucky?"

He pushed the button to close the slide.

"Always a chance, Trouble."

Chapter Fifty-two

"**T**his makes no sense." I sank down on to the sofa. "I had the lab double-check. John Doe can't be Charles Smiths. According to the medical examiner's report that your pal Peter managed to get us, both parents were B positive. The sample was A neg," Blue said.

"How can they be sure it's Charles's DNA?" I pulled my legs under the old T-shirt of Connor's I was wearing. I would have put it on in response to the knock on the door except people had once again stopped knocking. Connor had pulled on briefs and nothing else. Blue was fully dressed.

"Montoya took it from some silverware in the apartment. The only fingerprints in the place were yours, Rock's, and one unidentified. No match to the original report done on Charles Smiths for Esteban, but an eight-point match to the flea collar. Two types of saliva, one human, one canine.

"The dog's matched my competition there." Connor read from the report, nodding at Pavarotti, who was pushing her head between us on the couch.

I stroked the dog's fur. She yodeled and closed her eyes.

"Meaning John's probably not a murderer, either. He didn't kill his parents because they weren't his parents. Not even as part of some mental health problem. And he didn't have a reason to kill the maid. Or even a reason to know there was a maid."

"You were right about him, I think. He was troubled, not dangerous."

"Where is the real Charles Smiths?" I asked. "And who is John Doe?"

"Reed's claiming he didn't know John Doe wasn't Charles Smiths." Blue shrugged.

"Reed is sticking to his story," Blue said. "Abernathy was released on a decision by the prison medical review board based on good faith. It was only after he was free that Abernathy approached and threatened Jack. He wanted to steal an identity so he could get enough money to leave the country. According to Jack, Abernathy wanted to use one of Jack's rich patients because they were all mentally unstable and wouldn't be believed if they did complain. Jack went along because he was afraid for his life and his family."

"So Jack was just protecting Siobhan and not afraid he'd get caught bilking his patients?" I asked.

Blue shrugged.

"What does he say about the real Charles Smiths?" Connor asked.

"He says John Doe is the real deal. That he went on walkabout. That Gretchen convinced him if anyone found out that his star patient ran away he'd be held responsible. Then Abernathy showed up looking to become somebody else. Two birds with one stone." Blue scratched his chin. "I don't know. Hate to say it, but I'm buying it."

"The blood test says different," Connor protested.

"I'm not saying it's true. I'm saying Reed's not lying. Not about this, anyway."

"He's lying about everything," I cried.

"Yeah, but it's all shades of gray stuff. This one is a fact that can be checked. He's a doctor. He gets blood-type analysis. He wouldn't bullshit something that could bite him in the ass like that," Blue said.

"Do you believe that?" I asked Connor.

"I don't know, babe," Connor said. "Jack's not an original thinker. Maybe Gretchen manipulated him into switching them, because why quit a winner?"

"She'd done it before."

"Yeah, maybe."

"Think John's another patient? From back then, I

mean? He definitely has issues, but maybe he didn't before they got hold of him.''

"I don't know," Connor said.

"What do you think happened to the real Charles Smiths?" I asked.

"He was a messed-up kid. He killed his parents. The doctors who were supposed to help him had their own agendas. We might never know what happened to him," Connor said.

Blue smiled. "John Doe has been Smiths the longest. I say that makes him the real Charles Smiths. The dog'll vouch for him."

I smiled back. "I like that." Pavarotti slapped her head against my hand.

"Either way, Jack's laying it all off on Gretchen," Connor added.

"That's fair. She was planning on blaming him for everything," I said. Connor stared. "I'm not defending him. I'm just saying. I thought it was going to be Lily. John said 'she' the night of the polygraph, and Lily definitely had violent tendencies. She threatened me that day."

"What day?" Connor asked.

I gulped.

"The morning she used her key to wait for me. Blue didn't tell you?"

"Not the details." Connor looked thoughtful.

So Blue didn't tell him everything. Just as well. Less yelling all around. Blue rolled his eyes at me.

A couple of hours later, Pavarotti started her aria. Loud. Up and down her vocal register. Connor reached around me and lifted a sneaker from the floor. He flung it at the closed bedroom door. The song stopped. The dog breathed loudly in the hall, Connor breathed in my ear. I moved to get out of bed. He tightened his hold.

"She's not sleeping with us."

"Jealous of another woman? Really?"

"Yes."

"Oh, honey, that's sweet." I leaned over and kissed

him. He slid a leg over mine and opened his mouth, kissing me with a lot of wet heat.

"Um." I sighed.

He wrapped around me, rolling me beneath him. Warm and hard, and I pushed him off.

"What?" He lifted his head. His hair stood up. My work, I suspected.

"Can't you hear her?"

"Huh?"

Pavarotti was up to glass-shattering. "Maybe she has to go out."

"I'll go." He released me and reached for his jeans.

"No, that's okay." I dropped a T-shirt over my head and went to get my tennis shoe.

"Not while there are still crazies out there."

"There will always be crazies out there."

"Exactly."

"Fine. We'll go together." I opened the bedroom door. Pavarotti jumped up, nearly head height. "Sorry, girl, didn't realize we'd reached the red zone."

I patted her. She paced to the front door and back. Connor clipped her leash to her collar and we trooped to the elevator. Pavarotti practiced scales all the way to the ground floor. When the elevator doors opened, she pulled us to the front door.

"Didn't we take her out earlier?" I asked, trying to remember.

"Yeah. After dinner before . . ." He leaned down and kissed me.

I wrapped my arms around his middle and pushed the outer door open. Pavarotti yanked hard on the leash and was free. She ran to the walkway and down to the heavy shrubbery. In a pool of moonlight she stopped. The man stepped away from the shadows, his hand reaching for the dog. Pavarotti's tail pounded like a metronome.

"Jo—Charles?" I asked, nearly calling him John. He'd been Charles for years. If he wanted to be Charles, who was I to say different?

"Do you know me?"

"Yes." As well as anyone did.

"Does he know me?" John pointed at Connor. He nodded.

"Okay." John turned away.

"Charles?" I called after him.

"Yeah?"

"Do you know who else knows you?" I asked.

His hand reached out and grabbed fur, stroking. The dog vocalized low in her throat.

I brushed at the tear that slid down my cheek. "Your dog."

Read on for a sneak peek at the next
book in the Animal Instinct Mystery
series by Gabriella Herkert.

Available August 2009 wherever books
are sold or at penguin.com

"Not again," I sighed.

I knelt and reached for the man's wrist. Cold, pulseless. I used the beam of my flashlight to get a better look, then was sorry I had. Russ retched behind me.

"No. You are absolutely, positively not going to—" I jumped up.

Russ's breakfast spewed with the force of a geyser. I dodged but still got sprinkled with postconsumption huevos rancheros. The dead guy did worse. His flannel sleeve and the side of his face were doused with bile and eggs. A clump of green pepper stuck to one staring eye. Propped on his knees by the pitchfork sticking out of his chest, he looked like a praying Cyclops. Russ burped loudly. I danced a couple additional steps away from the mess.

"Sorry," he said, wiping his mouth with a snowy hand-kerchief. "I'm not good with"—he gestured toward the body—"reality."

I fixed him with the flashlight beam and he blinked, putting up a hand in defense. Russ's clothes were pristine. Brand-new down vest, pressed jeans, starched shirt, and Coach belt. Brushed-suede hiking boots that, except for the walk from the car to the barn, had never seen anything but concrete. Tall and blond, his autumn Seattle pallor replaced with a tanning-salon bronze, he could have been on a Ralph Lauren photo shoot. If he weren't my best friend, I'd hate him for it.

Not me. I was a vomit-dappled disaster in stained jeans, faded hooded sweatshirt, and battered running shoes. I clicked off the flashlight and put it into the front pouch of my sweatshirt. I pulled Russ toward the gloom outside the barn and away from the smell of horse apples and regurgitated breakfast.

"Just as well. You don't want to get too used to this sort of thing," I said, shaking my head. I hit *6 on my cell phone. I had the police on speed dial. What had my life become?

"He looks really dead," Russ said.

"Well, that makes sense since he *is* really dead." The phone rang on the other end.

"Sergeant Wesley."

"It's me."

Dial tone. I redialed. Two rings. Three. Four.

"Wesley."

"That wasn't nice," I told him. The early morning's light rain had given way to a bone-chilling deluge and the barn didn't have enough of an overhang to shield Russ and me. We'd parked the car in a wide area of the road's shoulder a half mile from the farm.

"Whatever it is," Wesley said gruffly, "I don't want to know. I've got two aggravated assaults, a push-in burglary, and some idiot who tried to rob an armored car by lying down in the middle of a busy street. Traffic's a mess."

"And it's raining," I offered. Russ tugged his collar up and looked snug if still a little seasick. I shivered in my cotton. "Did the armored car run over the moron in the road?"

"No."

"Then I'll take your dumb-criminal tricks and raise you a corpse with suspicious circumstances."

"Dammit." He sighed. "What is it with you? Most people go their entire lives without seeing a dead body outside a funeral home. Not you. You trip over them every time you leave the house."

"Helpful."

"Is that Connor?" Russ asked, too loudly. I slapped my hand over his mouth. The last thing I needed was for someone to find out I'd taken Russ on a work thing.

It was bad enough I was going to have to explain the dead guy.

"Who's with you?" Wesley demanded.

"TV," I said, taking my hand away with my sternest look and a pointed index finger.

"When is he coming? Because I've got to tell you, I'm through with this investigating gig. It's not for me." Russ's voice was a little higher than his usual tenor. He kept sneaking glances over his shoulder into the open barn as if this were a slasher flick and the guy might rise from the dead. "Your husband should be here. I should be someplace else. Like Bermuda."

I delivered a blow to Russ's solar plexus. His brown eyes widened and his lips pursed. He gasped for air. It hadn't taken much force. Connor's SEAL team took turns showing me antisocial moves. They had a running bet on which technique I found most useful in casual settings. The heel thrust that Connor's second in command, Blue, had shared was a definite front-runner. I turned my back and stepped away.

"Brother," Wesley muttered. "Where are you?"

"Stanwood," I said. "About forty miles north of Seattle on I-5."

"Way out of my jurisdiction." Wesley sounded happy about it. What kind of pal used a technicality to feed you to the local cops?

"But you're my cop," I protested, pulling up my hood. It was already heavy with rain but I remembered that most of my heat escaped through my head. When had I learned that? Probably around the same time I learned what a conjunction was. Damn. Now that song was going to be stuck in my head all day. *Conjunction Junction, what's your function?*

"We're not Social Security numbers. Every citizen doesn't get their own."

"But I need one."

He was silent. "Truer words were never spoken. Repeat the address."

I did. Russ reached into the front pocket of my sweatshirt and took the car keys. I stayed his hand.

Given his current state of mind, he might go in search of a medicinal triple no-foam espresso at Starbucks. We were beyond the civilization that put one on every street corner. In fact, we were past street corners altogether.

"I know a guy up there. I'll call him. You better be there, Sara, when he shows up."

Until that moment, I hadn't really thought about bailing. Now that he'd mentioned it, it was a much better idea than calling him had been.

"Don't worry about it. I'll just call the locals myself. I wouldn't want your friend to think you were taking advantage. Stepping on toes or anything. Forget I called."

"Did you kill the guy?" Wesley demanded.

"Do I need a lawyer?" I shot back.

"Did you kill him?"

"No."

"Then do not leave the scene. People who leave the scenes of crimes tend to get arrested. Prosecuted. Jailed."

Wasn't he painting a pretty picture? Not to mention fuzzing the legal niceties a little bit since I didn't think leaving the scene of a dead body was in itself a crime. Heck, it could be a simple farm accident. I leaned back into the barn to have another look. No chance.

"Fine," I sighed.

"You promise?"

"What am I, four years old?" I asked, my fingers crossed.

"Cooperate fully and cheerfully with the sheriff I send you."

"Fully and cheerfully."

"No lying."

"I never lie." Which was a lie in itself. Russ shook his head and clucked his tongue.

"Right." Wesley hung up.

"What were you thinking?" Russ asked. "Try 'I'm usually truthful.' He can hardly quantify. Go with 'I'll do my best.' That plays for poignancy. Even a distraction like 'Is that a fire bomb?' Which, by the way, is more believable given your track record, and would have a better chance of being believed than 'I never lie.' You're busted before the words are out of your mouth. After all I've taught you?" He *tsk*ed, *tsk*ed a little more.

"I'm not the one who tossed his cookies like a little girl at the amusement park."

"That's harsh. It's my first dead body. I'm not an old pro like you."

"As the old pro . . ." I began, "I'd suggest we get our stories straight."

About the Author

Gabriella Herkert is an evil corporate lawyer with endless opportunities to meet characters worthy of inclusion as victims, perpetrators, and comic relief. If she runs out, there are always her friends, family, and Koko, who bears a striking if fictional resemblance to a certain opera-singing, devoutly faithful canine companion in this book. Visit Gabi on her Web site at www.gabriellaherkert.com or send an e-mail to gabi_herkert@hotmail.com.